Thomas Warton

**The Life of Sir Thomas Pope**
*Founder of Trinity College, Oxford*

ISBN/EAN: 9783744725545

Printed in Europe, USA, Canada, Australia, Japan

Cover: Foto ©Raphael Reischuk / pixelio.de

More available books at **www.hansebooks.com**

Thomas Warton

# The Life of Sir Thomas Pope

Founder of Trinity College, Oxford

# THE
# L I F E

OF

Sir **THOMAS POPE,**

FOUNDER OF

TRINITY COLLEGE OXFORD.

CHIEFLY COMPILED FROM

## ORIGINAL EVIDENCES.

WITH

An **APPENDIX** of **PAPERS,**

NEVER BEFORE PRINTED.

THE SECOND EDITION,

CORRECTED AND ENLARGED.

By **THOMAS WARTON, B.D.**

FELLOW OF TRINITY COLLEGE, AND F.S.A.

## L O N D O N.

PRINTED FOR THOMAS CADELL IN THE STRAND.
M DCC LXXX.

# PREFACE.

BIOGRAPHERS, in the pursuit of information, are naturally betrayed into minute researches. The curiosity of the reader is seldom proportioned to that of the writer in this species of composition. Every incident, relating to a favourite character which the mind has long contemplated with attention, acquires importance. On these principles we may venture to found a plausible excuse, for the many trifling discoveries, and intricate discussions of insignificant circumstances, with which personal history so much abounds.

To this apology, which every biographer has a right to plead, the writer of the following memoirs presumes he possesses a peculiar

culiar

culiar claim, arifing from his fituation and connections. He defcribes the life of a perfon, whom the ftrongeft principles of gratitude, implanted in early years, have habitually taught him to regard with united veneration and affection. Under thefe circumftances, the flighteft events appear interefting; and the moft frivolous anecdotes of fuch a life are inveftigated with a pleafing enthufiafm.

In the mean time, a want of materials might have juftly been here alledged, in extenuation of an objection fo conftantly urged againft works of this kind. It will readily be granted, that to record the lives of men who have adorned their country by monuments of munificence, is a tribute indifpenfably due to public merit, and which cannot without public injuftice be witheld. But to difcharge this duty even imperfectly, and by thofe means, however inadequate, which the utmoft exertions of diligent enquiry can afford, is lefs unpardonable than to neglect

it

it entirely. When we cannot recover a perfect portrait of our friend and our benefactor,
we muft be contented with a few faint out-
lines. Abundance only implies rejection;
and where but little can be collected, it is
neceffary to retain every thing. We muft ac-
quiefce in anecdotes of inconfiderable confequence, while thofe of more importance cannot be procured.

Thefe inconveniencies might have eafily
been prevented. But our anceftors had no
regard for futurity. They trufted the remembrances of their heroes to chance and
tradition; or rather, to the laborious inveftigation of a diftant pofterity. For it is
the tafk of modern times to commemorate,
if they cannot imitate, the confpicuous examples of antiquity; and to compofe the
panegyric of thofe virtues which exift no
more. Inquifitive leifure is not the lot of
earlier eras. Ages of action are fucceeded by
ages of enquiry.

But

But that species of enquiry which properly belongs to the biographer, seems, in point of time, to be posteriour to that which forms the province of the historian. It does not grow fashionable till late: it begins to be the favourite amusement of cultivated nations at their most polished periods. When the more important and extensive stores of historical information have been exhausted, the growing spirit of curiosity, which increases in proportion as it is gratified, still demands new gratifications; it descends to particularities, and delights to develope circumstances of a subordinate nature. After many general histories have been written, inquisitive minds are eager to explore the parts of what they have hitherto surveyed at large. The ardour of research, which gathers strength from contraction, is exerted on distinct periods; and at length personal history commences. Characters before only represented in the gross, and but incidentally exhibited

hibited or fuperficially difplayed, now become the fubject of critical difquifition, and
a feparate examination. Occurences neglected or omitted by the hiftorian, form materials for the biographer : and men of fupe-
riour eminence are felected from the common
mafs of public tranfactions in which they
were indiftinctly grouped, and delineated as
detatched figures in a fingle point of view.

Nor was it till late after the reftoration of
literature, that biography affumed its proper
form, and appeared in its genuine character.
The Lives which were compiled at fome diftance after that period, are extremely jejune
and defective performances. The firft which
approached to perfection were thofe of Pei-
refkius, by Peter Gaffendus, and of Melancthon, by Camerarius. It was long, before
the perfeverance of inveftigation connected
with precifion, the patient toil of tracing evidences, authenticating facts, and digefting
fcattered notices, grew into a fcience : in a

word, before the accuracy of the antiquarian
was engrafted on the refearches of the biographer. The mafterly Life of William of
Wykeham will beft explain and illuftrate
thefe reflections : a work which I chufe to
produce as an example on this occafion, not
only becaufe it is here produced as an example with a peculiar degree of propriety,
but becaufe it is a pattern of that excellence
in this mode of writing, which I mean to
characterife and recommend.

As fir Thomas Pope bore fome fhare in
the national tranfactions of his time, to relieve the drynefs of perfonal and local incidents, I have endeavoured to render thefe
pages in fome meafure interefting to general
readers, by dilating this part of my performance, and by fometimes introducing hiftorical
digreffions, yet refulting immediately from
the tenour of my fubject. Amongft thefe, I
flatter myfelf that my relation of the perfecutions of the princefs Elizabeth may merit
fome

some attention: of which I have thrown together a more uniform and circumstantial detail than has yet appeared, with the addition of several anecdotes respecting that transaction not hitherto published.

On the whole I may venture to affirm, that I have at least attempted to make my work as entertaining as possible. My materials have not always been of the most brilliant kind; but they are such, as have often enabled me to enliven and embellish my narrative by presenting pictures of antient manners, which are ever striking to the imagination.

I have before hinted, that my resources for compiling this history were slender and insufficient. From books I could obtain scarce any information. Indeed, my chief assistance has been derived from manuscript authorities. I have not however in this respect found the success I wished. Yet I have carefully consulted every record that seemed

likely

likely to illuftrate my fubject; and my references will fhew, that I have fearched a
variety of authentic inftruments, preferved
in the Britifh Mufeum, the chapel of the
Rolls, and other repofitories of valuable
originals. Of thefe the more important are
printed at large in the Appendix.

Among my references to manufcript authorities, two fometimes occur which require
explanation. Thefe are, *MSS. Cotton. Vitellius*, F. 5. *MSS. Strype.* And, *MSS. F. Wife.*

In the year 1709, that induftrious and accurate annalift Mr. John Strype, communicated to doctor Arthur Charlett, mafter of
Univerfity college, originally fellow of Trinity college, an account of the Funeral
of fir Thomas Pope *. This account Strype
had tranfcribed from a manufcript of the

---

* See Ballard's Coll. of Letters, MSS. Bibl. Bodl. fol. xv.
pag. 31. Letter from Strype to Charlett, dated Lowlayton,
Effex, Apr. 20. 1709. See LIFE, infr. p. 178.

Cotton

Cotton library, which he perpetually cites in
in his Ecclesiastical Memoirs, marked
*Vitellius*, F. 5[b]. Soon afterwards it appears that
Strype fent to Charlett, perhaps at his requeft,
a few other notices relating to fir Thomas
Pope, extracted from the fame manufcript.

[b] In a letter from Strype to Charlett, dat. ibid. Apr. 5.
1709. MSS. ut fupr. vol. xv. p. 31. " The kindnefs you bear
" to the foundation of Trinity college, makes me inquifitive
" into the Founder's place of burial, which you find mentioned
" in my Annals, [p. 3. edit. i.] Though I cannot eafily re-
" collect every manufcript and particular place in them whence
" I have compiled every part of the hiftory. Yet it occurs to
" me, that fir Thomas Pope's Funeral, with the time and place,
" as alfo the reft of pages 30, 31, [viz.] the funerals in thofe
" pages mentioned, were taken from the volume, Vitellius
" F. 5. in the Cotton library, which is a certain brief journal
" of funerals, and as well of divers other occurrences, begin-
" ning at the year 1550, written, as it feems, by fome herald,
" or other diligent obferver of his own times. There the writer
" fets down all the particular ceremonies, the folemnities, and
" mourners, at that knight's interment. Which if you have
" any defire to know, I will tranfcribe out of my notes and
" fend you." This is an original. Then follows the letter before referred to, which is not the original, but a tranfcript by
the late Mr. Rawlins of Pophills in Gloucefterfhire, who became poffeffed of Charlett's extenfive correfpondence. See Append. p. 458. infr.

The

The late learned Mr Francis Wife, keeper of the archives, Radclivian librarian, and fellow of Trinity college, at Oxford, copied all the tranfcripts, about four or five in number, which Strype on this occafion had made from the Cotton manufcript, by permiffion of Charlett, among whofe curious and numerous papers they were·kept; and by Mr.Wife they were thus communicated to me. Fortunately for the prefent undertaking, the extracts had been made by Strype before the fire happened in the Cotton library, then placed in Afhburnham houfe at Weftminfter, by which fatal accident this valuable volume was particularly damaged; and, as far as I can judge from a curfory infpection, moft of the leaves, if not all, containing Strype's extracts, were either deftroyed or obliterated [c]. The reader is therefore defired to obferve, that the reference, viz. *MSS. Cotton. Vitell. F. 5. MSS. Strype,* fig-

[c] But fee APPEND. Numb. xxviii.

nifies

nifies Strype's transcripts from thence [d].  But whenever this Cotton manuscript is cited without the addition of *MSS. Strype*, the reader will remember, that such citations were faithfully transcribed by myself from that manuscript volume, now belonging to the British Museum.

Mr. Wise also transcribed, and communicated to me, two or three other papers from doctor Charlett's collections, beside those of Strype which I have just mentioned [e].  These I have called *MSS. F. Wise* [f].  Other refe-

[d] See pp. 46. 86. 89. 91.

[e] See pp. 185. 189.  And APPEND. Numb. xxix.

[f] Since my first edition, among the manuscript papers of the Rev. Thomas Wilkes, D. D. fellow of Trinity college, Oxford, and who died rector of Rotherfield Greys in Oxfordshire, in 1745, I have met with other notices by Mr. Wise, which are now first inserted in this edition, and are also styled, MSS. F. Wise.  These Mr. Wise seems to have had chiefly from Dr. Charlett's collections, and the family-papers of the late sir Harry Pope-Blount.

As to Charlett's collections, I learn that he derived many of his notices and informations on this subject, from Mr. Josiah Howe, a fellow of the college; a short account of whom will not be superfluous, as it may tend to establish their credit.  He was

was

rences will eaſily be underſtood, as care has been taken to give them with equal exactneſs and perſpicuity.

.

was born at Crendon in Bucks, and elected Scholar of Trinity college, June 12, 1632. Regiſtr. Coll. fol. 68. b. Admitted Fellow, being then bachelor of Arts, May 26, 1637. Ibid. fol. 72. b. By Hearne he is called, " a very great cavalier and " loyaliſt, and a moſt ingenious man." Rob. Glouc. Gloss. p. 669. He appears to have been a general and an accompliſh- ed ſcholar, and in polite literature eſteemed one of the ornaments of the univerſity. In 1644, he preached before king Charles the firſt at Chriſt-church cathedral Oxford. The ſermon was printed, and in red letters, by the king's ſpecial command. Only thirty copies were printed. One was purchaſed, in 1723, by Hearne from Dr. Charlett': library : the ſame, and that per- haps the only one extant, which is now among Rawlinſon's Books in the Bodleian. See Hearne's MSS. Coll. vol. 102. p. 8. Charlett bought this rarity many years before, at the high price of five ſhillings. Ibid. vol. 51. p. 176. In 1646, he was created Bachelor of Divinity by decree of the king, among others who were complimented with that degree for having diſ- tinguiſhed themſelves as preachers before the Court at Oxford. He was ſoon afterwards ejected from his Fellowſhip by the preſbyterians, but not in the general expulſion in 1648, accord- ing to Walker, Suff. Clerc. p. 134. Being one of the Bur- ſars of the college and foreſeeing its fate, having reſolved at the ſame time never to acknowledge the authority of Cromwell's viſitors, he retired, in the beginning of the year 1648, to a college-eſtate in Buckinghamſhire, carrying with him many ren- tals, rolls, papers, and other authentic documents, belonging

I muſt not here omit, what I am much
honoured in mentioning, that this work

to his office. He was invited to return to the college by Dr.
Harris the new preſbyterian Preſident, on a promiſe, that if he
would quietly give up the official books, his ſubmiſſion to the
viſitors ſhould be diſpenſed with, and he ſhould be permitted to
retain his fellowſhip without moleſtation. Harris by this artifice
having recovered the books, immediately ſigned an order for
Howe's expulſion; pretending to have received an unexpected
injunction from the viſitors, and profeſſing his regret at being
obliged to remove ſo valuable a member from the foundation.
Hearne, MSS. COLL. vol. 89. p. 195. He was reſtored to
his fellowſhip in 1660. He has a Copy of recommendatory
Engliſh verſes prefixed to the folio edition of Beaumont and
Fletcher, printed in 1647. Another to Thomas Randoph's
POEMS, reprinted at Oxford, in 1640. Another to Cartwright's
COMEDIES and POEMS, at Oxford, 1651. Theſe pieces in the
witty epigrammatic ſtyle which then prevailed, have uncommon
acuteneſs, and highly deſerve to be revived. Some others have
perhaps eſcaped me. In thoſe I have mentioned, he appears in
company with Denham, Waller, Jonſon, Corbett, Brome,
Shirley, Mayne, and others the moſt ingenious men of thoſe
times, who were of his intimate acquaintance. Wood ſays that
he wrote a copy of Engliſh verſes, which were much applauded,
ſpoken before the duke and ducheſs of York, in 1683, at Trinity college. MSS. Muſ. Aſhmol. fol. 57. D. 19. He lived
forty two years, greatly reſpected, after his reſtitution, and arriving at the age of ninety, died fellow of the college, where
he conſtantly reſided, Aug. 28, 1701. He is interred, under a
ſmall

is greatly indebted to the friendſhip of the
biſhop of Worceſter; who moſt obligingly
condeſcended to favour me with ſome valuable communications, from the family
papers of his lordſhip's father, the earl of
Guildford.

ſmall marble lozenge, with a ſhort inſcription, in the college-
chapel. Hearne ſays, that " he lived ſo retiredly in the latter
" part of his life, that he rarely came abroad; ſo that I could
" never ſee him, though I have often much deſired to have a
" ſight of him." GLOSS. ut ſupr. p. 670. Compare Wood,
ATH. OXON. ii. f. 56. And LIFE of BATHURST, pp. 154. 211.

THE

# THE

# L I F E

### O F

# Sir T H O M A S  P O P E.

---

### S E C T.  I.

THOMAS POPE was born at Dedington in Oxfordſhire, about the year 1508[a], and at the end of the reign of king Henry the ſeventh.

His parents were William and Margaret Pope[b], who lived at Dedington[c]: but the family, which ſeems at leaſt to have been that

---

[a] Computed from his age at the year of his death.

[b] E Statut. coll. Trin. Oxon. cap. xiii. " Majeſtatem tuam " oramus, O beata Trinitas, ut animarum Margarete uxoris " Fundatoris noſtri, et Gulielmi et Margarete parentum ejuſ- " dem, &c."

[c] Viſitation of Oxfordſhire, by Ric. Lee, Portcullis Marſhall to Clarencieux King at Arms, A. D. 1570. MSS. in Muſ. Aſhmol. Oxon. Codd. A. Wood. 4to. 8522. 60. pag. 32.

A                                    of

of a gentleman, was originally feated in Kent,
before the reign of Edward the third [d]. William appears to have been married to a former
wife, named Julian Edmondes [e]. His fecond
wife, Margaret, mother of THOMAS POPE,
was the daughter of Edmund Yate, of Stanlake in Oxfordfhire [f]: and after the death of

[d] Ex ftemmate Pope, MSS. in rotulo prægrandi pergamen.
penes honoratiff. Francifc. com. de Guildford. By which it
likewife appears, that the faid William Pope was the only fon
of John, fecond fon of Thomas Pope, and Grace Sampfon his
wife.

[e] Lee's MS. vifitation ut fupr. ibid. And MS. pedigree of
Pope, manu A. Wood, inter MSS. Rawlinf. bibl. Bodl. Compared with evidence occurring hereafter. One John Edmondes
of Dedington, is mentioned in Afhmole's Berkfhire, who, as I
collect, was her uncle. iii. 285. As alfo in Lee's MSS. ut fupr.
pag. 41. Her father was probably Robert Edmondes, one of
the executors of William Pope's will. Append. Numb. I. John
Edmondes is alfo a fubfcribing witnefs to an Inftrument, Append. No. XXII. John Edmondes, the elder, is mentioned in
an indenture of lands between Sir T. Pope, and Trinity college, Oxon. dat. Jun. 26. 1558. In regiftr. prim. fol. 20.

[f] From Lee's MS. vifitation, ut fupr. pag. 51. Compared
with pedigr. MSS. Rawlinf. According to Lee, Edmund Yate
of Stanlake was third fon and heir of Richard Yate of Charney,
co. Berks. He married Margaret, daughter of John Cornwall
of Stanlake. See the pedigree of Yate of Charney, which is
not altogether exact, in Afhmole's Berkfhire, iii. 321.

Wood fays, that Margaret Pope, in the text, was the daughter of —— Yate of *Stanford* in Wootton-hundred in Oxfordfhire. Hift. Antiq. univ. Oxon. ii. 301. But no fuch place
occurs in that hundred. Afhmole, Berkf. iii. 295. mentions
Yate of Stanford, Berks; which place Wood feems to have
confounded with *Sandford*, a village in Wootton-hundred.
Many

William Pope, fhe was again married, to John
Buftarde of Adderbury in the fame county [g].
Befide the abovementioned Thomas, the
principal fubject of thefe papers, the faid William and Margaret had one fon, John; and
three daughters, Elifabeth, Julian, and Alice [h]:
concerning all which I fhall fpeak more at
large hereafter.

William and Margaret Pope feem to have
lived in a decent and creditable condition, as
may be collected from the bequefts of William's will; which alfo partly fhews the circumftances in which his eldeft [i] fon was left.
He bequeathes his land to be divided between

Many of the family of Yate appear to have lived in, and about,
the villages of Charney, Buckland, and Stanford, Berks, and
Stanlake, Oxfordfhire; places all of the fame neighbourhood.
What ftill further confirms my fuppofition, that Wood is miftaken, and that the faid Edmund Yate, of Stanlake, was Margaret Pope's father, is; that Peter Yate of Stanlake, whom Sir
Thomas Pope in a letter, dat. 1557, calls his coufin, appears
to have been a tenant to Trinity college, Oxford. In indentur.
dat. Jul. 3. 1556. I find likewife one Barthol. Yate, co. Berks,
who I prefume was of fome of the places abovementioned, or
from that neighbourhood, elected fcholar of the faid college, in
1569. Ex regiftr. prim.' dicti coll. fol. 34. But it would be
needlefs, end trifling, to multiply proofs.

[g] Ex epitaph. infra citat.

[h] Lee's MSS. vifitat. ut fupr. 32. And from evidences occurring hereafter.

[i] See Append. I.

his wife and his fon Thomas [k] : one hundred pounds to the faid Thomas, and forty pounds to each daughter : a ftipend to a prieft to fing for his foul one year in the church of Dedington, in which he directs his body to be buried : three fhillings and four-pence, refpectively, to the torches, the bells, Saint Thomas's beam, and our Lady's beam, in the faid church : fix fhillings and four-pence to Clifton chapel near Dedington : three fhillings and four-pence to the mother church of Lincoln ; and to each of his god-children a fheep. He died in the year 1523 [l]. By an inquifition taken after his death, it appears, that he poffeffed eftates, at Whitehill and Hooknorton in Oxfordfhire, of the yearly value of fix pounds [m]. Margaret has wife furvived him many years, and died on the twenty-fifth day of Auguft, 1557 [n], at Wroxton, in Oxford-

[k] I find that Sir Thomas Pope fold'the manor of Dedington, with other poffeffions in the neighbourhood, to K. Henry viii. by indent. dat. Mar. 21. an. reg. 36. But the premiffes were no paternal eftate of the Popes; having been granted to Sir Thomas Pope, but a few years before, as parcel of the priory of Bicefter, viz. Pat. 28. Hen. viii. Teft. Feb. 11. par. 5.

[l] From the probate of his will, Append. No. I.

[m] See Append. No. *XII.*

[n] She is buried in the chancel of Wroxton church, with this epitaph on a brafs plate :

Here lyeth under this ſtone buryed Margaret Baſtarde, widowe, ſometyme the wif of William Pope of Dedingeton in the county of Oxford, Gent. and afterward married

to

ſhire, where ſhe ſeems to have lived during the latter part of her life with her younger ſon, John [o]; her ſecond huſband, John Buſtarde, dying in the year 1534 [p].

Their ſon THOMAS received the firſt rudiments of grammatical learning at the public ſchool of the neighbouring town of Banbury; at that time a celebrated ſchool, and kept by Thomas Stanbridge of Magdalen college in Oxford, an eminent inſtructor of youth [q], brother of John Stanbridge, who compiled a famous grammar, called Stanbridge-grammar [r].

to John Buſtarde, Gent. dwellinge at Atterbury in the ſaid county: which William and Margaret were father and mother to Sir Thomas Pope Knight, and John Pope, Eſquire. And the ſaid Margaret departed out of this worlde, the xxv day of Auguſt an. dni. 1557, and hopeth to ryſe and lyve agayne with Chriſte eternally.

[o] Ex indentura quadam quadripartit. in Theſauriario Coll. Trin. Oxon.

[p] From his monument at Adderbury, Co. Oxon. See Append. No. XXVI.

[q] He died 1522. Wood Ath. Oxon. Vol. 1. f. p. 26. col. 2. Ed. ii. and p. 18. col. 1

[r] Hugh Oldham, Biſhop of Exeter, about the year 1518, founded a ſchool at Mancheſter, and appointed the maſters to teach grammar after the uſe, manner, and form, of the ſchool at Banbury in Oxfordſhire; where Thomas Stanbridge taught the grammar compoſed by John Stanbridge. ibid. Oxford Biſhops, p. 658. col. 1. And Wood's School-Notes, MSS. Muſ. Aſhmol. 8518, 56. Mancheſter.

From hence he was removed to Eton college[s]: but I do not find that he completed his educa- tion at either of our univerſities.

It ſeems moſt probable, that he was imme- diately ſent from Eton ſchool to ſome of the inns of court. I believe, to Gray's-inn. That he was bred to the law is certain ; and there is undoubted evidence that he was employed, while very young, in ſome of the inferior offices of the court of chancery [t]. And that he was originally deſtined, and regularly train- ed, to this profeſſion, may be conjectured from his hand-writing ; many ſpecimens of which remain in his college at Oxford. Nor is it improbable, that he might be placed in his youth, for ſome time at leaſt, under the ſuper- intendence and inſtruction of ſome ſkilful practitioner in the law, perhaps a maſter in chancery ; as in his will he bequeathes to his *old maſter's ſon, maſter Croke* [u], his black ſattin

---

[s] For this we have his own teſtimony, in the ſtatutes of his college at Oxford. " Ex ſcholis Etonenſi, vel Banburienſi, in " quibus Ipſe olim in grammaticæ rudimentis educatus eram." Cap. vii.

[t] Apud Lit. pat. Hen. vii. an reg. 29. inf. citat. viz. " Grandes labores, laudabiliaque obſequia, quæ dilectus nobis " THOMAS POPE, attendens negociis noſtris in Cancellaria noſ- " tra predicta multipliciter impendebat, indieſque impendere " intendebat, merito contemplantes, &c." See Append. No.V.

[u] One Richard Croke is made comptroller and ſupervifor of the hanaper, in 1529, with a yearly fee of x. l. Bill. ſignat. Hen.

gown faced with Luferne-fpots ʷ. This Croke
or Crooke, his fuppofed Mafter, feems to have
been the chief of the fix clerks in chancery
who was ordered by Sir Thomas More, for the
fatisfaction of the judges, and his own juftifi-
cation, to make a docquet of all the Injunctions which he had given to the law courts
during the time of his chancellorfhip ˣ.

But whatever was our young adventurer's
fituation in early life, it is remarkable that a
perfon of his obfcure family and inconfiderable
fortune, fhould fo foon recommend himfelf to
public notice, and gain accefs even to the
royal favour. Vigorous abilities, and an active
mind, eafily furmounted all obftacles ; and he
quickly became a fuccefsful candidate in the
purfuit of riches and honour.

Hen. viii. anno reg. 20. Sep. 19. He has alfo more grants in
the law, under other years of the fame king. ˙

ʷ The fpotted fur of a Ruffian animal, called a Lucern,
antiently much in ufe and efteem. I find it mentioned in the
will of Sir John Wallop, an eminent captain and ftatefman in
the reign of Henry viii. May 22. 1551. " To the Sergeant
" of the kinges herthoundes my gowne furrid with *lucernes.*"
Regiftr. Buck. qu. 24. cur. Prær. Cant. It is fpecified in our
ancient ftatutes. See the word in Beaumont and Fletcher, vol.
ii. p. 399.

ˣ More's Life, by M. T. M. p. 218. 4to.

A 4                                          What

What was the firſt ſtep to his advance-
ment in life, and whether it aroſe from the
friendſhip of ſome private patron, from any
diſtinguiſhed merit in his profeſſion, a peculiar
caſt for buſineſs in general, or a lucky concurrence of all theſe cauſes, cannot be preciſely
determined, although from what follows it
may be partly conjectured. He was not much
more than twenty-ſeven years of age, when he
had ſufficient addreſs or intereſt to procure an
appointment to offices, which ſeem to have
been alternately beſtowed upon Henry's moſt
eminent favourites, and the moſt popular characters of thoſe times [y].

Having been early initiated, as I before obſerved, in the buſineſs of chancery, on the fifth
day October, 1533, he was conſtituted by letters patent of Henry the eighth, clerk of the
briefs in the ſtar-chamber at Weſtminſter [z],
On the fifteenth day of October in the ſame
year, he received by letters patent of the ſame
king, a reverſionary grant of the office of clerk

[y] Fuller in his quaint manner, obſerves concerning him,
" I behold him as fortunæ ſuæ fabrum ; the ſmith, who by
" God's bleſſing, hammered out his own fortune without any
" patrimonial advantage." Worthies of England, Article
London, p. 223. edit. 1662.

[z] See Append. No. IV.

of

of the crown in chancery. Of this poft, very foon afterwards, he became actually poffeffed ; with an annual fee of twenty pounds from the hanaper, and alfo a robe with fur at the feafts of Chriftmas and Pentecoft from the king's great wardrobe [a].

On the thirteenth day of November 1535, he was conftituted, by the king's letters patent, warden of the mint, exchange, and coinage, in the tower of London, on the voluntary re-fignation, in his favour, of John Coppynger, page of the great wardrobe [b]. How long he continued in this office I have not learned. It feems, however, that he had quitted it within eight years, and, as I fuppofe, for fome more valuable confideration [c]. On the twenty-third day of December, 1536, he was likewife by letters patent appointed, to exercife jointly with William Smythe, the office of clerk of all the briefs in the ftar-chamber at Weft-minfter [d].

[a] Pat. 29. Hen. viii. par. 5. See Append. No. V.

[b] Pat. 26. Hen. viii. par. 2. See Append. No. III. See more of John Coppynger, ibid. in the Notes.

[c] For in the Britifh Mufeum, there is, " Compotus Johan-" nis Browne, cuftodis Cambii, &c. a primo die Jul. an. reg. " Hen. viii. 34.". MSS. Harl. 698.—12.

[d] Pat. 26. Hen. viii. par. 1. Append. No. IV.

On

On February the twenty-eighth, 1538, he obtained, at his own inftance, a new royal licence for exercifing the office of clerk of the crown in conjunction with John Lucas[e], who was afterwards, in the reign of Edward the fixth, an eminent crown-lawyer, and employed by that prince in many important commiffions[f]. The firft of thefe grants he perhaps obtained by the recommendation of Sir Thomas More; who prefiding as Lord Chancellor in the court above-mentioned, where Sir Thomas Pope was employed when a young man, might have taken particular notice of his promifing diligence and abilities; and from which circumftance, a lafting friendfhip and intimacy between them both, as will be fhewn hereafter, feems to have originally commenced. Although there is equal reafon to fuppofe, as it will likewife appear in its proper place, that he was in no lefs favour and efteem with Sir Thomas More's fucceffor, the Lord Chancellor Thomas lord Audley; under whofe immediate infpection and authority he exercifed the office of clerk of the crown, and clerk of the briefs in the ftar-chamber: and to both of which

[e] Pat. 29. Hen. viii. ut fupr.

[f] Strype, Eccl. Mem. ii. 498. And ibid. B. ii. Ch. xxix. pafs.

depart-

departments, as I prefume, he muft have been appointed by Lord Chancellor Audley's nomination [g].

But thefe appointments were foon fucceeded by one of much greater confequence. For in the year 1536, he was conftituted, by the king, Treafurer of the Court of augmentations of the king's revenue, on its firft eftablifhment by act of parliament [h].

The principal defign of this court was for eftimating the lands of the diffolved monafteries, vefted in the Crown, and for receiving their revenues. It had moreover full power and authority to fell the monaftic poffeffions for the king's fervice [i]. It was fo called from the encreafe which the royal revenue received,

[g] Lord Audley was appointed Lord Keeper, May 20, 1532, on the refignation of Sir T. More: And Lord Chancellor, Jan. 26, 1533. Rym. Fœd. xiv. 435, 446. Dugd. Chron. Ser. pag. 82. Both offices, I apprehend, were in the appointment of the Chancellor, as the clerk of the crown is at prefent: although they paffed in the king's name. The ftar-chamber was a branch of chancery. Among Tanner's manufcripts there is an inftrument, without date, but while Audley was chancellor, relating to the monaftery of Furnefs, in Sir T. Pope's hand-writing. MSS. TANNER. 164. f. 44. Bibl. Bodl.

[h] Statut. Hen. viii. An. 27. Cap. xxvii. See STATUTES by Berthelette, in two vol. Lond. 1543. See vol. ii. ibid. 1551. fol. xli. b.

[i] From the act.

by

by this new acquifition of property. All perfons holding leafes and penfions, by former
grants, from any convent, exhibited their titles
before this court, and their pretenfions were
allowed in proportion to their validity. And
although the governors of the religious houfes,
forefeein , their fate, often contrived immediately before the diffolution of their refpective
focieties, to forge new contracts or indentures
in favour of their friends or kindred, few
frauds of this kind took effect. For the court
feems to have been very vigilant in preventing
and expofing fuch fpecious impoftures [k].

The officers of this court were a Chancellor, it's fuperior, a Treafurer abovementioned,
who was the fecond officer, a follicitor, ten
auditors, feventeen recievers, with others, belonging to the inferior departments. It was a
court of record, and poffeffed of two feals [l].

The Treafurer's office appears to have been
a poft of confiderable profit and diftinction,
and of equal truft and importance. He was
ranked with the principal officers of ftate in
the reign of Henry the eighth. For by ftatute
of the fame, he was privileged, together with

[k] Fuller Ch. Hift. B. vi. p. 349.
[l] From the Act of parl. ut fup.

the

the chancellor of the faid court, the chancellor
of the dutchy of Lancafter, the treafurer of
the king's chamber, the chancellor of the
court of firft Fruits and Tenths, the mafter of
the king's wards and liveries, the groom of the
ftole, the warden of the cinque ports, and
other honourable perfonages, refpectively, to
retain in his houfe one chaplain having a benefice with cure of fouls, who fhould not be
compelled to refidence [m]. The Treafurer was
allowed a limited annual falary for the exercife
of his office; as alfo perquifites for fuch fums
of money as he paid to the patentees of any
office, fee, or annuity, granted under the feal
of the court : and alfo, for fuch difburfements
as he made to any other perfons, by virtue of
the king's warrant or bill affigned, or by bill
affigned and fubfcribed by the chancellor, and
one other officer.

Thefe fees were regulated according to the
practice of the court of the dutchy of Lancafter [n]. The allowance of Sir John Williams,
afterwards Lord Williams of Tame, Treafurer
of this court in the reign of Edward the fixth,
was 320 l. A fum, which I prefume, was

---

[m] Statut. Hen. viii. an. 33. c. xxviii. And 21. xiii.

[n] Ex Statut. ut fupr.

then

then the full value of this place °: but which, although very confiderable, was much inferior to the emoluments of the fame office, when in the poffeffion of Sir Thomas Pope.

The Treafurer at his admiffion was fworn before the chancellor, that he would reafonably and honeftly procure the king's profit, adminifter juftice to the poor as well as the rich, faithfully keep and expend the king's treafure, and exhibit a true declaration of it without concealment. The receivers were ordered to pay into his hands the whole rents of all the diffolved monafteries : concerning which he accounted annually before the chancellor and two auditors. The chancellor, Treafurer, attorney, and follicitor, or any two of them were entrufted with power or licence to act without the king's warrant °.

On the diffolution of any greater abbey, fome of the auditors, who were employed in riding to furvey the manors and lands of the court, repaired thither, and were lodged and

---

° Fuller Ch. Hift. b. vi. p. 348. edit. 1651. In lieu of this falary, queen Mary granted Sir J. Williams a penfion of the fame value, when he quitted the treafurerfhip. Dugd. Bar. ii. 393. edit. 1675.

ᵖ Ex Statut. ut fupr.

accom-

accommodated in the houfe [q]; for the purpofe
of acquiring intelligence, and of tranfacting
the neceffary bufinefs relating to the feveral
eftates, with more convenience and certainty.
The firft chancellor of this court was Sir
Richard Rich, afterwards lord Rich, and lord
high chancellor of England [r].

Sir Thomas Pope held the treafurerfhip of
this court about five years, and was fucceeded
by Sir Edward North [s], privy counfellor and
executor to Henry the eighth, and created a
baron by queen Mary. About the fame time
he was appointed mafter, or treafurer, of the
jewel-houfe in the tower [t]. The yearly ftipend of this office, when in the poffeffion of
Thomas lord Cromwell, about five years before, was fifty pounds [u].

[q] Thus at the abbey of Evefham, fome of the principal
lodgings are ordered to be " referved for the king's officers of
" the court of augmentations when they fhall repair thither,
" &c." Stevens, Monaft. i. 402.

[r] Dugd. Bar. ii. 387. Sir Edward North appears to have
been chancellor of that court in 1545. From the dedication of
Sir Thomas Elliot's book, entitled, *Prefervative againft Death.*
Lond. 1545. 12mo.

[s] Dugd. Ibid. p. 394.

[t] Englifh Baronett. iv. 666. edit. 1741. From the infrma-
tion of Sir Henry Pope-Blount, cited in the margin. But this
does not appear by the patents.

[u] Dugd. ut fupr. p. 370.

It

It would have broken the thread of my narrative, if I had before obferved, that in 1535, June the twenty-fixth, beginning now to rife in the world, he received from Barker, otherwife garter king at arms, a patent for a new coat of arms, to be borne by him and his pofterity ᵂ; which are the fame that are now borne by Trinity college in Oxford: viz. Party per pale, or and azure, on a cheveron between three gryphons heads erafed, four fleur de lys, all countercharged ˣ. To which it may be added here, that in the latter end of the following year, viz. 1536, on the fifteenth day of October, he was knighted by Henry eighth ʸ, amid the folemnities attending the creations of the earl of Southampton, and the gallant Edward Seymour, earl of Hertford, afterwards the

ᵂ Penes honoratif. Francifc. com. de Guildford. See Append. No. II.

ˣ He ordered them to be placed in painted glafs, twice in the hall, and twice in the Prefident's lodgings, of that college. Thefe efcocheons were done by James Nicholfon, glafs-painter of London, each, at 6s. 8d. From a *Loofe Paper*, in Thefaur. Coll. Trin. Oxon. I prefume they were deftroyed under the adminiftration of the prefbyterians.

ʸ In an inftrument, in Thefaurar. coll. Trin. Oxon. dated 20 Dec. 1539. 31. Hen. viii. he is ftyled, " Egregius vir *magifter* Thomas Pope, Thefaurarius cur. augment. &c." In another, ibid. dated 28 Jan. 34. Hen. viii. he is called *miles.* But Dugdale ftyles him *knight*, in 1539. Warw. p. 416. b.

famous

famous duke of Somerfet. At which time Henry Howard, afterwards the celebrated and unfortunate earl of Surrey, alfo received the honor of knighthood [z].

A few years after the erection of the court of augmentations above-mentioned, the king perceiving that his exigencies required more expeditious returns of money than the annual revenues of the diffolved monafteries could produce, was neceffitated to fell by one extenfive commiffion a very confiderable part of their lands, for the purpofe of raifing prefent fupplies. By this ftep the court of augmentations was foon diminifhed. The caufes depending in it became few and inconfiderable, and the crown-profits arifing from thence decreafed; it's officers were numerous, and their penfions ample. On thefe confiderations he was induced to diffolve it; which he did by letters patent only: and on the fecond of January, 1546, created by the fame letters patent, a new court of augmentations, on a different and more confined plan.

In an original rough draught of this new eftablifhment [a], Sir Thomas Pope is nominated, by the king, mafter of the woods of the court

---

[z] Brit. Muf. MSS. Cotton Claudius. C. 3. fol. 127. b.
[a] In the Britifh Mufeum. MSS. Harl. 600. 1.

on

on this fide the river Trent, and Sir John Williams, Treafurer. The other principal patent-
officers, recited in the inftrument, are Sir Edward North, who is appointed chancellor, Sir
Walter Mildmay, and Sir Thomas Moyle, general furveyors, Robert Henneage mafter of
the woods beyond Trent, Richard Goodricke,
attorney, and John Gofnold, follicitor. The
reft are Geoffry Gates, and John Arnfcott, furveyors of the woods on each fide Trent, and
Richard Duke. The two mafters of the woods
on each fide Trent, are ftyled the fourth officers. At this time Sir Thomas Pope was one
of the king's privy-counfellors [b]. The total
fum of yearly fees belonging to this court, on
its fecond reduced eftablifhmemt, amounted to
7249 l. 10 s. 3 d. [c].

In the year 1553, the laft of the reign of Edward the fixth, the firft effort was made for the
actual abolition of this court, which by degrees
was become burthenfome, and at length fuper-
fluous. Accordingly, the fame year, at Mary's

---

[b] He is ftyled in the faid inftrument, " our truftie and well
" belovyd counfaillor." fol. 18. b. The firft notice I have
found of his being a privy counfellor, occurs in Pat. 36. Hen.
viii. par. 11. Teft. Mar. xxi. This was in 1545. Where he is
called, " dilectus et fidelis *confiliarius* nofter."

[c] Fuller, Ch. hift. vi. p. 349.

acceffion

acceſſion[d] it was incorporated into the exchequer[e]. Soon afterwards followed a grand ſale of lands, which formerly came within the cogniſance of this court, and continued in poſſeſſion of the crown, under the conduct of commiſſioners; one of which was the chancellor of the exchequer. This appears from three valuable manuſcript volumes in the Britiſh Muſeum[f], which the learned and accurate Wanley ſuppoſed to have belonged to the court of augmentations. But this could not be the caſe, as the firſt of them was made and begins ſo late as the year 1557, four years after the abolition of that court. They were however compiled in conſequence of that inſtitution, and may be conſidered among the laſt remains of its records[g].

[d] Statut. Mar. i. cap. x. But I find a renewal of Sir Richard Sackville's patent to the chancellorſhip of this court on queen Mary's acceſſion. Pat. 1. Mar. Teſt. Jan. xx. par. 2. Sackville was chancellor at the death of Edward vi. He was conſtituted pat. 1. Edw. vi. Teſt. Aug. ii. par. 2. on North's reſignation.

[e] See Statut, Edw. vi. 7. C. ii.

[f] Viz. liber primus de *lex rates* ann. 2, 3. Phil. Mar. fol. And the two following volumes, fol. MSS. Harl. 606, 607, 608. They are the originals.

[g] The CHAMBER of the *court of augmentations* was afterwards converted into the chamber of the *court of wards*, now long ſince diſſolved. Edward vi. at his coronation, when he came from York-Place, is ſaid to have robed himſelf in the chamber of the court of augmentations, " now called the *court of wards*," before he went into Weſtminſter-hall. TIME'S STORE-HOUSE,

B. 5.

It is commonly fuppofed, and it has been
faid in general terms, that Sir Thomas Pope
was appointed one of the commiffioners, or vifitors, under Cromwell, for diffolving the religious houfes. It is indeed true, that he was
one of thofe, into whofe hands the feal of the
magnificent and opulent abbey of Saint Alban's
was furrendered on the fifth day of December,
1539, by the laft abbot, Richard Stevenache[h].
This however is the only inftance I can find,
that he was ever concerned in this fort of bufinefs. His name does not appear among the
perfons fpecially appointed by Cromwell for
this purpofe; whofe names are recited by Dugdale[i] from an authentic manufcript in the

B. 5. ch. xix. pag. 502. fol. 1619. The chamber near the Exchequer, where the augmentation-records are at prefent repofit-
ed, is not the fame. Which was the court of wards, and confequently, which was the augmentation court, will appear, by
comparing the following paffage of Stowe, who wrote in the
reign of queen Elifabeth. " At the upper end of the great
" [Weftminfter] hall by the *King's Bench*, is a going up to a
" great chamber called the *Whitehall*, wherein is now kept the
" *court of wards and liveries*, and adjoining thereto is the *court*
" *of requefts*." Survey Lond. p. 892. edit. 1616. The chamber
therefore within or adjoining to Weftminfter-hall, at the upper
end, and called the *Whitehall*, was the COURT OF AUGMEN-
TATIONS.

[h] Stevens's Monafticon, i. 264. Weever's Fun. mon. p. 112.
edit. 1631.

[i] Warwickfhire, p. 800, feq.

Cotton

Cotton Library. Nor does his name occur in the private commiſſions, which, after a diligent ſearch, I have ſeen relating to this matter ; nor in any inſtruments of reſignation, letters of advice to the viſitor general, memorials, or other authentic papers, concerning the viſitation or ſuppreſſion of any monaſtery. My opinion is therefore, that he was only occaſionally employed at Saint Alban's, as being one of the principal officers in the court of augmentations, as the place was in the neighbourhood of London, and as the ſurrender of ſo famous an abbey was an affair of ſome importance. Thus we find that the priory, now the dean and chapter, of Canterbury, was not diſſolved in the ordinary way ; it being thought neceſſary, that the archbiſhop of Canterbury, the maſter of the rolls, Walter Henley attorney and Nicholas Bacon ſollicitor of the augmentation-court with four others, ſhould be ſent thither, to take the reſignation of the prior and monks [k]. However, if it can be proved, that he was ever engaged on other occaſions in theſe violent proceedings of an avaricious and arbitrary prince, it may at the ſame time be fairly preſumed, that in an employment which afforded ſo many obvious temptations to fraud, oppreſſion and rapacity,

[k] Somner's CANTERBURY, by Batteley, Append. p. 118. It was 31. Hen. viii.

B 3                                    he

he behaved with fingular decency, moderation, and honour. Of this we have the impartial evidence of a prejudiced hiftorian. For Fuller, who is remarkably fevere on the vifitors in general, and who is feldom fparing of his invectives, wherever he can difcover the flighteft foundation for abufe, mentioning Sir Thomas Pope as an agent in thefe affairs, immediately fubjoins : " However, by " all the printed books of that age, he ap- " peareth one of a candid carriage ; and in " this refpect ftands fole and fingle by himfelf. " That of the abbey-lands which he received, " he refunded a confiderable proportion for the " building and endowing Trinity college in " Oxford[1]." And in another place, he mentions him with honour on the fame fubject. " But " the moft pleafant object to entertain us at " this time in England, is the beholding of two " fair and frefh foundations in Oxford; the " one Trinity college, built by Sir Thomas " Pope, *principal vifitor* at the diffolution of " abbies[m]. Now as none were lofers employed " in that fervice, fo we find few refunding back " to charitable ufes; and perchance this man " alone the thankful Samaritane who made a " publick acknowledgement[n]." At the furren-

---

[1] Worthies. London, p. 223.

[m] This is a miftake, as we have before feen.

[n] Church-Hift. B. viii. p. 39.

der

der of Saint Alban's Abbey, he preferved by his intereft, and particular application to the king, the noble conventual church now ftanding, and made parochial °: one of the earlieft and moft venerable monuments of Norman architecture remaining in England ʹ.

On the whole, the circumftance of his having received grants of the lands of the monafteries, feems to have occafioned the miftaken fuppofition that he was frequently and profeffedly concerned as a Commiffioner in the diffolution of their foundations. That his prodigious property was accumulated in confequence of the deftruction of the religious houfes, is not denied : and the lucky oportunity of raifing an eftate from this grand harveft of riches which now lay open before him, feems to have diverted his thoughts from making a fortune by the law ; a profeffion which he moft probably would have otherwife continued to cultivate with the greateft fuccefs, and in which he might have undoubtedly claimed the moft opulent and diftinguifhed ftations. I could give a minute detail, from the moft authentic evidences, of the grants of abbey-land, which he

* From the information of the late Sir Harry Pope-Blount, of Tittenhanger in Hertfordfhire.

ʹ It was built by Paulin, the fourteenth abbot, a Norman, about the Year 1080.

received

recieved during the reign of Henry the eighth; but it may fuffice to obferve in more general terms, that before the year 1556, he appears to have been actually poffeffed of more than thirty manors in Oxfordfhire, Gloucefterfhire, Warwickfhire, Derbyfhire, Bedfordfhire, Hereford-fhire, and Kent; befide other confiderable eftates, and feveral advowfons. Some of thefe poffeffions were given him by Henry the eighth; but the greateft part was acquired by purchafe while he was connected with the court of augmentations [q]. Many of his eftates were bought of Queen Mary [r].

But let us fuppofe, what indeed cannot be proved, that Sir Thomas Pope was one of Cromwell's vifitors in the affair of the monaf-teries. For although I have infinuated above, that thefe vifitors were not on all occafions en-tirely juftifiable in their proceedings, I am yet

---

[q] See Dugdale's Warwickfhire.   And from the patents.

[r] Ex muniment. coll. prædict. And lib. prim. *lez rates*, ann. 3, 4. Phil. Mar. MSS. Harl. 606. 257. fol. 114. In the Britifh Mufeum, ut fupr. And lib. fecund. 607. 1. fol. 1.—13. fol 7. b. ibid. In the charter of foundation for his college at Oxford, dat. Mar. iv. 1554, are recited twenty-feven manors and thirteen advowfons : befide impropriations and penfions. With all which he is licenfed to enfeoff the college. Two years after-wards, viz. May 1, 1556, in the ftatutes of the college, he re-cites thirty-five manors. Cap. vi. Afterwards he made other acquifitions.

inclined

inclined to think, that their conduct and behaviour were in general lefs blameable than
has been commonly reprefented.

It is no wonder, that the monks fhould load
thofe whom they efteemed the inftruments of
their ruin with many calumnies; all which
were ftudioufly propagated and heightened by
their advocates of the catholic perfuafion. And
it fhould at the fame time be remembered, that
the king's injunctions, under which they acted,
were extremely fevere; infomuch, that many
fraternities defired their houfes might be rather
entirely fuppreffed, than reformed under fuch
rigorous conditions.

With regard to the vices and diforders *,
which they pretended to have detected in the

---

* Even in the Nunneries, where, among the fofter fex, fome
degree of delicacy, at leaft of decorum, might have juftly been
expected, the loweft vices, not to infift on the more criminal
irregularities, were too often practifed. In the Benedictine convent of Rumfey, in Hamfhire, at a vifitation by Bifhop Fox,
held in the year 1506, Joyce Rows the abbefs is accufed of im-
moderate Drinking, efpecially " tempore nocturno ;" and of
inviting the nuns to her chamber every evening, for the purpofe
of thefe exceffes, " poft completorium." The nuns are alfo forbidden to have fuch frequent and familiar accefs, at undue.
times, to the houfe of the bailiff or chief hind of the monaftery,
whence unfavourable fufpicions have arifen; and the faid bailiff
himfelf is ordered, no more to frequent the chambers of the
abbefs or nuns. Some of them are enjoined to abftain " a fo-
" cietate

monafteries, their reports fometimes perhaps
deferve credit, as thofe enormities are too naturally and unavoidably connected with the monaftic inftitution.   In this, as in all other cafes
of that fort, mutual oppofition produced mutual obloquy.         .

Nor fhould it be forgotten, that the vifitors
gave a favorable report of fome houfes.  They
interceded earneftly for the nunnery of Godftowe in Oxfordfhire: declaring that the nuns
were ftrict in their lives; and alledging that the
fuppreffion of this houfe would prove an irreparable inconvenience, as moft of the young
ladies of the beft families of that county were
fent thither for education '.  From the abbey of

"" cietate facerdotum ;"" and the abbefs in particular is commanded to avoid all communications with Seculars; efpecially
with fome whofe names are exprefsly mentioned, and who are
known to have "" acceffum et recurfum ad Eam."" One of the
injunctions to the nuns in general is, "" *Quòa fint* fobriæ, *et fe ab-*
"" *ftineant a* potu *poft Completcrium.*"" Apud Regiftr. Fox, Epifc.
Wint. Lib. i. fol. 42. b.  This was a rich convent, and filled
with ladies of the beft families.

' Burnet. Reformat. i. 238.  This was common in other nunneries.  Tanner, from the accounts of the cellarefs of Carhow
near Norwich, gives us a curious fpecimen of what was received
"" pro perhendinationibus"" or the board of young ladies, and
their fervants, for education.  "" *Rec.* de dom. Margeria Weder-
"" ley perhendinaut. ibid. xi feptimanas, xiii.s. iv.d.  Pro menfa
"" unius famulæ dictæ Margeriæ per iii. feptimanas, viii.d. per
"" fept. &c."" Not. Mon. fol. pref. p. xxxii. [Ex orig. Rot.
nunc in Bibl. Bodl. MSS. Tanner.]

faint

faint Edmondfbury in Suffolk they wrote to Cromwell, that they could find nothing fcandalous in the Abbot or any member of the convent ᵘ. After furveying the ftately and ancient abbey of Glaftonbury, they recommended it to the Lord Privy feal, that the buildings, at leaft, might be fuffered to remain undemolifhed; reprefenting, that the ftructure in general of this monaftery was fo magnificent, that it might very properly be fpared, and eafily be converted into a palace for the king ᵂ. Gyffard, in particular, one of the vifitors, petitioned in the ftrongeft terms for the abfolute continuance of the monaftery of Woolftrope in Lincolnfhire. I will infert the words of his letter to Cromwell; not only becaufe they contain an unexpected inftance of candour, compaffion, and honefty, but as they preferve a curious picture of a well-regulated religious houfe, of the fecond magnitude, at that period. " The gover-
" nor thereof [Woolftrope] is a verie good
" hufbande for the howfe, and well beloved
" of all the inhabitants thereunto adjoyn-
" ynge :—a right honeft man, having ryghte
" religious perfones, being prefts of ryght
" good converfacion, and lyvynge relygioufly :
" having fuch qualities of vertue as we have

ᵘ Burnet, ibid. 236.
ᵂ Willis's Mitr. Abb. i. 109.

" not

" not found the lyke in no place. For ther is
" not one religious perfon ther, but that he
" can and doth ufe, either embrotheryng,
" writinge bokes with verie fair hande, mak-
" yng their owne garments, carving, paynting,
" or graffing [graving]. The howfe wythout
" eny flaunder or ill fame, and ftandinge verie
" folitarie : keepinge fuch hofpitalitie, that,
" except fingular good provyfion, it could not
" be manytened with half fo much land more
" as they may fpend. Such a number of the
" pore inhabitants nigh thereunto daily reliev-
" ed, that we have not feene the lyke, havinge
" no more lands than they have. God be even
" my judge, as I do wryte unto yow the troth.
" Which verie pitie caufeth me to write. The
" premifes confidered, I befeche yow to be a
" meane. to the king's majeftie, for the ftand-
" inge of the fayde Wolftrope ˣ. The fame

---

ˣ Strype Eccl. Mem. i. 255. From the former part of this
letter, not printed by Strype, it appears, that the king had
been difgufted at the favorable reprefentation made by Gyffard and his affociates, of this and other monafteries : but that
his Majefty's difpleafure did not prevent him from telling the
truth. " And forafmuch as of late my fellowes and I wright
" untoo Mr. Chancellor of the augmentacions, in the favour
" of thabbey of feynt James, and the nunnerie of Catefbie in
" Northamptonfhire : which letters be fhewed unto the kynge's
" highnes in the favour of thofe howfes, where the kyngis
" highnes was *difpleafed*, as he fayd to my fervaunt, fayinge,
" that *it was like that we had receyved rewards, which caufed us*
" to

commiffioner, with three others of his affociates in the vifitation, pleaded in the fame be-
nevolent ftrain for the nunnery of Catefby in
Northamptonfhire. " This houfe we found in
" very perfett order. The priores a fure, wife,
" difcreet, and very relygious woman ; with
" ix nunnys under her obedyence, as relygious
" and devout, and with as good obedyence as
" we have in time pafte feen, or belyke fhall
" fee. The feid howfe ftandyth in fuch a
" quarter much to the releff of the king's peo-
" ple, and his grace's pore fubjects their [there]
" likewyfe moo relieved. —Wherefore yf yt
" fhuld pleafe the kyng's highnes *to have eny*
" *remorfe,* that eny fuch religious howfe fhall
" ftande ; we think his grace cannot appointe
" eny howfe more mete to fhewe his moft gra-
" cious charitie and pitey over than on the
" faide howfe of Catefby ʸ." I find alfo Gyffard interceding in the fame manner for the
nunnery of Polefworth in Warwickfhire.

---

" *to wright as we dyd*; which myght putt mee in feare to
" wright : notwithftanding the fure knowledge that I have had
" allway in your indifferens, gyveth me boldnefs to wright to
" you in the favour of the houfe of Woolftrope. *The Governor*
" *thereof*, &c." Dat. Jun. xix. 1537. Brit. Muf. MSS. Cott.
Claud. E. iv. fol. 213. The letter about Catefby will be cited
below.

ʸ Strype ibid. who has printed it incorrectly from Bibl. Cotton, MSS. Cl. iv. fol. 209. Brit. Muf. fee other letters of the
like kind in Collier, Eccl. hift. p. 2. b. iii. pag. 156.

" Wherein

" Wherein is an abbes namyd dame Alice
" Fitzherbert, of the age of lx yeares, a very
" fadde, difcreate, and religyous woman :—
" and in the fame howfe, under her rule, are
" xii vertuous and religyous nonnes, and of
" good converfation. —Wherefore ye myght
" do a ryght good and merytorious dede, to
" be medyatour to the kyng's highnes for the
" faid howfe to ftande and remayne unfuppref-
" fed.—And in the town of Polefworth are
" xliv tenements, and never a plough but
" one ᶻ : the refydue be artifycers, laborers,
" and victellers, and live in effect by the faid
" howfe, and the repayre and reforte that ys
" made to the gentylmens childern and ftu-
" diountes, that ther do lyf, to the nombre
" fometyme of xxx and fometyme xl and
" more; that their be ryght vertuoufly brought
" upp, &c. Written at Maxftocke befide Co-
" ventree the xxviii day of July ᵃ." [1537.]
Many others of the commiffioners alfo fhewed
a compaffionate concern for the religious at
their expulfion, in providing them proper pen-

---

ᶻ Nor was it likely there fhould be another, while the nunnery remained. The truth is, wherever there was a monaftery,
idlenefs was encouraged, and the ufual incitements to labour and
induftry were fuperfeded.

ᵃ MSS. Cotton. Claud. E. iv. ut fupr. fol. 210. b.

fions

fions, according to their age, infirmities, or other circumftances of diftrefs [b].

In the reign of Henry the eighth, Sir Thomas Pope was employed in various fervices and attendances about the court. He was appointed [c], April 21, 1544, together with Sir Edward North, afterwards Lord North, to convey the great feal of England, being refigned by the lord chancellor Audley then indifpofed, to the king at his new palace of Weftminfter, who delivered it into the cuftody of Sir Thomas Wriotheffey [d]. There is a circumftance

[b] Strype, ubi fupr. feq. Willis Mitr. Abb. &c. Dr. London, one of the vifitors, thus writes to lord Cromwell about the monaftery of De La Pre near Northampton. " Befechinge your " lordfhip to be gude lorde unto herre [the abbefs] and to herre " poor fifters in their penfions." MSS. Cotton. ut fupr. fol. 208.

[c] Perhaps as clerk of the crown.

[d] " Memorandum, quod die Lunæ, viz. vicefimo primo die Aprilis, anno regni Domini noftri Henrici octavi, dei gratia, Angliæ, &c, tricefimo quinto : Thomas Audeley miles, dominus Audeley de Walden, tunc Cancellarius Angliæ, infirmitate corporis debilitatus, magnum figillum .... præfato domino regi, per Edvardum North militem, et *Thomam Pope* militem, mifit ; qui quidem Edvardus, et *Thomas Pope*, figillum illud, in quâdam bagâ de albo corio inclufum, et figillo dicti Dom. cancellarii munitum, regiæ mageftati apud *Palatium* fuum *novum Weftmonafterienfe*, in camerâ fuâ privatâ .... in prefentiâ Thomæ Henneage militis, et Antonii Denny armigeri, præfentarunt et obtulerunt : humiliter fupplicantes .... eandem regiam mageftatem, quatenus idem D. rex figillum fuum prædictum

relating to this refignation which is not mentioned by any of our hiftorians. For the king
committed the feal to Sir Thomas Wriothefley,
with the title of keeper, only during the indif-
● pofition of lord Audley; with the refervation
of reinftating him in the chancellorfhip on his
recovery ᵉ. In 1547, he feems to have been
fummoned and examined by the privy council,
concerning certain treafonable expreffions which
had dropped from Thomas duke of Norfolk,
afterwards condemned with lord Surrey but
not executed, in reference to the Act of
Ufes ᶠ. He was a fingular and moft intimate
friend of fir Thomas More, who feems to
have taken early notice of him, as I before
hinted, when a young man in the court of
chancery; and was fent by the king, to notify
to that illuftrious fufferer in the caufe of miftaken confcience, the hour appointed for his
execution.   ·

dictum recipere et acceptare dignetur.  Super quo dictus D.
rex figillum illud, per manus ipforum Edvardi et *Thomæ Pope,*
recepit et acceptavit, &c. &c." Rymer, Fœd. Tom. xv. p. 20.
*Super deliberatione magni figilli.*

  ᵉ Rymer, ibid.

  ᶠ Herbert's Hift. Hen. viii. p. 564. edit. 1649. The hiftorian
fays, " *One* Thomas Pope informed the council, &c." It may
therefore be doubted whether he means fir Thomas Pope. But
it is the fame in Mafters's *Text* of this hiftory, in Jefus college
library. MSS. No. 2098. 79. vol. 3.

As

As the interview between thefe two friends, on this important occafion, is memorable and interefting, I fhall infert it at length.

On the fifth day of July [z], 1535, he waited on fir Thomas More, then under condemnation in the Tower, early in the morning; and acquainted him that he came by command of the king and council, to bring his unfortunate friend the melancholy news, that he muft fuffer death before nine of the clock the fame morning, and that therefore he fhould immediately begin to prepare himfelf for that aweful event. Upon this meffage, More, without the leaft furprize or emotion, chearfully replied; " Mafter Pope, I moft heartily thank you " for your good tidings. I have been much " bound to the king's highnefs for the benefits " of his honors that he hath moft bountifully " beftowed upon me; yet am I more bound to " his grace, I affure you, for putting me here, " where I have had convenient time and fpace " to have remembrance of my end. And fo " help me god. Moft of all am I bound unto " him, that it hath pleafed his majefty fo " fhortly to rid me out of the miferies of this " wicked world." Then Pope fubjoined, that it was the king's pleafure that at the place of execution he fhould not ufe many words. To this More anfwered, that he was ready to fubmit to the king's commands; and added, " I " befeech you good Mr. Pope, to gett the king " to fuffer my daughter Margaret to be prefent " at my burial." Pope affured him that he would ufe his utmoft intereft with the king for this purpofe : and having now finifhed his difagreeable commiffion, he folemnly took leave of his dying friend, and burft into tears. More perceiving his concern, faid with his ufual compofure; " Quiet yourfelf, good Mr. " Pope, and be not difcomforted; for I truft " that we fhall one day in heaven fee each " other full merrily, where we fhall be fure to " live and love together in joyful blifs eternal- " ly [h]." But this method of confolation proving ineffectual, More to divert the melancholy of his friend, and to difmifs him in better fpirits, called for a glafs; and applying it as an urinal, he held it up to the light, and with the prophetic air of a fagacious phyfician gravely declared, " This man might have lived longer " if it had pleafed the king [i]."

[h] Roper's Life of More, by T. Hearne, 4. 57.

[i] Thomæ Mori Vita et Exitus : by J. H. gent. Lond. 1652. pag. 127.

In

In confequence of fir Thomas Pope's in-
terceffion with the king, agreeably to More's
earneft and dying requeft, his favorite daughter, Margaret Roper, and others of his family
were permitted to be prefent at his interment,
which was performed immediately after the
execution in the chapel of the Tower. But
Margaret afterwards, and probably by the
fame intereft, begged the body of the king,
and depofited it on the fouth-fide of the choir
of the church of Chelfea, where a monument, with an infcription written by himfelf,
had been erected fome time before. This
affectionate daughter, whofe refolution equals
her pity, alfo found means to procure her
father's head, after it had remained, ignominioufly ftuck on a pole, on London brid;e,
for fourteen days. For this daring fact fhe
was apprehended and imprifoned; but declaring in her defence before the privy council, that fhe had bought it that it might not
in the end become food for fifhes in the
Thames, fhe was difcharged [k]. However fhe
carefully preferved it for fome time in a
leaden box, till an opportunity offered of con-

[k] Weever Fun. Mon. 505, 506, 522. Biograp. Brit. MORE.
pag. 3165.

veying

veying it to Canterbury, where fhe placed it
in a vault belonging to her hufband's family,
under a chapel adjoining to faint Dunftan's.
church in that city [1].

[1] Wood, Ath. Oxon. i. 39.

✝✝✝✝✝✝✝✝✝✝✝✝✝✝✝✝✝✝✝✝✝✝✝✝✝✝✝✝✝✝✝✝✝✝

## S E C T.  II.

IN the reign of Edward the fixth, when the religious and political affairs of the kingdom took another turn, and all public bufinefs fell into the hands of new miniſters and managers, ſir Thomas Pope did not comply with the times. He was appointed to no office, nor enjoyed any favor in this reign. He received indeed ſome grants of land from the crown about the firſt year of this king, with Cranmer archbiſhop of Canterbury, the duke of Somerſet, the earl of Warwick, the marquis of Northampton, and ſeveral other principal perſons of the court. But theſe grants were made for paſt ſervices, and in conſideration of other claims due from the deceaſed king [m].

[m] Strype Eccl. Mem. ii. 78.—Some of the particulars may perhaps be ſeen in pat. 1. Edw. vi. teſt. Jul. 24. par. 4.—Likewiſe, in this reign, ſir Richard Leigh is licenced to alienate a manor to ſir T. Pope, pat. 1. Edw. vi. teſt. Maii 27. par. 7.—Sir 'T. Pope is licenced to alienate a paſture in Bermondſey to Will. Gerrard, pat. 2. Edw. vi. teſt. Jan. 16. par. 3.—Sir T. Pope is licenced to alienate the manor of Broughton, co. Oxon. to William Godolphin and Henry Boothe, pat. 5. Edw. vi. teſt. Sept. 17. par. 7. Theſe are all the patents, of any ſort, which he received in this reign.

C 3                    The

The unlimited authority, and arbitrary do-
minion of Henry, had kept both proteſtants
and papiſts in ſubjection. Under ſuch a government they both acted uniformly, and neither
party preſumed to claim any apparent ſuperiori-
ty. But upon the deceaſe of that uncontroulable
monarch, the people diſcovered their real ſentiments without reſerve, and proteſtantiſm
manifeſtly began to be the prevailing religion.
The protector Somerſet, who had long been
a ſecret partiſan of the reformers, on the acceſſion of young Edward, publicly declared
his intention of forwarding and eſtabliſhing
the reformation. In this ſcheme he was happily ſeconded by moſt of the privy council,
who after the fall of Southampton ſeem entirely to have deſerted the catholic communion. The protector wiſely took care that
all perſons to whom he entruſted the education of the young king, ſhould be attached
to theſe rational principles ; and preferred and
encouraged thoſe alone that appeared active in
this profeſſion.

Thus moſt of the courtiers, yet more perhaps
in general from lucrative views than from real
conviction, became converts to the predomi-
nant party : amongſt which, however, I do
not find ſir Thomas Pope. This, at leaſt,
ſhews

fhews a fteadinefs and uniformity of mind in thofe days of change, which afford fuch frequent inftances of occafional compliance.

Nor let it be deemed any inconfiftency of character, that he, though a rigid papift, fhould have been in the preceding reign an agent for fuppreffing the monafteries, and a receiver of their poffeffions. For the demolition of thefe houfes was not an act of the church but of the ftate. It was prior to the reformation of religion, and effected by a king and parliament of the popifh communion. It was even confirmed by the parliament of queen Mary [n].

Very few papifts wrote or remonftrated againft the deftruction of thefe focieties. Without the leaft impeachment of their principles, or fufpicion of apoftacy, feveral others, the ftricteft members of the catholic perfuafion, and the moft refpectable characters of thofe times, among which, to mention no more, was the duke of Norfolk, accepted grants of the conventual eftates.

Even the clergy thought it no facrilege to fhare in thefe acquifitions. The dean and

[n] Statut, 1, 2. Phil. Mar. cap. viii. inf. citat.

chapter

chapter of Litchfield, and the abbot and convent of Weftminfter, made no fcruple of receiving manors alienated from other religious
corporations [o], lately diffolved. Burnet tells
us [p], that bifhop Gardiner was remarkably vehement in declaiming againft the monafteries;
and that in many of his fermons he commend-
ed the king for fuppreffing them [q]. Queen
Mary, in the very firft year of her reign, made
grants of the fite of twenty religious houfes,
and of very large quantities of abbey-land [r].
The bifhops and clergy in a catholic convocation, 1554, petitioned that the pope would
not infift on a reftitution of the ecclefiaftical
revenues, but rather confirm them to thofe
lords and gentlemen by whom they had been
obtained [s]. And it is notorious, that fome of
the popifh bifhops were no lefs alienators of
their epifcopal endowments [t], than many
other bifhops of the proteftant church proved
afterwards, in the reigns of Edward the fixth
and Elizabeth. The bifhop of Chichefter, in
opening the difputation of Henry the eighth

[o] See Tanner's Notit. Mon. fol. edit. pref. p. xxxix.
[p] Ref. i. 251.
[q] See Fox, vol. ii. p. 426.
[r] Tanner, ubi fupr.
[s] Wilkins's Councils. iv. 101.
[t] Tanner ubi fupr. And Collier Eccl. hift. xi. 324, 306.
Heylin p. 121.

with

with Lambert, in Weftminfter-hall, ranked the king's difincorporation of the monks with his rejection of the fee of Rome, his abolition of idolatrous adoration, and the introduction of the Englifh bible; as a matter of an external nature, and in no refpect interfering with the effentials of the catholic communion ⁿ. The monaftic inftitution was no part of the papiftic theology. Undoubtedly the fuppreffion of the convents facilitated the admiffion of proteftatifm : but it was evidently undertaken on other principles.

When queen Mary fucceeded to the throne, fir Thomas Pope was again taken into favour, and foon afterwards conftituted one of the queen's privy counfellors ᵛ. He is likewife faid to have been appointed cofferer to the houfhold ˣ.

But before I proceed further in this reign, it may be proper to obviate fome feeming difficulties and inconfiftences, by premifing, on what fecurity fir Thomas Pope, together with many others, held his church-revenues, under

---

ⁿ See MSS. C. C. C. C. cxxvii. 5.

ᵛ Hollingfhead, iii. 1159. Speed, 854.

ˣ MSS. Rawlinf. bibl. Bodl. Hiftory of Oxfordfhire, *Wroxtew*. But it does not appear by the patents. And Richard Frefton is made cofferer, pat. 3, 4. Phil. Mar. par. 2.

a bigotted

a bigotted catholic queen, and upon the reſtoration of the popiſh religion. By way of procuring new conceſſions in favour of Rome, and to prevent unſeaſonable alarms, at the beginning of this reign, both the queen and the pope had given repeated aſſurances that the church and abbey lands ſhould remain, forever unreclaimed, in the hands of their preſent poſſeſſors [y]. But that the tenure of theſe poſſeſſions ſhould not be fixed on ſo precarious a foundation as that of mere promiſes, in 1554, an act of parliament was paſſed; which, while it reſtored the pope's authority, gave abſolute ſecurity to the proprietors of the eccleſiaſtical eſtates, entirely confirmed their title beyond the power of reſumption, and, at the ſame time, exempted them from the danger of ſpiritual cenſures [z]. In the mean time, that this meaſure might receive the fulleſt ſanction, cardinal Pole, who was inveſted by the pope with legantine juriſdiction, ratified the parliament's decree : and, that the diſpenſation might be ſtill more ample and effectual, in conſequence of his maſter's commiſſion, the legate enſured even the property of future acquiſitions of church lands to the preſent receivers [a].

[y] Heylin Eccleſ. reſt. p. 41.
[z] Statut. 1, 2. Phil. Mar. cap. viii.
[a] Ibid. And Strype Eccl. Mem. iii. 159. ſeq. See alſo Harl. miſcell. vii. p. 264, 266.

Thus,

Thus, an equivalent was granted on both fides. The nobility and gentry were fettled in the quiet enjoyment of their eftates ; and the pope, although moft effentially weakened by the alienation of that wealth on which his power fo much depended, was reinftated in his fupremacy over the church.

During this reign fir Thomas Pope was often employed in. commiffions of confequence. On the twenty-ninth day of July, 1553, he was commiffioned by the council, together with fir Arthur Darcy, and others[b], to apprehend lord Ruffel, Anthony Browne of Effex, and feveral accomplices concerned in the duke of Northumberland's infurrection ; who, on the death of Edward, had raifed an army with an intent to place the lady Jane Gray on the throne, before Mary was proclaimed queen. The duke himfelf had been apprehended fome little time before. For after many fruitlefs efforts, and vain expectations of a reinforcement, he fuddenly changed his principles, difmiffed his troops, and tamely fubmitted to proclaim queen Mary with all external demonftrations of triumph and fatisfaction. Being immediately arrefted by the

[b] Burghley's State papers, by Haynes, p. 162.

earl

earl of Arundel, he fell on his knees and ab-
jectly begged his life [c].

In the fame year, on the twenty-third day of
February, I find him directed by the council,
together with lord Rich, the mafter of the
rolls, the lieutenant of the Tower, and others,
to appoint a certain number of the council,
who fhould conftantly remain, and difpatch
bufinefs, at London [d]. For the court, whom
the privy council always followed. and attended, was often held at different palaces in the
country; as at Oatelands, Richmond, Greenwich, and other places [e]. At the fame time he
is commanded, with the fame perfons, to give
orders for victualling and furnifhing the Tower
of London [f]. There was another commiffion,
the fame year, directed by the queen to fir
Richard Southwell, and others, for infpecting
the office of ordinance, and examining the
ftate of ammunition in the Tower [g]. By which

[c] Burnet, Ref. ii. 239.
[d] Q Mary's council book, MSS. Harl. Brit. muf. 643.
[e] In the reign of Henry the eighth, the principal places of
the royal refidence in the country were Richmond, Hampton
court, Wind.or, Eltham, and Woodftock. In a book of Injunctions for that king's houfhold, given by Cardinal Wolfey, it is
at thefe five palaces only, when the king is prefent, that the
folemnities of the Chapel and Hall are ordered to be kept.
MSS. Laud. K. 48.
[f] Council book.
[g] Strype Eccl. Mem. iii. 33.

it

it appears, that this department had been greatly neglected in the foregoing reign; or that the queen was willing to take the proper precautions againft any future attack on her title, from her factious and difcontented fub-jects. The fame year, on the twenty-ninth day of October, he was appointed, with the lord treafurer, the earl of Arundel, lord Rich, fir Francis Englefield, and feveral others, to examine certain offenders taken in Northumberland's rebellion, and to affefs their fines [h]. Soon afterwards, in the beginning of 1554, I find him prefent, together with fir Philip Denny, fir Thomas Brydges, and others, when fir Thomas Wyat, and his defperate affociates, after their rafh and abortive enterprife, were led prifoners into the tower of London. On which occafion fir Thomas Pope feverely reproached Brett, one of the principal rebels, for his complicated cowardice and treachery. A charge which the prifoner could not but acknowledge with much fhame and confufion. For Brett, being the captain of a detachment of archers in the queen's fervice, had privately revolted with all his party at a time of danger, and joined Wyat's army [i].

---

[h] Burghley's State papers, ut fupr. p. 193.

[i] *MSS. Annale of queene Marie her reigne.* MSS. Harl. 194. Brit. Muf.—This, and other particulars, have been tranfcribed by Stowe. Annals, ed. 1615. p. 621. col. 2.—The manufcript adds,

In the fame year, fir Thomas Pope was one
of the champions at a magnificent jufting exhibited before the queen at Weftminfter.  On
which occafion the horfes were richly capa-
rifoned with red velvet and filver boffes, and
the helmets of the knights were plumed with
oftrich-feathers.  Many Spanifh noblemen
were prefent [k].

On the fifteenth of March, 1554, he was
conftituted, with fir Robert Rochefter, comptroller of the houfhold, fir Richard Southwell,
fir Thomas Cornwallis, fir Edmund Peckham,
and fir Edward North, knights, a commiffioner, for examining, adjufting, and balancing
the accounts of fir Thomas Grefham, who
was agent to the queen at Antwerp for taking

adds, that during the fkirmifh of Charing-crofs in which Wyat
was taken, " there ftood upon the leades [of the white tower]
" the marques of Northampton, fir Nicholas Poines, Sir Tho-
" mas Pope, mafter John Seimer, and others." This paffage is
alfo tranfcribed by Stowe. This manufcript formerly belonged
to Stowe, who drew from it great part of queen Mary's reign :
yet omiting many paffages. It is cited by fir Simonds D'Ewes,
to whom it afterwards belonged, in his tract, entit. *Primitive
Practife for preferving Truth*. Lond. 1645. 4to. He fays it was
written " by a courtier under queen Mary,—the very auto-
" graph be'ng in my library, written with his own hand."
p. 13.

[k] MSS. Cotton. Vitell. F, 5. MSS. Strype.

up money of the merchants of that city[1]. The commiſſioners are ordered to examine, allow, and determine all receipts, payments, charges, and diſcharges, declarations, or employments, of ſir Thomas Greſham, or his agents ; to aſſign him, by deduction, an allowance of twenty ſhillings per day, with all incidental expences : and finally to acquit and diſcharge the ſaid ſir Thomas Greſham : to charge and diſcharge all allowances and defalcations in ſtating the account, according to their wiſdom and diſcretion, either of monies taken up for Edward the ſixth, or for the preſent queen. For this buſineſs ſir Thomas Pope was admirably qualified, from that knowledge and experience in ſtating extenſive and complicated accounts, which he muſt have acquired while he was concerned in the court of Augmentations. And for the ſame reaſon, in the ſucceeding reign, ſir Walter Mildmay was deputed by the lords, to make a general inquiſition of the royal revenue[m].

---

[1] Rymer's Fœd. tom. xv. p. 371. *Pro Thoma Greſham de commiſſariis ad computa examinanda.* " Mary by the grace of God, &c. To our right truſtie and wel-belovid counſaillors, ſir Rob. Rocheſter, comptroller of our houſe, ſir Rich. Southwell, knight, ſir Thomas Cornwallis, knight, and to our truſtie and right wel-belovid ſir Edward North, and ſir *Thomas Pope*, knights, Greetinge. . . . We having ſpecial truſt and confidence in your approvid fidelities, wiſdomes, and circumſpcctions, &c."

[m] Strype. Ann. Ref. i. 13. ſect. ii.

This

This expedient of borrowing money at an
exorbitant intereft of the merchants of Antwerp, was a meafure which Mary was obliged to put in practice more than once ". And
it had been to her honor, if fhe had ufed no
worfe. For indeed the chief object of government, which for fome time engaged her
attention, was to raife large fums by the moft
irregular methods, or to extort money from
her fubjects. She fometimes endeavoured to
recruit her exhaufted exchequer by retrench-
ing the public expences at home. She demolifhed feveral forts on the river below
Gravefend, which were filled with fuperflu-
ous garrifons; fhe broke all the body guards,
half the band of penfioners, the gentlemen
of the ftables, and the pages of honor:
and propofed to difband the hundred archers
of the guard. But to frugality fhe added
oppreffion, and her unhappy neceffities frequently compelled her to the moft violent and
unjuftifiable experiments. She levied fixty
thoufand marks from feven thoufand yeomen,
and thirty-fix thoufand pounds from the merchants. This was exacted, becaufe they had
not contributed to a former loan of fixty thoufand pounds levied on a thoufand perfons, in

---

" Council-book. MSS. Brit. Muf. ut fupr.

whofe

whofe compliance, either on account of their loyalty or their riches, fhe firmly confided. But that tax not being found fufficient, fhe exacted a general loan of an hundred pounds each, on all who poffeffed an annual income of twenty pounds. This impofition obliged many of the gentry to reduce their domeftic expences, and to difmifs many of their fervants, that they might, at leaft more prudently, comply with her commands. And as thefe fervants, having no means of fubfiftence, by too common a tranfition from that ftate of idlenefs, betook themfelves to theft and robbery, the queen knew no better method of redreffing the grievance, than to publifh a proclamation, obliging their former mafters to take them back to their fervices. In order to gratify the city of London for paft favors, and to engage them to affift her with future fupplies, fhe iffued an edict, at their inftance, prohibiting for four months, the exportation of Englifh clothes into Flanders. By this iniquitous combination, a good market was procured in that country for fuch as had already fent thither large quantities of that fort of merchandife °.

Her extravagancies proved a perpetual ob-ftruction to the commercial interefts of the

° Carte, iii. 330, 331, 337, 341.

D          kingdom.

kingdom. Her own bigottry was not always a
fufficient reftraint on her confcience, to prevent her from expofing to fale the revenues ?
of that church, in defence of which fhe had
facrificed in the flames fo many victims. But
it would be endlefs and impertinent here, to
mention at large her multiplied extortions;
and the various imprudent or fraudulent
fchemes, which her exigencies invented for
obtaining money. It may be fufficient to
add, that thefe expedients were employed, not
to carry on an expenfive war, for fhe was in
profound peace with all the world; nor to
promote the national welfare by any new efta-
blifhments or improvements : but to fatisfy
the unjuft demands of a hufband, who flighted
her love, neglected her interefts, and folely
confulted his own convenience.

On this occafion one cannot help obferving
the weaknefs of the human mind under the
moft powerful and importunate of paffions.
Mary regarded her hufband Philip with all the
fondnefs and follicitude of an uncertain lover.
This attachment produced ftrange contradic-
tions in her fentiments and behaviour. She
was naturally too phlegmatic to be profufe;
yet, from a penurious and economical habit

P See fupr. pag. 40.

of

of mind, she suddenly became rapacious and expensive. She persecuted the reformed with the most barbarous severities, yet alienated the riches assigned to support her favorite superstitions. In this situation, she was at once deserted by that cold and stoical inflexibility which distinguishes her character; and the sedate and gloomy queen suffered herself to be betrayed into greater inconsistencies of conduct, than even the most unaccountable caprice of her father Henry could have dictated.

Before the reign of queen Mary, it was the common practice with our English princes to have recourse to the city of Antwerp for voluntary loans; and we generally find their credit so low, that they were obliged to engage the city of London to join in the security. But this business seems never to have been so effectually conducted as by that public-spirited and enterprizing merchant, sir Thomas Gresham, who began to be employed in this agency by Edward the sixth[q]. He was likewise employed by queen Elizabeth for the same purpose; one of whose first steps, at her accession, was to procure money. She

_____

[q] See Burghley's State papers, by Haynes, p. 185. And Ward's Life of Gresham, p. 7.

D 2                                                      sent fent Grefham to Antwerp to borrow two hundred thoufand pounds, in order to enable her to reform the coinage, at that time extremely debafed. But, as a moft fenfible and acute hiftorian obferves ', fhe was fo impolitic as to make herfelf an innovation in the coin; by dividing a pound of filver into fixty-two fhillings, inftead of fixty, the former ftandard.

In the year 1557, on the eighth of February, fir Thomas Pope was joined by the queen, in a famous commiffion for the more effectual fuppreffion of heretics ', in concert with Bonner, bifhop of London, Thirlby, bifhop of Ely, the Lords Windfor and North, fecretary Bourne, fir John Mordaunt, fir Francis Englefield, fir Edward Waldegrave, fir Nicholas Hare, fir Roger Cholmeley, fir Richard Read, fir Thomas Stradling, fir Rowland Hill, ferjeant Raftall, Cole, dean of faint Paul's, William Cooke, Thomas Martin, John Story, and John Vaughan, doctors of law, and William Roper and Ralph Cholmeley, efquires. Thefe commiffioners were empowered to enquire after all perfons fufpected of heretical

---

' Hume, hift. Eliz. p. 731. edit. 4to.

* Burnet's Reformation, Coll. of records, part. ii. b. ii. p. 311. " Having fpecial truft and confidence in your fidelities, " wifdoms, and difcretions, &c."

opinions :

opinions: to fearch for and feize feditious
and heterodox books, either expofed to fale,
or fecreted in private houfes: to invefti-
gate and examine concealments, contempts,
confpiracies, and calumnies, againft the government. They were ordered to detect thofe
perfons who refufed to preach the facrament
of the altar, to hear mafs, to take holy bread
or holy water, to frequent their refpective
public churches, and to affift in the folemn
proceffions. They were likewife privileged
to fummon what witneffes they judged moft
proper, and to tender oaths to the parties
profecuted, for anfwering fuch queftions as
might be deemed moft convenient for dif-
covering the truth, In this injunction however, there is a remarkable claufe of reftraint
upon the commiffioners. For it is expreffly
commanded, that if any perfon brought before them for heretical doctrines or opinions,
fhould ftill obftinately perfift in his error,
" He fhould immediately be committed to
" his ordinary, there to be ufed according to
" the fpiritual and ecclefiaftical laws."

Bifhop Burnet, whofe imagination was perpetually haunted with the horrors of popery,
fuppofes, that fomething more dreadful was
intended by this commiffion than appears at
firft fight, and that it was undoubtedly de-

figned

figned as the tribunal of an Inquifition in England [t]. But a fuperficial reader may plainly perceive, that there is nothing of the form, procefs, or power, of an Inquifition contained in this inftrument. The commiffioners receive no authority to try heterodoxy, nor to put the offenders upon *making an act of faith*. On the contrary, they are directed to deliver up all delinquents to the ordinary. And even here the procefs is to be regulated by the laws of the church. Thefe circumftances feem fufficiently to exclude the idea of an inquifitorial tribunal. For the proceedings of the commiffioners, however rigoroufly they might have been conducted, were not unlimited and arbitrary; but finally determinable by the proper ecclefiaftical officer, who was himfelf controlled by the fpiritual conftitutions of the land, which did not at leaft on this occafion, receive any degree of extenfion. The zealous bifhop makes the matter ftill more alarming, where he tells us, that in fupport of fuch meafures, " he finds it faid, that fome ad- " vifed that courts of inquifition, like thofe in " France and Spain, might be fet up in " England [u]." But he does not inform us by whom this is faid, nor can I find this advice

[t] Hift. Ref. ii. 347.
[u] Ubi fupr. p. 346.

in

in any of our hiftorians. Even Fox, who omits nothing that can expofe the papifts, who has ftudioufly recorded all the idle reports of the times, and who fuppofed that the papifts worfhipped one god and the proteftants another ᵂ, is filent on this important fubject. And indeed if we confider the queen's late expoftulation with the pope, in which fhe declared her refolution of maintaining the prerogative and the conftitution ˣ; if we re-collect that Philip's confeffor, Alphonfus, ex-preffly declaimed againft perfecutions in the pulpit, by the king's own defire ʸ : and if to thefe reafons we add the diftinguifhed lenity, moderation, and candor of cardinal Pope ; this project of an Englifh inquifition muft appear altogether improbable.

But whatever was the real ftate of the cafe, we find that the commiffioners, fenfible that perfecution naturally counteracts its own pur-

---

ᵂ He thus rallies the devotion of the people, for praying for Mary's happy delivery of a child, " Cry up louder you priefts, " peradventure ʏᴏᴜʀ ɢᴏᴅ ɪs ᴀsʟᴇᴇᴘ. Vol. iii. p. 116.

ˣ When the Pope would have obtruded a new legate, in the place of cardinal Pole, and while he was actually on his journey to England, the queen abfolutely refufed his admiffion into the kingdom. Collier, Eccl. Hift. ii. 403.

ʸ Neal's Hift. Pur. i. 99. Strype Eccl. Mem. iii. 239. Hey-lin, p. 56. Burnet, Ref. ii. 305.

pofe,

pofe, and averfe to meafures which might probably end in the moft inhuman punifhments,
did little or nothing in this bufinefs [z]: efpecially as to the detection of prohibited books.
For fo inactive were they, that on the fixth
of June, 1558, the queen was obliged to publifh a proclamation [a]; in which fhe complains, that not only numberlefs feditious and
treafonable treatifes, were printed at home and
difperfed without controul, but even imported from abroad. As the provocation was great,
fo the proclamation is conceived in the moft
defpotic and unconftitutional terms. It fets
forth, amonft other extraordinary menaces,
that if thofe perfons who find fuch unlaw-
ful books do not immediately deftroy them,
they fhall be reputed rebels, and executed
accordingly by martial law. The queen indeed had fome reafon for complaint, and for
fubftituting fomewhat more effectual in the
place of her former commiffion by this recent
injunction. For during the actual fubfiftence
and authority of that commiffion, Knox and
Goodman printed, and imported from Geneva,
a piece entitled, *The firft Blaft of the Trumpet
againft the monftrous Regimen of Women* [b]. In

[z] Heylin, ubi fupr.
[a] Heylin, ubi fupr. Strype, Eccl. Mem. iii. 459.
[b] Genev. 8vo. 1558.

this

this performance, which is full of paradox and enthufiafm, they call the queen *Trait-refs, Baftard, Proferpine*; with other terms of illiberal and ridiculous abufe. Goodman alfo publifhed about the fame time, *How fuperior Powers ought to be obeyed of their Subjects, and wherein they may be lawfully by God's Word difobeyed and refifted* [c]. But thefe treatifes, written chiefly for the gratification of Calvin then living at Geneva, were not more invectives againft the invincible bigottries of Mary, and the grofs abfurdities of popery, than they were openly fubverfive of all eftablifhed government and religion. Juft before, a book of very pernicious tendency had appeared [d], called a *Treatife of politick Power* [e]. Plays and enterludes ridiculing the queen's perfon and

[c] Genev. 16to. 1558. printed by John Crifpin. Unluckily, Mary herfelf while princefs, in 1548, yet certainly without any heretical intention, had publifhed a piece, which of courfe fell under the cenfure of this commiffion. It was a tranflation of Erafmus's paraphrafe on St. John, and done by defire of queen Catharine Parr. The preface is written by Udall, mafter of Eton-fchool; in which he much extolls, and I believe not without reafon, Mary's proficience in literature.

[d] Collier, Eccl. Hift. p. ii. p. 404.

[e] Suppofed to be written by Poynett, the deprived bifhop of Winton. infra citat. Stowe reports, that Poynett was in Wyatt's army; but that finding that enterprife likely to mifcarry, he fled, and embarked for Germany, where he joined his reformed brethren, the religious exiles. Stowe, Ann. per Howes, p. 620.

govern-

government were exhibited [f]. Libels and fatires were thrown into the houfes of the privy counfellors ; and even dropped in the queen's own chamber.

Amongft other pafquinades, there were prints, or pictures, reprefenting her majefty, naked, meager, withered, and wrinkled, with every aggravated circumftance of deformity that could difgrace a female figure, feated in a regal chair ; a crown on her head, furrrounded with M. R. and A. in capital characters. In the firft of thefe was written, in fmall letters, *Maria*, in the fecond *regina*, and in the third *Angliæ*. The additional figures were a great number of Spaniards fucking her. Underneath, in Italian characters, were legends, fignifying that the Spaniards had fucked her to fkin and bone ; as alfo fpecifying minutely the money, rings, jewels, and other prefents, with which fhe had fecretly gratified her hufband Philip. The queen was highly incenfed at this infolent and popular piece of ridicule; efpecially as fhe fufpected fome of her own council, who alone were privy to thefe tranfactions, and acquainted with her fecrets [g].

[f] Council book, MSS. Harl. and Strype. Burnet.
[g] Carte, iii. 331.

With

With regard to the perfecutions of this reign, which occafioned the commiffion in which Sir Thomas Pope was concerned, relating to the fuppreffion of heretics, we will allow that the queen and her friends had fuffered, what they thought the moft injurious treatment; and, no doubt, when power returned into their hands, were but too naturally difpofed to retaliate in their own way. Thefe oppreffions, perhaps injudicioufly conducted, prepared the way for popery : juft as the feverities of Mary, at the fucceffion of Elifabeth made the proteftants more violent againft the papifts. In the reign of Henry the eighth, the monafteries were deftroyed, and the wealth of the church, in which it's ftrength confifted, was diffipated. Three of the abbots, in the courfe of that tranfaction, were unjuftly put to death [h]. Six bifhops, amongft which were Mary's favorites, and the great champions of her religion, Bonner and Gardiner, were deprived, infulted, and imprifoned, during the reign of Edward the fixth [i]. In the fame reign, the queen, while princefs, was abfolutely forbidden to hear mafs ; a misfortune, in her ideas, almoft equal

[h] Collier, Eccl. Hift. ii. 164.
[i] See Heylin, Ecclef. Reft. fub. ann. 1551.

to

to the lofs of life [k] : and her friends who privately interpofed to defeat the execution of this dreadful interdiction, were fent to the Tower [l].

But as no religion can expiate, fo no provocation can juftify, no refentment can excufe, that uninterrupted feries of deliberate barbarity which marks every page of her unprofperous annals with martyrdoms, hardly to be paralleled in the pagan perfecutions of primitive chriftianity. If in the two preceding reigns, many venerable prelates of Mary's communion had been injurioufly treated, or even put to death, for confcientious difobedience, yet none of them were inhumanly dragged to the flames like the meek Latimer or the learned Ridley. It is alfo allowed, that to burn heretics was an eftablifhed doctrine of the catholic religion. But in what age of the fame religion, or in what country, were thefe punifhments ever executed with fo many circumftances of cruelty ? Her attempt to reftore the monafteries, however conformable to her fyftem, was a meafure, which tended only to bring back national poverty with national fuperftition : for

[k] See MSS. Harl. Brit. Muf. 6195. 26. " Mary had rather lofe her life than part with the mafs."
[l] Strype, Eccl. Mem. iii. 253. feq.

it

it is certain, that Henry's diftribution of the monaftic revenues into private hands, although dictated by felfifh and fordid motives, founded the prefent greatnefs of England. In the mean time it will be but charitable to grant, that her private life was confeffedly blamelefs and un-blemifhed. I will not fay whether it was her fault or her unhappinefs, that the conftancy of her attachments feldom met with fuitable re-turns of gratitude and affection. In this at leaft fome goodnefs of heart appears, that no-thing affected her fo much, as the unkindnefs of thofe whom fhe beft loved. She poffeffed a firmnefs of mind, which deferved better times ; and a vigour of underftanding, which was im-peded by religious prejudices. Her merits, whatever they were, feem to have been over-looked in her misfortunes: and as the latter were aggravated, fo the former were obliterat-ed, by that blaze of profperity which fur-rounded the fucceeding reign.

S E C T.

✝✝✝✝✝✝✝✝✝✝✝✝✝✝✝✝✝✝✝✝✝✝✝✝✝✝✝✝✝✝✝✝✝✝✝✝✝

## S E C T.   III.

IN the year 1555, the princefs Elizabeth, afterwards queen, having been before treated with much infolence and inhumanity, was placed under the care and infpection of fir Thomas Pope [a]. Mary cherifhed that antipathy to the certain heirefs of her crown and her fucceffor, which all princes who have no children to fucceed naturally feel. But the moft powerful caufe of Mary's hatred of the princefs, with whom fhe formerly lived in fome degree of friendfhip [b], feems to have arifen from Courtney, earl of Devonfhire.

The perfon, addrefs, and other engaging accomplifhments [c] of this young nobleman, had

[a] Fox, edit. 1684. iii. 798. Speed, &c.

[b] Strype, Eccl. Mem. iii. 14. 17. 82. At queen Mary's coronation, the lady Elizabeth rode in the firft chariot, with lady Anne of Cleves, after the queen's litter, in the proceffion from the tower to Weftminfter. Strype, ib. 36. See alfo Hollingfh. Chron. iii. 1152. col. 1.

[c] He was polite, ftudious, and learned ; an accurate mafter of the languages, fkilled in the mathematics, painting, and mufic. He lived a prifoner in the tower, from fourteen to twenty-fix years of age ; when he was fet at liberty by queen Mary, at her acceffion. Strype, Eccl. Mem. iii. 339.

made

made a manifeſt impreſſion on the queen[d]. Other circumſtances alſo contributed to render him an objeCt of her affeCtion ; for he was an Engliſhman, and nearly allied to the crown ; and conſequently could not fail of proving acceptable to the nation. The earl was no ſtranger to theſe favorable diſpoſitions of the queen towards him[e]. Yet, he ſeemed rather to attach himſelf to the princeſs ; whoſe youth and lively converſation had more prevailing charms than the pomp and power of her ſiſter[f]. This preference not only produced a total change in Mary's ſentiments with regard to the earl, but forced her openly to declare war againſt Elizabeth.

The ancient quarrel between their mothers remained deeply rooted in the malignant heart of the queen[g] : and ſhe took advantage from the declaration made by parliament in favor of Catharine's marriage[h], to repreſent her ſiſter's birth as illegitimate. Elizabeth's inclination to the proteſtant religion ſtill further heightened Mary's averſion : it offended her bigottry, diſappointed her exſpeCtations,

[d] Burnet, Ref. ii. 255.
[e] Goodwyn, p. 339.
[f] Burnet, Ref. ii. 273. Collier, Eccl. Hiſt. ii. 352, 362.
[g] Camden, Eliz. per Hearne, i. *Apparatus*, pag. 19.
[h] Statut. Mar. i. cap. i.

and

and difconcerted her politics. Thefe caufes of diflike, however, might perhaps have been forgotten by degrees, or, at leaft, would have ended in fecret difguft. But when the queen found that the princefs had obftructed her defigns in a matter of the moft interefting nature; female refentment, founded on female jealoufy, and exafperated by pride, could no longer be fuppreffed.

So much more forcible, and of fo much more confequence in public affairs, are private feelings, and the fecret undifcerned operations of the heart, than the moft important political reafons. Monfieur Noailles, however, the French embaffador at the court of England during this period, with the true dignity of a myfterious ftatefman, feems unwilling to refer the queen's difpleafure to fo flight a motive : and affigns a more profound intrigue as the foundation of Courtenay's difgrace. Domeftic incidents operate alike in every ftation of life ; and often form the greateft events of hiftory. Princes have their paffions in common with the reft of mankind.

Elizabeth being now become the public and avowed object of Mary's averfion, was openly treated with much difrefpect and infult. She was forbidden to take place, in the
prefence-

prefence chamber, of the countefs of Lenox and the dutchefs of Suffolk, as if her legiti-macy had deen dubious.[i]. This doctrine had been infinuated by the chancellor Gardiner, in a fpeech before both houfes of parliament [k]. Among other arguments enforcing the necef-fity of Mary's marriage, he particularly in-fifted on the failure of the royal lineage; art-fully remarking, that none of Henry's defcen-dants remained, except the queen, and the *princefs* Elifabeth [l]. Her friends were neglect-ed or affronted. And while her amiable qua-lifications every day drew the attention of the young nobility, and rendered her univerfally popular, the malevolence of the vindictive queen ftill encreafed. The princefs therefore thought it moft prudent to leave the court: and before the begining of 1554, retired to her houfe at Afhridge in Hertfordfhire [m].

In the mean time, Sir Thomas Wyat's rebel-lion, abovementioned, broke out, in oppofition

[i] Goodwyn.

[k] Seff. fec. ann. prim. Mar.

[l] Avoiding the term *fifter*. Amb. de Noailles, apud Carte, iii. 310.

[m] " Wherein our moft worthie and ever famous queen " Elifabeth lodged as in her owne, beinge then a more ftately " houfe, at the time of Wyatt's attempte in queen Maryes " dayes." Norden's *Difcription of Hartfordfhire*, written 1596. pag. 12. edit. 1723.

E                                                              to to the queen's match with Philip of Spain. It was immediately pretended, that the princefs Elifabeth, together with lord Courteney, was privately concerned in this dangerous confpiracy, and that fhe had held a correfpondence with the traitor Wyat. Accordingly [n], fir Edward Haftings, afterwards lord Loughborough, fir Thomas Cornwallis, and fir Richard Southwell, attended by a troop of horfe, were ordered to bring her to the court. They found the princefs fick, and even confined to her bed, at Afhridge [o]. Notwithftanding, under pretence of the ftrictnefs of their commiffion, they compelled her to rife: and, ftill continuing very weak and indifpofed, fhe proceeded in the queen's litter by flow journies to London [p]. At the court, they kept her confined and with-

[n] See Hollingfhed's Chron. iii. 1151. feq. From Fox.

[o] Amb. de Noailles, whofe papers are cited by Carte, calls this a *favorable illnefs*. " Since, he adds, it feems likely to " fave Mary from the crime of putting her fifter to death by " violence." Carte, iii. 306.

[p] Her manner of coming to London is thus defcribed in a manufcript chronicle, often cited hereafter, " The fame tyme " and daye, between four and fyve of the cloke at night, my " lady Elifabeth's grace came to London, through Smithficlde, " untoo Weftminfter, with c. velvet cotts. after her grace. " And her grace rod in a charyt opyn on both fydes: and " her grace [had] ryding after her a 100. in cotts of fyne " redde gardyd with velvett; and fo through ftetftrete unto the " court through the quenes garden, hir grace being fycke." MSS. Cotton, Vitell. F. 5.

out

out company, for a fortnight: after which, bifhop Gardiner, who well knew her predomi-
nant difpofition to cabal and intrigue, with
nineteen others of the council, attended to
examine her concerning the rebellion of which
fhe was accufed. She pofitively denied the
accufation. However they informed her, it
was the queen's refolution fhe fhould be committed to the Tower, till further enquiries
could be made [q]. The princefs immediately
wrote to the queen, earneftly entreating that
fhe might not be imprifoned in the Tower,
and concluding her letter thus: " As for that
" Traytor Wiat, he might paraventur write
" me a letter; but on my faith I never re-
" ceved any from him. And as for the copie
" of my letter fent to the Frenche king, I
" pray *God confound me eternally*, if ever I
" fent him word, meffage, token, or letter,
" by any menes [r]." Her oaths, and her repeated proteftations of innocence were all ineffectual. She was conveyed to the tower, and
ignominioufly conducted through the Traitor's
gate [s].

At her firft commitment, only three men
and three women of the queen's fervants, were

[q] Hollingfhead, ut fupr.
[r] Camden's Eliz. per Hearne, vol i. editor. præfat. p. 78.
[s] May 18. As MSS. Cott. Vitell. F. 5.

appointed

appointed for her attendants. But even thefe were forbidden to bring her meat; and fhe was waited on, for this purpofe, by the lieutenant's fervants, or even by the common foldiers. But afterwards, two yeomen of her chamber, one of her robes, two of her pantry and ewry, one of her buttery, one of her cellar, another of her larder, and two of her kitchen, were allowed, by permiffion of the privy council, to ferve at her table. No ftranger, or vifitor, was admitted into her prefence. The conftable of the tower, fir John Gage, treated her very feverely, and watched her with the utmoft vigilance. Many of the other prifoners, committed to the fame place on account of the rebellion, were often examined about her concern in the confpiracy : and fome of them were put to the rack, by way of extorting an accufation. Her innocence however was unqueftionable : for although Wyat himfelf had accufed her, in hopes to have faved his own life by means of fo bafe and fcandalous an artifice, yet he afterwards denied that fhe had the leaft knowledge of his defigns ; and left thofe denials which he made at his examinations might be infidioufly fuppreffed, and his former depofitions alledged againft her adopted in their ftead, he continued to make the fame declarations

tions openly on the scaffold at the time of his execution [t],

There was a pretence, much infisted on by Gardiner, that Wyat had conveyed to her a bracelet, in which the whole scheme of the plot was inclosed. But Wyat acquitted her of this and all other suspicions [u]. After a close imprisonment of some days, by the generous intercession of lord Chandois, lieutenant of the tower, it was granted that she might sometimes walk in the queen's lodgings [w], in the presence of the constable, the lieutenant, and three of the queen's ladies; yet on condition that the windows should be shut. She then was indulged with walking in a little garden, for the sake of fresh air: but all the shutters which looked towards the garden were ordered to be kept close.

Such were their jealousies, that a little boy of four years old who had been accustomed every day to bring her flowers, was severely threatened if he came any more; and the child's father was summoned and rebuked by

[t] Hollingshead, ut supr.
[u] Strype, Eccl. Mem. iii. 97.
[w] Concerning these apartments in the Tower, see the very judicious and ingenious Mr. Walpole's *Historic Doubts concerning Richard the Third.*

E 3
the

the conftable. But lord Chandois being obferved to treat the princefs with too much
refpect, he was not any longer entrufted with
the charge of her; and fhe was committed to
the cuftody of fir Henry Bedingfield, of Ox-
burgh in Norfolk [x], a perfon whom fhe had
never feen nor knew before. He brought with
him a new guard of one hundred foldiers,
cloathed in blue; which the princefs obferving, afked with her ufual livelinefs, *If lady
Jane's fcaffold was yet taken away?*

About the end of May fhe was removed
from the tower under the command of fir
Henry Bedingfield, and lord Williams of
Thame, to the royal manor or palace at Woodftock [y]. The firft night of her journey fhe
lay at Richmond; where being watched all
night by the foldiers, and all accefs of her
own private attendants utterly prohibited, fhe

[x] He was firmly attached to the queen's interefts. Befide
his Government of the Tower, he was knight marfhal of the
queen's army, captain of her guards, vice-chamberlain to the
queen, and a privy counfellor. She alfo granted him a yearly
penfion of 100 l. for life, and part of the forfeited eftate of fir
Thomas Wyat. Blomefield's Norfolk, iii. 481. He is often,
by miftake, written *Beningfield, Benfield,* &c.

[y] MSS. Cotton. Vitel. F. 5. "The xx daye of May my
"ladie Elifabeth, the quenes fifter, came out of the tower, and
"toke hir barge at the tower-wharffe and fo to Rychmond,
"and from thens unto Wyndfor, and fo to Wodftoke."

began

began to be convinced, that orders had been
given to put her privately to death. The
next day she reached Windsor, where she
was lodged in the Dean's house near saint
George's collegiate chapel. She then passed
to lord Williams's seat at Ricot in Oxfordshire, where she lay; and " was verie prince-
" lie entertained both of knights and ladies."
But Bedingfield was highly disgusted at this
gallant entertainment of his prisoner. During
their journey, lord Williams and another gentleman playing at chess, the princess accident-
ally came in, and told them she must stay to
see the game played out; but this liberty Bedingfield would not permit [z].

Arriving at Woodstock, she was lodged in
the gatehouse of the palace; in an apartment
remaining complete within these fifty years
with it's original arched roof of Irish
oak, curiously carved, painted blue sprinkled
with gold, and to the last retaining it's name
of *Queen Elizabeth's chamber* [a]. Hollingshead

[z] Hollingshead, ut supr.

[a] The old royal manor, or palace, at Woodstock, was be-
sieged in the grand rebellion, and much damaged in the siege.
The furniture was afterwards sold, and the buildings portion-
ed out by Cromwell, or his agents, to three persons. Two
of them, about 1652, pulled down their portions for the sake
of the stone. The third suffered his part to stand, which con-
sisted

gives us three lines which fhe wrote with a
diamond on the glafs of her window; and

fifted of the gatehoufe in which the princefs Elizabeth was
imprifoned, and fome adjoining ruinous buildings. After the
rebellion, lord Lovelace turned this gatehoufe into a dwelling
houfe, and lived in it for many years. As to its adjoining
ruins, perfons now living remember ftanding, a noble porch,
and fome walls of the hall ; the walls and magnificent windows
of the chapel ; feveral turrets at proper diftar.ces ; and could
trace out many of the apartments. Sir John Vanbrugh, while
Blenheim palace was building, had tafte enough to lay out
2000 l. in keeping up the ruins. But afterwards lord treafurer
Godolphin obferved to Sarah, dutchefs-dowager of Marlborough, that a pile of ruins in the front of fo fine a feat, was an
unfeemly object, all the old buildings, and amongft the reft,
the princefs Elizabeth's gatehoufe, were entirely demolifhed and
erafed. Aubrey, the antiquarian, acquaints us that in the old
hall there were two rows of pillars, as in a church ; and that
the arches were of the zigzag Norman fhape. He has left us in
his manufcript, Drawings of the windows in the larger apartments, and in the chapel and hall. Aubrey's CHRONOLOGIA
ARCHITECTONICA, MSS. in Muf. Afhmol. Oxon. fol. pag. 7.
Of fair Rofamond's *Bower*, which literally fignifies no more
than a *chamber*, and which was a kind of pleafure-houfe on the
fouth-weft fide of the old palace, fome ruinous remains are ftill
remembered : particularly, an apartment over Rofamond's-well.
This *well*, which is a large, clear, and beautiful fpring, paved
and fenced about the infide with ftone, was undoubtedly a bath,
fountain, or refervoir, for the convenience of the *Bower*, or
perhaps of the palace. The author of the hiftory of Allchefter,
written 1622, tells us, that " the ruins of Rofamond's Bower
" are ftill to be feen againft the court-gate." Apud Kennet's
PAROCH. ANTIQ. p. 694. Henry vii. built much here : particularly the front and principal gate of the palace. On this gate
was his name, and an Englifh rhyme, importing that he was the
founder. Wake's REX PLATONICUS, edit. Oxon. 1607. pag.
6. 4to.

Hentzner, in his itinerary of 1598 [b], has recorded a sonnet, which she had written with a pencil on her window shutter. In the Bodleian Library at Oxford [c], there is an English Translation of saint Paul's Epistles, printed in the black letter, which the princess used while she was here imprisoned; in a blank leaf of which, the following paragraph, written with her own hand, and in the pedantry of the times, yet remains. " I walke " many times into the pleasant fieldes of the " holye scriptures; where I plucke up the " goodliesome herbs of sentences by pruning, " eate them by reading : chawe them by mus- " ing : and laie them up at length in the hie

6. 4to. It was a favorite seat of our kings, who all resided here from Henry I. to Charles I. Queen Elisabeth in particular, notwithstanding her imprisonment here, parhaps on that account, was remarkably fond of living at this palace : and she became a considerable benefactress to the town of Woodstock. I have a small etching of a prospect of the *Princess Elizabeth's chamber* and its adjoining ruins ; done, a few years before they were destroyed, in 1714, by J. Whood.

[b] Edit. Noriberg. 1629. pag. 215.

[c] Inter MSS. 242. 12mo. In the same library is a translation by the princess Elizabeth into Latin, of an Italian sermon of Occhini. Calligraphy was a requisite accomplishment of those times, and it is accordingly written, on vellum, with uncommon elegance, in her own hand. It is dedicated in Latin, to her brother king Edward, to whom she sends it as a new-year's gift. The dedication is dated *Enfield*, December xxx. Bibl. Bodl. Arch. D. 115. 8vo.

seate

" feate of memorie, by gathering them to-
" gether. That fo having tafted the fweetenes,
" I maye the leffe perceave the bitterneffe of
" this miferable life." The covers are of black
filk; on which fhe had amufed hesfelf with
curioufly working, or emboffing, the following infcriptions and devices in gold twift.
On one fide, on the border, or edge, CÆ-
LUM PATRIA. SCOPUS VITÆ XPVS.
CHRISTO VIVE. In the middle a heart;
and about it, ELEVA COR SURSUM IBI
UBI E. C. [i. e. *eft Chriftus.*] On the other
fide, on the border, BEATUS QUI DIVI-
TIAS SCRIPIURÆ LEGENS VERBA
VERTIT IN OPERA. In the middle a
ftar, and about it, VICIT OMNIA PER-
TINAX VIRTUS E. C. [i. e. *Elifabethæ
Captivæ*; or, *Elifabetha Captiva.*] One is
pleafed to hear thefe circumftances, trifling
and unimportant as they are, which fhew us
how this great and unfortunate lady, who became afterwards the heroine of the Britifh
throne, the favorite of her people, and the
terror of the world, contrived to relieve the
tedious hours of her penfive and folitary confinement. She had however little opportunity for meditation or amufement. She was
clofely guarded: yet fometimes fuffered to
walk into the gardens of the palace. In this
fituation, fays Hollingfhead, " no marvell, if
" fhe

" fhe hearing upon a time out of hir gardin
" at Woodftocke a certaine milkmaide fing-
" ing pleafantlie, wifhed herfelf to be a milk-
" maide, as fhe was ; faying that her cafe was
" better, and life merrier ᵈ."

After being confined here for many months,
fhe procured a permiffion to write to the
queen : but her importunate keeper Bedingfield intruded, and overlooked what fhe wrote ᵉ.
At length, king Philip interpofed, and begged
that fhe might be removed to the court ᶠ. But
this fudden kindnefs of Philip, who thought
Elifabeth a much lefs obnoxious character than
his father Charles the fifth had conceived her

---

ᵈ This circumftance has given occafion to an elegant ballad
by Shenftone.

ᵉ Hollingfhead ut fupr.

ᶠ When fhe came to the crown, fays Hollingfhead, fhe difcharged Bedingfield from the court, telling him, that whenever fhe fhould happen to have a ftate-prifoner who required
to be " hardlie handled and ftrictlie kept," fhe would fend for
him. Hollingfhead, p. 117. col. 2. But there is fome reafon
to fufpect, that Fox, from whom Hollingfhead tranfcribes, has
aggravated, in his account, fir Henry's ufage of the princefs.
After fhe was queen, he was very often at court, and her majefty vifited him in a progrefs, 1578. And though fhe frequently called him her *Jaylor*, yet this feems rather to have been a
term of royal familiarity than of contempt. Though I doubt
not that he treated the princefs with no great compaffion or delicacy ; a circumftance which reflects honor on her forgivenefs.
See Blomefield's Norfolk, iii. 481.

to

to have been, did not arife from any regular principle of real generofity, but partly from an affectation of popularity [g]; and partly from a refined fentiment of policy, which made him forefee, that if Elifabeth was put to death, the next lawful heir would be Mary queen of Scots already betrothed to the dauphin of France, whofe fucceffion would for ever join the fceptres of England and France, and confequently crufh the growing interefts of Spain [h].

In her firft day's journey, from the manor of Woodftock to lord Williams's at Ricot, a violent ftorm of wind happened; infomuch, that her hood and the attire of her head were twice or thrice blown off. On this, fhe begged to retire to a gentleman's houfe then at hand: but Bedingfield's abfurd and fuperabundant circumfpection refufed even this infignificant requeft; and conftrained her, with much in-

[g] He affected to treat the princefs with much refpect. In an examination, cited by Hollingfhead, it appears, that accidenttally paffing her in a chamber of the palace, he paid her fuch obeifance as to fall with one knee to the ground, notwithftanding his ufual ftate and folemnity. Chron. iii. 1160. col. 1.

[h] Camden, Eliz. per Hearne, vol. i. *Apparatus*, pag. 21. However, it is faid, that out of gratitude for her prefervation, fhe conftantly kept Philip's picture by her bed-fide; even to her death, notwithftanding his perfidy after fhe became queen. Ballard's Mem. of L. ladies, p. 217.

decorum

decorum, to replace her head-drefs under a hedge near the road. The next night they came to Mr. Dormer's, at Winge, in Buckinghamfhire; and from thence to an inn at Colnebroke, where fhe lay. At length fhe arrived at Hampton-court, where the court then refided, but was ftill kept in the condition of a prifoner. Here bifhop Gardiner, with others of the council, frequently perfuaded her to make a confeffion, and fubmit to the queen's mercy. Diffimulation appears to have been a confpicuous feature in Elifabeth's character. One night, when it was late, the princefs was unexpectedly fummoned, and conducted by torch light to the queen's bedchamber : where fhe kneeled down before the queen, declaring herfelf to be a moft faithful and true fubject. She even went fo far, as to requeft the queen to fend her fome catholic treatifes, which might confirm her faith, and inculcate doctrines different from thofe which fhe had been taught in the writings of the reformers. The queen feemed ftill to fufpect her fincerity : but they parted on good terms. During this critical interview, Philip had concealed himfelf behind the tapeftry, that he might have feafonably interpofed, to prevent the violence of the queen's paffio-

nate

nate temper from proceeding to any extremities [i].

One week afterwards fhe was releafed from the formidable parade of guards and keepers [k]. A happy change of circumftances enfued ; and fhe was permitted to retire with fir Thomas Pope [l] to Hatfield-houfe in Hertfordfhire, then a royal palace [m]. At parting the queen began to

[i] Hollingfhead ut fupr.

[k] Burnet, Fox, Speed, &c.

[l] Maifter Gage, who is called the queen's gentleman-ufher, or mafter of the ceremonies, is faid by Fox and others, to have been joined with fir Thomas Pope in this appointment. But he feems to have acted only as an affiftant or inferior. Probably this was fir Edward Gage, to whom the queen granted in 1556, thirty retainers. Strype, Eccl. Mem. iii. 480. Sir *John* Gage was conftable of the tower ; and died in 1556. Anftis, Regift. Gart. i. 423. *Notes.* He [Sir John] was alfo chancellor of the dutchy of Lancafter. chamberlain of the houfhold, and a privy counfellor. Anftis, ibid.

[m] The prefent noble ftructure was erected by Robert, firft earl of Salifbury, about 1610. James the firft exchanged Hatfield, with lord Salifbury, for Theobalds. It originally belonged to the bifhops of Ely, and was built by bifhop Morton about 1480. The chapel was confecrated in 1615. See Le Neve, Prot. Bifh. vol. 1, 2. pag. 144. Peacham tells us, that this chapel was adorned with paintings, by Butler, and other eminent artifts. GENTLEMAN'S EXERCISE, Lib. i. c. 3. " Robert earl of Salifbury, " lord high treafurer of England, who as he favoreth all learn- " ing and excellencies, fo he is a principal patron of this art ; " having lately imployed M. Butler and many other excellent " artifts for the beautyfying his houfes, efpecially his chappell " at Hatfield." pag. 310. edit. 1661.

fhew

fhew fome fymptoms of reconciliation: fhe recommended to her fir Thomas Pope, as a perfon with whom the princefs was well acquainted, and whofe humanity, prudence, and other valuable qualifications were all calculated to render her new fituation perfectly agreeable [n]; and at the fame time fhe prefented her with a ring worth feven hundred crowns [o].

But before I proceed further in this part of my narrative, I ftop to mention a circumftance unnoticed by our hiftorians: which is, that fir Thomas Pope in conjunction with others, had fome concern about the perfon of the princefs Elizabeth, even when fhe firft retired from the court, in difgrace, to her houfe at Afhridge; and before her troubles commenced, occafioned by Wyat's rebellion; all which I have already related at large. When that rebellion broke out, Mary wrote to the princefs then fick at Afhridge, artfully requefting her immediate attendance at the court. Elizabeth's governors at this time, whofe names are no where particularly mentioned, waiting every day for her reco-

[n] See Thomas Heywood's ENGLAND'S ELIZABETH. Lond. 12mo. 1631. p. 202.
[o] Carte, iii. 326.

very,

very, very compaſſionately declared it unſafe yet to remove her. And the princeſs herſelf in the mean time, ſignified by letter her indiſpoſition to the queen ; begging that her journey to the court might be deferred for a few days, and proteſting her abhorrence of Wyat's ſeditious practices. Her governors likewiſe, on their parts, apprehending that this tenderneſs towards their miſtreſs might be interpreted in a bad ſenſe, diſpatched a letter to biſhop Gardiner, lord chancellor ; acquainting him with her condition, and, avowing their readineſs to receive the queen's commands. An original draught or copy of this letter in Sir Thomas Pope's own hand,, with ſeveral corrections and interlineations by the ſame, is now preſeved in the Britiſh Muſeum P : from which circumſtance it is manifeſt that he was at this time one of theſe

P Brit. Muſ. Bibl. Cotton. MSS. Titus. B. ii. fol. 159. After it, follows the letter from the privy council to ſir Thomas Pope, cited below. The paper which contains both is endorſed, " *Minute of the lady Elizabeth's Officers to the Queen's counſail.*" The letter here mentioned in the text, begins thus.

" It may pleaſe your good lordſhip. That albeit we at-
" tende on my ladie Elizabethes grace our miſtres, in hope
" of her amendement to repair towardes the queenes highnes,
" whereof we have as yet none apparaunt likelyod of helthe ;
" yet conſideringe this daungerouſe worlde, the perillous at-
" temptes and the naughty endevours of the rebelles, which
" we dayly here of againſt the queenes highnes our ſovereigne
" ladie,

governors or attendants; but in what department or capacity, I know not. However it

" ladie, we do not forgeate our moſt bounden dewty, nor yet
" our readynes in worde and dede to ſerve her highnes by all
" the waies and meanes that may ſtande in us, both from her
" grace our miſtres, and of our owne partes alſo. Which thing
" although my ladie's grace our ſaid miſtres hath tofore this
" ſignified unto the queenes highnes, of her behalffe, by meſ-
" ſage ; it might nevertheles ſeame to your good lordſhip, and
" the lordes of the councel, ſome negligence, that we did not
" make you alſo privy herunto. We have therefore thought
" it our deuties to declare this unto your lordſhip, &c." The
whole is printed in Strype's Mem. Eccl. iii. 83. From MSS.
Petyt, *Now in the Inner-Temple library.* Strype ſays only, that
it was written by the lady Elizabeth's governors ; or, " by
" thoſe that had the care and government of her." Among
the princeſs Eliſabeth's domeſtics or attendants was John
Aſtley, one of Roger Aſcham's literary friends, and to
whom many of his Latin letters are written. Prefixed to
Aſcham's very ſenſible Engliſh political tract on the Affairs of Germanie, and addreſſed to Aſtley, is an Engliſh letter, dated 1553, from Aſtley to Aſcham, in which the
latter ſpeaks feelingly of their frequent agreeable converſations
on learned ſubjects at Hatfield-houſe. Aſcham was preceptor to
the princeſs. Sir Thomas Pope, in a fragment of a letter to
the preſident of Trinity-college Oxford, and dated Hatfield,
ſays, that he had procured an Office in the Tower of London
for *Maiſter Aſtley.* Probably this is the ſame perſon. Aſcham
in ſome of his Epiſtles complains, that he was unjuſtly driven
from his tuition of Eliſabeth, in a conſequence of a party formed againſt him in the family of the princeſs. My principal
reaſon for mentioning theſe particulars is to ſhew, that ſir Thomas Pope could not have been one of Aſcham's enemies on this
occaſion ; for, had that been the caſe, it is not very probable
that he ſhould promote Aſcham's friend. He was huſband of
Catharine Aſteley, the governeſs of the princeſs. See below,

F P. 99.

is evident that he was removed from this charge, when the princefs, notwithftanding her infirm ftate of health, was hurried up to the court by Southwell, Cornwallis, and Haftings: nor do we find, that from that time he had the leaft concern with her during her imprifonment in the tower and at Wood-ftock, and the reft of thofe undeferved per-fecutions, which preceded her enlargement and final removal to Hatfield.

To this lady fir Thomas Pope behaved with the utmoft tendernefs and refpect: re-fiding with her at Hatfield, rather as an indulgent and affectionate guardian, than as an officious or rigorous governor. Although ftrict orders were given that the mafs alone fhould be ufed in he family, yet he connived

p. 99. Afcham mentions this Catharine Afteley in very re-fpectable terms, in a Letter to the princefs, on the death of her tutor Grindall. "Hunc dolorem, magis apud te renovando " augere, quam confolando lenire vererer, nifi perfpecta effet " mihi prudentia tua, fic confiliis prudentiffimæ Feminæ do- " minæ Catharinæ Aftlex munita, &c." EPIST. Lib. ii. p. 95. a. edit. 1581. See alfo ibid. p. 89. b. This Aftely was made matter of the Jewel houfe at queen Elifabeth's acceffion, with a falary of fifty pounds. Decembr. 23. LIT. PAT. i. Eliz. He wrote a treatife on HORSEMANSHIP, printed without his name, in 1586. 4to. By the way, it appears from what has been faid, that the princefs before her final fettlement at Hatfield under fir Thomas Pope's care, was occafionally fhifted about to various royal feats, of which Hatfield was one.

at

at many proteftant fervants, whom fhe retained
about her perfon [q]. Yet Sir John Harrington
fays, that his father, a proteftant, was imprifoned in the tower for twelve months, and
fined one thoufand pounds, for carrying a letter to the princefs, and expreffing his good
wifhes for her profperity : and that, as if the
herefy of a maid of honor could do any great
harm, his mother, who was one of her favorite attendants, was removed from that fituation, as a profeffed heretic, by the command of
bifho pGardiner [q].

Nor was fir Thomas Pope wanting on proper occafions, in ftudioufly fhewing her fuch
marks of regard and deference as her ftation
and quality demanded. This appears from
the following anecdote, which alfo marks his
character [r].

Two of the fellows of Trinity college in
Oxford, juft founded by him, had violated one
of it's ftricteft ftatutes, and were accordingly
expelled by the prefident, and Society. Upon

[p] Britifh View of the State of the church of England, &c.
Written in the year 1608. Lond. 1653. 12mo. p. 45. He adds,
that when his mother was difmiffed, her own father durft not
take her into his houfe. p. 46.
[q] Strype, Eccl. Mem. iii. 216.
[r] See Append Numb. XV.

F 2                                    this

this they repaired to their founder, then at
Hatfield with the princefs Elifabeth, humb-
ly petitioning a readmittance into his college.
Sir Thomas Pope probably was not a little
perplexed on this occafion ; for although difpofed to forgivenefs, yet he was unwilling to
be the firft who fhould openly countenance or
pardon an infringement of laws which himfelf
had made. But perceiving a happy opportunity of adjufting the difficulty, by paying at
the fame time a handfome compliment to the
princefs, with much addrefs he referred the
matter to her gracious arbitration ; and fhe
was pleafed to order, that they fhould immediately be reftored to their fellowfhips. In
confequence of this determination, he wrote
the following letter to the Prefident of the
college.

"  *Maifter Prefident, with my hertie commen-*
"  *dations,*

"  Albeit Sympfon and Rudde ' have com-
"  mitted fuch an offence, as whereby they
"  have juftlie deferved, not onlie for ever to
"  be expulfed out of my collegge, but alfo to
"  be ponifhed befides in fuch fort as others
"  myght fere to attempt the like : never-
"  theleffe, at the defier, or rather commande-

* The two delinquents.

"  ment

" ment, of my ladie Elizabeth her grace;
" and at my wiffes requeſt, who hath both
" ſent and written to me very erneſtlie; and
" in hope this will be a warnyng for theym
" to lyve in order hereafter: I am content
" to remytt this fault, and to diſpence with
" theym towching the ſame. So always,
" that they openly in the hall, before all the
" felowes and ſcolers of the collegge, con-
" feſſe their faultes; and beſides paye ſuch
" fyne, as you with others of the collegge
" ſhall think meate. Which being don, I
" will the ſome be recorded yn ſome boke;
" wherein I will have mencion made, that
" for this faulte they were clene expelled
" the collegge; and at my ladye Elizabeth
" her graces deſier, and at my wiffes requeſt
" they were receyved into the houſe again.
" Signifying, that if eny ſhall hereafter com-
" myt the lyke offence, I am fully reſolved
" ther ſhall no creature living, the quenes
" maieſtie except who maye commaunde me,
" cauſe me to diſpence withall. Aſſuring
" yow, I never dyd eny thing more agaynſt
" my hert, then to remytt this matter: the
" poniſhment whereoff to the extremyte, I
" beleve wold have don more good, then in
" this forme to be endyd; as knoweth the
" holye goſt, who kepe you in helth. Writ-

F 3                    " ten

" ten at *hatfelde* the xxiith of Auguſt, anno
1556.

" *Your own aſſuredly,*

THO. POPE.

" [*P. S.*] Sir, I requyre you above all
" thinges, have a ſpeciall regard there be
" peace and concorde in my collegge ¹."

Nor did ſir Thomas Pope think it inconſiſtent with his truſt, to gratify the princeſs
on ſome occaſions with the faſhionable amuſe-
ments of the times; even at his own expence, and at the hazard of offending the
queen.   This we learn from a paſſage in a
curious manuſcript chronicle ᵘ.   " In Shrove-
" tide, 1556, ſir Thomas Pope made for the
" ladie Eliſabeth all at his owne coſtes, a
" greate and rich maſkinge in the greate halle
" at Hatfelde; wher the pageaunts were
" marvellouſly furniſhed.   There were thar
" twelve , minſtrels antickly diſguiſed; with
" forty-ſix or more gentlemen and ladies,

---

¹ Ex autograph. in Theſaur. coll. Trin. Oxon.   Superſcribed
" *To his loving friend,* Mr. Slythurſt, *preſident of Trynitie Collegge*
" *in Oxford.*"   And in regiſtr. prim. ejuſdem coll. fol. xvi. b.

ᵘ MSS. Cotton. fol. Vitellius. F. 5. Brit. Muſ. MSS. Strype.
See Append. Numb. XXVIII.

" many

" many of them knights or nobles, and ladies
" of honor, apparelled in crimfin fattin, em-
" brothered uppon with wrethes of golde
" and garnifhed with bordures of hanging
" perle. And the devife of a caftell of clothe
" of gold, fett with pomegranates about the
" battlements, with fhields of knights hang-
" ing therefrom, and fix knights in rich
" harneis turneyed. At night the cuppboard
" in the halle was of twelve ftages main-
" lie furnifhed with garnifh of gold and
" filver vefful, and a banket of feventie
" difhes, and after a voidee of fpices and fut-
" tleties with thirty fpyfe plates, all at the
" chardgis of fir Thomas Pope. And the
" next day the play of HOLOPHERNES. But
" the queen percafe myfliked thefe folliries, as
" by her letters to fir Thomas Pope hit did
" appear, and fo their difguifinges were
" ceafed."

The princefs was notwithftanding fometimes fuffered to make excurfions, partly for '
pleafure, and partly for paying her compliments at court : and on thefe occafions fhe
was attended in a manner fuitable to her
rank. Strype tells us, from the fame manufcript journal of memorable occurrences, writ-

ten

ten about thofe times ʷ, that on February
the twenty-fifth, 1557, "The lady Eliza-
" beth came riding from her houfe at Hat-
" field to London, attended with a great com-
" panie of lords, and nobles, and gentle-
" men, unto her place, called Somerfet-place
" beyond Strond-bridge, to do her duty to
" the queen. And on the twenty-eighth fhe
" repaired unto her grace at Whitehall with
" many lords and ladies." And again, in
March, the fame year. " Aforenoon the lady
" Elizabeth's grace took her horfe and rode to
" her palace of Shene; with many lords,
" knights, ladies, and gentlemen, and a good-
" ly companie of horfe ˣ." In April the fame
year, fhe was efcorted from Hatfield to En-
field-chafe, by a retinue of twelve ladies clothed
in white fattin on *ambling palfries*, and twenty
yeomen in green, all on horfe back, that *her
grace* might *hunt the hart*. At entering the
chafe, or foreft, fhe was met by fifty archers in
fcarlet boots and yellow caps, armed with
gilded bows; one of whom prefented her a
filver-headed arrow, winged with peacock's
feathers. Sir Thomas Pope had the *devifing*
of this fhow. By way of clofing the fport,
or rather the ceremony, the princefs was grati-

ʷ Strype Eccl. Mem. iii. 444, 445.
ˣ Strype Eccl. Mem. iii. 336.

fied

fied with the privilege of cutting the throat of a buck [y]. In the fame month fhe was vifited by the queen at Hatfield : when the great chamber was adorned with a fumptuous fuit of tapeftry, called the *Hanginge of the fiege of Antioch*, and after fupper a play was performed by the choir-boys of Saint Paul's [z].

In the fummer of the fame year, the prin-cefs paid a vifit to the queen at Richmond. She went by water from Somerfet-place in the queen's barge ; which was richly hung with garlands of artificial flowers, and cover-ed with a of canopy green farcenet wrought with branches of eglantine in embroidery, and powdered with bloffoms of gold. In the barge fhe was accompanied by fir Thomas Pope, and four ladies of her chamber. Six boats attended on this proceffion, filled with her highnefs's retinue, habited in ruffet da-mafke and blue embroidered fattin taffelled and fpangled with filver, with bonnets of cloth of filver plumed with green feathers. She was received by the queen in a fump-tuous pavilion, made in form of a caftle, with cloth of gold and purple velvet, in the labyrinth of the gardens. The walls, or

[y] Vitell. F. 5. MSS. Cotton. MSS. Strype ut fupr.
[z] MSS. Ibid. See HIST. ENG. POETRY. ii. 392.

fides

fides of the pavilion were chequered into
compartments, in each of which was alternately a lily in filver and a pomegranate in
gold. Here they were entertained at a royal
banquet ; in which was introduced a *fottletie* [a]
of a pomegranate· tree bearing the arms of
Spain. There were many minftrels, but no
mafking or dancing. Before the banquet, the
queen was long in confultation with fir Thomas Pope. In the evening the princefs with
all her company returned, as they came, to
Somerfet- place ; and the next day retired to
Hatfield [b]. During her refidence at Hatfield,
the princefs was alfo prefent at a royal
Chriftmas, kept with great folemnity by the
queen and king Philip at Hampton-court.
On Chriftmas-eve, the great hall of the palace was illuminated with a thoufand lamps
curioufly difpofed. The princefs fupped at
the fame table in the hall with the king and
queen, next the cloth of ftate : and after fupper, and ferved with a perfumed napkin and
plates of confects by the lord Paget. But
fhe retired to her ladies, before the revels,
mafking, and difguifings began. On faint
Stephen's day fhe heard mattins in the queen's
clofet adjoining to the chapel, where fhe was

[a] A curious devife in cookery or confectionary.
[b] MSS. Cotton. Vitell. F. 5. MSS. Strype, ut fupr.

attired

attired in a robe of white fattin, ftrung all over with large pearls. On the twenty ninth day of December, fhe fate with their majefties and the nobility at a grand fpectacle of jufting, when two hundred fpears were broken. Half of the combatants were accoutred in the Almaine, and half in the Spanifh fafhion [c]. Thus our chronicler, who is fond of minute defcription. But thefe and other particularities, infignificant as they feem, which he has recorded fo carefully, are a vindication of Queen Mary's character in the treatment of her fifter : they prove, that the princefs, during her refidence at Hatfield, lived in fplendor and affluence, that fhe was often admitted to the diverfions of the court, and that her prefent fituation was by no means a ftate of oppreffion and imprifonment, as it has been reprefented by moft of our hiftorians.

We have before feen that fir Thomas Pope, during his attendance on this lady, was engaged in the foundation of his college. An undertaking of fuch a nature, could not fail of attracting the attention of the young Elifabeth ; whofe learned education and prefent fituation naturally interefted her in the progrefs of a work fo beneficial to the in-

[c] Vitell. F. 5. Cotton. MSS. Strype, ut fupr.

creafe.

creafe of her favorite purfuits, and carried on by one with whom fhe was fo nearly connected. Accordingly this fubject was often matter of converfation between them, as appears from part of a letter written by fir Thomas Pope : which alfo ftill further proves the friendly terms on which they lived together. " The princefs Elifabeth her grace, whom I " ferve here, often afkyth me about the courfe " I have devyfed for my fcollers : and that " part of myne eftatutes refpectinge ftudie I " have fhewn to her, which fhe likes well. " She is not only gracious, but moft lerned, " as ye right well know [d]."

[d] Dat. Hatfield, 1556. To the Prefident. Ex Autograph. ubi fupr. Afcham, in one of his Latin Epiftles, gives the following interefting account of Elifabeth's progrefs in literature, when fhe was very young, under the year 1550. Among the learned daughters of Sir Thomas More, he fays, the princefs Elifabeth fhines like a ftar of diftinguifhed luftre ; deriving greater glory from her virtuous difpofition, and literary accomplifhments, than from the dignity of her exalted birth. I was her preceptor in Latin and Greek for two years. She was but little more than fixteen, when fhe could fpeak French, and Italian, with as much fluency and propriety as her native Englifh. She fpeaks Latin readily, juftly, and even critically. She has often converfed with me in Greek, and with tolerable facility. When fhe tranfcribes Greek or Latin, nothing can be more beautiful than her handwriting. She is excellently fkilled in mufic, although not very fond of it. She has read with me all Cicero, and great part of Livy. It is chiefly from thofe two authors alone, that fhe has acquired her knowledge of the Latin langnage. She begins the day

While fir Thomas Pope was concerned in this fuperintendance of the princefs, he received a letter from Heath, archbifhop of York and lord chancellor, the bifhops of Rochefter and Ely, lord Arundel, and fir Henry Jernegan, dated July the thirtieth, 1556, by which it appears, that the privy council placed much confidence in his penetration and addrefs, and greatly depended on

day with reading a portion of the Greek teftament, and then ftudies fome felect Orations of Ifocrates and the tragedies of Sophocles. From thefe authors, I was of opinion, that fhe would adorn her ftyle with the moft elegant diction, enrich her mind with the moft fuitable precepts, and frame her high ftation of life to every fortune. For her religious inftruction, after the Scriptures, fhe adds to the claffics Saint Cyprian and the Common Places of Melancthon, with other writers of that fchool, who teach purity of doctrine with elegance of expreffion. In every compofition, fhe is very quick in pointing out a far-fetched word, or affected phrafe. She cannot endure thofe abfurd imitators of Erafmus, who mince the whole latin Language into proverbial maxims. She is much pleafed with a Latin Oration naturally arifing from its fubject, and written both chaftly and perfpicuoufly. She is moft fond of tranflations not too free, and with that agreeable clafh of fentiment which refults from a judicious comparifon of oppofite or contradictory paffages. By a diligent attention to thefe things, her tafte is become fo refined, and her judgment fo penetrating, that there is nothing in Greek, Latin, and Englifh compofition, either extravagant or exact, carlefs or correct, which fhe does not in the courfe of reading accurately difcern; immediately rejecting the one with difguft, and receiving the other with the higheft degree of pleafure. Afcham. Epistol. Lib. i, p, 18. a. edit. Lond. 1581.

his

his fkilful management of her highnefs at
this critical period.

In confequence of Wyat's unfuccefsfull attempt, new efforts were made to foment a
fecond infurrection. Many of Wyat's adhe-
rents, of which the principal was one Dudley
Afhton, had fled into France where they were
well entertained. Afhton being connected
with both kingdoms fent over from France
one Cleyberye, a condemned perfon, who pretended to be the earl of Devonfhire. The
confpirators at the fame time, in the letters
and proclamations which they difperfed, made
ufe of the lady Elifabeth's name, and propagated many fcandalous infinuations againft
her reputation and honour [e]. They proceeded
fo far, as at Ipfwich to proclaim lord Courteney and the princefs, king and queen of England [f]. In how licentious a manner her character was abufed, appears from a curious
manufcript paper preferved in the Britifh Mufeum, entitled, " A relation how one Cleber,
" 1556, proclaimed the ladie Elifabethe quene,
" and her beloved bedfellow, lord Edwarde
" Courtneye, kynge [g]." It was thought pro-

[e] Strype Eccl. mem. iii. 336.
[f] Carte iii. 327.
[g] MSS. Harl. 537. 25.

per that the truth of this affair fhould be made known to the princefs; and as the communication of it was a matter of fome delicacy, and that mifreprefentations might be prevented, the council above-mentioned order fir Thomas Pope, " Becaufe this mat-
" ter is fpread abroad, and that paradventure,
" many conftructions and difcourfes will be
" made thereof, we have thought meet to
" fignifie the whole circumftances of the
" cafe unto you, to be by you opened to the
" ladie Elifabeth's grace at fuch time as ye
" fhall thinke moft convenient. To the end
" it may appear unto her, how little thefe
" men ftick, by falfhood and untruthe, to
" compafs their purpofe : not letting, for that
" intent to abufe the name of her grace, or
" any others : which their devifes neverthe-
" lefs are (god be thanked) by his goodnefs
" difcovered from time to time, to their ma-
" jefties perfeverance, and confufion of their
" enemies. And fo we bid you hertily well
" to fare. From *Eltham* the xxxth of July,
" 1556. *Your loving friends,* &c [h]."

In confequence of fir Thomas Pope's explanation, the queen herfelf wrote a letter to

[h] Burnet Hift Ref. RECORDS, Numb. xxxiii, pag. 314. And Hift. p. 351.

the

the princefs, in which fhe expreffed her abhorrence and difbelief of thefe infamous for-
geries. It was anfwered by the princefs,
who declared her deteftation of the confpirators, and difclaimed the leaft knowledge of
their malicious defigns. Undoubtedly having
fuffered fo feverely, and perhaps unjuftly, in
the affair of Wyat, fhe judged it expedient
to clear her character even from the moft
improbable fufpicions. Commiffioners were
immediately appointed for examining into
this confpiracy, fir Francis Englefield the
comptroller, fir Edward Waldegrave, fir
Henry Jernegan, fir Edward Haftings, and
Cordall the queen's follicitor; and feveral of
the parties were apprehended, and condemned
at Guildhall[l]. When war was next year proclaimed againft France, this fecret concurrence
of the French court, with the machinations of
Dudley Afhton and his accomplices, was ex-
preffly fpecified, amongft other articles in the
declaration[k].

Soon afterwards, Eric king of Sweden
fent by his ambaffador, a meffage fecretly to
the princefs at Hatfield, with a propofal of
marriage. King Philip had juft before pro-

[l] Strype, Eccl. Mem. iii. 336, 337.
[k] Camden, Eliz. per Hearne. i. *Apparat.* pag. 22.

pofed to the queen, to marry her to the duke of Savoy [1]; with a view perhaps of retaining the duke who was an able general, in his interefts againft France, with which Philip was at this time engaged in open hoftilities. This propofal of the king of Sweden fhe wifely rejected, becaufe it was not conveyed to her by the queen's directions. But to this objection the embaffador anfwered, that the king of Sweden his mafter, as a man of honor and a gentleman, thought it moft proper to make the firft application to her-felf: and that having by this preparatory ftep obtained her confent, he would next, as a king, mention the affair in form to her majefty. But the final anfwer of princefs was an abfolute denial: and fhe defired the meffenger to acquaint his mafter, that as fhe could not liften to any propofals of that na-ture, unlefs made by the queen's advice or authority; fo fhe could not but declare, that if left to her own will, fhe would always pre-fer a fingle condition of life. The affair foon came to the queen's ears; who fending for fir Thomas Pope to court, received from him an entire account of this fecret tranfac-tion; ordering fir Thomas at the fame time to write to the princefs, and acquaint her

---

[1] Strype, Eccl. Mem.. iii. 317.

how

how much fhe was fatisfied with this prudent
and dutiful anfwer to the king of Sweden's
propofition.　Sir Thomas Pope very foon
afterwards returned to his charge at Hatfield;
when the queen commanded him, not only to
repeat this approbation of the conduct of the
princefs relating to the propofed match from
Sweden, but to receive from her own mouth
the refult of her fentiments concerning it;
and at the fame time to take an opportunity
of founding her affections concerning the
duke of Savoy, without mentioning his name.
The imperial ambaffadors Mountmorency lord
of Courieres, and Bouchard, were ftill in
England, waiting for the event of the latter negociation [m]. For the Emperor Charles
the fifth [n], who was now become her friend,
and had before interefted himfelf in her favor, was anxious, by fuch an important
connection, to form a potent and lafting
alliance between the Britifh and Imperial
crowns. But I fhall infert fir Thomas Pope's
letter, written in confequence of this commiffion, to the queen or council; by which he
feems perfectly to have underftood Elifabeth's
real thoughts and difpofition.

[m] Carte, iii. 307.

[n] See Hume, Hift. iii. 386. feq. Ed. 4to.　And Dr. Robert-
fon's mafterly Hiftory of Charles the fifth.

" Firft

" Firſt after I had declared to her grace,
" how well the quene's majeſtie liked of her
" prudent and honorable anſwere made to
" the ſame meſſenger; I then opened unto
" her grace the effects of the ſayd meſſengers
" credence : which after her grace had hard,
" I ſayd, the queenes highnes had ſent me
" to her grace, not onlie to declare the ſame,
" but alſo to underſtande how her grace
" liked the ſayd motion. Whereunto after
" a little pauſe taken, her grace anſwered
" in forme following. Maiſter Pope, I re-
" quyre you, after my moſt humble com-
" mendacions to the quenes majeſtie, to
" render untoo the ſame lyke thankes, that
" it pleaſed her highnes of her goodnes, to
" conceive ſo well of my anſwer made to the
" ſame meſſenger ; and herwithal, of her
" princelie confyderation, with ſuch ſpeede
" to command you by your letters to fig-
" nyfie the ſame untoo me : who before re-
" mained wonderfullie perplexed, fering that
" her majeſtie might miſtake the ſame : for
" which her goodnes I acknowledg myſelf
" bound to honour, ſerve, love, and obey
" her highnes, during my liffe. Requyring
" you alſo to ſaye untoo her majeſtie, that
" in the king my brothers time, there was
" offered me a verie honorable marriage or

" two

" two : and ambaſſadors ſent to treat with
" me touching the ſame°; whereupon I made
" my humble ſuite untoo his highnes, as
" ſome of honour yet livinge can be teſti-
" monies, that it would lyke the ſame to
" give me leave, with his graces favour, to
" remayne in that eſtate I was, which of all
" others beſt lyked me or pleaſed me ᴾ.    And

° Viz. in 1552, the eldeſt ſon of the king of Denmark.
Heylin, Eccl. Reſt. Eʟɪᴢ. p. 99.

ᴾ She was not however perfectly ſatisfied with this ſtate,
at that time ; as appears from many curious anecdotes of
her early coquetry with lord Thomas Seymour, high ad-
miral, who married Catharine Parr, widow of Henry viii.
Burghley's State Papers, vol. i. by Haynes. p. 96.  " From
" the confeſſion of Thomas Parrye her cofferer.  I do remember
" alſo ſhe [Catharine Aſhley] told me, that the admirall loved
" her but too well, and had done ſoo a great while : and
" that the queen was jealouſe on hir and him, inſomuche,
" that one tyme the quene ſuſpecting the often acceſſe of the
" admirall to the lady Elizabeth's grace, cam ſodenly upon
" them, when they were all alone, he having her in his armes.
" From the confeſſion of Catharine Aſhley, her waiting woman,
" or governeſs.  She ſaith at Chelſy he would come many
" mornyngs into the ſaid lady Elizabeth's chamber, before ſhe
" were redy, and ſometyme before ſhe did riſe.—And if ſhe
" were in hir bed, he wold put open the curteyns, and bid hir
" good morrow, &c.  And one morning he ſtrave to have
" kiſſed her in bed.—At Hanworth, in the garden, he wrated
" with her, and cut her gown in an hundred pieces, being
" black cothes.  An other tyme, at Chelſey, the Lady Eliza-
" beth hearing the pryvie-lock undo, knowyng that he would
" come in, ran out of hir bed to hir maydens, and then went
" behynd the curteyn of the bed, &c.—At Seymour-place, . . .
                                                    " he

" in good faith, I pray you fay untoo her
" highnefs, I am even at this prefent of the
" fame minde, and fo intende to continewe
" with her maiefties favour : and afiuringe
" her highnes, I fo well like this eftate, as
" I perfwade myfelfe ther is not anie kynde
" of liffe comparable unto it. And as con-
" cerning my lyking the fayd mocion made
" by the fayd meffenger, I befeeche you fay
" unto her maieftie, that to my rememb-
" raunce I never hard of his mafter before
" this tyme; and that I fo well lyke both

" he did ufe a while to come up every mornyng in his nyght-
" gowne, barelegged in his flippers, where he found com-
" monly the lady Elizabeth up at hir boke.—At Hanworth,
" the queene told this examinate, that my lord admirall look-
" ed in at the galery wyndow, and fe my lady Elizabeth
" caft hir armes about a man's neck. The which heryng,
" this examinate enquyred for it of my lady's grace, who de-
" nyed it weepyng, and bad ax all hir women. Thei all
" denyed it. And fhe knew it could not be fo, for ther came
" no man but Gryndall, the lady Elizabeth's fcholemafter.
" Howbeit, thereby this examinate did fufpeft, that the quene
" was jelous betwixt them ; and did but feyne this, to then-
" tente that this examinate fhould take more hede, and be,
" as it were, in watche betwixte hir and my lord admirall.
" She faith alfo,- that Mr. Afhley, hir hufband, hath divers
" tymes given this examinate warnyng to take hede, for he
" did fere that the lady Elizabeth did ber fome affeftion to
" my lord admirall, fhe femyd to be well plefed therwith,
" and fometyme fhe wold blufh when he were fpoken of."
Ibid. p. 99. This was in 1548. Parrye was afterwards made
treafurer of her houfhold.

" the

" the meſſage and the meſſenger, as I ſhall
" moſt humblie pray God upon my knees,
" that from henceforth I never hear of the
" one nor the other : aſſure you, that if it
" ſhould eftſones repaire unto me, I would
" forbeare to ſpeak to him. And were there
" nothing els to move me to miſlyke the
" mocion, other than that his maſter would
" attempte the ſame, without making the
" queen's maieſtie privie therunto, it were
" cauſe ſufficient."

" And when her grace had thus ended,
" I was ſo bold as of myſelfe to ſay unto her
" grace, her pardon firſt requyred, that I
" thought few or none. would beleve, but
" that her grace could be ryght well con-
" tented to marrie, ſo ther were *ſome ho-*
" *norable marriage* offered her by the queen's
" highnes, or her maieſties aſſent. Wher-
" unto her grace anſwered, What I ſhall do
" hereafter I knowe not : but I aſſure you
" upon my truthe and fidelitie, and as God
" be mercifull unto me, I am not at this
" tyme otherways mynded, than I have de-
" clared unto you ; no, though I were offered
" the greateſt prince in all Europe.—And
" yet perçaſe the queen's maieſtie may con-

" ceive

" ceive this ⁹ rather to proceed of a maidenlie
" fhamefaftnes, than upon anie fuch certaine
" determination.

## THOMAS POPE '."

Courtney earl of Devonfhire being now
dead ', the queen grew lefs jealous of the
princefs, and feemed almoft perfectly reconciled. In November, 1556, fhe was invited
to court; and accordingly came to London
with much parade '. The principal reafon

⁹ In MSS. Harl. [ut inf.] it is, " this *my anfwer* rather,
" etc." As if it was the fpeech of the princefs continued.

ʳ Brit. Muf. MSS. Harl. 444. 7. viz. " The ladye Eliza-
" beth hir graces aunfwere made at Hattfield, the xxvi of
" Aprill 1558, to fir T. Pope knt. being fent from the quenes
" majeftie to underftand howe hir grace lyked of the mocyon
" of marryage, made by the kynge ellect of Swethelandes
" meffenger." fol. 28. See alfo the fame, ibid. MSS. Cotton, Vitell. xii. 16. 8. It is alfo among Petyt's Manufcripts,
now in the Library of the Inner Temple : from whence it is incorrectly printed by Burnet, ubi fupr. No. 37. p. 325. See
ibid. Hift. p. 361.

ˢ He was imprifoned in Fotheringay-caftle, on fufpicion of
being concerned with the princefs Elifabeth in Wyat's rebellion. Being releafed, he travelled into Italy, and died at Pa-
dua, aged thirty. He was the laft earl of Devonfhire, of the
noble family of Courtenay. Strype, Eccl. Mem. iii. 338, 339.
Some fay he was poifoned.

ᵗ " The xxviiith daye of November, came ryding thrugh
" Smythfelde and Old Balee, and thrugh Fleet-ftreet, unto
" Somerfett-plafe, my good lade Elifabeth's grace the quenes

" fyfter ;

of this invitation, was formally to propofe to her in perfon a marriage with Philibert Emanuel, the duke of Savoy, which fir Thomas Pope, by the queen's commands, had before hinted at a diftance, as we have feen in the preceding letter. This propofal the princefs declined; but difguifed her refufal with the fame earneft profeffions of her unchangeable devotion to a ftate of virginity, which fhe had before made to fir Thomas Pope on account of the Swedifh match. Great court was paid to the princefs during her abode at Somerfet-houfe ". Her amiable condefcenfion, obliging addrefs, and agreeable converfation, procured her new interefts and attachments, and even engaged the beft part of the lords of the council in her favor.

Her beauty perhaps had no great fhare in thefe acquifitions; fuch as it was, it ftill retained fome traces of ficknefs, and fome fhades of melancholy, contracted in her late fevere but ufeful fchool of affliction.

---

" fyfter; with a grate company of velvett cotts and chaynes, " hir graces gentyllmen : and aftyr, a grate company of her " men, all in redd cotts gardyd with a brod gard of blake " velvett and cutts, &c." Vitell. MSS. Cott. F. 5. ut fupr. Strype cites a part of this paffage, Eccl. Mem. iii. 309.

" Carte, iii. 331.

She

She found however that retirement best suited her circumstances, as it did her inclinations ; and although she had been invited to pass the whole winter in London, after a short stay of one week only, she returned to her former situation at Hatfield ".

One should have expected that the queen would have parted in difgust with the princess, at this rejection of a match, recommended by Philip, and so convenient to his purposes. But it appears, that the queen was extremely backward in promoting her husband's desire of marrying Elisabeth to the duke of Savoy. On this account, Philip employed Alphonsus, a franciscan frier, his confessor, to confer with her majesty on the subject of this marriage. She told him, that she feared, without consent of parliament, neither her husband Philip, nor the nation would be benefited by this alliance. She added, that she could not in point of conscience press this match upon her sister ;

---

" " Hir grace did loge at hir plase [Somerset house] till the " iii day of Deffember. The third day of Deffember cam ryd- " ing from hir plase my ladie Elifabeth's grace from Somerset " plase down Fleetftrete, and thrugh Old Bailee and Smyth- " felde, &c. And so hir grace toke hir waye towards byfhope- " hatfeld plafe," MSS. Cott. Vittell. F. 5. ut fupr.

meaning

meaning perhaps that it would be unjuſt, to
force the princeſs to be married, after her
reſolute declarations againſt wedlock; or improper and diſhonorable, to match her beneath the dignity of a crowned head.  The
theological reaſonings of Alphonſus were too
refined for the underſtanding, or too weak
for the conſcience, of the queen, who ſtill
remained inflexible in her former opinion.
Upon this, Philip wrote to her in his uſual
authoritative ſtyle, adviſing her to examine
her own conſcience, and to conſider whether
her opinion was founded in truth or in ob-
ſtinacy; adding, that if the parliament op-
poſed his requeſt, he ſhould lay the blame
upon her [x].  The queen, in her anſwer, begged that he would, at leaſt, defer the matter till he returned into England: and that
then he might have a better opportunity
of judging, what attention her reaſons de-
ſerved.  That otherwiſe, ſhe ſhould live in
jealouſy of his affections, a ſtate of mind
to her worſe than death; but which, to her
great diſquietude, ſhe had already began to
feel.  She obſerved, with many expreſſions
of deference to his ſuperior judgment and
authority, that, whatever her conſcience might
have determined, the matter could not be

[x] Strype, Eccl. Mem. iii. 317. ſeq.

poſſibly

poffibly brought to any fpeedy conclufion, as the duke would be immediately ordered into the field.

This letter which is in French, and printed by Strype [y], is no lefs a fpecimen of her implicit fubmiffion to Philip, than the whole tranfaction is, at the fame time, an inftance of that unconquerable perfeverance which the queen exerted on certain occafions. Philip perfifted in his defign : and with a view to accomplifh it more effectually, difpatched into England the duchefs of Parma and the duchefs of Lorraine, whom he commiffioned to bring back with them the princefs Elifabeth into Flanders. Philip was in love with the duchefs of Lorain ; and the fplendor of her table and retinue, which fhe was unable to fupport of herfelf, made the queen extremely jealous. She was therefore, whatever her companion might have been, a very improper fuitrefs on this occafion. The queen would not permit the two ducheffes to vifit the princefs at Hatfield ; and every moment of their ftay gave her infinite uneafinefs. But they both foon returned, without fuccefs [z].

[y] Strype, Eccl. Mem. iii. Append. Numb. LVI.
[z] Carte, iii. 358.

Perhaps

Perhaps the growing jealoufy of the queen, a paffion which often ends in revenge againft the beloved object, might at leaft have fome fhare in dictating this oppofition to Philip [a]. At length the remonftrances of the queen, and the repeated difapprobation of the princefs, prevailed; and it is certain, whatever Mary's real motives might be, that the propofal was fuddenly laid afide. But Mary fo far concurred with Philip's meafures, as the next year to declare war againft France [b]; in which the duke of Savoy was Philip's chief commander at the battle and fiege of faint Quintin [c].

As to the king of Sweden, he afterwards, in the year 1561, renewed his addreffes to Elifabeth, when fhe was queen of England: at which time, he fent her a royal prefent of

[a] Philip, while abroad, had fhewn her fo many marks of indifference, and had trifled with her fo frequently about his return to England, that once, in a fit of rage, fhe tore his picture. Carte, ibid. 329.

[b] Yet the public finances were at this time fo low, that fhe could not procure a fingle vote from her privy-council for the declaration of war: and fhe therefore threatened to difmifs them all from the board, and to appoint counfellors more obfequious. Hume, iii. 391. ed. 4to.

[c] Strype, Eccl. Mem. iii. 317. Hollingfhead, Chron. iii. 1134. col. 1, 2.

eighteen

eighteen large pyed horfes, and two fhips laden with riches [d]. At the fame time, fome ftationers of London had publifhed prints of her majefty Elifabeth and the king of Sweden in one piece. This liberty, as it was called, gave great offence to the queen, who ordered fecretary Cecil to write to the lord mayor of London, enjoining him diligently to fupprefs all fuch publications; as they implied an agreement of marriage between their majefties. Cecil takes occafion to add, " her majeftie hitherto cannot be induced, " whereof we have caufe to forrow, to allow " of any marriadg with any manner of per- " fon [e]." Soon afterwards the king of Sweden was expected to pay the queen a vifit at Whitehall; and it is diverting to obferve the perplexity, and embarraffment of the officers of ftate about the manner of receiving him at court, " the queenes majeftie *being* " *a maide* [f]."

But fhe ftill perfifted in thofe vows of virginity which fhe had formerly made, to fir Thomas Pope at Hatfield; and conftantly refufed not only this, but other advantageous

---

[d] Strype, Ann. Ref. i. p. 271.

[e] Burghley's State Papers, by Haynes. p. 367.

[f] Ibid. p. 371.

matches.

matches. One of them was with the Duke
D'Alenzon, whom fhe refufed, yet after fome
deliberation, becaufe he was only a boy of
feventeen years of age, and fhe almoft in her
fortieth year *. A hufband, I fuppofe, although a young one, would have been at
that time perhaps inconfiftent with her private attachments ; and the formalities of marriage might have laid a reftraint on more
agreeable gallantries with the earl of Effex
and others, Bayle ʰ affigns a curious phyfical
reafon for Elifabeth's obftinate perfeverance in
a ftate of virginity.

The four laft years of queen Mary's reign,
which the princefs Elifabeth paffed at Hatfield with fir Thomas Pope, were by far the
moft agreeable part of her time during that
turbulent period. For although fhe muft
have been often difquieted with many fecret
fears and apprehenfions, yet fhe was here perfectly at liberty, and treated with a regard
due to her birth and expectations. In the
mean time, to prevent fufpicions, fhe prudently declined interfering in any fort of
bufinefs, and abandoned herfelf entirely to

* Camd. Eliz. p. 269. per Hearne.
ʰ Diſt. Artic. Elizabeth.

books

books and amufements[i]. The pleafures of folitude and retirement were now become habitual to her mind; and fhe principally employed herfelf in playing on the lute or virginals, embroidering with gold and filver, reading Greek, and tranflating Italian. She was now continuing to profefs that character which her brother Edward gave her, when he ufed to call her his *fweet fifter Temperance*[k]. But fhe was foon happily removed to a reign of unparalleled magnificence and profperity.

Upon the acceffion of the new queen, who was refident at Hatfield when her fifter Mary died on November the feventeenth, 1558, it does not appear that fir Thomas Pope was continued in the privy-council. This circumftance may juftly be interpreted to his honor. Elifabeth, to prevent an alarm among the partifans of the catholic communion, had prudently retained thirteen of Mary's privy counfellors. Thefe were, Heathe, archbifhop of York, and lord chancellor; the marquis of Winchefter, lord treafurer; the earls of Arundel, Shrewfbury, Pembroke, and Derby; the lords Clinton, and Howard; fir Thomas Cheyney, fir William

[i] Burnet, Hift. Ref. ubi fupr. p. 363.

[k] Camd. Eliz. per Hearne, APPARAT. vol. i. p. 14.

Petre,

Petre, fir John Mafon, fir Richard Sackville, and Doctor Wootton, dean of York and Canterbury[1]. But moft of thefe had complied with all the changes which were made in the national religion fince the latter end of Henry's reign; and were fuch dexterous adepts in the fafhionable art of adapting their principles to the variable complexion of the times, that they were ftill employed in every new revolution.

[1] Burnet, Reformat. ii. 375.

++++++++++++++++++++++++++++++++++++++++++++

## S E C T.  IV.

WE have now done with fir Thomas Pope's political character; and are entering on that moft memorable circumftance of his life, before incidentally mentioned, by which he fecured immortality to his name, and conferred a perpetual emolument on his country; I mean, the foundation of Trinity college in Oxford. His good fenfe and good difpofition led him to reflect, that he could not beftow a competent proportion of thofe riches which he had fo largely received, with greater propriety, utility, and generofity, than in the fervice of the public. I fhall therefore make no apology for delivering at large a hiftory of his proceedings in forming and completing this liberal defign.

And perhaps there are fome of my readers, who will be more pleafed to view him in the milder and more amiable light of the father of ingenuous education, difpenfing rewards to fcience and virtue, than in the more active yet turbulent fcenes of public life, diverfified only

H                                    by

by the vain viciffitudes of human affairs, or fraught with the crimes and misfortunes of mankind.

About the year 1290, Richard de Hoton, prior, and the monks, of the cathedral convent of Durham, erected a college in the northern fuburbs of Oxford, for the education of the novices of their monaftery; to which it was confidered as an appendage[a]. This was afterwards increafed, with the addition of revenues and books, by Richard of Bury, bifhop of Durham, in the year 1345. It was at length entirely rebuilt, more effectually eftablifhed, and more amply endowed, for eight benedictine monks and eight fecular ftudents, in the year 1370, by the munificence of Thomas Hatfield, bifhop of the fame fee[b]. About the year 1541, this college was diffolved by Henry the eighth[c]: at which time, all its eftates, its fite, precinct, chapel, bellfry, buildings of all forts,

[a] See grant in the Appendix, Numb. VI. Which, as it probably contains the firft and early feparation of the ground on which Trinity college now ftands, with its precincts, or of the greateft part of thefe, to the purpofes of learning, was thought too curious to be omitted among the original papers.

[b] The monks were allowed annually ten pounds each, and the feculars five marcs. It is remarkable, that the ftipend of thefe monks is treble to moft of the fellowfhips then in Oxford.

[c] See Stevens's Monaft. vol. i. p. 343. from MSS. A. Wood.

with

with the entire appurtenances of the fame, were granted by the king to his new dean and chapter of Durham cathedral, which, as I prefume, they now poffefs [d]. Its fite only reverted to the crown; for Edward the fixth, in the feventh year of his reign, by letters patent dated February the fourth, 1552 [e], granted the fite of this college to George Owen, of Godftowe, the king's phyfician, and William Martyn, gentleman.

On this ground fir Thomas Pope determined to found his intended college. Accordingly, by indenture, dated February the twentieth, 1554 [f], he purchafed the premifes of the faid Owen and Martyn. In the fame year he obtained from Philip and Mary a royal licence, or charter, dated March the eigthth, 1554 [g], empowering him to create and erect a certain college within the univerfity of Oxford, confifting of one prefident a prieft, twelve fellows, four of whom fhould be priefts, and eight fcholars [h]: and liberally and fufficiently to endow the fame and their fucceffors with certain manors, lands, and revenues. In the fame

---

[d] See Append. Numb. *VII*.
[e] See Append. Numb. VIII.
[f] See Append. Numb. IX.
[g] See Append. Numb. X.
[h] This Number he afterwards encreafed to *twelve*.

charter,

charter, and with the eftates and poffeffions therein recited, he likewife obtains licence of the king and queen to found and endow a fchool at Hokenorton in the county of Oxford, to be called *Jefus Scolehoufe*; and to give ftatutes as well to the college, as to the firft and fecond mafters of the faid fchool [l]. On the twenty-eighth day of March, 1555, by deed fo dated [k], he declares his actual erection and eftablifhment of the faid college : and configns the fite and place above-mentioned, to Thomas Slythurfte, S. T. B. Prefident : Stephen Markes, A. M. Robert Newton, John Barwyke, James Bell, Roger Crifpin, John Richardfon, Thomas Scotte, George Sympfon, Bachelors of Arts, Fellows : And John Arden, John Comporte, John Perte, and John Langfterre, Scholars. In the morals, learning, and ftudious diligence of all which perfons, he therein declares that he much con-

[l] " Ac eciam ulterius damus et concedimus eidem Thomæ
" Pope, militi, plenariam facultatem et auctoritatem condendi
" et fanciendi, pro bono regimine dictorum COLLEGII et SCOLÆ,
" ac terrarum, tenementorum, hereditamentorum, bonorum et
" catallorum, eorundem, quecunque ftatuta, ordinationes, et
" regulas, per dictos, Prefidentem Socios et Scholares, *Archidi-*
" *dafcalum, Hypodidafcalum, et eorum quemlibet, obfervanda, &c.*"
EX CHART. ut fupr.

[k] See Append. Numb. XI.

fides.

fides. Referving to himfelf, at the fame time, the right of nominating the remainder.

With this deed the founder himfelf, the fame day, came to Oxford; and in confequence of it, in his own perfon delivered poffeffion of the college to the faid Prefident, Fellows, and Scholars, in the prefence of John Warner, vice-chancellor of the univerfity, warden of All Souls college, and archdeacon of Cleveland, and of Ely[1]; Owen Oglethorp, prefident of Magdalene, and dean of Windfor[m]; Robert Morwent, prefident of Corpus Chrifti; Walter Wryght, archdeacon of Oxford; John Browne, canon of Windfor[n]; Edmund Powel, efquire[o], Edward Love, John Bylling, Simon Perrot, John Heywood, Henry Bryan, Arthur Yeldard, John Myleward, John Edmundes, John Beresford, Ralph Dodmer, John Lawrence, Bartholomew Plott, Humfrey

---

[1] He was alfo or had been, profeffor of Phyfic in Oxford, and prebendary of Winchefter and Salifbury. He died Dean of Winchefter. A fmall Hiftory of All Souls college occurs in his hand-writing, about the year 1560, in Cod. MSS. Rawlinf. 236. fol. Bibl. Bodl.

[m] Afterwards bifhop of Carlifle : in which character he crowned queen Elizabeth.

[n] See Wood, Ath. Oxon. i. F. p. 65. edit 2.

[o] Of Sandford, near Oxford.

H 3                    Edmundes,

Edmundes [p], gentlemen, and many others [q]. In confequence of this laft-mentioned deed, by an inftrument dated the fame day and year, Thomas Slythurfte appoints Stephen Markes and Robert Newton, his lawful attornies, to enter, in his name and ftead, into a certain meffuage or building, with its appurtenances, in Oxford, called Trinity college, of the foundation of fir Thomas Pope, knight; and of the fame to take full and peaceable poffef-fion; and to keep and retain it for the ufes and purpofes of the faid Thomas Slythurfte, according to the force, form, and effect, of a certain grant made to him and others by the faid fir Thomas Pope [r].

In May following, the founder furnifhed his college with neceffaries and implements of every kind [s]. To the library in particular he gave no inconfiderable collection of valu-able and coftly. books, both printed and ma-nufcript [t]. But above all, he adorned the

[p] Indorfed on the inftrument cited Append. Numb. XI.

[q] Many of thefe perfons occur in different parts of thefe me-moirs; and their characters, and connections with fir Thomas Pope, are explained in their proper places.

[r] See Append. Numb. XII.

[s] Ex indent. dat. Maii 5. ii. iii. Phil. Mar. In Thefauriar. et Regiftr. prim. Coll. fol. 5.

[t] Ibid.

chapel,

chapel, as appears by a deed dated the fifth of May, 1555 ", with filver veffels, embroidered veftments, copes of tiffue, croffes, and illuminated miffals ". The next year, he tranfmitted to the fociety a body of ftatutes, dated the firft of May, 1556. On the eighth of the fame month, he gave them one hundred pounds for a ftock to begin with ˣ. Matters being thus duely prepared and adjufted, and his endowment ʸ of the college confifting of manors, lands, and impropriations, having effectually taken place before or upon the feaft of the annunciation, 1556 ˣ; the firft prefident, fellows, and fcholars, nominated by himfelf, were formally and ac-

---

ᵘ See Append. Numb. XVI.

ʷ The altars of the chapel were dedicated the following year, as appears from the following entry, in Comp. Burff. 1556, anno primo Coll. " Sol. pro Obfoniis datis Dom. Epif- " copo Gloceftrenfi et Miniftris ejus in confecratione altarium, " xviij s. x d. ob."

ˣ Ex acquietantia in Regiftro primo, fol. 6. b.

ʸ See an inftrument figned with his own hand, viz. " *A* " *Valewe of all the Manors, Londes, Tenements, and Heredita-* " *mentes, which I Sir* Thomas Pope, *Knighte, Founder of Trinitie* " *colledge within the Univerfitie of Oxford, have given to the Pre-* " *fidente, Fellowes, and Schollers, of the fame, and to their Succef-* " *fors for ever. As well at the firft Erection of the colledge, as here-* " *after followithe,* &c." Ad. Calc. vet. Libri Statutor. in pergamen. penes Præfid. fol. 109. b. etc.

ˣ Comput. Burff. anno primo Coll.

H 4 tually

tually admitted within the chapel, on the thirtieth day of May, being the eve of Trinity Sunday, the fame year, yiz. 1556. They were all, the graduates at leaft, taken from different colleges in Oxford; except one, who was of Cambridge. Their names, dignities, colleges, degrees, counties, and appointments in the new fociety, as far as notices have occurred, are here fpecified *.

## P R E S I D E N T.

*Thomas Slythurfte*, S. T. B. Canon of Windfor. County, Berkfhire.

## F E L L O W S.

*Arthur Yeldarde*, Fellow of Pembroke-Hall, in Cambridge, A. M. Northumberland.—Appointed philofophy-lecturer by the founder.

*Stephen Markes*, Fellow, and Rector, of Exeter College, in Oxford, A. M. Cornwall.—Appointed vice-prefident by the founder.

*John Barwyke*, of Magdalen College, in Oxford, A. M. Devonfhire. — Appointed dean by election.

* See Append. Numb. XIII.

*James*

*James Bell*, Scholar of Corpus Chrifti College, in Oxford, A. B. Somerfetfhire.—Appointed rhetoric-lecturer by election.

*John Richardfon*, Scholar of Queen's College, in Oxford; A. B. Cumberland.—Appointed burfar by election.

*George Sympfon*, Scholar of Queen's College, in Oxford, A. B. Cumberland.

*George Rudde*, Scholar of Queen's College, in Oxford, A. B. Weftmoreland.

*Thomas Scotte*, Scholar of Queen's College, in Oxford, A. B. Cumberland.

*Roger Cryfpin*, Fellow of Exeter College, in Oxford, A. B. Devonfhire.

*Roger Evens*, A. B. Cornwall.

*John Perte*, A. B. Warwickfhire.—Appointed burfar by election.

*Robert Bellamie*, of Exeter College, in Oxford, A. B. Yorkfhire.

## S C H O L A R S.

*John Langfterre*, of Brafen-Nofe College, in Oxford, A. B. Yorkfhire.

*Reginald Braye*, A. B. Bedfordfhire.

*John Arden*, or *Arderne*, Oxfordfhire.

*John Comporte*, Middlefex.

*Robert*

*Robert Thraske,* Somerfetfhire.

*William Saltmarfhe,* Yorkfhire.

*John Harrys,* Gloucefterfhire.

———    ———    ———[b].

On faint Swithin's day, being the fifteenth of July, in the fame year, the founder paid a vifit to his college. He was accompanied by the bifhops of Winchefter and Ely, and other eminent perfonages. He difmounted from his horfe at the college gate, where he was received by the prefident, who ftood at his ftirrup. At entering the gates he was faluted in a long and dutiful oration by the vice-prefident : after which the burfars offered him a prefent of embroidered gloves. From thence he was conducted with the reft of the company into the prefident's great chamber : the fellows and fcholars ftanding on either fide, as he paffed along the court. Having viewed the library and Grove, they proceeded to dinner in the hall, where a fumptuous entertainment was provided. The prefident fate on the left hand of the founder,

[b] One *Starkie* was alfo nominated; but he not appearing, Edmund Hutchins, the founder's nephew, was admitted in his room by the founder's mandate, Octob. 3. Regiftr. Coll. prim. fol. 3. b. And Regiftr. Kettell. citat. apud Append. Numb. XXV.

yet

yet at fome diftance, and the reft of the guefts, and the fociety, were placed according to their rank, and in their proper order. There were twelve minftrels prefent in the hall; and among other articles of provifion on this occafion, four fat does, and fix gallons of *Mufcadel*, are mentioned. The whole expence of the feaft amounting to xij *l.* xiij *s.* ix *d.* After dinner they went to evening mafs in the chapel, where the prefident celebrated the fervice, habited in the richeft cope : and the founder offered at the altar a purfe full of angels. They then retired to the Burfary; where the founder paid into the hands of the Burfars all the cofts incurred by this vifit: and gave them befides, at the fame time, a filver goblet gilt, which being filled with hypocraffe, he drank to the Burfars, and to all the company prefent. He then departed towards Windfor : but before he left the college, gave with his own hands, to each of the fcholars, one marc *.

In November following, I find a letter to the prefident from the founder; in which, as likewife in eighteen others written after-

---

ᶜ See Append. Numb. XXIX.

wards

wards [d], are many marks of his attention to the affairs and economy of his college, and of his follicitude about fettling every article of the new foundation in the moft effectual manner : as alfo of his readinefs to affift on all neceffary occafions. In the letter juft mentioned, among feveral other particulars, he tells the prefident, in confequence of a converfation which had lately paffed between them both at Tyttenhanger in Hertfordfhire, by what expedient certain extraordinary expences of the college, in the late vifitation [e] of

[d] Fourteen of thefe letters are the originals in his own hand, preferved in the treafury of the college. The reft are copies in the firft regifter.

[e] Concerning which I find the fo'lowing entries, in Comp. Burff. 1556. " Expensæ equitantium.—Sol. per dom. " Perte in equitando ad fundatorem primo. ij s. ij d.—Sol. dom. " Bellamie equitanti ad Mag. Love [the founder's receiver] ut " certiorem eum redderet de adventu vifitatorum, et pro ex- " penfis propriis. xj d.—Sol. pro obfoniis, aliifque rebus, pro " vifitatoribus reverendiffimi Cardinalis Pole. xxiv s. ix d. Sol. " in regardo miniftris vifitatorum. xxv s."—For an account of this vifitation, fee Wood, Hift. Antiq. univ. Oxon. Lib. i. p. 278. col. ii. The vifitors were Brookes bifhop of Glocefter, Cole dean of Saint Paul's, Morwent prefident of Corpus, Wright archdeacon of Oxford, and Ormanet the pope's datary. Their defign was to reftore the pope's authority in the univerfity, and to ejeft all ftudents who were difaffefted to the catholic cere- monies. The vifitation feems to have ended in burning a con- fiderable number of Englifh bibles, and in removing the body of Peter Martyr's heretical wife from the cathedral of Chrift- church.

the

the univerſity by the deputies of cardinal Pole, and in ſome other inſtances, ſhould be diſcharged. He commiſſions him to thank maſter Rawes, a canon of Windſor [f], for a preſent of books intended for the library. He deſires the preſident would bargain for him with maſter Freere [g], for one thouſand load of ſtone, to

[f] He lies buried under the fourth arch of the ſouth ile, on the choir ſide, of St. George's chapel, at Windſor, with a plate of braſs on his grave, much injured; having the figure of a prieſt in a canon's mantle, with St. George's arms on his left ſhoulder, with this inſcription.

Orate pro anima Magiſtri Thomæ Rawes hujus ſacri collegii Canonici, qui obiit xii. die Maii anno dni milleſimo quingenteſimo quinquageſimo ſexto. Cujus anime propicietur deus. Amen.

In Rymer's FOED. Tom. xv. p. 463. is queen Mary's grant of his canonry to Richard Brewarne, canon of the firſt ſtall of Chriſt Church, Oxford, dated May 24, 1557, in which inſtrument he is called " nuper defunctus." According to Frithe's Catalogue of canons of Windſor, in Aſhmole's Berkſhire, vol. iii. p. 260. he was alſo vicar of Wantage, Co. Berks. His books, conſiſting of near fifty volumes in folio, came to the college in 1557. He was of Oxford, where he occurs determining in Arts, 1518. Wood MSS. Aſhmol. E. 6.

[g] William Freer, of the city of Oxford, whoſe father Edward married Anne the daughter of John Buſtarde, ſecond huſband of the founder's mother. Lee's MSS. Viſitation, ut ſupr. pag. 24. I find one Thomas Freer, admitted Probat. Soc. of Trin. coll. Jun. ix. 1560. Dioceſ. Lond.—Regiſtr. coll. prim. I find alſo the following article, in Comp. Burſſ. 1561.--2.

" Sol. xxvii. Novemb. pro expenſ. Dni Freer perferentis col-
" legii literas et librum ſtatutorum ad epiſcopum Wynton,
" vij ſ. viij d.

He

be carried to the college for beginning a wall round the Grove. He talks of having moved my lord cardinal Pole's grace, for licence for three of the fellows to preach [h]: a matter concerning which very rigid injunctions had been published, at the reftoration of the catholic religion by queen Mary. He mentions having fent to the college, for the fervice of the chapel, two pair of cenfers of one fafhion, two cruets, two candlefticks for the high altar, one fhip, and one pax of ivory: " trufting, or it be longe, ye fhall have the " lyke thynges of *fylver*." He adds, " and " forafmoch as it is evill carriage of my " organes this wynter, Mr. White [i], at my

He was afterwards M. D. and gave to the college-library, in 1566, a beautiful and valuable MS. on vellum, in folio, of Gregory Nazianzen. Edward Freer, above-mentioned, was buried in the church of All Saints Oxon. Jan. 27, 1564. Regiftr. *Parochial.* ecclef. prædict.

[h] " Concerning Lycence for Mr. Markes, Mr. Yeldard, and " Mr. Barwyke, to preach, I have already moved my lord Car-" dinall's grace ;; who anfwered the bufhop might give ly-" cence : but underftonding fyns by Mr. Yeldard the contrary, " I fhall eftfones move his grace therein." Queen Mary, Aug. 29, 1553, commiffioned Gardiner bifhop of Winchefter, Lord Chancellor, to grant Licences for preaching. Rym. Fœd. xv. 337. See form of a licence for this purpofe in Collier, Eccl. Hift. ii. Records, Numb. 78. pag. 82.

[i] Sir Thomas Whyte, who at this time was engaged in founding St. John's college. I find him entertained at Trinity college more than once, viz. in Comp. Burff. Coll. Trin. 1562.--3.

" Sol.

" requeſt, is content you ſhall have [keep]
" his littell organs till the beginning of ſo-
" mer ᵏ, when I may convey myne to you
" without hurtyng them. And bycauſe ye
" write, ye have grete nede of a ſtanding cup
" to drynke wyne in ; Mr. Sowtherne's ' mo-
" ney ſhall be beſtowed in ii. ſtanding cuppes
" gilt with covers, or ells in one faire ſtond-
" ing cupp with a cover, and ii. ſylver ſaltes
" with a cover ; and if they come to more
" money, I will pay the ſame myſelf. Ye
" ſhall receive by maſter Yeldard a rentall
" of all ſuch londes as I have given your col-
" lege ; which, till I appoint more ſcollers,
" as, god ſuffering I intend ſhottely, is a iuſt
" proportion to bear all the charges of your

" Sol. ex bellariis inſumptis in Fundatorem Collegii ſancti
" Johannis, iiij ſ. ix d." And again the ſame year, " In datis
" Fundatori Collegii ſancti Johannis cum viſeret collegium." .

The two founders ſeem to have been intimately acquainted
and connected ; as appears not only from this, but fiom another paſſage, in the letter before us. " Mr. [Sir] Thomas White
" and I ar almoſt at a point with ſir John Maſter for his woode ;
" and I believe ſhall conclude for the ſame within this ii. or iii,
" dayes."

ᵏ Accordingly, his own being received, ſir Thomas Whyte's
organ was returned to St. John's college, as appears from Comp.
Burſſ. coll. Trin. 1556.–7. viz.

" Sol. pro organorum ad Collegium ſancti Johannis vectura,
" iiij d."

¹ See an account of him, Append. Numb. XIII. Notes.

" colledge.

" colledge. And thus befeeching you with
" my hertie commendacions to all the fel-
" lowes and fcollers of my college, defiring
" the fame to remember me with their
" prayers, I bid you farewell. Wrytten at
" Clerkynwell the xxviith of *November*,
" 1556. Your affured loving friend,

## " THOMAS POPE<sup>m</sup>."

From other letters, written to the prefident, it appears that during his life-time he
paid all the univerfity expences of degrees,
regencies and determinations, for the fellows
and fcholars [n].

On the twentieth of January 1557, he
fent to the college for the fecond time [o], and
again on the twelfth of April following for
the third time [p], various articles of coftly furniture for the chapel and hall, confifting of
rich copes, fervice books, &c. as before; and
feveral pieces of filver plate. The whole
quantity of plate which he gave them at

[m] Ex autograph.

[n] I find him paying, at once, to Proceeders of his college,
perhaps for the whole year, the fum of vj *l.* xiij *s.* iv*d.* From
letter, dat. *St. Thomas's day, at Tyttenbanger, without the year.*

[o] See Append. Numb. XVII.

[p] See Append. Numb. XVIII.

_ thefe

thefe three feveral times, is as follows. A ftanding cup of filver gilt, with a cover, em-boffed with pomegranates⁹, and a fheaf of arrows, weighing thirty-three ounces. Two gilt faltes, weighing thirty-nine ounces. Three cups of filver gilt, weighing more than thirty-one ounces. Twelve filver fpoons befide one before fent, parcel-gilt, with knobs of fculp-ture. Thefe were for the hall. For the chapel they received, two cruets of filver gilt, weighing nine ounces. An holy-water-ftop and afpergoire of filver parcel-gilt, weighing more than eighteen ounces. A facring bell of filver gilt, weighing five ounces. A pax of filver gilt, with a crucifix, and the images of Mary and John, weighing near feventeen ounces. Two pair of cenfers, for frankin-

⁹ The *Pomegranate* firft became an ornament on filver plate, particularly on filver emboffed ftanding cups, in the reign of Henry vii. It was in compliment to prince Arthur who matched with Spain. Among the badges on his tomb in Worcefter Cathe-dral, Pomegranates are introduced with his father's portcullis and fleur de lis. In the reign of Henry viii. who married Ca-tharine of Spain, Arthur's widow, they were often ufed as an ornament in the furniture of mafques and pageants, exhibited for the entertainment, and in honor, of the queen. See Hol-lingfhed, Chron. iii. 802, 807, 808, 839, &c. Hence they became alfo a decoration in architecture ; as in the turrets of the great gate of Chrift Church, at Oxford, built by Wolfey. They were again revived, and grew very fafhionable, in the reign of queen Mary, after her marriage with Philip of Spain.

I                                                 cenfe,

cenfe, of filver parcel-gilt, weighing feventy. ounces. A fhip of filver with a fpoon for frankinfence, parcel-gilt, weighing near eighteen ounces. Two chapel-bafons of filver parcel-gilt weighing more than thirty feven ounces. A fair crofs of filver gilt, with images of Mary and John, garnifhed with chryftal and precious ftones, with a foot of filver gilt, weighing together, befide the chryftal and ftones, twenty-four pounds and five ounces. Two candlefticks of filver, for the high altar, parcel-gilt, weighing near thirty-two ounces. A monftrans of filver gilt, weighing twenty-pne ounces. A patin with a chalice of filver gilt, weighing twenty ounces. Another patin with a chalice of filver parcel-gilt, weighing thirteen ounces. A pipe of filver parcel-gilt, weighing thirteen ounces. He gave them befides, by his laft will, feveral other pieces of plate, for the fervice of the hall, which I fhall enumerate hereafter.

In September, 1557, he made confiderable additions to the foundation ; on the tenth of which month, he conveyed ', or rather confirmed to the Society the manors of Dun-

---

' With a condition of exchange : and he afterwards exchanged them for poffeffions of greater value in Effex and Gloucefterfhire, 1558. ADDITAM. ut infr. fol. 115.

thorp

thorp and Seawell in Oxfordſhire. With theſe new revenues he ordains and endows five obits, or dirges, yearly to be ſung and celebrated as feſtivals, in his college'. Theſe are, for queen Mary and her moſt noble progenitors, on the day of the aſſumption of the holy virgin; for dame Margaret his late wife, and Alice his daughter, deceaſed, on the day of the conception of the holy virgin; for dame Elizabeth his preſent wife, on the day of the nativity of the holy virgin; and for William and Margaret, his father and mother, on the day of the annunciation of the holy virgin. And on Jeſus day, the ſeventh of Auguſt, he appoints an.

---

' " ADDITAMENTUM ex liberalitate dom. Thome Pope, Funda-
" toris collegii ſanctæ et individuæ Trinitatis, in univerſitate Oxon.
" poſt erectionem dicti collegii ; tam pro augendo numero ſcholarium,
" quam pro aliis rebus in eodem peragendis."

" Cum, haud multum poſt collegii mei erectionem, ingente
" tum et inſolita rerum omnium caritate et penuria, miſere
" ubique ſæviente ; Ego de exequiis et hujuſmodi aliis re-
" bus ſtatuendis, quæ oblivione in initio erant prætermiſſæ,
" nonnulla præterea alumnis meis perquam neceſſaria deeſſe
" adhuc viderem : Perpetuam ejuſdem collegii mei perduratio-
" nem conſervationemque in omnibus ex animo cupiens at-
" que volens, precedenti Beneficio meo hoc inſuper addidi,
" &c."—" Dat. in Ædibus meis Clarkenwell, Septemb. 10·
" 1557." ADDITAM. ad calc. libri Statutorum. fol. 97. · Notwithſtanding, he had before thought of many of theſe particulars. They were not, however, till now, fully and effectually
eſtabliſhed.

I 2                                               Obit

Obit or dirge ', annually to be celebrated, as well during his life, as after his deceafe, for himfelf and all chriftian fouls. At which time, during his dirge and mafs, he orders that twelve poor men and twelve poor wo-men fhall be prefent in the chapel, and after-wards receive each a competent allowance of money, bread, and drink, within the col-lege at the entrance into the hall : and after the mafs of his obfequie was fung ", that bread and drink be annually diftributed the fame day among the poor prifoners in Oxford. From the fame revenues he likewife grants a

---

' By deed dat. Decemb. xxiv, 1 Eliz. 1558, he likewife founded a dirge on the fame day, in the church of Much-Waltham in Effex ; for which he gave a penfion of xxvjs. viijd. to Bryan Needham, vicar of Much-Waltham, and to his fuc-ceffors, " That the faid Bryan Nedeham, and his fucceffoures, " fhall yerly for ever, upon the feaft day of Jefus in the monthe " of Auguft, fay, or caufe to be faid, one *Dirige* ; and the " next day following one Maffe, for the fowle of fir Thomas " Pope, and all criften fowles : And after the faid maffe fy-" nifhed, that then the faid Bryan Nedeham, and his fuccef-" foures, fhall ymmediatelie gyve unto fyve poore folkes, " which fhall be prefent at the faid *Dirige* and Maffe, to pray " for the fowle of the faid fir T. Pope, and all criften fowles " to eueric of them, four-pence."—" Sig. S. and D. in the Pr. " of John Bersford, and John Milward." In Thefauriar. coll. Trin. Oxon. I find the faid Bryan Needham fupplicating for the degree of M. A. at Oxford in the year 1556. Regiftr. I. Congreg. et Convoc. fol. 169. a. fol. 160. b. In Turri Scho-larum.

" Regiftr. Coll. ut fupr. fol. 14. feq.

weekly

weekly allowance to the said prisoners; with various other improvements, and augmentations of former appointments. And because he once intended to found a School at Hokenorton in Oxfordshire ; with the endowment intended for that purpose, he now founds from these lands, four additional scholars in his college : By which judicious alteration of his original plan, the number of the scholars was increased to twelve, and equalled to that of the fellows. He tells us that he rejected the scheme of founding a school ʷ as an appendage to the college, being persuaded that it would prove more beneficial to the public, to restore in some measure, and encrease the number of scholars in the university of Oxford, of late much diminished and still continuing to de-

---

ʷ " Cum ante annos aliquot decreveram, unam perpetuam
" ac liberam SCHOLAM apud Hokenorton, in com. Oxon. erigere
" et stabilire ; ejusque rei Licentia, quemadmodum et fundandi
" mei collegii, ab illustriss. Phil. et Mar. &c. mihi facta sit.—
" Atque a gravissimis prudentissimisque hominibus, Reipublicæ
" me consultius facturum sit indicatum, si numerum scholarium
" Oxoniæ jam multum diminutum, ac indies magis magisque
" deficientem, augerem ac restaurarem, quam si hujusmodi
" Scholarum multiplicarem numerum ; præsertim cum constet
" in oppidis illi loco vicinis, varias Scholas, easque doctis or-
" natas instructoribus, ob discipulorum accedentium paucitatem,
" non satis frequentatas. Illorum rationibus atque consilio
" ductus, &c." EX ADDITAMENTO, ut supr. He first intended to found this school at Dedington, his native town. For an
account of it, see Append. No. XIV.

cay

cay, than to multiply the number of grammar fchools; efpecially as thofe fituated in
the neighbourhood of the place abovementioned, although properly filled with learned
mafters, were fo little frequented and encouraged.

In December, the fame year[x], he declares
his intention of building a commodious edifice at Garfington near Oxford, to which the
fociety might retire in time of peftilence,
then no uncommon malady. For this purpofe, in cafe he fhould not accomplifh it in
his life-time, as he intended, he left by his
will five hundred marks, and the building,
confifting of a fair quadrangle of ftone, was
accordingly raifed after his death[y].

When fir Thomas Pope had founded his
college, the univerfity of Oxford complimented him with their letters of thanks and
acknowledgment, in confideration of his hav-

---

[x] Indent. dat. Dec. 1. 1557. Regiftr. prim. fol. 16. b.
And Append. XXIII. XXIV.

[y] See articles of his will, infr. Great part of it has been
demolifhed, as ufelefs. One range, or fide, of the building now
remains; containing an arched entrance, with many large apartments having arched windows, and the kitchen at one end with
a fpacious fire place as in our colleges. It was not completely
finifhed till 1570. Ex comp. Burff. 1570.--1.

ing

ing added a new college to the former number; which were delivered to the founder
by the prefident ². Indeed they had no fmall
reafon, at this time, to acknowledge with
pleafure and gratitude this acceffion to their
conftitution. Heylin very juftly remarks, that
queen Mary, in rebuilding the public fchools
at Oxford " gave encouragement to two
" worthy gentlemen to add two new col-
" leges to the former, Trinity and faint
" John's. Had it not been for thefe Foun-
" dations, there had been nothing in this
" reign to have made it memorable, but only
" the misfortunes and calamities of it ª."
He might have added, that this liberality

---

² The letter was accompanied with a prefent of rich gloves,
viz. Ex comp. Burff. coll. Trin. 1556.—" Sol. per dom. Bel-
" lamie pro deferendis LITERIS et CHIROTHECIS ab univerfi-
" tate ad præfidem pro Fundatore. ij s. xj d."—The prefident,
I fuppofe, was then in London, waiting for this purpofe. Bellamie is one of the fellows. See Append. Numb. XXV. Article, BELLAMIE. In a Computus of Dr. W. Trefham, commiffary
of the univerfity in the aforefaid year, I find the following article, viz. " Here folowith other charges which I William Trefham
" as commiffarie have leyde out for the univerfitie of Oxford fithence
" the xxiitie day of April an. dni 1556.—ITEM for gloves fent
" to fir THOMAS POPE, and my lady his wife, with letters of
" thankefgiving from the univerfitie, vj s. viij d." Among the
auditors of this computus are Thomas White, Walter Wryght,
Thomas Slythurft, and Robert Morwent. Ex orig. in Bibl.
Bodl. Codd. MSS. A. Wood.

ª Ecclef. Reftaurat. Hift. of Q. Mary. p. 84.

I 4                                         could

could not have been conferred at a more feafonable time on the univerfity. And of this
fir Thomas Pope was very fenfible, as we
have before feen, when he fubftituted an additional number of academical ftudents in the
place of a grammar fchool.

But that it may further appear, how much
thefe encouragements were now wanted, it
will be neceffary to look backwards upon the
ftate of learning in England, particularly at
Oxford; and from thence to trace its progrefs,
and the caufes of its decline, down to the
times with which we are concerned. An enquiry not lefs inftruftive than entertaining,
and naturally connefted with the prefent
fubjeft.

About the clofe of the fifteenth century,
a tafte for polite letters, under the patronage
of the popes, began to be revived in Italy.
But thefe liberal pontiffs did not confider at the
fame time that they were undermining the pa-
pal intereft, and bringing on the Reformation. This event is commonly called the
Reftoration of Learning; but it fhould rather
be ftyled the reftoration of good fenfe and
ufeful knowledge. Learning there had been
before, but barbarifm ftill remained. The
moft

moſt acute efforts of human wit and penetration had been exerted for ſome centuries, in
the diſſertations of logicians and theologiſts;
yet Europe ſtill remained in a ſtate of ſuperſtition and ignorance. What philoſophy could
not perform, was reſerved to be completed by claſſical literature, by the poets and
orators of Greece and Rome, who alone
could enlarge the mind, and poliſh the manners. Taſte and propriety, and a rectitude
of thinking and judging, derived from theſe
ſources, gave a new turn to the general ſyſtem of ſtudy : mankind was civilized, and religion was reformed. The effects of this happy
revolution by degrees reached England. '

We find at Oxford, in the latter end of
the fifteenth century, that the univerſity
was filled with the jargon and diſputes of
the Scotiſts and Thomiſts; and if at that
time there were any ſcholars of better note,
theſe were chiefly the followers of Wicliffe;
and were conſequently diſcountenanced and
perſecuted. The latin ſtyle then only known
in the univerſity, was the technical language
of the ſchoolmen, of caſuiſts, and metaphy-
ſicians. At Cambridge, about 1485, nothing
was taught but Alexander's *Parva Lo-
gicalia*, the trite axioms of Ariſtotle, which
were never rationally explained, and the profound

found queftions of John Scotus [b]. At length fome of our countrymen, the principal of which were Grocyn, Latymer, Lillye, Linacer, Tunftall, Pace, and fir Thomas More, ventured to break through the narrow bounds of fcholaftic erudition, and went over into Italy with a defign of acquiring a knowledge in the Greek and Latin languages [c]. The Greek, in particular, was taught there with much perfection and purity, by many learned Greeks who had been driven from Conftantinople. In 1488, Grocyn and Linacer left Oxford, and ftudied Greek at Florence under the inftruction of Demetrius Chalcondylas, and Politian; and at Rome under Hermolaus Barbarus [d]. Grocyn returned an accomplifhed mafter in the Greek, and became the firft lecturer of that language at Oxford, but without any fettled endowment [e]. Elegance of ftyle began now to be cultivated, and the ftudy of the moft approved antient writers became fafhionable.

[b] Erafm. Epift. H. Bovillo. dat. Roffæ. 1516.
[c] Leland. ENCOM. pag. 74. edit. 4to. 1589. viz.
Omnes Italiam petierunt fydere faufto,
Et nituit Latiis terra Britanna Scholis.
[d] Wood Ath. Oxon. i. 15, 19, 20. See Stapleton de tribus THOMIS. cap. i.
[e] Wood. Hift. Antiq. univ. Oxon. i. 246.

In 1496, Alcock bifhop of Ely, founded Jefus college in Cambridge, partly for a certain number of fcholars to be educated in grammar [f]. Degrees in grammar, or rhetoric, had been early eftablifhed at Oxford. But the pupils of this clafs ftudied only fyftems of grammar and rhetoric, filled with empty definitions and unneceffary diftinctions, inftead of the real models [g]. In 1509, Lillye, the famous grammarian, who have learned Greek at Rhodes, and afterwards improved himfelf in latin at Rome under Johanes Sulpitius and Pomponius Sabinus, was the firft teacher of greek at any public School in England. This was at faint Paul's fchool in London then newly eftablifhed, and of which Lillye was the firft Mafter [h]. And that ancient pre-

[f] See Lit. Pat. Hen. vii. quod Johannes Epifcopus Elienf. fundare poffit quoddam collegium de uno magiftro, et fex fociis, et certo numero fcholarium in *Grammatica* erudiendorum. Rymer. Fœd. xii. 633. and Knight's Life of Colet, p. 19.

[g] Walter de Merton, in the ftatutes of Merton college at Oxford, appoints a grammarian in that fociety. " Sit etiam " in ipfa congregatione grammaticus unus, qui ftudio gram- " maticæ totaliter vacet.— Et eorum qui ftudio grammaticæ " fuerint applicati curam habeat : et ad ipfum etiam provectio- " res in dubiis fuæ facultatis fine rubore habeant regreffum, " &c." Statut. coll. Mert. cap. ii. Thefe ftatutes were given in Auguft, A. D. 1274.

[h] Knight's Life of Colet, p. 19.

judices

judices were fubfiding apace, and a national tafte for critical ftudies and the graces of compofition began to be diffufed, appears from this circumftance alone; that from the year 1502, to the reformation, within the fpace of thirty years, there were more grammar fchools founded and endowed in England than had been for three hundred years before[1]. Near twenty grammar fchools were inftituted within this period; before which moft of your youth were educated at the monafteries [k].

[l] Knight ubi fupr. p. 100.

[k] It is not to be doubted, that William of Wykeham's ample foundation at Winchefter, formed on a plan perfectly original, and that of Henry vi. at Eton, its tranfcript, were very conducive, although diftant, inftruments in preparing and facilitating this great work. And indeed long before the period at which we began, William of Wainflete, fenfible of the expediency of grammar learning, had founded two confiderable fchools.——John Leland, or Leilont, taught grammar in Peckwater-inn at Oxford, of which he was principal, about the reign of Henry vi. He wrote a *Grammar*, which I have feen, in the black letter, entitled GRAMMATICA NOVA. Prefixed are fome recommendatory epigrams " *Carmeliani pottæ.*" One of thefe is entitled " *In reverendum dominum Gulielmum epifcopum* " *Wintonienfem.*" That is, William of Waynflete. It is clofed with this diftich :

Hoc opus auctor enim, *te perfuadente,* Joannes
    Edidit, &c.

Whence it appears that John Leland, the author, wrote this *Grammar* by the advice and encouragement of William of Waynflete ;

In 1517, that wife prelate and bountiful patron, Richard Fox, founded his college [l] at Oxford, in which he conftituted,
with competent falaries, two lectures for the
latin and greek languages [m]. This was a new
and noble departure from the narrow plan of
academical education [n], The courfe of the latin lecturer was not confined to the college,
but open to the ftudents of Oxford in general. He is exprefly directed to drive *barbarifm* from the new college [o]. And at the fame
time it is to be remarked, that Fox does not
appoint a philofophy-lecturer in his college,
as had been the practice in moft of the previous foundations ; perhaps thinking, that
fuch an inftitution would not have coincided

Waynflete ; probably while the latter was mafter of Winchefter fchool, as Leland died in the year 1428.

[l] Statut. C. C. C. Oxon. dat. Jun. xx, 1517. Cap. xx. fol.
51. Bibl. Bodl. MSS. Laud. I. 56.

[m] Befide a third in theology.

[n] It is not however to be forgotten here, that at the foundation of Chrift's college in Cambridge a lecturer was eftablifhed,
who, together with logic and philofophy, is ordered to read
" vel ex poetarum vel oratorum operibus." Cap. xxxvii. Thefe
ftatutes were given in the year 1506. In the ftatutes of King's
at Cambridge, and New college at Oxford, both much more
antient, an inftructor is appointed by the general name of *Informator* only, who taught all the learning then in vogue.

[o] " Lector feu profeffor, artium humaniorum . . . *barbariem*
" e noftro alveario extirpet."

with

with his new fyftem of doctrine, and that it would be encouraging that fpecies of fcience which had hitherto blinded mens underftandings, and kept them fo long in ignorance of more ufeful knowledge. The greek lecturer is ordered to explain the beft greek claffics ; and thofe which the judicious founder, who feems to have confulted the moft capital fcholars of his age, prefcribes on this occafion, are the pureft, and fuch as are moft efteemed at this day.

Thefe happy beginnings were feconded by the munificence of cardinal Wolfed. About the year 1519, he founded a public chair at Oxford for rhetoric and humanity ; and foon afterwards another for the greek tongue : endowing both with ample ftipends [p]. But thefe innovations in the plan of ftudy were greatly difcouraged and oppofed by the fcholaftic bigots, who called the greek language herefy. Even bifhop Fox when he founded the greek lecture above-mentioned, was obliged to cover his excellent inftitution under the venerable mantle of the authority of the church, left fhe fhould feem to countenance a dangerous novelty. For he gives it as a reafon, or rather as an apology, for this new

[p] Wood Hift. Antiq. univ. Oxon. i. 245, 246.

lecture-

lecturefhip, that the facred canons had commanded, that a knowledge of the greek
tongue fhould not be wanting in public feminaries of education [q]. The univerfity of
Oxford was rent into factions on account of
thefe attempts; and the defenders of the new
erudition, from difputations, often proceeded
to blows with the rigid champions of the
fchools. But thefe animofities were foon
pacified by the perfuafion and example of
Erafmus, who was about this time a ftudent
in faint Mary's college at Oxford, oppofite
to New-Inn [r]. At Cambridge however, which,
in imitation of Oxford, had adopted greek,
Erafmus found greater difficulties. He tells
us himfelf that at Cambridge he read the

[q] " Quem præterea in noftro alveario collocavimus, quod
" facrofancti canones commodiffime pro bonis literis et impri-
" mis chriftianis inftituerunt·ac jufferunt, eum in hac univer-
" fitate Oxon. perinde ac paucis aliis celeberrimis gymnafiis,
" nunquam defyderari. Nec tamen eos *hac ratione* excufatos
" volumus, qui Græcam lectionem in ea fuis impenfis fuftentare
" bebent." Statut. C. C. C. ut fupr. By thefe *facri canones*
he means a decree of the council of Vienne; which enjoined
that profeffors of Greek, Hebrew, and Arabic fhould be inftituted in the univerfities of Oxford, Paris, Bononia, Salaman-
ca, and the court of Rome. Gregory Typhernas, one of the
learned greek fugitives, about the year 1472, offered to teach
greek in the univerfity of Paris, and afked a ftipend for his labour, under this canon. Naud. apud Hod. de Græc. illuftr.
lib. ii. c. 3. pag. 234. See alfo Hod. ibid. pag. 233.

[r] Wood Hift. Antiq. univ. Oxon. i. 237.

greek

greek grammar of Chryfoloras to the bare
walls': and that having tranflated Lucian's
dialogue called Icaro-menippus, he could
find no perfon in the univerfity able to tranfcribe the greek with the latin'. His edition
of the greek teftament was entirely profcribed
there; and a decree was iffued in one of the
moft confiderable colleges, ordering that if
any of the fociety was detected in bringing
that impious and fantaftic book into the college, he fhould be feverely fined". One
Henry Standifh, a doctor in divinity and a
mendicant frier, afterwards bifhop of faint
Afaph, was a vehement opponent of Erafmus
in this heretical literature; calling him in a
declamation, by way of reproach, *Græculus
ifte*, which afterwards became a fynonymous
term for an heretic ".

But neither was Oxford, and for the fame
reafons, entirely free from thefe contracted
notions. In 1519, a preacher at faint Mary's
church harangued with much violence againft
thefe pernicious teachers, and his arguments
occafioned no fmall ferment among the ftu-

* Epift. cxxiii. Ammonio dat. 1511. tom. iii. p. 140. Opp.
' Epift. cxxxix. dat. 1512. Ibid. p. 120.
* Epift. cxlviii. H. Bovillo. dat. 1513. Ibid. p. 126.
" Knight's Life of Colet. p. 14. See Erafm. Op. tom. ix. 1440.

dents.

dents. But Henry the eighth, who was luckily a patron of thefe improvements, being then refident at the neighbouring royal manor of Woodftock, and having received a juft ftate of the eafe from Pace and More, immediately tranfmitted his royal mandate to the univerfity, ordering that thefe ftudies fhoud not only be permitted but encouraged <sup>x</sup>. Soon afterwards one of the king's chaplains preaching at court, took an opportunity to cenfure the new, but genuine, interpretations of fcripture which the grecian learning had introduced. The king, when the fermon was ended, which he heard with a fmile of contempt, ordered a folemn difputation to be held, in the prefence of himfelf; at which the preacher oppofed, and fir Thomas More defended, the ufe and excellence of the greek tongue. The divine, inftead of anfwering to the purpofe, fell upon his knees, and begged pardon for having given any offence in the pulpit. After fome little altercation, the preacher, by way of a decent fubmiffion, declared that he was now better reconciled to the greek tongue, becaufe it was derived, from the hebrew. The king, amazed at his ignorance, difmiffed him, with a charge that he fhould never again prefume to preach

<sup>x</sup> Erafm. epift. ccclxxx. ut inf.

K.                                          at

at court[y]. In the grammar-fchools eftablifhed in all the new cathedral foundations
of this king, a mafter was appointed with a
competent fkill not only in the latin, but
likewife in the greek language[z]. This was
an uncommon qualification in a fchool-
mafter.

At length ancient abfurdities univerfally
gave way to thefe encouragements : and at
Oxford in particular, thefe united efforts for
eftablifhing a new fyftem of rational and manly
learning were finally confummated in the
magnificent foundation of Wolfey's college,
to which all the Learned of Europe were
invited.

But thefe aufpicious improvements in the
ftate of learning did not continue long. A
change of the national religion foon hap-

[y] Erafm. epift. P. Mofcllano. dat. 1519. ccclxxx. pag. 408.
tom. iii.

[z] " Statuimus præterea, ut per Decanum, &c. unus [*Archi-*
" *didafcalus*] eligatur, latine et *Græce* doftus, bonæ famæ, &c."
Statut. ecclef. cathedr. Roffenf. cap. xxv. They were given
Jun. 30, 1545. In the fame ftatute, the fecond mafter is required to be only *Latine* doftus. It is remarkable, that cardinal
Wolfey does not order greek to be taught in his fchool at Ipfwich, founded 1528. See Strype's Eccl. Mem. i. Append.
xxxv. pag. 94. feq.

pened,

pened, and difputes with the Lutherans enfued, which embroiling the minds of learned men in difference of opinion, difunited
their endeavours in the caufe of literature,
and diverted their attention to other enquiries.

Many of the abufes in civil fociety are
attended with fome advantages. In the beginnings of reformation, the lofs of thefe advantages is always felt very fenfibly; while
the benefit refulting from the change, is the
flow effect of time, and not immediately
percieved or enjoyed. Scarce any inftitution
can be imagined lefs favorable to the interefts of mankind than the monaftic. Yet
a great temporary check given to the progrefs
of literature at this period, was the diffolution of the monafteries. For although
thefe feminaries were in general the nurferies
of illiterate indolence, and undoubtedly deferved to be deftroyed, yet the ftill contained
invitations and opportunities to ftudious leifure and literary purfuits. On this important event therefore, a vifible revolution and
decline in the ftate of learning fucceeded.
Moft of the youth of the kingdom betook
themfelves to mechanical or other illiberal
employments, the profeffion of letters being
now fuppofed to be without fupport and reward.

ward. By the abolition of the religious houſes, many towns and their adjacent villages were utterly deprived of their only means of inſtruction. What was taught in the monaſteries was perhaps of no great importance, but ſtill it ſerved to keep up a certain degree of neceſſary knowledge. Hence provincial ignorance became almoſt univerſally eſtabliſhed.

Nor ſhould we forget, that ſeveral of the abbots were perſons of public ſpirit : by their connection with parliament, they became acquainted with the world ; and knowing where and how to chuſe proper objects, and having no other uſe for the ſuperfluity of their vaſt revenues, encouraged, in their reſpective circles, many learned young men.

It is generally thought, that the reformation of religion, the moſt happy and important event of modern times, was immediately ſucceeded by a flouriſhing ſtate of learning. But this, in England at leaſt, was by no means the caſe ; and for a long time afterwards an effect quite contrary was produced. Yet, in 1535, the king's viſitors ordered lectures in humanity to be founded in thoſe ſocieties at Oxford where they were yet wanting : and
theſe

thefe injunctions were fo warmly feconded and approved by the fcholars in the largeft colleges, that they feized on the venerable volumes of Duns Scotus, and other irrefragable logicians, and tearing them in pieces, difperfed them in great triumph about their quadrangles, or gave them away as ufelefs lumber [a]. The king himfelf alfo eftablifhed fome public lectures, with large endowments [b]. Notwithftanding, the number of ftudents at Oxford daily decreafed : infomuch that, in 1546, there were only ten inceptors in arts, and three in jurifprudence and theology [c].

In the mean time, the greek language flourifhed at Cambridge, under the inftruction of Cheke and Smyth [d]; notwithftanding the unreafonable interpofition of their chancellor, bifhop Gardiner, about pronunciation. But Cheke being foon called up to court, both univerfities feem to have been reduced

---

[a] See Dr. Layton's Letter to Cromwell. Strype's Eccl. Mem. i. 210.

[b] Wood. Hift. Antiq. univ. Oxon. i. 261. col. 1. ii. 36. col. 2.

[c] Wood. ibid. fub. anno.

[d] Strype's Lives of Cheke and Smyth.

to

to the fame deplorable condition of indigence and illiteracy[e].

During the reign of Edward the fixth, whofe minority, which promifed many virtues, was abufed by corrupt counfellors and rapacious courtiers, little attention was paid to the fupport of literature. Learning was not the fafhion of the times : and being difcouraged or defpifed by the rich who were perpetually grafping at its rewards, was neglected by thofe of moderate fortunes. Avarice and zeal were at once gratified in robbing the clergy of their revenues, and in reducing the church to its primitive apoftolical ftate of purity and poverty[f]. A favorite nobleman of the court held the deanery and treafurerfhip of a cathedral, with fome of its beft canonries : while his fon enjoyed an annual income of three hundred pounds from the lands of a bifhoprick[g]. In every robbery of the church, the interefts of learning fuffered. Exhibitions and penfions were fub-

---

[e] Roger Afcham acquaints us, that about this time, the doctrines of Original Sin and Predeftination were much canvaffed at Cambridge. But he *laments*, that in thefe enquiries they followed *Pigbius*, whom yet he much *commends*, rather than faint *Auftin*. Afch. Epiftol. lib. ii.

[f] See Collins's Eccl. Hift. Records, 67. pag. 80.

[g] Eurnet, Ref. P. ii. 8.

ftracted

ſtracted from the ſtudents in the univerſities [h]. At Oxford the public ſchools were neglected by the profeſſors and ſcholars, and allotted to the loweſt purpoſes [i]. All academical degrees were abrogated as antichriſtian [k]. The ſpiritual reformers of thoſe enlightened days proceeded ſo far, as to ſtrip the public library, eſtabliſhed and enriched by that noble patron Humphrey duke of Glouceſter, of all its books and manuſcripts; to pillage the archives, and diſannul the privileges of the univerſity [l]. From theſe meaſures many of the colleges were in a ſhort time entirely deſerted.

His ſucceſſor, queen Mary, took pains to reſtore the ſplendor of the univerſity of Oxford. Unamiable as ſhe was in her temper and conduct, and inflexibly bigotted to the glaring abſurdities of catholic ſuperſtition, ſhe protected, at leaſt by liberal donations, the intereſts of learning. She not only con-

[h] See Wood ibid. ſub. ann. 1550. ſeq. See alſo a letter to ſecr. Cecyl. dat. 1552. In Strype's Life of Cranmer, Append. Numb. xciii. p. 220.

[i] " In ſcholis artium pannos exſiccabant mulierculæ lotrices." Wood, ibid. p. 273. col. 2.

[k] Catal. MSS. totius Angliæ. fol. edit. 1697. In Hiſt. Bibl. Bodl. ibid. Præf.

[l] Wood, ut ſupr.

K 4                    tributed

tributed large fums for rebuilding the public
fchools, but moreover granted the univerfity
three confiderable impropriations.    In her
charter reciting thefe benefactions, fhe declares it to be her determined refolution, to
employ her royal munificence in reviving its
ancient luftre and difcipline, and recovering
its privileges. Thefe privileges fhe reefta-
blifhed with the addition of frefh immuni-
ties ⁿ : and for thefe good offices the univerfity decreed for her, and her hufband Philip,

ⁿ See Wood, ut fupr. i. 274. 278. ii. 17. 426. She gave alfo to Trinity college in Cambridge, where fhe rebuilt the chapel, ccclxxvj *l.* per annum.    Fuller Hift. Cambr. p. 122.  Parker's Scel. Cant. ed. Hearne, p. 245.   And to Chrift-Church,
Oxon. lxxiv *l.* viij *s.* iv *d.* per annum.  Strype Ann. Ref. iv. 243.
Willis, Cathedr. *Oxford.* pag. 429.

Sanders flourifhes on this fubject, in his ufual declamatory
ftrain.  " Ita ergo academia, et reliqua refpublica, ab heref-
" eos fæcibus, quantum tam brevi potuit, fpatio, purgatis,
" reftituuntur et ornantur paffim ecclefiæ, altaria eriguntur et
" confecrantur, COLLEGIA NOVA *ampliffima dote* fundantur,
" cœnobia. . . . reædificantur."  De Schifm. Angl. edit. Col.
" Agrippin. 1628. lib. ii. pag. 246.  It is true, that fhe re-
founded, or founded anew, fome confiderable monafteries : re-
eftablifhed faint Patrick's cathedral in Dublin, the bifhoprick
of Durham, and the hofpital of the Savoy.  She reftored to the
clergy the firft-fruits and tenths, impropriations, and many
eftates alienated from diverfe epifcopal fees.  Burnet, Ref. ii.
340.  Collier, Eccl. Hift. ii. 398.  Biogr. Brit. artic. *Bafnet.*
Strype's Grindal, p. 158.  Willis's Cathedrals, *Durham.* Stat.
2. 3. Phil. Mar. cap. iv. Afhmole's Berkf. ii. 426. Heylin, &c.

an

an anniverſary commemoration [n]. I need not recall to the reader's memory, that ſir Thomas Pope, and ſir Thomas Whyte, were ſtill more important benefactors by their reſpective foundations. Without all theſe favors, although they did not perhaps produce an immediate improvement, the univerſity would ſtill have continued to decay : and they were at leaſt a balance, at that time, on the ſide of learning, againſt the pernicious effects of . returning popery.

In the beginning of the reign of Eliſabeth, which ſoon followed, when proteſtantiſm might have been expected to produce a ſpeedy change for the better, puritaniſm began to prevail, and for ſome time continued to retard the progreſs of ingenuous and uſeful knowledge. The Engliſh reformed clergy, who during the perſecutions of queen Mary had fled into Germany, now returned in great numbers ; and in conſideration of their ſufferings and learning, many of them were preferred to eminent ſtations in the church. They brought back with them thoſe narrow principles about church-government and ceremonies, which they had imbibed, and which did well enough, in the petty ſtates and republics

[n] Wood, ut ſupr. i. 278. col. 2.

abroad,

abroad, where they lived like a ſociety of philoſophers; but which were inconſiſtent with the genius of a more extended church, eſtabliſhed in a great and magnificent nation, and requiring a ſettled ſyſtem of policy, and the obſervance of external inſtitutions. However, they were judged proper inſtruments to be employed at the head of eccleſiaſtical affairs, by way of making the reformation at once effectual. But unluckily this meaſure, ſpecious as it appeared at firſt, tended to draw the church into the contrary extreme. In the mean time their reluctance or abſolute refuſal to conform, in many inſtances, to the eſtabliſhed ceremonies, and their ſpeculative theology, tore the church into violent diviſions, and occaſioned endleſs abſurd diſputes, unfavorable to the progreſs of real learning, and productive of an illiterate clergy, at leaſt unſkilled in liberal and manly ſcience.

In fact, even the common ecelefiaſtical preferments had been ſo much diminiſhed by the ſeizure and alienation of impropriations, in the late depredations of the church, which were not yet ended, that few perſons were regularly bred to the church, or, in other words, received a learned education. Hence almoſt any that offered themſelves,

were

were without diſtinction admitted to the ſacred function. Inſomuch, that in 1560, an injunction was directed to the biſhop of London from his metropolitan, ordering him to forbear ordaining any more artificers, and other unlearned perſons who had exerciſed ſecular occupations [o]. But as the evil was unavoidable, this caution took but little effect. About the year 1563, there were only two divines, the dean of Chriſt Church, and the preſident of Magdalene college, who were capable of preaching the public ſermons at Oxford [p]. Many proofs have been mentioned of the extreme ignorance of our clergy at this time: to which I ſhall add one, which is curious and new. In 1570, Horne biſhop of Wincheſter enjoined the Minor canons of his cathedral to get by memory, every week, one chapter of ſaint Paul's epiſtles in latin: and this taſk, beneath the abilities of an ordinary ſchool-boy, was actually repeated by ſome of them, before the biſhop, dean, and prebendaries, at a public epiſcopal viſitation of that church [q].

The taſte for latin compoſition, and it was faſhionable both to write and ſpeak in that

[o] Strype's Life of Grindal. b. i. ch. 4. pag. 40.

[p] Wood, ut ſupr. i. 285.

[q] Regiſtr. Horne, Epiſcop. Winton. fol. 80. b.

language,

language, was much worfe than in the reign of
Henry the eighth, when jufter models were
ftudied. One is furprized to find the learned
archbifhop Grindal, in the ftatutes of a fchool
which he founded and amply endowed, pre-
fcribing fuch ftrange claffics as Palingenius,
Sedulius, and Prudentius, to be taught in
the new feminary '. Much has been faid
about the paffion for reading Greek which
prevailed in this reign. But this affectation
was confined to the queen, and a few others :
and here it went no farther than oftentation
and pedantry. It was by no means the national ftudy ; nor do we find that it improved
the tafte, or influenced the writings, of that
age. But I am wandering beyond the bounds
which I firft prefcribed to this neceffary digreffion.

Yet I muft add an obfervation or two.
In government, many fhocks muft happen
before the conftitution is perfected. In like
manner, it was late in the reign of Elifabeth,
before learning, after its finews had been re-
laxed by frequent changes and commotions,
recovered its proper tone, and rofe with new
vigor, under the genial influence of the

' Strype's Life of Grindal. B. ii. ch. 17. pag. 312. This
was A. D. 1583.

proteftant

proteftant religion. And it may be further remarked, that, as all novelties are purfued to excefs, and the moft beneficial improvements often introduce new inconveniencies, fo this influx of polite literature deftroyed philofophy. On this account, fir Henry Savile, in the reign of James the firft, eftablifhed profeffors at Oxford for aftronomy and geometry; becaufe, as he declares in the preamble of his ftatutes, mathematical ftudies had been totally deferted, and were then almoft unknown in, England'. Logic indeed remained; but that fcience was ftill cultivated, as being the bafis of polemical theology, and a neceffary inftrument for conducting our controverfies againft the church of Rome.

---

' See Rym. Fœd. xvii. 217. It is obfervable, that he entirely interdicted the teaching of judicial aftrology to his profeffor of Aftronomy. Statut. Savil. cap. ii. Thefe ftatutes are dated Aug. 11. 1619.

✝.✦✝✦✝✦✝✦✝✦✝✦✝✦✝✦✝✦✝✦✝✦✝✦✝✦✝✦✝✦✝✦✝✦✝✦✝✦✝✦✝✦✝✦

## S E C T.  V.

IN the year 1556, fir Thomas Pope having now finifhed the foundation of his college, made his laſt Will[a], which is dated the fixth of February the fame year, he being then no more than forty-feven years of age. Of the feveral bequeſts and appointments contained therein, and in the codicil annexed dated the twelfth of December 1558, I fhall infert a fummary[b].

He defires to be buried in the church of faint Stephen's Walbrook, London, in the tomb, or vault, in which his firſt wife dame Margaret, and his daughter, were interred. His funeral to be without pomp, " or herfe of " wax," and only two tapers of virgin wax with branches, to burn on his hearfe, in the church of the parifh in which he fhall happen to die, for the fpace of one week.

[a] Regiſtr. Cheyney, qu. 10. 86.  In cur. Prærogat. Cant.

[b] The probate is dated May vi. 1559. About three months after his death. Before Dr. Walter Haddon, keeper of the fpiritualities and commiffary, in the vacancy of the archbifhoprick.

He

He gives " blacke cootes or gownes," to all his executors, his retainers, his houfehold fervants; and all fuch of his overfeers, friends, and kindred, as fhall happen to be in his houfe at the time of his deceafe.

He bequeaths xx *l.* or more to be diftributed in alms to the Poor, in general, at his burial : and at the fame time, xl *s.* befides, to twenty poor men, and as many poor women, in parricular, with " a gowne of good " mantill fryfe each :" and when his obfequies were finifhed, v *l.* more at leaft, to be diftributed in alms. He gives alfo xx *s.* to a difcreet preacher for two funeral fermons : one to be preached in the church of the parifh in which he fhall die ; and the other in the church of faint Stephen's Wallbrook, at the time of his interment.

To the prifons of Newgate, Ludgate, Counter of Bread-ftreet, Poultry-Counter, the Fleet, King's Bench, Marfhalfea, New Counter in Southwark, Gate-houfe, faint Alban's, and Hertford, xviij *l.* To be given within one month after his death.

To

To feveral of his kindred cccccclxxxiij *l.*
v *s.* and xl. marks <sup>c</sup>. Befide certain fmaller bequefts to fome others.

To his coufin Jane Hankes one new gilt
ftanding cup of filver, with a cover, weighing twenty-five ounces. To his fon in law
John Basford, or Beresford, the third part of
all his <sup>d</sup> armour " and artillerie <sup>e</sup>," his beft
gauntlets and target, and his beft horfe.

To Mr. Thomas Abrydge, " his ftele fad-
" dill gilte, and all the harnes of crymfyn

<sup>c</sup> Amongft others, he leaves to the children of William
Hyde, of Denchworth, co. Berks, xx *l.* He is buried in the
church of Denchworth ; where on a brafs-plate it is faid, that
he and his wife Margery had xxx children. He was related to
fir T. Pope, by means of *Hyde* marrying into *Yate* of Berks.
This I chiefly mention, to confirm what is faid above, pag. 2.
concerning the family of fir Thomas Pope's mother. See Afhmole's Berkf. iii. 322. There is another William Hyde, who
died 1567, with Alice his wife, buried in the fame church.
They had ten children.

<sup>d</sup> " My harneys."

<sup>e</sup> That is *Bows and arrows,* and perhaps crofs-bows, lances,
guns, &c. See Afcham's TOXOPHIL. f. 19. a. edit 1571. But
the word ARTILLERY, that is *Ars telaria,* as appears from
many other paffages in Afcham, was originally and properly re-
ftrained to the *Bow and Arrow.* Compare Engl. Bibl. i. SAM.
xx. 38. 40. And Maundrell's TRAVELS, p. 19. Sund. Mar.
7. See alfo Du Cange, GL. Lat. V. ARTILLARIA. edit. 1733.

" velvett

" velvett belonging to the fame." To miftrefs Staveley, his mother in law, and to three
others of his kindred, each, a fair new cup,
or bowl, of filver, weighing each twenty
ounces. To his fon in law, John Dodmer,
fifty angels to make him a chain; and his
mother's picture in the bracelet of gold,
" which I ware about my arme, and the ring
" of gold hanging at the fame; which brace-
" lett was the firft tokyn that ever his mo-
" ther gave me."

To nine of his fervants by name,
lviij *l.* xiij *s.* iv *d.* Befide gratuities to all the
reft of his fervants, of every fort, living in
his houfe at the time of his deceafe[f]. Praying his executors, that if his wife fhould
not find it convenient to retain them after his
death, they would help the faid fervants to
fome worfhipful man's fervice[s].

To Trinity college in Oxford, by him
founded, c*l.* for building a wall round the
Grove of the faid college.

[f] To many of them, v*l.* To others, vj *l.* xiij *s.* iiij *d.* To
None, lefs than xl *s.*

[s] But he permits all his fervants to remain, and to be maintained, in his houfe, for one quarter of a year after his death;
in which time they may provide themfelves with other fervices.

L                           To

To the said college five hundred marcs for building at Garsington near Oxford [h], a house to accommodate the said college, in time of the plague at Oxford; in case he should not live to accomplish the same : And then charging his wife, if the said sum should not be found sufficient, as he believes and intends it to be, fully to supply the defect.

To the said college, beside those which he before gave for the service of the hall, the following pieces of silver plate, viz. Three goblets gilt, weighing together threescore and three ounces. Six plain cups gilt, each with one handle, weighing together seventy-seven ounces and an half. Three other goblets parcel gilt, with covers, weighing sixty ounces. Thirteen spoons, one completely gilt, weighing together forty ounces and an half. All the foregoing to be new made. He likewise bequeathes to the said college, the largest of his standing cups with a cover, completely gilt, weighing twenty-three ounces and a half. Also one of his

[h] He repeats this charge to his wife at the end of his Will. " I beseech my good wife most hartely, that in case I do not in " my life make a Howse for my Scolers of my College to re- " pare thereto at Garsington in sicknes tyme, that she will in " as convenyent spede, &c."

basons

bafons and ewers parcel-gilt, weighing three-
fcore and fifteen ounces [i].

To the Nuns of the convent of Syon v /.
To the Friers Obfervants in the chapel of the
Holy Crofs at Greenwich, v /. To the Black
Friers at London, v /.

To faint Bartholomew's hofpital in Weft-
Smithfield, cc /. To be beftowed in con-
ftructing a conduit for conveying water to
the faid hofpital. Otherwife, to be expended
in purchafing an eftate of x /. per annum, for
providing coats, fhirts, and gowns, for the
fick and poor at their firft reception into the
houfe [k].

To the repair of the church of Clerkenwell, London, xl /. To Wallbrook church
for opening the vault therein for his fepul-
ture, xx s. To the vicar of Clerkenwell
church, x s. And to the vicar of Ridge in
Hertfordfhire, x s.

[i] They were received May 25, 1564. Ex acquietant. in
Regift. prim. fol. 22.

[k] " For fuch as from tyme to tyme fhall enter into the faid
" hofpitall, being difeafed and wanting the fame things at
" their entre."

To

, To John Heyward[1], his "trewe frynd," one of his gowns of filk. To Mr. Croke, his old mafter's fon, his gown of black fattin faced with luferne fpots[m]. To lord Vaulx, c*l*. To fir Nicholas Shirley, 1*l*. in abatement of cccl *l*. owed, and payable at Midfummer next. Befide debts forgiven to fome of his poor relations.

[1] See Append. Numb. IX. In the Notes.

[m] He is painted in fuch a gown by Hans Holbein. At Trinity college, there are five portraits of him, all of the fame dimenfions, drefs, and attitude. A fixth, a moft high-finifhed old portrait, was lately given by the college to the picture gallery at Oxford, inftead of another now in the library. One of thefe fix, and the oldeft, came to the college 1596. Ex *Comp. Anni.* Another is mentioned as hanging in the chapel 1634. Ex *Comp. Anni.* One of all thefe which is now in the Hall, was painted by Francis Potter, a curious mechanic and mathematician, and a member of the college, about 1637. Another, mentioned above, was painted in 1665, at the expence of the college, for the picture gallery. This is now in the college library. Another lately purchafed, a copy of Holbein, the painter unknown, is in the Burfary. There is a feventh at Tyttenhanger in Hertfordfhire. They are all fuppofed to be copies from a valuable picture by Hans Holbein, in the poffeffion of lord Guildford at Wroxton. It is not, however, quite improbable that Holbein might have painted fome of the fuppofed copies.—Sir Thomas Pope fate to Hans Holbein, for his picture, in the chamber within the gallery gate-houfe at Whitehall, defigned by Hans Holbein, and lately demolifhed. Hans Holbein painted many of his pictures in this chamber, which was ufed by king Henry the eighth as a ftudy or library.

To

To Mr. Gerrard, the queen's attorney general, one ring of fine gold. To Thomas Slythurſte, clerk, preſident of Trinity college aforeſaid, one ring of fine gold. Another to Sir Arthur Darcy, knight. Each ring to weigh one ounce, with the initials of his name on one ſide, and a Death's head on the other.

To the children of ſeveral poor tradeſmen and others, xxx *l.* and five marcs.

Of this his laſt will and teſtament, he conſtitutes his wife Eliſabeth, his moſt true and aſſured friend Nicholas Bacon, eſquire, afterwards ſir Nicholas, and his wife's brother, William Blount, eſquire, Executors. He alſo appoints his moſt truſty, worſhipful and loving friends, ſir Thomas Cornewallys, knight, comptroller of the king's and queen's houſhold, ſir Francis Englefield, knight, ſir Edward Waldegrave, knight, ſir Richard Southwell, knight, ſir Robert Southwell, knight, William Cordall, eſquire, ſollicitor general to the king and queen, Richard Goodryck, eſquire, John Wyſeman, eſquire, and Antony Wayte, gentleman, overſeers of the ſame. To each of the ſaid overſeers he gives a ring of gold, of the faſhion of thoſe

L 3

before-

before-mentioned. To Nicholas Bacon, one of his executors, he gives his whiftle, fhaped like a dragon [n], and fet with ftones, which he commonly wore at his chain [o]. To his other executor, William Blount, he gives xl angels, to make him a chain [p].

[n] He is painted by Hans Holbein with a whiftle hanging to his chain, fhaped like a mermaid.

[o] John de Veer, earl of Oxford, by Will dat. Apr. 10, 1508, devifes his " chain with the whiftell, having fix fcore " and one links, weighing xcviii ounces, to be fold." Regiftr. FETTYPLACE, Cur. Prær. qu. 11.—Sir Edw. Howard by will, dat. 1512, bequeathes to " fir Charles Brandon the roope of " bowed nobles that he wore his great whiftle by, and to the " kings grace his greate whiftle." Ibid. qu. 18. About the year 1519, Hall mentions the earl of Surrey " on a great " courfir richely trapped, and a greate whiftle of gold fet with " ftones and perle, hanging at a great and maffy chayne bau- " drick-wife." Hall's CHRONICLES, p. 65. a. The curious Mr. Anftis endeavours to prove, by thefe and other inftances, that the *Whiftle* was the badge, or emblem, of admirals. OR- DER of the Garter, ii. 121. But it is certain, from the paffage in the text, and other places, that it was often indifcriminately ufed. It was perhaps even a common ornament. Robert Ar- derne, a gentleman of Oxfordfhire, bequeathes his *beft* whiftle, filver and gilt : and his *fecond* whiftle, filver and gilt. Aug. xx. 1593. Regiftr. Cur. Cancell. Oxon. G G. fol. 203.

[p] He heartily defires the faid executors, and overfeers, " not " to waye my fimple gifts any other than as a remembrance of " my unfayned good will and difpofition towards theym in my " lyfe tyme." He at firft had bequeathed to each of the Overfeers " a fair jugge of filver," to be new made, weighing xxiv ounces : With a death's head in a roundell, and the ini- tials of his name, graven on the covers. But this bequeft was afterwards altered in the codicil, as in the text.

To

To Elifabeth his wife, and Executrix, whom he declares ever to have found, honeft, true, faithful, loving, and obedient, he bequeathes the refidue of his moveable goods, leafes and debts : praying her heartily that fhe would beftow part of the fame among the Poor [q]. He commiffions his faid wife, to furnifh Trinity college aforefaid, with copes, veftments, and ornaments for divine fervice, and houfhold neceffaries. But all thefe things he completely accomplifhed himfelf, in his own life-time, as has been already related. He requires his faid wife, in cafe John Pope, his only brother, fhould be without a male heir when Elifabeth Pope, daughter of the faid John, marries, to beftow ccc marcs, otherwife bequeathed to the faid Elifabeth Pope for a marriage-portion, in deeds of charity.

As to his eftates, not fettled on Trinity college, he wills that they fhould remain, as is expreffed and covenanted in a certain pair of quadripartite indentures, dated April the firft,

[q] " Being hartely fory I am able to give her no more, to re-
" compens her moft honeft, obedient, and womanly behaviour
" towardes me in my life tyme, which hath byn fuch as well
" hath meryted a thowfand tymes more than I am able any
" waye to give her, &c."

1554.

1554 '. By which indentures it appears, that the princpal demifes of the fame were made to Elifabeth his wife, John Pope his brother, John Edmondes his uncle, and Edmund Hutchins his nephew '.

He further wills, that all manors, lands, tenements, and hereditaments, whatfoever, by him lately given to the prefident, fellows, and fcholars, of Trinity college aforefaid, fhall for ever remain under the firft affurances by which they were by him fettled upon the faid college ; without interruption or claim of heirs, executors, and affigns, or difturbance of any other perfon claiming in in their right, name, or title.

During the time of founding his college, he chiefly refided at Clerkenwell, Lon-

---

' In Thefauriar. coll. Trin. Oxon. Sæpius citat. Between fir Thomas Pope, and Elifabeth his wife, on the one part ; And fir Arthur Darcy, Richard Catelyn ferjeant at law, deceafed, Richard Goodrick, and Antony Waite, on the other. Dat. April i. i Phil. Mar.

' But in cafe of non-performance of covenants and conditions therein fpecified, he orders many of them to be given to " king Henry the eighth's houfe of poor in Weft-Smithfield," i. e. faint Bartholomew's hofpital ; to which he actually bequeathed, as above, 200 l. After his death, an inquifition was taken of all his lands and poffeffions, at Chipping-Norton, com. Oxon. In which the faid quadrip. indenture is recited.

don,

don', within the diffolved priory of Black nuns ': to the repair of the conventual church of which, being left ftanding at the diffolution, he gave the fum of forty pounds". The buildings and fite of this religious houfe, containing fourteen acres, had been granted by king Henry in 1545, to fir William Henley and fir John Williams'. In the country, he lived much at Tyttenhanger, in the parifh of Ridge, in Hertfordfhire'; which had been the country-feat of the abbots of faint Alban's, and was conveyed to fir Thomas Pope by Henry the eighth, in the laft year of his reign, 1547, but not confirmed to him till by letters patent of Edward the fixth, dated July the twenty-fourth, in the following year'. However, it appears that he bought

---

' From his letters to the college. And other evidences. ibid.

' In a deed of dame Elif. Paulett, dated Feb. i. 35 Eliz. infra citat. This manfion is called the " capital meffuage and " fcyte of the late diffolved monaftery of Clerkenwell." It was granted him by queen Mary, Pat. Phil. Mar. an. 3, 5. Febr. i. par. 4. " Rex et Regin. conceff. T. Pope, et al. Pardonatio- " nem alienationis pro fcitu monafterii de Clerkinwell in com. " Middl." In an indenture dat. May xxx, 1538. 30 Hen. viii. he is ftyled Thomas Pope *of London*, efquire.

" See pag. 163. fupr.

' Weever, Fun. Mon. p. 428. Tanner Not. Mon. fol. p. 299.

' The Statutes of his college are dated there.

' Liber fecundus de *Les Rates*, ann. 3, et 4. Phil. Mar. fol. MSS. Harl. 607. 1. fol. 1. Brit. Muf.—See alfo pat. Edw. vi. an. 1. Jul. xxiv. par. 4. Where the grant fpecifies " Scitum " *Capitalis*

this eftate of Queen Mary, June the fixteenth, 1557, for twenty years purchafe[a]:
notwithftanding, in a deed dated 1555, he
ftyles himfelf of Tyttenhanger[b], and in the
charter of his college, 1554, mentions Tyttenhanger as one of his manors. The houfe
was built by John Moot, one of the abbots
of faint Alban's, in 1405[c], and much enlarged and adorned by his fucceffors, particularly the learned and munificent John
Whethamftede, in the reign of Henry the
fixth[d]. The chapel was an elegant edifice :
and the wainfcott, behind the ftalls, was
beautifully painted with a feries of the figures
of all the faints who bore the name of John.
The windows were enriched with painted
glafs, which fir Thomas Pope brought hither
from the choir of faint Albans abby, when
that church was, by his interpofition, preferved from total deftruction. Sir Thomas
Pope alfo erected over the veftibule of the
great hall a noble gallery for wind-mufic[e].
This houfe was fo large, that in the year

" *Capitalis manfionis* de Tyttenhanger, ac Manerium de Tyt-
" tenhanger, &c.
  [a] Ibid. MSS. Harl.
  [b] See Append. Numb. XI.
  [c] Willis Mitr. Abb. i. 22.
  [d] Weever Fun. Mon. p. 565. edit. 1631.
  [e] From the Information of Sir Harry Pope-Blount, ut fupr.

1528,

1528, King Henry the eighth and his queen, with their retinue, removed hither from London, during the continuance of the Sweating ficknefs[e]. But this antient and ftately manfion was intirely pulled down, and that which is now ftanding built in its place, about 1654, by fir Henry Blount, the famous traveller[f]. Of this county, and of Effex, fir Thomas Pope was twice fheriff, in the years 1552, 1557[g].

I muft not here forget, that the learned and candid John de Feckenham, the laft abbot of Weftminfter, and a great friend to the princefs Elifabeth, about the reign of Edward the fixth, often vifited fir Thomas Pope, at Tyttenhanger-houfe; who never fuffered him to depart without a prefent. Once in particular he gave Feckenham, at parting, a purfe filled with twelve angels, his picture in enamel, a filver crucifix ftudded with pretious ftones, and a large miffal richly ornamented with thirty-fix hiftorical pictures[h]. On the mention of Feckenham, I ob-

[e] Hollinfh. Chron, vol. iii. p. 906. 10. col. 2.

[f] Engl. Baronet. iv. 669. edit. 1741.

[g] Chauncy's Hertfordfhire, p. 23. Fuller, WORTHIES, p. 31. fays, that as to their Sheriff, Hertfordfhire and Effex were united till the ninth of Elifabeth, 1567.

[h] From the information of fir Harry Pope-Blount, ut fupr.

ferve

ferve here, perhaps out of place, that Sir Thomas Pope is faid to have joined with abbot Feckenham in an application to queen Mary, to fpare the life of fir John Cheek; in confideration of Cheek's eminent learning and integrity, and on condition that he would renounce the herefies of the reformation[1]. It is certain that this admirable fcholar, the reftorer of the Greek tongue, would otherwife have been executed in the flames. Yet he did not long furvive the remorfe of a recantation. His own confcience had all the feverities of a martyrdom.

To refume the courfe of our narrative. He feems alfo, for fome time, and fo early at leaft as 1546, to have been fettled at Bermondfey in Southwark[k]; at which place, and in the neighbourhood, he had acquired a very confiderable property[1]. Here,

---

[1] MSS. F. Wife.

[k] Ex indentura dat. May xiii.'38. Hen. viii. MSS. F. Wife.—He alfo ftyles himfelf of Bermondfey, in a deed without date: which however appears to have been made after 7 Edw. vi. In Thefauriar. coll. Trin. The earlieft notice of his connection with this place appears from the Patents. Pat. Hen. viii. an. 33. Jan. xvi. par. 5. Edward Powell is licenfed to alienate a meffuage in Bermondfey to Thomas Pope, knight. This year the monaftery there was diffolved.

[1] Pat. fupra citat.

as

as I conjecture, he built a houfe on the ruins of the diffolved abbey of Cluniac monks which he probably purchafed of his friend fir Robert, or fir Richard, South-well, to one of whom that monaftery was granted at the diffolution[m]. This houfe, which Stowe calls "a goodly houfe builded of ftone and timber," afterwards came into the poffeffion of the earls of Suffex[n].

What was fir Thomas Pope's laft illnefs, or the particular circumftances of his death, I have not found. It is not improbable, but that he was carried off by a peftilential fever, which began to rage with uncommon violence in the autumn of the year 1558, and before the end of the fucceeding winter, feized three parts in four of the people of England[o]; deftroying in the general devafta-tion, thirteen bifhops, and feveral other per-fons, both men and women, of the moft emi-nent rank and quality[p]. His laft letter to his college, which having eftablifhed by his munificence, he lived near five years to pro-

---

[m] Tanner, Not. Mon. fol. p. 535.

[n] Stowe ubi fupr. p. 344. Aubrey's Surrey. V. 39.

[o] Cooper's, or Lanquette's Chronicle, 4to. 1560. p. 377.

[p] Godwyn, p. 340. Engl. edit. 1630. Stowe, by Howes, 634. Strype, Ann. Ref. i. 30, 31.

tect

tect and affift with his patronage, is dated Auguft the eighth, 1558 [p]. While he meditated further benefactions for the encreafe of its endowment [q], he died the twenty-ninth day of January following, 1559, on Sexagefima Sunday, at his houfe in Clerkenwell, in the fiftieth year of his age [r].

He was magnificently buried, with the following folemnities [s]. His body was firft carried to the church of Clerkenwell in London, where it was laid under a herfe, or fhrine, illuminated with wax tapers, for the fpace of one week. On the feventh day of February, began his funeral proceffion to the church of faint Stephen's Wallbrook : to which he was conveyed with a ftandard, a Coat, a penon or banner of arms, a target, helmet, fword, and four dozen of arms, with twelve for the branches of wax tapers, and fix for the body, or fhrine. He was attended by two heralds at arms, Clarencieux and York. The firft bore the coat, and the latter the helmet and creft. Twenty poor men

[p] Regiftr. prim. Coll. prædict. fol. 23. b.
[q] See Append. No. XXV. Under JOHN PERTE.
[r] From an infcription on his Picture, in Trin. coll.—And Wood, Hift. Antiq. Univ. Oxon. ii. 301. col. 2.
[s] MSS. Cotton. Vitell. F. 5. In the Britifh Mufeum. See Append. Numb. XXVIII.

and

and twenty poor women, carried torches. The men were cloathed in mantle frieze gowns, and the women in ' rails, which he gave them. Sir Richard Southwell, and fir Thomas Stradling, knights, and diverfe gentlemen and others, all in black, where mourners, to the number of fixty or more. All his houfe at Clerkenwell, and the church, were hung with black, with efcotcheons of his arms. After the heralds had offered the fword, target, coat, and helmet at the high altar, and other ceremonies were performed, the company returned back to his houfe to a banquet, where they were refrefhed with fpiced bread and wine. The next day followed his morrow mafs, in the faid church; at which were three Songs, two being pricked fongs, and the third the mafs of requiem, all fung by the Clerkes of London. He was then buried; after which they went back to his houfe to dinner, " being, as my manu-
" fcript fays, a very great dinner, and plenty
" of all thinges." Then followed a great dole of almes diftributed among the Poor.

Stowe infinuates, that he was interred in

----

' A fort of white veil, often mentioned as part of the mourning-drefs of women, at antient funerals. See Strype, Eccl. Mem. iii. 385.

the north ile of the choir of Wallbrook church. Here was a vault, in which before had been buried his wife Margaret, his daughter Alice, and Anne Pope his fister in law. Stowe adds the following infcription, which was evidently placed there before his death, and I fuppofe immediately upon the deceafe of dame Margaret. It was deftroyed with the old church.

Hic jacet Thomas Pope Primus Thefaurarius Augmentationum, et domina Mar-
gareta uxor ejus, quæ quidem Marga-
reta obiit xvi Jan. MDXXXVIII ".

But in 1567, eight years after his death, his body and the body of dame Margaret afore-faid, were removed from faint Stephen's Wallbrook to the chapel of Trinity college in Oxford; where they were again interred on the north fide of the altar, under a ftate-ly tomb of good gothic workmanfhip, on which are the recumbent figures of fir Thomas Pope in complete armour, and of his fecond wife Elifabeth, large as the life, in alabafter, with this infcription.

" Fol. edit of Stowe's Survey. 1633. p. 245.

Hic

Ḣic jacent corpora Ḣome Pope militis fundatoris ḣujus collegii Ḣrinitatis et do= mine Elizabeḣe et Margarite uroris ejus. Ḋui quidem Ḣomas obiit xxix. die Ja= nuarii, M.D. LUIII.

*Quod tacitum velis nemini dixeris* [u].

That the body of the founder was actually removed hither, appears unqueſtionably from the Will of Elizabeth his ſecond wife, who deſires expreſſly to be buried in a vault or tomb in Trinity college chapel in Oxford, " wherein lieth the corps of my late good " huſband ſir Thomas Pope [w]." This is alſo further confirmed from the teſtimony of Anthony Wood : who in the Appendix ſubjoined to his Hiſtory of the Univerſity of Oxford, containing omiſſions and miſtakes of the tranſlator in the Text of that elaborate work, obſerves ; that notwithſtanding the inſcription in ſaint Stephen's Wallbrook, his Tranſlator, according to the original Engliſh copy, ought to have expreſſly inſerted, in the place

---

[u] It originally ſtood within a grate of iron. *Arms, &c.* by Lee, ut inf. f. 74. The greateſt part of its elegant workman-ſhip is now concealed, and the effect of the whole deſtroyed, by an alcove, correſponding to another on the oppoſite ſide : both which, conſidered in a general view, are moſt injudiciouſly in-troduced, and are perhaps the only blemiſhes of the preſent beautiful chapel.

[w] Infra citat.

M                                    where

where fir Thomas Pope's burial is mentioned, " Sed fepultus fuit in capella coll. S. S.
" Trinitatis *". In the mean time, it is extraordinary that no mention fhould be recorded of this Removal of the founder's body
in any regifter of the college. That this
tomb in the college chapel was ftanding in
the year 1567, at leaft, that the founder was
then removed thither, may be fairly concluded from the two following entries in the
computus of the Burfars of that year, and
they are the only notices that any where
occur concerning it, viz.

" Sol. *Mar.* 10. *tribus Operariis laboran-*
" *tibus per quatuor dies in facello circa*
" *fepulcrum fundatoris,* x s. xiij d.
" Sol. *pro quinque modiis calcis circa fe-*
" *pulcrum fundatoris,* ij s. xjd ʸ.

---

* In Appendic. Hift. Antiq. Oxon. p. 447. Although this
point needs no further authentication, I will add part of a letter written from Strype to Dr. Charlett, mafter of Univerfity
college, Oxford. " The funeral of fir Thomas Pope, as it is
" fett down in the Cotton volume, [fee Append.] I mention-
" ed to you in my laft, you fhall have at the foot of this letter.
" His body, I find, was foon removed from Clerkenwell
" [Walbroke] to the college which he founded, and honoured
" defervedly with a monument there." Dated Low-Layton,
April xx, 1709. This letter, as I am informed by the very learned and communicative Dr. Ducarrell, was given by Dr. Charlet
to Dr. Dobfon, prefident of Trinity college. The fame, being
the original, is now in the Burfary of Trinity college. A copy
of it is among Cod. MSS. Ballard. Bibl. Bodl. vol. xv. 31.
    ʸ Comp. Burff. 1566.--7.

This

This monument was probably given by Elizabeth his fecond wife in her life-time. It was certainly erected after his death, viz. after 1559, as the infcription, which is wrought in large gothic characters out of the fubftance of the ftone, minutely fpecifies the date of his deceafe. Elizabeth furvived her hufband more than thirty years; and, if at all, fhe muft have erected it before 1567, when it appears to have exifted. But of this I fhall have occafion to bring further evidences.

SECT.

# S E C T.  VI.

I Now proceed to throw some collateral light on sir Thomas Pope's history, by giving a detached and distinct account of his brothers, sisters, wives, and friends : most of which have already been occasionally mentioned in the course of this narrative.

His brother John Pope, who was one of his heirs, and to whom he granted large estates, appears to have been settled at Wroxton in Oxfordshire, in the reign of Edward the sixth [z]. I find John purchasing of Henry the eighth, in the year 1544, estates belonging to the dissolved canons of Kenilworth in Warwicshire, for 1501 _l._ 13 _s._ 8 _d_ [a]. In the same year he recieved a grant of the site of the house of Francican friers at Lincoln [b] : as also, jointly with others, the site of the black friars at Beverly in Yorkshire [c]. In

[z] Ex Indentur. dat. Aug. 1. 5 Edw. vi. Wroxton was a priory of Augustine Canons. See Append. Numb. XVII.

[a] Dugd. Warw. p. 474.

[b] Tanner's Not. Mon. fol. p. 281.

[c] Ibid. p. 689.

1545,

1545, he received some lands belonging to the priory of Bileigh in Essex [d]. I could give many more instances from the patents, and privy seals. I find him often entertained at Trinity college, Oxford: and once with his second wife Elizabeth Brockett [e]. He was three times married. But as a further account of him, his marriages, issue, and their descendants, would take up too much of our time here, and on other accounts requires a

---

[d] Newc. Rep. ii. 610.

[e] Comp. Burff. 1561.--2. " Sol. pro vino, pyris, aliisque
" bellariis, insumptis in Magistrum Pope visitantem colle-
" gium. ij s. vj d.

Comp. 1562.--3. " Sol. ex cerasis, fragis, vino, potu, et sac-
" caro, datis Magistro Pope et uxori ejus visentibus colle-
" gium. iij s. x d.

Comp. 1562.--3. " Sol. 7 Mart. pro vino, pomis, etc. datis
" Magistro Pope visenti collegium. xviij d.

Comp. 1563.--4. " Sol. 23 Feb. ex bellariis insumptis in
" Magistrum Pope visentem collegium. xviij d.

——" Sol. Magistro Pope invisenti collegium. xix d.

Comp. 1564.- 5. " Sol. in bellariis Magistro Pope, et quibus-
" dam advenis, visentibus collegium. xxij d.

Comp. 1568.--9. " Allocat. in epulis Magistri Pope et Ma-
" gistri Billinge in temp. sessionum. iij s. viij d.

Comp. 1572.--3. " Allocat. pro epulis pro Magistro Johanne
" Pope fratre fundatoris quum hic nos invisceret. vj s.
" vij d. ob.

Comp. 1573.--4. " Allocat. in epulis pro Magistro Pope fra-
" tre fundatoris invisente collegium. vj s. viij d.

Comp. 1581.--2. " Allocat. in epulis pro Magistro Pope.
" x s. vj d."

more minute and feparate confideration, thefe
particulars fhall form an article for the
Appendix [f].

Sir Thomas Pope's fifters were Alice, Elizabeth, and Julian, as I before obferved.
Alice was married to Edward Love, gentleman, of Aynhoe, in Northamptonfhire [g];
whofe name often occurs in the affairs of
Trinity college aforefaid about the time of
its foundation, and who appears to have acted as the founder's receiver in Oxfordfhire
and other counties [h]. She died 1534, and
they are both buried in the church of Stoke-
Lyne near Bicefter in Oxfordfhire, with an
infcription on a brafs-plate [i]. Elizabeth his

[f] Numb. XXVI.

[g] Ex Evident. in Coll. antedict.

[h] Regiftr. prim. dicti Coll. fol. 7. b. Et alibi. See Append. Numb. XXI. in the Notes. Among Rawlinfon's antient
original charts, there is an indenture, by which John, Prior of
Nottley Abbey in Bucks, and his convent, leafe their appropriate
parfonage of Stokelyne to this Edward Love, for fixty one
years. Dat. in Dom. Capitul. Mar. 6. A. D. 1524. MSS.
Rawli f. Bibl. Bod. 1522. Ch. ult. in pergamen. The leffee
is herein difcharged from an annual penfion, which the convent
paid from the faid church to faint Fridefwyd's priory at Oxford.

[i] Over this infcription are the images of a man in armour,
and of a woman, both kneeling before defks : behind *bim* five
boys, and behind *ber* three girls. Over their heads, *Delicta ju-
ventutis noftræ et ignorantias ne memineris domine.* Arms, viz.

*fecond*

fecond fifter was married to Richard Hutch-ins, of Chipping-Norton in the fame county, and afterwards to John Orpewood of the fame place[k]. The third fifter Julian was, as I conjecture, a nun at Godftowe ; and upon the diffolution of that convent, received a grant of an annual penfion of vj *l.* xiij *s.* iv*d*[l].

*Quart.* } A lyon ramp. with a crofs patee on his fhoulder. Love.
} Parti p. fefs indent. in chief 3 martlets..

*Impal.* } Love. *ut fupra.*
} Erm. a fefs chequee, a crefcent for a difference.
} Arden.

One of their daughters, Elizabeth, was married to Simon Parrot, or Perrot, fellow of Magd. coll. Oxon. Who are both buried, with an infcription on a brafs-plate, in faint Peter's, Oxon. For this Simon Parrot, fee Wood, Hift. et Antiq. ii. 59. and ib. 421. And Smith's Annals Univ. coll. p. 247. See alfo Append. Numb. XXI. The name of one Parrot, undoubt-edly this Simon Parrot, often occurs in papers and accounts re-lating to the affairs of Trinity college, at its foundation; viz. Append. Numb. XVII. " Three antiphoners of parchmente " bought by Mr. Parrot for the queere." And Comp. Burff. 1556.--7. " Sol. pro Campanæ fecundò reportatione a Ma-" giftro *Parrot*." That a perfon, at leaft of this name, was one of the founder's agents in this bufinefs, with Edward Love, I find in other articles : and from the following paffage of one of the founder's letters to the prefident, 27 Nov. 1556. " In " your next letters fend me a bill declaring, particularly, fuch " bokes, and other thinges, as ye have receyved ether from me " or els of Mr. *Perrot*." See fupr. p. 117.

[k] By the firft fhe had one fon Edward, or Edmund : and four daughters, Anne, Bridget, Jane, and Mary. By the fecond, two daughters, Frances and Winifred. Ex teftam. T. P. And Lee's MSS. Vifit. Oxf. f. 32.

[l] Willis, Mitr. Abb. ii. 179. And Append. ibid. 23.

M 4                                        which

which fhe continued to poffefs, 1553. This is a larger penfion than was ufual : which probably fhe got by the intereft of her brother fir Thomas Pope. And this is more probable, as among other notices, it appears from an in-dorfement on a fragment of a rental of that nunnery in the hand-writing of fir Thomas Pope, that on their difperfion, he gave a gratuitous donation of forty marcs to twelve of its nuns, who were friendlefs and born in Oxfordfhire ᵐ. She, if the fame, was however married, before the year 1556, to Henry Bryan of Cogges in Oxfordfhire ⁿ, who feems to have been but in moderate circumftances ᵒ.

As to the wives of fir Thomas Pope, he was three times married. His firft wife was Elifabeth Gunfton, from whom he was di-vorced by Richard Gwent, doctor of decrees, archdeacon of London, and principal official in the court of Canterbury, July the eleventh 1536, by the authority of the king and par-

---

ᵐ I know not exactly whether it is of Godftowe or Bicefter Priory, both in Oxfordfhire. Of the latter, in the Burfary of Trinity college, are two beautiful Audit rolls on vellom, one of the year 1393, the other of 1443.

ⁿ Teftam. Dom. T. Pope.

ᵒ Comp. Burff. 1562.-3. " Sol. in vino infumpt. in Magiftrum " Breanum de Cogges. 24 Jun. xiij *d*.

Comp. 1569.--70. " Sol. pro prandio Magiftri Bryan fratris " domini fundatoris. xij *d*.

liament.

liament [p]. His ſecond wife was Margaret Dodmer, widow, to whom he was married at London, July the ſeventeenth, 1536 [q], by licence from archbiſhop Cranmer; authoriſed by parliament for this purpoſe [r]. Margaret Dodmer's maiden name was Townſend, and ſhe was a native of Stamford in Lincolnſhire [s]. She was the relict of Ralph Dod-

[p] Collectan. MSS. F. Wiſe.

[q] From ſir T. Pope's BREVIARY §, written and illuminated, given by John Aubrey the Antiquarian to the Aſhmolean Muſeum. No. 55. In it, among others, are the following entries.

"Memorand. quod Margaretta uxor Thomæ Pope equitis "obiit die Lunæ viz. xvi°. die Januarii, A. Dni M. D. "xxxviii. circa horam decimam ejuſdem dici poſtmeridianam, "et ſepulta erat die dominical. ſequent. in ecclia Sti Stephani "in Walbroke.

"Alicia filia Thomæ Pope nata erat die dominicæ, viz. "xvi. die Aprilis, A°. xxviii°. dom. H. viii. circa horam no-"nam ejuſdem die poſt meridiem, A°. Dom. M. D. xxxvii.

"Matrimonium inter Thomam Pope primarium Theſaurari-"um augment. Revent. coronæ Dom. R. et Dnam Margaretam "Dodmer, Viduam, ſolemnizatum erat in London. xvii. die "Julii A°. xxviii. Dom. Hen. viii. Anno Dni. M. D. xxxvi. "t°.—Quod tacitum velis nemini dixeris.—THOMAS POPE, "*Miles*.

[r] "Authoritate Parliamenti ad infra ſcripta fulcitus." Collectan. MSS. F. Wiſe. Ex Licent.

[s] So indorſed on the ſaid licence.

§ This Breviary Aubrey had intended to place in its proper repoſitory, Trinity college Library; but having conceived ſome prejudice againſt Dr. Bathurſt the preſident, he changed his deſign and gave it to the Aſhmolean. From his LETTER to A. Wood, dat. 1674. Cod. BALL. Bibl. Bodl. vol. xiv.

mer,

mer, mercer and fheriff of London, 1524.; afterwards knighted ᵗ, and mayor of London, 1529 ᵘ. She was married to the faid Ralph, by licence from cardinal Wolfey, dated November the twentieth, 1527 ʷ. By this fir Ralph Dodmer, fhe had two fons Ralph and John, both living 1554ˣ, and two daughters, Ann and Mary ʸ. By fir Thomas Pope, her fecond hufband, fhe had only one

ᵗ At Yorke-place, 21 Hen. viii. MSS. Bibl. Cott. Claud. c. 3. fol. iii. The fame fir Ralph Dodmer was alfo *major of the ftaple* at Weftminfter, 23. Feb. 23 Hen. viii. Madox, Formul. Angl. pag. 20.

ᵘ Stowe's Survey of London Edit. fol. 1633. p. 580, 579. He was alfo fheriff of London 1529. See edit. 1599. 4to. p. 444, 445. Ralph's father was Henry, of Pickering-Leigh, Yorkfhire. Stowe, ibid.

ʷ Collectan. MSS. F. Wife.

ˣ Ex indentura quadripartit. prædict.—John is mentioned in Teftam. T. P. 1556.

ʸ Thefe two daughters, with the two fons aforefaid, are all mentioned in a grant of lands to fir T. Pope, pat. 28. Hen. viii. Teft. Mar. i. par. 5.—" Prolibus Rad. Dodmer militis, " civis London." Sir T. Pope, in his will, requefts his executors, &c. " to help to fett forward" the children of his late wife Marg. Dodmer, " which be fryndlefs."————Stowe informs us that, " near Thames ftreete is Grantham lane, fo call-" ed of John Grantham fometime mayor and owner thereof, " whofe houfe was very large and ftrong, builded of ftone, as " appeareth by gates arched yet remaining. Ralph Dodmer " firft a brewer, than a mercer, mayor 1529, dwelled ther, " and kept his mayoralty in that houfe, &c." SURVEY, ut fupr. edit. 1599. p. 183.

daughter

daughter Alice, born April the fixteenth, 1537.[z], who died very young. Lee, in a book of arms, chiefly of Oxfordfhire, drawn by himfelf in 1574, gives us the arms of *Dodmer* impaling *Pope*, from an efcocheon of painted glafs in a window at Trinity college, fince deftroyed with many others: viz. Four lozenges meeting in point, gules, between four rofes of the fame : Upon a chief, gules, a wheat fheaf between two annulets, Or [a]. But thefe arms do not agree with an engraving of the arms of fir Ralph Dodmer given by Stowe [b], With this lady Margaret, fir Thomas Pope feems to have lived in the greateft harmony and happinefs; for in his Will he mentions with much affection, " her " womanlie behaviour, trewth, and honeftie, " ufed towards me," and makes this the fole caufe of his kind remembrances and gifts to her fon; befeeching his executors, and honorable friends, to treat all her children as his own. She died the fixteenth day of January, 1538[c].

[z] From fir T. Pope's BREVIARY, ut fupr.

[a] Muf. Afhmol Oxon. MSS. Codd. A. Wood. D. 14. pag. 74. His arms are not tricked (as thofe of other knights are) in the manufcript cited above, viz. Claud. c. 3. fol. 111, bibl. Cotton.

[b] Ubi fupr.

[c] From fir T. Pope's BREVIARY, fupr. And her Tomb.

His

His third wife, who deferves more particular notice, was Elizabeth the daughter of
Walter Blount, efquire, of Blount's Hall in
Staffordfhire, and Mary his wife, defcended
from the illuftrious family of Dudley Sutton,
of which were the famous, John Dudley
duke of Northumberland, and Robert earl
of Leicefter. The faid Elizabeth when married to fir Thomas Pope, was relict of
Anthony Basford, or Beresford, efquire, of
Bentley in Derbyfhire, by whom fhe had
an only fon John⁴. It is faid by one who

---

⁴ The true name is *Beresford*, as appears from a pedigree
of the family in MSS. Vifitation of Derbyfhire, taken by
Flower and Glover, 1562, fol. 25. b. Muf. Afhmol. Codd.
Afhmol. 728. As alfo from a deed recited above, where John
*Beresford*, probably her fon, mentioned in the text, is a fubfcribing witnefs. I likewife find one *Beresford*, perhaps the
fame, buried as it feems in the college, 1567. Comp. Burff. ut
fupr. An. 1566.--7.

"Alloc. in prandium famulis dominæ fundatricis cum per-
"folverentur jufta Magiftro *Beresford*, x s.

This refpectable family came originally from Staffordfhire,
where is a village fo called : and flourifhes ftill in Derbyfhire.
See *Vifitation of Staffordfhire*, in 1963, and 1664. By Dugdale
Norr. Herald. MSS. Coll. Armor. C. 36. fol. 114. And
Lodge, Peer. Ireland, ii. 210. ed. 1754. As to her fon John,
the founder fent him to Trinity college, Oxford, to be educated under Arthur Yeldard one of the fellows : with a letter
printed in Append. Numb. XXV. In another letter, to the prefident, the founder defires the lecturers, " to tech him and to
" rede him Erafmus piftells and Tully's piftells, which he fhall
                                                        " lerne

knew her well[e], that fir Thomas Pope was
induced to marry this lady principally on
account of her charitable difpofition, and
and other excellent qualifications; and that fhe
heartily concurred with her hufband's pious
intention of founding a college. They
were married by licence from archbifhop
Cranmer, the firft of January, 1540[f]. They
had no iffue. After the death of fir Thomas
Pope in January 1559, fhe was married, for
the third time, before or in December following[g], to fir Hugh Powlett of Hinton
faint George in Somerfetfhire: concerning
whofe life and character, it may not perhaps
be thought too great a digreffion to mention
fome few particulars.

Sir Hugh Powlett was the fon of fir Amias
Powlett knight, of whom it is remembered,
that having incurred the difpleafure of cardinal Wolfey, to produce a reconciliation, he

" lerne to tranflate well." He is a witnefs to the codicil of fir
T. Pope's will.

[e] Dr. Ralph Kettell, prefident of the college. See Append.
Numb. XXX.

[f] MSS. Collectan. F. Wife.

[g] As appears from Comp. Burff. coll. Trin. 1560.--1. viz.

" Sol. Decemb. i. pro pari Chirothecarum dat. dom. Powlett

" et dominæ fundatrici. xvj s.

This prefent, I prefume, was a compliment on their marriage.

re-edified the gate of the middle temple, where he was treafurer, in a moft fuperb manner, introducing among other decorations, the cardinal's arms, cognifance, and badges[h]. Sir Hugh, during the reign of Henry the Eighth, was much in favor with that king. He was invited, in 1537, with the principal nobility, to attend the magnificent baptifm of prince Edward[i]. He was knighted for his gallant fervices againft the French in the wars of that reign : particularly for his behaviour at taking the Brey, at the fiege of Boloigne, in the prefence of the king[k]. He was treafurer of the king's army at the fiege of Boloigne[l]. In confideration of thefe merits, he was rewarded by Henry the eighth with feveral grants of manors and lands[m]. By that king he was likewife appointed furveyor of the rents of the diffolved

[h] Dugd. Orig. Jurid. p. 188. In the Britifh mufeum, there is a tranflation of a French romance into Englifh, entitled *L' Hiftoire de la Ducheffe de Savoye*, by fir Hugh Powlett. *Par Hugues le fils des Monf. Aime Powlett*, &c. MSS. Harl. 1215. 4to. It is probably one of his juvenile exercifes in the French language.

[i] Strype, Eccl. Mem. ii. 5.

[k] Collins, Peer. iii. 223. ed. 2. He was knighted Octob. 18. 1536. MSS. Cotton. Claud. iii. c. fol. 127. b.

[l] Falle's Jerfey, edit. 1694. p. 91.

[m] Collins, ut fupr.

monaftery

monaſtery of Glaſtonbury[n]. In the third
year of Edward the ſixth, he was knight-
marſhal of the army commanded by lord
Ruſſel lord privy ſeal, and ſent againſt the
rebels of Cqrnwall and Devonſhire, whom
he totally defeated[o]. For theſe ſervices he
was, the year following, appointed, for life,
governor of the iſle of Jerſey and Mount-
Orgueil-caſtle[p]. In 1551, the fifth year of
the laſt-mentioned king, he was inſtalled
knight of the garter, at a chapter held in the
royal palace of Greenwich[q]. In 1559, the
the firſt year of queen Elizabeth, the privy
council conſtituted him vice-preſident of the
marches of Wales, in the abſence of lord
Williams, preſident[r]. In 1563, he was
made governor of Havre de Grace[s], then in
the hands of the Engliſh. The next year, he
was one of the principal commanders who
ſo bravely defended Newhaven againſt the
French. On this occaſion, when Montmo-
rency, conſtable of France, ſent a trumpet

[n] May ii. Priv. Sig. Ann. 37. Hen. viii.

[o] Hollingſhed, Chron. iii. 1026.

[p] Pat. 4. Edw. vi. Teſt. Mar. xx. par. 9. In Q. Mary's council-book, MSS. Harl. ut ſupr. are many letters to him from
the privy-council, relating to this office.

[q] Anſtis, Order of the Garter, vol. ii. 446.

[r] Strype's Ref. i. 23.

[s] Falle, ibid.

to

to the earl of Warwick fummoning him to
furrender, fir Hugh Powlett was deputed
by the earl to affure the Conftable, that the
Englifh were prepared and refolved to fuffer
the laft extremity before they would yield
the town, without the queen's exprefs orders.
And when the Englifh army was at length
fo miferably reduced by a peftilence, that her
majefty in compaffion to thofe gallant foldiers who ftill furvived, gave directions to
lord Warwick to deliver up the place; fir
Hugh Powlett was the chief of the commiffioners who conducted the conferences with
the conftable of France for the capitulation [t].
He was in a word, befide the character of
fingular prudence and integrity, one of the
moft intrepid and experienced officers of his
time [u]. He was father, by a former wife, of
fir Amias Powlett [w], a privy counfellor and
an eminent ftatefman, in the reign of queen
Elizabeth [x]. Sir Hugh died in 1571, being

---

[t] Stowe, per Howes, 665. Camden. Eliz.

[u] See Burghley's State-papers, by Haynes, p. 407. Stowe
ut fupr, 653.

[w] Falle, ibid.

[x] In the year 1586, Mary queen of Scots was committed to
his cuftody. This truft he fo honourably difcharged, that when
fecretary Walfingham perfuaded him to fuffer one of his fervants to be bribed by the agents of the queen of Scots, for the
fake of better intelligence, he rejected the propofal with indig-
nation. Camd. Eliz. ed. Hearne, ii. 533. 488. Fuller's Wor-
THIES.

then reprefentative in parliament for the county of Somerfet[y], and without iffue by this lady.

This Lady, whom we muft now call Dame Elizabeth Powlett, did not, however, from her new connection difcontinue that previous and natural attachment, which, in the character of foundrefs, fhe bore to the foundation of her former hufband fir Thomas Pope. She poffeffed indeed no fmall jurifdiction over the tranfactions of the fociety: for the founder had delegated to her the authority of nominating it's fcholars, and prefenting to it's advowfons, during life[z]. And this power,

THIES. *Somerfetfhire.* I find him, before he was knighted, vifiting the fellows and fcholars of Trinity college, Oxford, at Garfington, in time of the plague. Comp. Burff. 1571.--2.

" Alloc. pro epulis quo tempore Magiftre Amifius Powlett " veniebat ad collegium Garfingtoniæ. iv*s.* iv*d. q.*"

Lord Bacon, when very young, attended him on an embaffy into France. Dugd. Bar. ii. 438. See Strype's Ann. Ref. iii. 360. Where is a letter written to him by the queen, with her own hand, fuperfcribed, *to my faithfull Amyas,* and in which fhe calls him, *my Amyas.* Compare Hearne, Rob. Glouc. p. 673. feq. And MSS. Harl. 6994. 29. 30. And Ballard's Learned Ladies. In Add. and Corr.

[y] Willis, Notit. Parl. p. 94.

[z] Once, by the fame authority, fhe nominated a prefident. See Append. Numb. XXV. It appears, however, that the college once rejected her nomination to a fcholarfhip, and chofe another candidate. Upon this fhe appealed to Cooper bifhop of

N                                                    Winchefter,

yet with fóme interruptions ᵃ, fhe continued
to exercife till her death ᵇ. Nor was fhe
wanting in proper marks of affeftion to a
place, to which fhe was by the ftrongeft
ties fo nearly related. She engaged her
hufband, fir Hugh Powlett, to join with her
in protefting the interefts óf the college.
She added, in part, to the founder's endowment, after his death, the reftory of Ridge
in Hertfordfhire, and the advowfon to the
vicarage ᶜ. She freely fulfilled the founder's
unlimited charge, in which fhe was bound to
finifh the houfe at Gàrfington abovementioned; the coft of it having exceeded the
five hundred marcs which he fpecified by
will for that purpofe : and accordingly we
find her, from time to time, advancing without referve, the neceffary fupplies of timber
and money ᵈ. She appears often to have in-

Winchefter, the vifitor, who fuperfeded the perfon elefted by
the college, and decreed that her nomination fhould take place.
Aug. ii. 1592. Regiftr. prim. dift coll. fol. 48. b.

ᵃ Particularly, from 1563 to 1578 inclufive, it does not appear by the regifter, that fhe ufed her privilege of nominating
to the fcholarfhips. But fhe afterwards refumed it. She fometimes nominated the fellows.

ᵇ Regiftr. prim. coll. antedift. paffim.

ᶜ Ex indentur. dat. April. 1. 22 Eliz. apud coll. prædift.
See Append. Numb. XXX. And regiftr. prim. fol. 46.

ᵈ Viz. the fum of 28 l. 9 s. 3 d. in 1566. Ex Regiftr. in
4to. ut fupr. And Comp. 1566.--6. Befide timber in 1561.--2.
and

terefted herfelf in the affairs of the fociety,
and to have lent her affiftance and advice on
many occafions : for which fhe frequently received their teftimonies of refpect and regard ᵉ. Once I find her prefent at the college

and 1564. Ex Comp. et Regiftr. prædict. ˙ She alfo glafed the
houfe. Comp. 1570.--1. " Sol. pro expenf. Magiftri Præfidis
" et magiftri Chambrelen proficifc. Londinum ad dom. funda-
" tricem ad parandum vitrum pro domo apud Garfington.
" xxx *s*. v *d*." Glafs, at this time, was neither a cheap nor a
common commodity. The glafing of a large building was a
confiderable work.

 ᵉ From the following articles, among many others.
Comp. Burff. 1560.--1. " Sol. pro expenf. Magiftri Præfidis
  ` " equitantis ad dom. fundatricem de vifitatione futura.
  " xxxix *s*. vj *d*."
Comp. 1563.--4. " Sol. Maii 24. pro expenf. Magiftri Præfi-
  " dis et duorum famulorum dominæ fundatricis venien-
  " tium Londino, circa neceffaria collegii negotia, et Ma-
  " giftri Præfidis illuc eadem de caufa profecti. xx *s*. x *d*.
——" Sol. eod. die pro expenf. eorundem [famulorum] dum
  " Oxoniæ manerent. x *s* vij *d*."
Comp. 1563.--4. " Sol. Jan. 27. ex pari chirothecarum dat.
  " dom. fundatrici. iv *s*. iv *d*. -
Comp. 1566.--7. " Alloc. in prandium famulis dom. funda-
  " tricis. x *s*.
Comp. 1568.--9. " Sol. pro duobus paribus chirothecarum
  " miffis ad domini Powlett et fundatricem. x *s*.
——" Sol. pro epulis famuli fundatricis. ij *s*. ob. *q*.
Comp. 1569.--70. " Sol. pro chirothecis miffis ad dom. fun-
  " datricem. vj *s*. ,
Comp. 1570.--1. " Sol. pro epulis famuli fundatricis. iij *s*.
  " ix *d*.
Comp. 1574.--5. " Dat. famulo fundatricis adferenti feri-
  " nam. ij *s*.

N 2                                          Comp.

in 1565, viz. " *Sol.* pro Refectione data Fun-
" datrici, liij *s.* iiij *d'*." Sir Edward Hoby,
an eminent statesman and scholar, in the
reigns of queen Elizabeth and James the
first, styles her in a latin epistle *, " præno-
" bilis heroina;" and adds the great obliga-
tion she had conferred upon him in admitting
into the college, Bernard Adams [h], afterwards

Comp. 1579.--80. " Sol. pro chirothecis dom. epifcopi Wyn-
" ton, et dominæ fundatricis. xviij *s.* vj *d.*

Comp. 1589.--90. " Sol. Magiftro præfidi proficifcenti ad
" dom. fundatricem. iij *l.* xv *s.* v *d.*

Comp. 1590.--1. " Sol. pro chirothecis dom. fundatricis. vj *s.*
——" Sol portanti ftrenam [a new year's gift] ad dom. fun-
" datricem. vj *s.*

In a letter written to her by the fociety, dated June xvii.
1573. they tell her, " Wysfhyng you hartily that it wold
" pleafse your ladiship to vifytt your college, and us your
" daily orators, now in your journey downe into Summerfett-
" fhyre, which thynge would be a greate comforte to us all."
In Thefauriar. prædict. I have feen a fermon, preached at St.
Paul's, dedicated to this Lady, by Bartholomew Chamberleyn,
an eminent preacher, and fellow of the college. Lond. 8vo.
1589. [One *Mr. Chamberlayne of Oxford* occurs among many
eminent divines who preached in the Churft of Stevington.
[f. Berks,] from A. D. 1573, to 1578. MSS. Harl. 2396. 123.
f. 157.]

   f Comp. Burff. 1565.

   g MS. To Dr. Ralph Kettell, abovementioned. Dat. 1613.
In Bibliothec. Coll. antedict.

   h Schol. Maii 30. 1583. Soc. Jun. 3. 1588. E Regiftr. prim.
—Confecrat. Epifc. Limericenf. 1604. Wood, Ath. Oxon. i.
730. Hoby's words are, " Arctiori etiam vinculo conftrinxit
                                                    " præno-

bishop of Limerick. Sir Hugh Powlett affis-
ted the college with his patronage, in a trou-
blesome and expensive law-suit against lord
Rich, and enabled them to overthrow their

" *prænobilis heroina* Fundatrix vestra, quo tempore Bernardum
" Adamium, ·nunc Limbricensem Episcopum, pro *amore in me*
" *suo*, in Albo vestro conscripsit, sustentavit, aluit." I find this
notice occurring, concerning bishop Adams, in Comp. Burss.
coll. Trin. 1619.--20. " Exp. quardo collegium recepit rev.
" in Christo patr. Episcop. Limbricens.¹ iij *l.* i *s.* vij *d.*" Ware
says, that Adams adorned his cathedral with a new organ, and
other costly furniture. Præsul. Hibern. p. 189. His picture, a good old portrait on board, is at Trinity college.

When queen Elisabeth visited Oxford, 1566, a book was presented to her majesty, by Nele, the Hebrew Professor, entitled
*Collegiorum Scholarumque Publicarum Acad. Oxon. Topographica
Delineatio.* With verses under each. Under Trinity College
are the following·lines, some of which particularly respect this
lady, as a patroness of her husband's foundation.

Urbis at egresso jam mænia, proxima sedes
Occurrit, Thomæ sumptibus aucta Popi :
Quam sacro-sanctæ Triados cognomen habere
Jussit inauratus Miles, Equestre Decus.
Hujus adhuc teneros Fœtus pia mater adauget      ,
Conjux, tam digno Conjuge digna suo.            .

Vid. H. Dodwelli Parm. equestr. by Hearne, pag. 142. And
J. Bereblock's Relation of the queen's visit to Oxford, apud
Hist. Ricard. ii. per Hearne, p. 283. See also Miles Wind-
sore's Europæi Orbis Academiæ, Lond. 1590. A copy of
these pictures and verses is in the archives of the Bodleyan Library, probably the same which was presented to the queen.
The verses were written by Nele ; and the buildings delineated by John Bereblock abovementioned, a fellow of Exeter
college.

N 3                    powerful

powerful antagonist[i]. He generously gave them a present of twenty pounds in silver, in 1566, for finishing the stone wall round their Grove[k]. I find him entertained with them on Trinity Sunday the preceding year[l]. I find him also visiting them 1567, viz. " *Allocat.* Jun. xxviii. pro dapibus domini " Paulett visentis collegium, vj *s.* viij *d.* " Item pro cerasis et vino eodem tempore, " ij *s.* iv *d.* [ix *s.*][m].

But I proceed to some other particulars concerning Dame Elizabeth Powlett. In the year 1560, she placed in rich painted glass in a window of the choir, or chancell, of the church of Broadwell in Oxfordshire, an image of the Holy Trinity, with the figures

---

[i] About 1561. From a latin epistle of the college to him, dat. Jun. xiv. 1566. ut infr.

[k] For these things they tell him, " Maximum quod a nobis " dari potuit munus, Dominationi tuæ detulimus : ut primas tu " quidem post Fundatorem nostrum, cujus laudes nulla obli- " vionis ærugine exedi, nullis unquam sordibus obsolescere po- " terunt, inter omnes qui de nobis benemerendo nominis im- " mortalitatem consequuntur, tuo jure teneres." From the same latin epistle. It is addressed " Ornatissimo viro et patrono nos- " tro dignissimo D. Hugoni Paulett." In Thesaur. ut supr. In the law-suit, they acknowledge themselves assisted, " tuo consilio et industria."

[l] From a foul copy of the said latin epistle.

[m] Comp. Burss. 1566.--7.

of

of herfelf and Sir Thomas Pope[n], both kneeling in their heraldic furcoats of arms. But
this window was removed or deftroyed the
following year by own her command, being
cenfured as fuperftitious[o]. In the following
year, fhe gave a great clock to the late conventual church of Clerkenwell in London[p].
This was a confiderable benefaction, and not
unworthy to be mentioned here; as clocks,
if of any fize, were at that time uncommon
and very expenfive. In 1564, fhe placed a new
pair of organs, with a picture of the Paffion
of Saint Sebaftian, in the chapel of Tyttenhanger-houfe[q]. In the year 1592, being defi-
rous of perpetuating her affection to her
native town of Burton upon Trent in
Staffordfhire, by the memorial of fome
public benefaction, fhe gave an annuity of

[n] Probably the reafon why fhe did not place here the figure
of her prefent hufband Sir Hugh Powlett, rather than that of
Sir Thomas Pope, was becaufe this picture was intended as a
memorial of the college to which the church belonged. In the
large old manfion houfe at Filkins, a hamlet of Broadwell,
pulled down about fifty years ago, there were on the fpouts the
initials E. P. for Elifabeth Powlett, and the date 1592.

[o] MSS. F. Wife.

[p] MSS. F. Wife.

[q] MSS. F. Wife. This article, and the two foregoing, I believe,
were communicated to Mr. Wife by the late fir Harry Pope-
Blount, who feems to have had them from fome family papers
or memoirs.

fifteen

fifteen pounds iſſuing from her eſtate in
Clerkenwell, and all her lands and poſſeſſions
at Bentley in Derbyſhire, for improving the
ſalaries of the firſt and ſecond maſters of the
free-ſchool, and alſo for the perpetual maintenance of five poor women, aged and unmarried, in that town [q]. At length this pious and reſpectable lady having lived to a
very great age, died the following year 1593,
on the twenty-ſeventh day of October, at
Tyttenhanger in Hertfordſhire [r]. When her
body was carried from thence, to be buried
at Oxford, five pounds in money, and large
proviſions of meat and drink were diſtributed

[q] Ex indentura, dat. 1 Feb. 35 Eliz. apud Burton prædict.
By this benefaction, the ſchoolmaſter is to receive yearly, iij *l.*
And the uſher v; *l.* The poor women are provided with a lodg-
ing each : fewel, with other neceſſaries ; one frieze gown, one
apron, one ſmock, and xxvj *s.* viij *d.* in money, yearly. She
refers to theſe charities in her will.

[r] From Wood's original Engliſh of *Hiſtory and Antiquities of
the Univerſity of Oxford*, MSS. Autograph. olim in Archivis
Univ. Oxon. Nunc Bibl. Bodl.——She chiefly lived at Tyttenhanger and Clerkenwell. There are three of her letters to
Trinity c llege ; the firſt of which is dated Tyttenhanger, Sept.
23. 1559. Regiſtr. prim. fol. 24. b. The ſecond, Tyttenhanger, Sept. 5. 1570. Ibid. fol. 23. The third, Clerkenwell, Jun. 12. 1590. fol 46. Ibid. In the year 1578, ſhe was
viſited at Tyttenhanger by queen Elizabeth, in a royal progreſs. Blomefield's NORFOLK. iii. 481. See alſo Strype, ANN.
REF. ii. p. 542. ed. 2. And W. Lilly's LIFE, p. 11. edit.
1774.

to

to the Poor, at the gate of Tyttenhanger-
houfe'. On the firft of November following,
the corpfe arrived at Oxford, where, not fo
much on account of her rank, as in regard to
that public relation which her former hufband
fir Thomas Pope bore to the univerfity, it
was laid in ftate, in faint Mary's church'.
The next day it was conveyed with proper
folemnity to Trinity college, attended by the
prefident, fellows, and fcholars of the fame,
all cloathed in mourning at her own charge";
where with great pomp fhe was interred in
the chapel, with fir Thomas Pope and his
former wife Margaret. Three pennons, con-
taing impalements of all her three huf-
bands, Beresford, POPE, and Powlett, were
hung up over the tomb". Twenty-five of
the pooreft women which could be found in
Oxford, were ordered to be prefent at the interment, habited in black gowns of frieze.
On this occafion, a fumptuous dinner was
provided in the hall of the college, for the
whole fociety, and attendants of the funeral.
The remains of the entertainment were diftributed to the poor at the college-gate, and

* Ex teftam.
᠂ Wood, MSS. ut fupr.
ᵘ Ex teftam.
▼ From MSS. Harl. Brit. Muf. Num. 1724.

five

five pounds in money. At the fame time, a
legacy of ten fhillings was delivered to each
of the fcholars. All this was by her own directions [x]. She bequeathed xj *l.* v *s.* to feveral prifons : and to every fingle prifoner at
Oxford one ftone of beef. To the pooreft
and moft difeafed patients in the hofpital of
faint Bartholomew [y] in Weft-Smithfield, xl *s.*
to be delivered to each of them refpectively,
within one week after her deceafe. Among
other bequefts to her honorable friends and
relations, fhe leaves, to lord keeper Pucker-
inge a ftanding cup with a cover, of filver
gilt. To lord treafurer Burleigh a ring of
gold garnifhed with a diamond, pointed up-
wards and downwards, which was fometime
the ring of lord keeper fir Nicholas Bacon,
and by him fold to fir Arthur Darcy, who
fold the fame to fir Thomas Pope for one
hundred pounds. To the earl of Ormond
her black ambling horfe. [z] To the countefs
of Warwick, aunt of fir Philip Sydney,
two long cufhions of red cloth of gold, for
the furniture of a bow window; and an ewer

---

[x] Ex teftam.

[y] " Amongeft the pooreft, moft ficklye and difeafed people
" within that houfe."

[z] Thomas earl of Ormond lord high treafurer of Ireland, and
the queen's General in the Irifh rebellion. See Carte's OR-
MOND, vol. i. INTRODUCT. p. liii. edit. fol. 1736.

of

of filver, fuitable to the bafon which fhe gave
her at the laft " New yeres tide," for a new
year's gift [a]. To lady Stafford, lady of the
queen's privy chamber, a candleftick of filver,
weighing twenty two ounces, fuitable to two
others before given [b]. To lady Scudamore, a
very fair cafting bottle of filver gilt, weighing
fifteen ounces [c]. To her fifter lady Sydenham,

[a] She was Anne, daughter of Francis earl of Bedford, third
wife of Ambrofe Dudley earl of Warwick, high in favor with
queen Elifabeth, and who died in 1595. Dugdal. WARW. p.
339. See the large infcription on this earl's tomb in the Virgin
Mary's chapel at Warwick. To his countefs, the fame that is
mentioned in the text, fir Philip Sydney bequeathed one of his beft
jewels, in 1589. See MEM. prefixed to Collins's SYDNEY-PAPERS,
p. 111. And ibid. p. 42. She is often mentioned in the SYDNEY-
PAPERS, and on important occafions. She died in 1603. Collins's
MEM. ut fupr. p. 42. See Norden's HARTFORDSHIRE, p. 20.
Strype, REF. iii. 598. Ames, HIST. PRINT. p. 425.

[b] Mary daughter of Edward earl of Darby, wife of Edward,
Baron lord Stafford. See Dugdal. BARON. i. 171.

[c] This lady occurs more than once in the SYDNEY-PAPERS.
—Rowland Whyte to Sir Robert Sydney, 1597. " Upon fun-
day in the afternoone, my Lady Skudamore gott the QUEENE
" to reade your letter, who afked of her how yt came to her
" handes. She anfwered, that my lady Sidney defired her to
" delyver yt to her majeftie from her hufbande. Do you know
" the contents of it, fayd the queene ? No, madam, fayd fhe.
" When her majeftie fayd, here is much ado about the CINQUE
" PORTS. I demanded of my lady Skudamore, what fhe ob-
" ferved in her majeftie while fhe was a reading of it : who
" fayd, fhe read yt all over with two or three pughs." vol. ii.
p. 97. Again, Whyte to fir Robert Sydney, 1599. " Yefter-
" day the countefs of Leicefter fent to the queene a curious
" fyne gowne, which was prefented by Lady Skudamore, &c."
ibid.

a neſt of ſilver bowls, two trencher Salts of ſilver, and her bed, with all its rich furniture, of cloth of [d] ſtamel colour [e]. Theſe particulars acquaint us with her connections, and ſhew the manners of the times.

She had two brothers; William Blount [f] an executor, with Nicholas Bacon, of ſir Thomas Pope's will: and Walter Blount, nominated a ſcholar of Trinty college, Oxford, by the founder, and admitted January the ninth, 1557 [g]. Her ſiſters were Mary,

ibid. p. 174. Some of the court hiſtory of this family is probably couched under the adventures of Syr Scudamore in Speſ.ſer's Faerie Queene.

[d] A light red. See Steevens's Shakespeare, vol. i. p. 62, 63. edit. 1779. Dr. Borde, in his Dietarie of helthe, written i◗1541, ſays, under the chapter of Apparel, "in ſomer uſe to "weare a ſkarlet petycote of ſtamel or linſie wolſie." ch. viii.

[e] Ex teſtam. dat. April. xvi. 1593. Probat. Feb. viii. 1594. In Regiſtro Dixey, 83. 15. Cur. Prærog. Cant. The executors are, William Weſton, P.pe Blount, Edward Blount, and Edward Blount.

[f] He married Frances, one of the three daughters of Edward Love, and Alice his wife, ſiſter of ſir Tho. Pope abovementioned. He was ſettled at Oſberſton, co. Leiceſter, and dying 1592. Nov. xxvi. was buried in the church of Ridge, the pariſh church of Tyttenhanger, co. Hertford. See Burton's Leiceſterſhire. p. 210. 211.

[g] Regiſtr. prim. fol. 4. See Append Numb. XXV. He left the college ſoon afterwards, as appears from the following extract of one of the founder's letters. " I am content to diſ- " pens with my wiffs brother for his ſcholers rome, which I

"do

Anne and Ellen [h]. William Blount's heir Thomas [i], who was settled at Tyttenhanger in Hertfordshire about 1593, prefixed Pope to the name of Blount, in remembrance of

" do the rather, for that I believe he ment to lefe his rome
" [place] by his abfens. I wold he fhold be broken of fome
" part of his witt ; affuringe you from henceforth I will for no
" mans pleaffure living breke my ftatutes, neither in that, nor
" in eny other poynt. For when I fhall goo about to breke my
" eftatutes in my owne life, howe maye I hope to have theym
" kept after I am gone ?" To the *Prefident, without Date.*
But my chief reafon for citing this paffage, is to fhew his im-
partiality and difintereftednefs, and at the fame time his refolution and prudence, in keeping up the ftatutes of his college
which he had once given, even againft the benefit and convenience of his own relations, and in a cafe where he might have
acted juft as he pleafed.

[h] Ex Teft. T. P.———Mary was married to———Siden-
ham knight, perhaps fir George, of Combe Sydenham, co.
Som. as appears by *Anne* Blount's epitaph in the church of
Clerkenwell. Stowe's SURVEY, edit. 1618. p. 819. Alfo from
lady Powlett's Will ; and thefe notices in Comp. Burff. coll.
Trin.

    Comp. 1574.--5. " Sol. pro duobus paribus chirothecarum
    " pro domina fundatrice et domino Sydenham. xj *s.*

    Comp. 1573.--4. " Alloc. pro cena Magiftri Sydenham,
    " fratris fundatricis, nos invifentis. v *s.*

Ellen, as I guefs, was married to———Goodwyn. Anne, buri-
ad as above, died unmarried.

[i] He was knighted by James I. at Theobalds, 1603. And
offered by him the dignity of a baronet. Collins's Bar. iv. 667.
—He occurs matriculated of Trin. coll. Oxon. by the name of
Thomas Pope-Blount, Æt. 18. Nov. xi. 1574. Wood MSS.
Muf. Afhm. E. 5.

fir

fir Thomas Pope; as many of his lineal defcendants have done.

Of this family of Blount there were afterwards three eminent writers : fir Henry
Blount knight, fir Thomas Pope-Blount
knight, and baronet, and Charles Blount,
efquire. Concerning whom a few words
may not be perhaps impertinent or unaccepta-
ble. Sir Henry Blount was admitted a gentleman-commoner of Trinity college Oxford,
in 1615[1], under the tuition of the learned
Robert Skynner one of the fellows, afterwards fucceffively bifhop of Briftol, Oxford,
and Worcefter, in the fourteenth year of his
age : where, at that early period of life, he
attracted the peculiar attention and efteem of
the fociety, more from his own perfonal and
intrinfic accomplifhments, his amiable difpofition, lively converfation, engaging addrefs,
genius, and tafte for polite literature, than
from his family connections, and his near relation to the founder[m]. In 1636, He publifhed his VOYAGE INTO THE LEVANT,
which became exceedingly popular, and was

[1] Ex Regiftro in 4to. apud Coll. Trin. fupr. citat. I find
his elder brother Thomas, admitted with him a CONVICTOR of
the fuperior rank. ibid. Thomas quitted the college in 1615.
Henry in 1619. ibid.
[m] Wood, ATH. OXON. ii. 712.

frequently

frequently reprinted. But to fay the truth, this little work is the voyage of a fceptic: it has more of the philofopher than the traveller, and would probably never have been written, but for the purpofe of infinuating his religious fentiments. Yet his reflections are fo ftriking and original, and fo artfully interwoven with the thread of his adventures, that they enliven, inftead of embarraffing, the narrative. He has the plaufible art of colouring his paradoxes with the refemblance of truth. So little penetration had the orthodox court of Charles the firft, that merely on the merit of this book, he was appointed one of the band of Penfioners[m]. Sir Thomas Pope-Blount his eldeft fon was born in 1649, and was educated under his father's infpection. His CENSURA CELEBRIORUM AUTHORUM, which is a compilation of great erudition and labour, is well known to the critic and the literary hiftorian. Niceron unfortunately compares the CENSURA with Baillet's JUGEMENT DES SAVANS[n]. But Baillet has the vanity and injuftice to report the opinions of other writers in his own words: our author has the modefty and fidelity to tranfcribe and

---

[m] For fome of his other pieces, fee Wood's ATH. OXON. ii. 712. And Langbaine's DRAM. POETS, p. 327.

[n] MEMOIRES *pour fervir*, &c. tom. xxiii. p. 399.

to cite his authorities. His Essays on various subjects are learned and judicious, and they have the ease and freedom, without the singularity, of Montaigne. Another of his works, which has been superseded by those who have used its materials, is Remarks on Poetry. Of this piece it will be sufficient to say, that it was honoured with the approbation of lord Mulgrave, the most elegant critic of the author's age. Charles Blount, or Pope-Blount, esquire, second son of sir Henry abovementioned, inherited his father's philosophy. From an abhorence of superstition, he appears to have adopted the most distant extremes of the theistic system. His Anima Mundi, Oracles of Reason, Life of Appollonius Tyanaeus, and Diana of the Ephesians, written with great learning, sagacity, wit, and force of reasoning, are the consolation of infidels, and are melancholy monuments of admirable abilities abused in the defence of a futile but dangerous cause °. In conformity to these principles, he died by his own hand in 1693. Bayle has inaccurately represented the affecting story of his death ᴾ.

---

° See the Miscellaneous Works of Charles Blount, published by Charles Gildon in 1693. And Wood, ubi supr.

ᴾ Artic. Appollonius Tyanaeus. The true story is this. Mr. Blount, on the death of his wife, fell in love with her sister, a

lady

I clofe my account of Dame Elizabeth'
Powlett, and her nearer relations, with a few.
words concerning the antiquity and dignity of
her family. Its anceftor was Le Blound lord
of Guifnes in Normany, whofe fons Robert
and William le Blound, both entered England with William the conqueror. William
was one of the captains in that expedition,
and quartered, with other Norman knights,
on the monks of Ely. Robert was created by
the conqueror, baron of Ixworth in Suffolk;
in which county he received a grant of thirteen lordfhips. Gilbert, his fon, founded an
Auguftine priory at Ixworth, in the reign of
William Rufus, which he endowed with
fourteen knights fees. One of Gilbert's defcendants was killed at the battle of Lewes,.

lady of great beauty and accomplifhments : fhe was not infenfi-
ble to his attachment, but was fcrupulous about the legality of
marrying her fifter's late hufband. On his application to the
moft learned civilians, and the archbifhop of Canterbury, he
was informed, that fuch a match could not take place. On this,
the lady pofitively refufed her confent, and Mr. Blount in a fit
of defpair fhot himfelf through the head. The wound not immediately proving mortal, he lived five days : during which
time, he received no fuftenance or medicines but from the hands
of the lady, who attended him with the moft fympathetic tendernefs till his laft moments. This account I received from the
late fir Harry Pope-Blount, baronet, the laft of the family, and
a diligent and faithful antiquary.

O                                        in

in the reign of Henry the third, where he was ftandard-bearer to Mountford earl of Leicefter. In the progrefs of it's defcent, this family numbers many perfons of fingular eminence and high ftation[q]; and is, befides, nobly connected by marriages. On the fides of the tomb in Trinity college chapel above-mentioned, are two coats : Pope impaling Quarterings of Blount, viz. Barry, Nebule of fix, Or, and fable; And of Roger de Sutton, anceftor of Elizabeth's mother, viz. A lyon rampant. This is one coat. The other con-fifts of quarterings of Blount, Of the faid Ro-ger de Sutton; and, Of Nicholas de Wichard lord of the manor of Ofberfton aforefaid in the reign of Henry the third, marrying into the faid Roger, viz. Azure, a cheveron Ar-gent, between three martlets[r] Or. Thefe arms are an additional and evident proof, that Dame Elizabeth Powlett erected this monument; in decorating which, fhe was fo ftudious to introduce the enfigns and ho-nors of her own family[s].

[q] See Peacham's COMPLEAT GENTLEMAN, edit. 1661. pag. 230.   And Eng. Baronet. iv. 665. 675. 576.   And ii. 367.

[r] See Burton's Leicefterfhire, p. 211.

[s] There is an old portrait of lady Powlett, in the Burfary at Trinity college, painted, as I judge from the drapery and the age of the countenance, about the middle of Q. Elifabeth's reign; by which fhe appears to have been handfome.   This picture

picture was in the college at leaft before 1613. It is mentioned in Comp. Burff. coll. 1612.--13. I have been told that this picture was painted by fir Antonio More, portrait and hiftory painter to Philip and Mary. Several of his pictures were in the collection of king Charles the firft, and at fir Philip Sydenham's at Brympton in Somerfetfhire, a family (as we have feen) nearly related to Lady Powlett. More had one hundred ducats for his common portraits. He died in 1575. I rather think this picture is a copy of an original by More.

++++++++++++++++++++++++++++++++++++++++

## S E C T.  VII.

IT may be neceſſary to ſpeak of ſir Thomas Pope's friends, and of thoſe with
whom he ſeems to have maintained any particular intimacy, connection, or intercourſe:
notwithſtanding moſt of their names have
before occurred incidentally. Theſe were
ſir Thomas More, lord Audley, ſir Richard
Southwell, ſir Thomas Stradling, ſir Nicholas Bacon, ſir Thomas Cornewallys, ſir Francis Englefield, ſir Robert Southwell, ſir Edward Waldegrave, William Cordall, eſquire,
Richard Gooderick, John Wyſeman, ſir Arthur Darcy, ſir Gilbert Gerrard, lord Vaulx,
ſir Thomas Brydges, cardinal Pole, Thirlby
biſhop of Ely, ſir Thomas Whyte, lord Williams of Thame, Whyte biſhop of Wincheſter, and Thomas Slythurſte, preſident of Trinity college ſo often mentioned.

I need not repeat his laſt interview with
ſir THOMAS MORE : of whom it will be
ſufficient to add here, that he was the greateſt ornament of the Engliſh nation at the reſtoration of polite literature ; that he was a
man

man whofe life and death are equal prodigies, and whofe valuable virtues and untimely fate are alike 'admired and lamented ᵃ. THOMAS lord AUDLEY, made lord high chancellor of England on fir Thomas More's refignation in 1533, was probably fir Thomas Pope's particular patron, and perhaps not a little inftrumental towards his rife in the world, as has been already hinted. In how great confidence and efteem fir Thomas was held by lord Audley, is further manifefted, from his being appointed, with fir Edward North, and two others, an executor of lord Audley's will ᵇ; in which, among feveral other directions, they are requefted to deliver, the next new year's day after his deceafe, one hundred pounds to the king; from whom the teftator profeffes to have received *all his reputations and benefits* ᶜ. Few of the favorites of Henry the eighth appear to have more fuccefsfully recommended themfelves to their fovereign than

---

ᵃ Erafmus who always preferved the higheft opinion of More, has, with great elegance and truth, drawn his character at full length, EPIST. 447. See alfo 605. More was among Erafmus's moft intimate friends.

ᵇ Regiftr. Allen. Cur. Prærog. qu. i. dat. April. xix. 1544

ᶜ He bequeathes the *refidue* of his plate, goods, and chattels, to lady Elizabeth his wife, fir Edward North, and fir THOMAS POPE, knights, and his fervants Edmond Martyn and Thomas Barbour. And " the fum of cclj *l.* to either of the " faid fir Edward and fir THOMAS."

lord

lord Audley. But although by his perfeverance in the bufinefs of the Divorce, and the
diffolution of the monafteries, he fo gratified
the kings private views, as " to fuftain, ac-
" cording to his own declaration, much da-
" mage and infamy ;" yet the beft hiftorians,
admit, that he oppofed the dangerous defigns
of his arbitrary mafter in a matter of the
higheft importance. In 1539, many fevere
acts were made, in which thofe ftyled the fix
bloody articles were included ; and the prerogative was carried to fuch an enormous
height, that the king's proclamation was allowed to attain the force of a law. It does
not very plainly appear who were his majefty's
principal counfellors in this affair : but we
are affured, by concurrent and undoubted
authorities, that the rigorous execution of
thofe laws which the king had at firft intended, was prevented by the fpirited interpofition of lord Audley[d]. But I forbear entering further into the hiftory of this diftinguifhed ftatefman and lawyer ; who bore fo
confiderable and fo public a fhare in the moft
impôrtant tranfactions of the reign of Henry
the eighth. I fhall only add, that with fir
Thomas Pope, he was an encourager of literature ; and the founder, or reftorer, of

[d] See BIOGRAPH. BRIT. Vol. i. AUDLEY.

Magdalen

Magdalen college in Cambridge [e]. Sir Richard Southwell was one of the chief
mourners at fir Thomas Pope's burial. He was
educated at Bennet college in Cambridge, and
from thence removed to the inns of court [f].
He was fummoned, in 1537, with many
lords and knights, to attend the baptifm of
prince Edward [g]. He was a vifitor at the
diffolution of religious houfes [h], privy counfellor to Henry the eighth, and an executor
of his will [i]. In 1545, although a ftrict catholic, he protected, in his houfe called
the Charter-houfe at London, his tutor at
Cambridge, one John Loude, a polite fcholar, who was perfecuted for herefy, being a
friend to his literature notwithftanding his
religion [k]. When fir Thomas More was
committed to the tower, he was fent by the
king, with Rich the follicitor-general, to take
away More's books [l]. Henry the eighth left
him by will two hundred pounds [m]. In the

---

[e] Fuller, Hift. Cambr. pag. 120.

[f] Strype, Eccl. Mem. i. 385.

[g] Ibid. ii. 5.

[h] Rymer, Fœd. xiv. 558.

[i] Mafters's Hiftory of C. C. C. p. 373.

[k] Strype, ut fupr. i. 386.

[l] See this whole tranfaction in the State Tryals.

[m] Rymer, Fœd. xv. 117.

reign

reign of Edward the fixth, he was appointed one of the counfellors to the young king, during his minority [n]. In 1551, he was concerned with lord Wriothefley, and others, in bringing about the fall of the protector Somerfet; who was become odious to the people on accont of his ambitious views, and the riches he had amaffed in plundering the revenues of the church and crown. But in confequence of this intrigue, which was deemed a faction, he was imprifoned, but pardoned. At the acceffion of Mary, he received a grant from the queen of an annual penfion of one hundred pounds [o], for his fervices in oppofing the duke of Northumberland who difputed her title, and was accordingly beheaded for rebellion [p]. In the fame reign, 1553, he was mafter of the ordinance and armory [q]; the nature of which, at that time, appears from the following warrant, requiring him to deliver, " towardes the fur-

[n] Strype, Eccl. Mem. ii. 457.

[o] This affair is related, perhaps with fome partiality, in an old treatife entitled, " A fhort treatife of politike power and " of the true obedience, etc. Compyled by D. J. P. B. R. VV. " 1556." 12mo. It is fuppofed to be written by Doctor John Poynet bifhop of Rochefter, then of Winchefter. See fignat. iiii. The book appears to be printed abroad. See fupr. p. 58.

[p] Rymer, Fœd. xv. 355.

[q] Viz. Maii 2. Lit. Pat. Mar. an. reg. i. Par. 4. With a falary of cc marcs.

niture

" niture of the bande of horfemen, appoint-
" ed prefently to attend upon her Grace,
" theis parcells of armour; four hundred
" demy launces, with all their furniture, five
" hundred corfeletts, one hundred and fiftie
" fhirtes of mail, with morions to the fame."
Afterwards mention is made of " two hun-
" dred bowes, with fheffs of arrowes, two
" groffe of bowftringes, fifty partizans [hal-
" berds] and five hundred pikes'." In 1554,
the queen gave him a licence for forty retainers', an honor only granted to perfons
of uncommon diftinction. In this reign he
was alfo one of the privy council, and repeatedly joined in the moft important commiffions'; one of which he executed in conjunction with fir Thomas Pope. In the
firft year of queen Elizabeth, he was continued mafter of the ordinance and armory; when he made fuit to the lords,
that he might exhibit a declaration of the
ftate of his office, and of the military ftores
then remaining in his pofeffion. In a letter
to Slythurfte, the firft prefident of Trinity
college, dated Whitmonday 1558, fir Thomas Pope propofes to place his fon in law

---

' Burghley's State Papers, p. 166. 169.
' See Eccl. Mem. iii. 480.
' Burghley's Pap. ut fupr. paffim. And Strype, Rymer, &c.

John

John Beresford abovementioned, a ſtudent in
his college, and concerning whoſe ſucceſs in
life he appears to have been very ſollicitous, as
a page with ſir Richard Southwell, and his
brother ſir Robert, " to lerne there amonge
" his [ſir Richard's] childern, the Latin
" tonge, the French tonge, and to playe at
" wepons ᵘ." Theſe at this time, were
probably the ſole and complete accompliſh-
ments of a gentleman. Sir THOMAS STRAD-
LING ʷ, another of the chief mourners at ſir
Thomas Pope's funeral, was of ſaint Donat's caſtle in Glamorganſhire. When queen
Mary ſucceeded to the crown ˣ, 1553, he
was appointed, with others, a muſter-maſter
to the queen's army ʸ, and a commiſſioner
for the marches of Wales ᶻ. In the ſame

ᵘ Sir Richard Southwell's children were placed, in his own
houſe, under the care of John Loude. Of whom he uſed to ſay,
" He will make my boy, like himſelf, too good a Latiniſt, and
" too great a heretic." Strype, Eccl. Mem. i. 386.

Tuſſer the poet, in his HUSBANDRIE, mentions ſir Richard
Southwell, as a moſt bountiful patron. Edit. 1593, 4to. pag.
159.

ʷ Knighted Feb. 17. 3 Edw. vi. MSS. Cotton. Claud. C.
3. fol. 190.

ˣ In the reign of Henry viii. the king grants " Thomæ
" Stradlyng, uni Dapiferorum ſuorum, officium Bedelli" of
certain lordſhips in Glamorganſhire, &c. Bill. Signat. Hen.
viii. An. 17. Sept. 19.

ʸ Burghley's State Papers, p. 158.

ᶻ Ibid. 201.

year

year he was reprefentative in parliament for
Eaft-Grinftead in Suffex; and, the following year for Arundel in the fame county *.
In 1558, he was joined with fir Thomas
Pope, and others, in a commiffion, before
mentioned at large, for the fuppreffion of
heretics [b]. He was father of fir Edward Stradling, remarkable in the reign of Elizabeth,
for his critical fkill in the Britifh language,.
and his patronage of the Welch antiquarian
literature [c]. Sir Thomas Stradling magnificently repaired the ancient caftle of faint
Donat's [d]; and built faint Mary's chapel,
adjoining to faint. Donat's church, in which
he was buried [e].

Sir NICHOLAS BACON, one of the executors of fir Thomas Pope's will, in which
he likewife remembers him with a token of

---

[a] Willis, Notit. Parl. p. 30. 38.

[b] See fupr. p. 52.

[c] See *Joannis Stradlingi* EPIGRAMMATUM *libri quatuor*. Lond.
1607. 8vo. He was nephew to fir Edward. lib. i. pag. 3. See
alfo Wood's ATH. OXON. i. 350, 351.

[d] As appears from an epitaph upon him in Stradling's epigrams, where are the following lines. p. 10.

Hic Donatæa quondam fulgebat in arce,
. Caftra diu proavis nobilitata fuis.
Omnia quæ vincit, caftra hæc abfumpferat ætas,
Hujus at ingenio pæne novata vides.

[e] Wood, ut fupr.

affection

affection, calling him moreover " his moſt " true and aſſured friend," was ſir Thomas Pope's neighbour at Gorhambury near ſaint Alban's ; where he built in 1566, a beautiful houſe, which ſtill remains a monument of ancient magnificence and manners, with much of its original furniture and decorations ᶠ. He was likewiſe ſollicitor ᵍ, while ſir Thomas was treaſurer, of the firſt court of Augmentations. During the reign of Henry the eighth, having enjoyed many marks of royal favor, more from virtuous induſty than from mean ſubmiſſion, he was made by queen Elizabeth, 1559, lord keeper of the great ſeal, and a privy counſellor ʰ. In theſe ſtations, he behaved with that wiſdom and integrity which their importance and dignity required. To this character it may be ſuperfluous to add, what alone might ſupply the place of a prolix panegyric, that he was the father of Francis lord Verulam.

Sir THOMAS CORNEWALLYS, one of the Overſeers of ſir Thomas Pope's will, all

---

ᶠ In Aubrey's MSS. LIVES, Muſ. Aſhmol. is a particular deſcription of it.—It is now deſtroyed, 1779.

ᵍ Batteley's edition of Somner's CANTERBURY. App. p.118. Birch's Mem. of Q. Elizabeth, i. 10.

ʰ Dugd. Bar. ii. 437. And Orig. Jurid. Chron. ſer. p. 90.

whom

whom he ftyles his moft *trufty and loving
friends*, was fheriff of Norfolk juft before
queen Mary's acceffion, where he raifed a
confiderable force againft thofe difaffected
and factious fubjects who oppofed her title.
For this feafonable and ferviceable affiftance,
he was immediately made one of her privy
council, treafurer of Calais[i], and comptroller of her houfhold[k]. When it was debated
in council to fend the princefs Elizabeth out
of the kingdom, in order that fhe might be
excluded from the fucceffion, he boldly dif-
fuaded the queen from a proceeding at once
unjuft and imprudent[l]. Sir FRANCIS EN-
GLEFIELD, a fecond overfeer of fir Thomas
Pope's will, and joined with him in a commiffion, was knighted by Edward the fixth[m],
but afterwards imprifoned in the Tower by
the protector Somerfet, becaufe he concurred
with fir Edward Waldegrave, and others, in
fuppreffing the commands of the privy council for the prohibition of mafs in the family
of his miftrefs the princefs Mary, with whom
he then refided at Copped-hall in Effex[n].

[i] Viz. Maii 7. Lit. pat. 1 Mar. par. 7.
[k] Dugd. BAR. ii. 480. And from his monument in the
church of Brome, co. Suffolk. See Wever, FUN. MON. p. 764.
[l] Camden's Eliz. edit. Hearne. Vol. i. APPARATUS, p. 21.
[m] Dugdale's Warw. ed. 2. ii. 891.
[n] Strype, Eccl. Mem. ii. 253. feq.

But

But when Mary, fucceeded to the throne, he was conftituted a privy-counfellor, conftable of Windfor caftle, and mafter of the great wardrobe °. She alfo granted him one hundred retainers [b]. In the reign of Eliza-beth, he left the kingdom, and retiring into Spain, became a zealous advocate to king Philip in favor of Mary queen of Scots [q]. But Elizabeth, highly provoked at the info-lence of a man who prefumed to plead the caufe of a lady more beautiful than herfelf, commanded him to be outlawed and attaint-ed [r]. This bigotted knight was much of-fended at the fingular forbearance and indul-gence fhewn to the celebrated Roger Afcham, whom he looked upon as a moft dangerous heretic, during the rigid reign of queen Mary: but there are papers to prove, that it was principally by fir Thomas Pope's influence and earneft interpofition, that Englefield was perfuaded to abandon a violent profecution which he had commenced againft Afcham [s].

---

° Burnet, Ref. ii. 308. Collins Peer. iii. 259. ed. 2.—And Lit. pat. Mar. an reg. i. par. 6. Et ibid. par. 10.

[p] Strype, Eccl. Mem. iii. 480.

[q] Strype, Ann. Ref. i. 371.

[r] See cafe in Coke's Reports, p. vii. fol. 11.—And Strype, Ann. Ref. ii. 26. 538. iii. 246, &c.

[s] See Strype's Life of ❀ T. Smyth, p. 65. I was informed by the late fir Harry Pope-Blount, that a moft valuable portrait

Sir ROBERT SOUTHWELL, another of the overſeers of ſir Thomas Pope's will, and brother to ſir Richard, was made maſter of the rolls, 1542, by Henry the eighth[t], and continued in that office till about the middle of Edward the ſixth, 1550[u]. In 1542, he was repreſentative in parliament for the county of Surrey, and often afterwards for the county of Kent, and ſeveral boroughs, in the reigns of Edward and Mary[w]. He was a receiver of abby lands from Henry the eighth[x]. He died in November, 1559[y]. Queen Mary granted him twenty retainers[z]. He was appointed a delegate and commiſſary in the firſt year of queen Mary, with many civilians, and others of the firſt honor and quality, for the reſtitution of biſhop Bonner[a]. He was one of the attornies, while ſir Thomas Pope was treaſurer, of the court of aug-

of Roger Aſcham, painted by Hans Holbein, was removed from Tyttenhanger-houſe, about the reign of king William. This had undoubtedly been placed there by ſir Thomas Pope. See ſupr. p. 81.

[t] Dugd. Orig. Jurid. Chron. Ser. p. 85.
[u] Ibid. p. 89.
[w] Willis, Notit. Parl. p. 7, 20, 21, 27, 49, 56.
[x] Tanner, Notit. Mon. fol. edit. p. 228, 535, 560.
[y] Strype, Ann. Ref. i. 193.
[z] Strype, Eccl. Mem. iii. 480.
[a] Strype, Eccl. Mem. iii. 23. See alſo ibid. 289.

mentations.

mentations[b]. Sir EDWARD WALDEGRAVE, another of the overſeers of ſir Thomas Pope's will, was a principal officer in the houſhold of the princeſs Mary, and committed to cloſe impriſonment to the Tower, with ſir Francis Englefield, and ſir Robert Rocheſter, for omitting to forbid the celebration of maſs in her houſe[c]. The princeſs when ſhe ſucceeded to the crown, had him much in eſteem; and in conſideration of his ſufferings and unſhaken conſtancy, ſhe conſtituted him a privy-counſellor, maſter of the great wardrobe[d], and chancellor of the duchy of Lancaſter[e]. He was created knight of the carpet, by lord Arundel, the day following her majeſty's coronation[f]. He was appointed one of the executors of cardinal Pole's will; in which the cardinal aſſigns him a gratuity of fifty pounds[g]. In the year 1561, he was ordered, with his lady, to the Tower, for hearing maſs in his family[h]. Strype, in the ſpirit of his honeſt ſimplicity, tells us[i],

[b] Weever, Fun. Mon. pag. 109.
[c] Strype, Eccl. Mem. ii. 253. ſeq.
[d] Viz. Jan. 16. Lit. pat. Mar. an. reg. 1. par. 2.
[e] Collins, Peer. iii. 553. ed. 2.
[f] Collins, ibid. But ſee Strype, ut ſupr. iii. Append. p. 11.
[g] Life of Pole, P. ii.
[h] Strype, Ann. Ref. i. p. 233.
[i] Ibid.

that

that " this knight and his lady had the cha-
" racter of very good alms-folks, in refpect
" of their great liberality to the Poor."
Three other Overfeers of fir Thomas Pope's
will were fir William Cordall, Richard
Gooderyke, and John Wyfeman. Sir William Cordall was lent reader of Lincoln's inn, 1553[k], and afterwards frequently
governor of that houfe[l]. In the fame year
he was appointed follicitor-general, by queen
Mary[m]; and in 1557, mafter of the rolls[n].
Sir Thomas Pope mentions him in this capacity, in a letter to the prefident of his college, dated at Clerkenwell, on Whitmonday,
1558. " I fhall buy of the mafter of the
" rolles, ii fayre manors with two advowfons
" in Lyncolnfhere which I entende to gyve
" to my collegge, &c[o]." He was one of
Mary's privy counfellors[p], who granted him
the privilege of twelve retainers[q]. He was
one of the executors of cardinal Pole's will,

---

[k] Dugd. Orig. Jurid. p. 252. col. 2.

[l] Ibid. 260. col. 1.

[m] Ibid. Chron. Ser. p. 81.—In the patent he appears to have
belonged to the court of Augmentations. Lit. pat. Mar. an.
ieg. 1. par. 8.

[n] Dugd. ibid. p. 91.

[o] Ex Orig. Thef. coll. Trin. ut fupr.

[p] Council-book, MSS. Harl. ut fupr.

[q] Strype, Eccl. Mem. iii. 480.

with

with a bequeſt of fifty pounds[r]. He was likewiſe an executor, and is ſtyled a beloved friend, of the great earl of Dorſet[s]. In 1558 he was ſpeaker of the houſe of Commons[s]. The maſterſhip of the rolls he kept late in the reign of Elizabeth, with much reſpect, till 1581[t]. William Lambarde's famous book, entitled ARCHAIONOMIA or ſyſtem of Saxon laws, tranſlated into Latin, and printed at London in 1568, is dedicated to this ſir William Cordall; and in the dedication, the learned editor acknowledges the many obligations and encouragements he had received from ſir William's patronage in the proſecution of that valuable work. Abraham Fleming alſo dedicates his tranſlation of *The General Doctrine of Earthquakes* to this worthy patron[w]. He is ſaid to have been a great encourager of Saxton, who publiſhed maps of England, in the reign of queen Elizabeth[x]. He was appointed viſitor of ſaint John's college in Oxford, during life, by the founder ſir Thomas Whyte; and is ſuppoſed to have

[r] Life of Pole, P. ii.

[s] Ex teſtam. 8 Eliz. apud Collins Peer. i. 517. ed. i.

[t] Willis, Not. Parl. SPEAKERS, pag. 113.

[u] Dugd. ubi ſupr. p. 97.

[w] Lond. 1580. 8vo.

[x] Hearne's coll. MSS. Bibl. Bodl. vol. 123. p. 143.

drawn

drawn up the ftatutes of that fociety by the founder's defire [y]. He lived at Long-Melford in Suffolk [z] : and, in 1578, gave example for the magnificent feafting of queen Elizabeth in that county ; into which her majefty was received by three troops, one of two hundred young gentlemen cloathed in white velvet, another of three hundred gentlemen of the county apparelled in black velvet coats and coftly chains, and a third of fifteen hundred attendants well mounted on horfeback [a]. RICHARD GOODERYKE appears to have been a lawyer of great eminence ; and his name is frequently mentioned, with other chief lawyers and noblemen, in various commiffions and proclamations, during the reigns of Henry the eighth, Edward, Mary, and Elizabeth [b]. Leland, in

[y] His arms were in the windows of the chapel and hall of faint John's college. Hutton's Collections, MSS. Bibl. Bodl. p. 202. In Mufeol. Bibl. They have been long fince deftroyed. There is a curious old picture of him, in faint Jchn's college, by one *Cornelius de Zeem.* Thefe ftatutes are digefted from thofe of New-College in the fame Univerfity.

[z] Collins, Peer. ii. 266. ed. i. He founded a hofpital, at Long-Melford, for a warden and twelve brethren. Strype's PARRER, p. 23. B. i. ch. vi.

[a] Hollingfhed, Chron. iii. 1287. Compare Weever, p. 748. And Camd. ELIZ. vol. ii. p. 322. edit. Hearne.

[b] Strype, Eccl. Mem. and Ann. paffim.

the

the ENCOMIA [c] of illuſtrious perſons, compliments him when a young man, for his pro-
miſing virtues and abilities; and from thence
infers his future reputation in the profeſſion
of the law [d]. He was an attorney [e], while
ſir Thomas Pope was maſter of the woods,
of the ſecond court of Augmentations. Edward the ſixth, in 1551, granted him an annuity of one hundred pounds [f]. He was often a repreſentative in parliament [g]. He was

[c] *Principum ac illuſtrium aliquot et eruditorum in Anglia virorum* ENCOMIA, *&c.* edit. 1589. qu. pag. 108. In the preface
to Aſcham's SCHOLEMASTER, printed 1589, ſir Richard Sackville at a conference with Aſcham about education, mentions,
" our deare frende, good maſter *Goodericke*, whoſe judgment I
" cold well beleeve, &c." This is perhaps the ſame.

[d] Ad RICARDUM GOODERICIUM.
Magnificum retines, GODERICI candide, nomen,
    Quod vel Saxonicum recte idioma probat.
Sic bonus ac dives diceris jure latino;
    Moribus hoc nomen convenit omne tuis.
Nominis illa tui, tam bella notatio non te
    Conſtituit ditem, conſtituitve bonum.
Splendida felicem te virtus reddidit una,
    Macte hac virtute, et dona beata feres.
Cauſidico ſic fama foro tua, lauſque nitebit,
    Et te patronum percolet ipſe cliens.
Nec ſic contentus virtuti imponere morem,
    Suſpice doctrinæ lumina clara piæ.
Illa tuas poſſunt ad cœlum tollere laude,
    Te quoque per niveas condecorare notas.

[e] Rym. Fœd. xv. 334.
[f] Strype, Eccl. Mem. ii. 498.
[g] Willis, Notit. Parl. pp. 12. 73. 91.

born

born in Yorkſhire 1524 [b], and was high-
ſheriff of that county 1579 [i]. He was nearly
related to Goodryke biſhop of Ely, high
chancellor of England [k]. JOHN WYSEMAN [l]
was of Canfield-Hall in Eſſex [m]. I find him
one of the commiſſioners for certifying to
Henry the eighth, the value of all the mo-
naſtic and other ſpiritual foundations in the
county of Eſſex [n]. He was a member of parliament, in 1554, for Malden in Eſſex: and
in the following year, for Eaſt-Grinſtead
in Suſſex [o].

Sir ARTHUR DARCY, to whom ſir Thomas
Pope bequeathes a valuable memorial in his
will, and with whom he was joined in a commiſſion, is ſaid to have been " a ſoldier of
" great fidelitie and truſt [p]." Upon informa-

[b] Collins, Bar. ii. 259.

[i] Drake's Eborac. p. 354.

[k] Collins, ubi ſupr. See Strype's CRANMER, p. 221.

[l] Sir Thomas Pope is licenced to alienate to this John Wyſeman, and others, the manors of Ditton, Brampton, and Syfling-
ton, in Kent. Pat. Phil. Mar. 3. 4. Teſt Apr. 9. Par. 8.

[m] Collins, Peer. p. 530. *Waldegrave.* Ed. ii.

[n] In the inſtrument he is ſtyled *Auditor.* I ſuppoſe of the exchequer, or augmentation office. Dated 26 Hen. viii. Jan. 30.
MSS. Tanner. Bibl. Bodl.

[o] Willis Not. Parl. p. 42. 51.

[p] Letter of ſir Ph. Hoby in Burghley's State papers, ut ſupr.
p. 125.

P 3                                                    tion

tion given to Henry the eighth, that the
emperor Charles the fifth had threatened war
againſt England, in 1532, and by ſome ſecret
negotiations, engaged James the fourth of
Scotland to his aſſiſtance; he entered Scotland
with an army, and waſted the country. In the
ſame year he was deputed captain of the Iſle
of Jerſey; and afterwards, in 1551, by Edward the ſixth, lieutenant of the tower of
London[q]. He was moreover an encourager of
polite learning, then begining to grow faſhionable, as we learn from Leland; who addreſſes
a copy of verſes to him in the ENCOMIA[r];
and ſays, that ſir Arthur Darcy was preſent,
and countenanced him when he preſented, in
1545, his new years gift to the King[s]. Sir
GILBERT GERARD, to whom ſir Thomas
Pope alſo leaves a memorial, was autumnal
reader of Gray's-inn, 1553[t]; and in the following year, treaſurer of that ſociety with
Nicholas Bacon[u]. He was appointed, by

q Dugd. Bar. i. 374. ſeq. And MSS. Harl. Brit. Muſ. 284.
—61. fol. 94. He was made knight of the garter at Greenwich, Apr. 23. 6 Edw. vi. Anſtis, Ord. Gart. i. 446.

r Leland calls him,
      Doctrinæ eximium POLITIORIS
       Cultorem.———p. 36. edit. ut ſupr,

s Leland, ibid.

t Dugd. Orig. Jurid. p. 293. col. 2.

u Ibid. p. 298. col. 1.

queen

queen Elizabeth, at her acceffion, 1559, attorney general [w], and on the death of fir William Cordall, in 1588, mafter of the rolls [x]; in which ftation he remained till 1594 [y], when he probably died. The memorable William Herbert, earl of Pembroke, appointed him in 1569, with others his good lords and friends, an overfeer of his will, with a reward of fifty pounds, to be given him in money, plate, or jewels [z]. WILLIAM Lord VAULX, of Harwedon, to whom fir Thomas Pope leaves a legacy of one hundred pounds, was fummoned to parliament 1557. He founded an hofpital at Irtlingburgh in Northamptonfhire [a]. In 1582, he was accufed before lord Burghley and fir Walter Mildmay, and heavily fined, for harbouring Campion the jefuit, but was afterwards reconciled to the queen [b]. Notwithftanding this popifh attachment, he was one of the noblemen appointed to conduct her majefty from Hatfield

---

[w] Ibid. Chron. Ser. p. 91.

[x] Dugd. ubi fupr. p. 97.

[y] Ibid. p. 99. He was knighted at Greenwich, 1579. 5 Jul. MSS. Cotton. Claud, C. 3. fol. 245. b.

[z] Regiftr. LYON. Cur. Prær. Cant. qu. 15.

[a] Dugd. Bar. ii. 305.

[b] Strype, Ann. Ref. iii. 126. And MSS. Harl. Brit. Muf. 859. 4.

to

to London, on the Death of her fifter Mary[c].
Sir THOMAS BRYDGES, to whom, by the
name of Mr. Thomas Abrydge, fir Thomas
Pope alfo bequeathes a remembrance, was
brother to John firft earl of Chandois[d]. In
Mary's reign he was lieutenant of the Tower
of London[e]. Fox mentions a friendly religious · conference between him, fecetary
Bourne, and Bifhop Ridley, in the Tower[f].
When the princefs Elizabeth was confined
in the tower, he faved her life, by detecting
and communicating a plot which bifhop Gardiner is faid to have contrived for her immediate execution[g]. When he led, as lieutenant
of the tower, lady Jane Gray to the fcaffold,
he begged her to beftow on him fome fmall
prefent, which he might keep as a perpetual
memorial of her[h]. She gave him her table-
book, where fhe had juft written three fenten-
ces on feeing her hufband's headlefs body

[c] Strype, ibid. i. Append. p. 2.
[d] See Strype, Eccl. Mem. iii. 62. 478.
[e] Both fir John and fir Thomas Bridges, knights, occur lieu-
tenants of the tower in Q. Mary's reign. Baker's Collectan. ex
MSS. Camden. Brit. Muf. 7033. Vol. vi. pag. 341. As was
Edmund, the fecond earl. Dugd. Bar. ii. 595. See Hollingfhead, iii. 1099 1100. 1103. In one of which places fir *John*
is put for fir *Thomas.*
[f] Martyrol. ii. 1297.
[g] Hollingfh. ut fupr. pag. 1130.
[h] Ibid. 1100.

carried

carried back to the tower in a cart. They were written one in Greek, another in Latin, and a third in Englifh [1]. That fir Thomas Pope was nearly connected with CARDINAL POLE,. appears from paffages in his letters. I have before mentioned his application to the cardinal, for obtaining a licence for three. of his fellows to preach. Sir Thomas Pope in a letter to the prefident of his college, 1558,

[1] Heylin, 167. But by miftake he fays it was fir John Gage. See what is faid of fir Thomas Brydges, fupr. p. 45. And of John lord Chandois, p. 69. It may be added, that this Thomas, or fir, Bridges, who was of Cornebury in Oxfordfhire, occurs in a grant of lands to fir T. POPE, Pat. 31. Hen. viii. par. 4. And fir Thomas Bridges is mentioned as one of the gentlemen of Oxfordfhire, prefent at Cranmer's execution. Strype's Cran-. mer, pag. 384. b. iii. ch. 21. I prefume he had fome appoint-ment in the court of Henry viii. For he attended at the funeral of the king; on which occafion he bore the dragon-ftandard between two ferjeants at arms with their maces. Strype, Eccl. Mem. ii. Append. Numb. x. He was a confiderable fharer of abbey lands in Oxfordfhire, with Sir T. POPE; particularly of the lands of the monaftery of Bruerne: As appears by the patent above cited. In his Will, he mentions the *Manfion-houfe* of Bruerne; which, I fuppofe, was the monaftery. Alfo the demefnes of that houfe, and feveral of its eftates. In the fame will he bequeathes to lord Chandois twenty corflets: to his fon Henry the reft of armour, and his beft chain of gold. To lord Grey of Wilton, in confideration of his lofs by being ap-prehended at Gynes, 50 l. TESTAM. Th. Brydges. dat. Octob. 18, 1559. Probat. Feb. 13, 1559. In. Cur. Prærog. Cant. regiftr. Melerfh, qu. 13. He received from Edward vi. a grant of the abbey of Keinfham near Briftol. Tanner's Not. Mon. edit. fol. pag. 469.

fpeaks

ſpeaks of procuring a prebend for one Heywood, and adds, " my lord cardinalls Grace
" and my lord of Elie [Thirlby] are both
" willing." In another letter to the ſame,
dated 1557, he ſays, " Towching Mr. Hey-
" wood's recompens, I wold be glad to un-
" derſtonde what he wold have ; and therup-
" pon wold make my ſute to my lord cardi-
" nall's Grace, and my lord of Elie, accord-
" inglie [k]." In another to the ſame, and
on the ſame buſineſs, without date, he ſays,
" my lord cardinall's grace has promiſed me
" a prebend of xx *l.*" In another to the
ſame, dated July the ninth, 1558, he tells
the preſident, that if his ſon in law John
Bereſford, or Basford, mentioned above, then
at Trinity college, ſhould prove a good pro-

[k] This Mr. Heywood was *Richard Hayward*, rector of Gar-
ſington, in Oxfordſhire, to which he was preſented by the crown
about Auguſt, 1556. Rym. Fœd. xv. p. 442. The next year ſir
Thomas Pope purchaſed the ſaid rectory of Philip and Mary,
and annexed it to the preſidentſhip of Trinity college. This
application to cardinal Pole, and the biſhop of Ely, was undoubtedly to diſpoſſefs Hayward, by procuring him ſome equivalent, that the preſident might immediately ſucceed to the
rectory. Which appears to have been done, yet not without
ſome difficulty, nor in conſequence of theſe applications. Regiſtr. prim. coll. Trin. fol. 122. b. Arthur Yeldard, Preſident,
was inſtituted to this rectory, on the reſignation of R. Hay-
wood, Sept. 8. 1562. REGISTR. Epiſcopat. Oxon. SEDE VA-
CANT. fol. 219.

ficient

ficient in the latin tongue, " I will not fail
" to fue to my lord cardinall's grace for
" him :" in order that he " might, as is faid
" in another letter, attende uppon his grace."
Of the cardinal's character it will be fufficient to obferve, that he is more endeared to
pofterity by private virtues and amiable qua-
lifications, than ennobled by birth and dignities. Inftead of imbruing his hands in the
blood of martyrs, and loading the confciences
of mankind with arbitrary decrees and unna-
tural edicts, he correfponded with learned
men, and introduced into England the pure
and ufeful elegancies of claffical compofition [l].

[l] I have before referred the reader to Wood's HISTORY and
ANTIQUITIES of the univerfity of Oxford, for an account of
Pole's vifitation of the univerfity. I will here add an anecdote
relating to that tranfaction not mentioned by Wood. The cardinal finding faint Mary's college, (where Erafmus had ftudied,
but which had been diffolved as a feminary for various monafteries of auguftine canons,) although very ruinous, a place
which might be made convenient f..r the reception of ftudents,
ordered it to be repaired and fitted up for that purpofe, Sept.
17. 1556. Accordingly, a principal was appointed to it: yet
on condition, that he fhould refign his office, in cafe the cardinal fhould ever be difpofed to convert the faid college into a
houfe of religious. The principal's name was Alexander El-
cocke, A. M. But John Wayte *lord of the foil* of the faid college refufed entry to the new principal into the premiffes, " ut
" paret cubicula ftudiofis." Regiftr. Cur. Cancell. Oxon. GG.
fol. 63. in Archiv. Univ. Oxon. I know not what was the
immediate confequence of this procceding : but it is certain
that

Sir Thomas Pope fubmitted to the cardinal the ftatutes of his college, as appears from a letter to the Prefident : which, while it pays a compliment to the cardinal's tafte, likewife illuftrates what has been before obferved about the ftate of literature at this period. " My lord cardinall's grace has had " the overfeeinge of my ftatutes. He much " lykes well that I have therein ordered the- " latin tonge [m] to be redde to my fchollers. " But he advyfes me to order the greeke to " be more taught there, than I have provyd- " ed. This purpofe I well lyke : but I fear " the tymes will not bear it now [n]. I re- " member when I was a yong fcholler at " Eton, the greeke tongue was growing " apace : the ftudie of which is now alate " much decaid [o]." The paffages in the letters above cited likewife inform us, how far

that neither of the cardinal's fchemes took effect. Erafmus in fome of his Epiftles fpeaks feelingly of the repofe which he enjoyed, and the felicity with which he profecuted his ftudies, for two years, in this retired houfe. The chapel, no inelegant fabric, containing the curious monuments of the founder Thomas Holden and his wife, together with the cloifter, was not completely demolifhed till the year 1656. Nothing now remains but a part of the gatehoufe, which fronts weftward.

[m] The claffics.

[n] Vid. fupr. p. 156.

[o] To the prefident. dat. Hatfield. 1556.

fir

fir Thomas Pope was connected with THIRL-
BY, bifhop of Ely[p]. He was conftituted the
firft, and only bifhop of Weftminfter by
Henry the eighth[q]. He was, by Edward
the fixth, tranflated to Norwich, and afterwards by queen Mary to Ely; by whom he
was alfo appointed a privy counfellor[r], and
joined in commiffion with fir Thomas Pope
and others for the fuppreffion of heretics[s].
By all thefe princes he was much efteemed
for his experience in political affairs, and frequently employed as an envoy to foreign
courts. In the reign of Elizabeth he was
ejected and imprifoned for perfevering in popery; but was afterwards received into the
family of archbifhop Parker, who, not more
on account of his former dignity, than of
his learning, candor, and affability, treated
him with due refpect and humanity[t].
WHYTE, bifhop of Winchefter, became the
firft vifitor of Trinity college in Oxford. It
is reafonable to fuppofe, that fir Thomas
Pope's real motive for appointing the bifhops
of Winchefter to be vifitors of his college,

[p] See alfo Append. Numb. xix.
[q] Burnet, Ref. *Records*. i. 246.
[r] Goodwyn, ut fupr. p. 333.
[s] See fupr. p. 52.
[t] Goodwyn, ubi fupr.

originated

originated from Gardiner, who was the bishop
of Winchester when the foundation was pro-
jected; and who, moreover, had been governor of a college at Cambridge; was now
chancellor of that university, a learned civilian, a scholar of the first rank, an eminent
patron of literature ", and bore the greatest

---

" Gardiner's literary character has been commonly overlooked
in his political, and is rarely regarded or acknowledged. He
was admirably skilled in the Greek language, at a time when
it was cultivated in England only by a few neglected scholars.
His ideas of pure Latinity were refined to a fault; and he carried his notions of the chaste Roman phraseology to such a
nicety, as to be esteemed a Ciceronian by his cotemporaries.
Leland, the most polite classical writer in England at that period, congratulates some of his elegant friends, on their being
educated in the college over which Gardiner presided at Cambridge; and which, under such a governor, had become the
seat of eloquence and of the choir of the Muses. Leland also
characterises Gardiner by the epithet DISERTUS, or the master
of genuine Latinity; and calls him the restorer of classical
composition, and the study of philology, at Cambridge. EN-
COM. p. 100. edit. 1589. Le'and paid these compliments
before Gardiner was a bishop, and when there were no temptations to flattery. Many of Ascham's terse Latin epistles are addressed to this prelate: in which, his distinguished learning, his
sollicitude for the revival of ancient letters, and his general patronage, are repeatedly displayed in the highest yet unaffected
terms of panegyric. In one of these, Ascham expresses his
great satisfaction, that Gardiner, who excells all others in critical discernment, had so warmly approved his TOXOPHILUS,
then just published, and written with a view to teach a just
English style; and desires that the bishop, *pro es amore quo literas et earum cultores unice amplecteris,* would recommend that
book

fway in all civil and ecclefiaftical affairs. But
Gardiner dying while the ftatutes were yet

book to the king. Lib. ii. p. 85. b. edit. 1581. In another,
he thanks the bifhop for honouring him with fo many marks of
notice and attention, when he came, an unknown and obfcure
academic, to court. He recommends a tutor to the duke of
Norfolk's nephew; and wifhes that Gardiner, who is fo eminent a judge and protector of literary merit, would ratify the
choice. Ibid. p. 92. a. In a third, lamenting the untimely
death of king Edward the fixth, he petitions Gardiner among
other requefts, to intercede with queen Mary, for the continuance of his penfion originally granted by king Henry the
eighth, as a reward for his Toxophilus : profeffing his confidence in the bifhop's known erudition, authority, liberality,
prudence, and activity, to quiet the diftractions which not only
the civil but literary ftate of the kingdom would probably fuffer,
from that unexpected and calamitous event. Ibid. p. 154. b.
Dat. 1553. In the next, he prefents the bifhop, then juft releafed from imprifonment in the Tower at the acceffion of
Mary, with a Greek Translation of the Psalms, probably
the Metaphrase of Apollinarius : enforcing the propriety
of his prefent by obferving, that it was written in a language
in which the bifhop fo much delighted, and that poetry had
been his chief amufement during the tedious hours of his late
confinement. Ibid. p. 157. b. See alfo, p. 65. a. With the
next, dated 1554, as a flender remembrance of the numerous
favors he had recently received, he fends the bifhop an antient
golden Roman coin. Ibid. p. 163. a. In three or four others,
evidently written during the reign of Mary, he complains of
many unjuft taxations and oppreffive exactions, impofed by fome
late innovators on the univerfity of Cambridge; fupplicating
the affiftance of Gardiner as their Chancellor, and expatiating
largely on his accuftomed indefatigable endeavours to fupport
the rights and promote the honour of the univerfity. Ibid. p.
194. b. feq. In another letter, to one of Margaret Roper's
learned daughters, dated 1554, Afcham fpeaks of being called

from

under confideration, and Whyte fucceeding
to the bifhoprick, although not confirmed till

from Cambridge by the fpecial favour and appointment of
bifhop Gardiner, to ferve the queen in the very liberal office of
Latin fecretary. Ibid. p. 162. b. In a letter to the learned
Sturmius, dated at Greenwich 1555, he declares, " I would
" not exchange the Office of Latin Secretary for any fituation
" in life. Bifhop Gardiner has treated me with the greateft
" kindnefs and indulgence in this affair : and I can hardly fay,
" whether Lord Pagett has fhewn more readinefs in naming me
" to the queen, or the bifhop in pleading my caufe and recom-
" mending my character. There are fome who have endeavour-
" ed to ftop the courfe of the bifhop's benevolence, on account
" of my religious principles, but without effect. I therefore
" am deeply indebted to his humanity, and it is a debt which
" I willingly owe. I am indeed but one among many who
" have experienced his generofity. I have often thought of
" talking to him about your noble work of the ANALYTICS.
" For I well know his predilection to polite letters, and think
" his patronage would be of fervice on this occafion, &c."
Ibid. p. 45. b. feq. It appears alfo, that Gardiner procured
from queen Mary for Afcham, a renewal of the royal penfion
for his TOXOPHILUS, with the annual addition of ten pounds.
IBID. ibid. p. 45. b. And Grant's VITA, p. 21. Afcham's
LATIN. EPIST. edit. Oxon 1703. By the fame intereft, Afcham
was fuffered to keep his fellowfhip and public orator's place at
Cambridge, during a long abfence from the univerfity, while
he was Latin fecretary and abroad in Germany. Ibid. p. 22.
Nor was Afcham the only learned proteftant whom Gardiner
countenanced in the reign of queen Mary. Throughout the
perfecutions of that unhappy period, he permitted Sir Thomas
Smith, one of the reftorers of Greek, and fecretary of ftate in the
reign of Edward the fixth, to enjoy the comforts of a ftudious
retirement with a penfion of one hundred pounds. Strype's SMITH,
p. 60. feq. I forbear to enlarge on Gardiner's high celebrity as a
civilian and canonift : and fhall only add on that head, that

Henry

after they were actually delivered to the new
fociety ᵂ, the founder by this unexpected
change of circumftances was not fo far reduced,
to a ftate of indetermination and indifference,
as to wifh to depart from his appointment.
Sir Thomas Pope in a letter to the prefident of
the college, dated May the twenty-fixth, 1558,
acknowledges a very particular favor, which
" my lord of Wynchefter and others the
" commiffioners for fpiritual matters,"
had promifed to grant him for the college.
In another letter, dated the fame year, to the
fame, he fays " my lord of Wynchefter
" has bene fycke with me at Tyttenhanger,
" but now returns to the corte. He has pro-
" myfed to give his coat-armur for the grete

Henry the eighth would take no ftep in the bufinefs of his divorce, however eager for a decifion, till Gardiner could be confulted, who was abfent at Rome. I fufpect he was but moderate-
ly fkilled in fcholaftic theology.

ᵂ Gardiner died in Novemb. 1555. The ftatutes of Trinity
college were given May i. 1556. The bulle of pope Paul iv.
for Whyte's tranflation and inthronifation is dated, Prid. Non.
Jul. 1556. He was inthroned Sept. 21. 1556. Regiftr. WHYTE,
Epifc. Winton. fol. 1. a. feq.

Some fay, that upon Gardiner's deceafe it was intended cardinal Pole fhould hold the fee of Winton with that of Canterbury in commendam. But this fcheme being found unpo-
pular or impracticable, Whyte was bound to pay Pole yearly
1600 l. out of his epifcopal revenues, for the better fupport of
the cardinal's dignity. See Wood, Athen. Oxon. i. 132. Collier, Eccl. Hift. ii. 387. Goodwyn de Præful. ut fupr.

Q                              " glas-

" glas-windowe ther in my hall[x]." In a manuſcript greek pſalter on vellum, in the college library, I find the following entry in ſir Thomas Pope's own hand. " *Mem.* that " the reverend father in god, John buſhop of " Wynton gave me three bokes. Tho. Pope[y]." Whyte, who was firſt ſchoolmaſter [z], and afterwards warden of Wincheſter college [a], was 'made ſucceſſively biſhop of Lincoln [b] and Wincheſter[c] by queen Mary[d]. He was a man of learning and eloquence[e]; but his

---

[x] I preſume in the hall of his houſe at Tyttenhanger. It was cuſtomary for gueſts of rank, after a long viſit, to give an eſcocheon of their arms in painted glaſs to the bow-window of the hall. An eſtimate of the price of painted glaſs, particular-ly of Arms, in the preceding century, may be partly gathered from the following diſburſement for painting the Arms of biſhop William of Wykeham, founder of New-college Oxford, in win-dows of the churches of Newton-Longueville, Whaddon, and Great-Horwood, Bucks. " Solutum Vitriario de Aylſbury " pro Armis domini fundatoris poſitis in Eccleſiis de Newnton, " Whaddon, et Horwoode, xiij ſ. iiij *d.*" Comp. Burſſ. Collegii Novi Oxon. A. D. 1479. See ſupr. p. 16.

[y] See Append. Numb. XXIX.

[z] A. D. 1534. Tanner, Bibl. 761.

[a] A. D. 1541. Willis, Mitr. Abb. i. 333.

[b] Conſecrat. April. 1. 1554. Le Neve, Faſt. p. 141.

[c] See ſupr. p. 237.

[d] Goodwyn, p. 300.

[e] He was not an inelegant latin poet. As a ſpecimen of his latin poetry, he has left Diacosio-Martyrion, *ſive ducentorum virorum teſtimonia de veritate corporis,* etc. Lond. 4to. in æd. R. Cali, 1553. See alſo his verſes on the marriage of Philip and Mary,

religious prejudices of courfe difqualified him from retaining his preferments after the firft year of Elizabeth; who was much offended at the panegyric which he too liberally be-ftowed on Mary, when he preached at her funeral [f]; and foon afterwards commanded him to be imprifoned for making a public appearance in his pontifical veftments [e]. He had alfo incurred no fmall fhare of the queen's difpleafure for his behaviour at the folemn conference held in Weftminfter-hall, before her majefty, the privy council, and both houfes of parliament; at which, with three other catholic bifhops, he was appoint-ed to difpute againft a felect number of the reformed party [h]. He was a benefactor to

Mary, Hollinfh. Chron. iii. 1120. Wood, ubi fupr. mentions one book of latin epigrams, MS. Fox has preferved many of his difputations, orations, &c. Fox and Pits, according to cuftom, have both equally gratified their refpective prejudices in reprefenting the character of this prelate. Pits fays, " Erat " fane vir pietate et doctrina confpicuus. Acutus poeta, orator " eloquens, Theologus folidus, concionator nervofus." Angl. Script. Parifiis, 1619. pag. 763. The learned and candid arch-bifhop Parker ftyles him, " ambitiofiffimus antiftes." Antiq. Eccl. pag. 527. edit. Drake.

[f] Council-book, MSS. Harl. ut fupr. viz. Jan. 19. 1559. See Wood, Ath. Oxon. i. 131. feq. Strype, Eccl. Mem. iii. App. 277. who has printed the fermon.

[g] Strype, Ann. Ref. i. p. 145.

[h] See Strype, ibid. ch. 5.

both

both Wykeham's colleges[i] in which he had
the happinefs to be educated. Of fir Thomas
Pope's intimacy with fir THOMAS WHYTE,
the founder of faint John's college in Oxford,
I have before mentioned proofs[k]. And to
thefe evidences we may add, that their interefts and attachments tended the fame way:
for we find fir Thomas Whyte affording fig-
nal fervices to queen Mary againft the rebel
Wyat and his followers, while lord mayor of
London[l]; in confequence of which, he was
knighted by the queen[m]. But a fimilitude of un-
dertakings for the propagation of letters might
otherwife have naturally produced a friendfhip
between fir Thomas Whyte and fir Thomas Pope; as they were both, at the fame

[i] To New College, Oxon. he gave the manor of Hall-place
in Hampfhire. Wood, Hift. Antiq. univ. Oxon. ii. 131. To
Winchefter college he gave his mitre and crofier, a filver goblet
gilt, a bafon and ewer of filver, a rich carpet, with other valuable prefents. E Regiftr. Benef. coll. Winton. In the warden's
lodgings at Winchefter, there was lately a bedchamber, with
a curious old pannelled cieling; having in each compartment
a cypher of the initials of Whyte's name, and of king Henry
viii. It was put up by him in that reign. His epitaph, written
by himfelf, remains on a large brafs plate, under which he intended to de buried, in the antechapel of the college. But dying 11. Jan. 1559, he was interred in his cathedral.

[k] See fupr. p. 124.

[l] Hollinfhed, Chron. iii. 1096.

[m] MSS. Rawlinf. Bibl. Bodl.

time

time, employed in the fame acts of public and literary beneficence. Lord WILLIAMS of THAME generoufly concurred with fir Thomas Pope in treating the princefs Elizabeth, amidft her unmerited and oppreffive perfecutions, with proper regard[a]. He is mentioned in a letter of fir Thomas Pope to the prefident of Trinity college[o]: " I wold " be glad to lerne whether my lord Williams " and Mr. Afhfeld[p], gave the ii Buckes to " my college at the [act] commenfement." Lord Williams having enjoyed many eminent favors from Henry the eighth, and Edward the fixth, was by queen Mary created a baron in reward for his faithful fervices at her acceffion. He continued to receive frefh honors from queen Elizabeth, and was appointed prefident of the council in the principality of Wales[q]. Bifhop Ridley, when bound to the ftake, requefted lord Williams then prefent, to follicit queen Mary, that the epifcopal leafes which he had granted, while bifhop of London, to many poor tenants, might remain and be confirmed. This was

[a] See fupr. p. 71.
[o] It is without date. Lord Williams is mentioned in ancther of his letters concerning a purchafe.
[p] Probably fir Edmund Afhfield of Tame co. Oxon.
[q] Dugd. Bar. ii. 393.

Q 3 the

the fole anxiety that difquieted the compofure of the dying martyr. But lord Williams
promifed to recommend this petition to the
utmoft of his power, and it was accordingly
performed[r].

It is natural to fuppofe, that fir Thomas
Pope was nearly connected with feveral other
perfons of eminence and diftinction in the
courts of Henry the eighth and queen Mary.
That he was in high confidence and efteem
with the latter, may, befide many other arguments, be concluded from a paffage in the
ftatutes of his college : by which it appears,
that he expected her majefty, who profeffed
herfelf fo zealous a patronefs to the univerfity, together with king Philip, would honor the college with a royal vifit[s].

But among his friends I muft not forget
to mention THOMAS SLYTHURSTE[t], whom
he appointed the firft Prefident of his college ; and had before probably preferred, by

[r] Fuller's Worthies, p. 109.   Fox, Martyrolog.

[s] Statut. coll. Trin. Oxon.   " Nifi quando forfan Angliæ
" Reges et Reginæ, eorumve primogeniti, Collegium invifere
" dignabuntur : quos fic quidem advenientes, cum omni honore
" et obfequio excipiendos præcipio et ftatuo." cap. xxvi.

[t] See more of him in Append. Numb. XXV.

his

his intereſt with the queen, to a canonry of Windſor. He ſeems to have conceived a high opinion of Slythurſte's learning and prudence; whom, from the truſt committed to his charge, we reaſonably may imagine to have been a perſon of diſtinguiſhed worth and abilities. In a general Addreſs to the new ſociety, annexed to the ſtatutes of the college, he particularly compliments the preſident for his remarkable moderation of temper, his eminent learning, experience, prudence, and probity; obſerving moreover, in juſtification of his choice, that he ſhould have acted in vain, if he had not added to the benefit of his foundation ſuch a governor, ſo properly qualified in every requiſite accompliſhment; one completely fitted for the difficult and critical taſk of conducting the firſt beginnings of a recent inſtitution, and to whom therefore, borrowing the character of a father in that of a founder, he with pleaſure entruſted the education of his children. On various occaſions, ſir Thomas Pope appears to have placed the greateſt confidence in his friendſhip, advice, and judgement. Many of the founder's letters to Slythurſte contain free conſultations about adjuſting the

Q 4 ˮendow-

endowment, amending the ſtatutes ", and re-
gulating other articles of his young ſociety;
and ſometimes relate to the domeſtic con-
cerns of his own family. I find him frequently viſiting the founder at Clerkenwell
and Tyttenhanger. The ſudden revolution,
however, of religion, at the acceſſion of
queen Elizabeth, prevents us from knowing
much more of his chaaraſter and behaviour
in this ſituation : for in September, 1559, he

---

" In the firſt copy of the ſtatutes, dated 1556, ſigned by the
founder, are ſeveral eraſures and interlineations in the hand of
Slythurſte, made by the conſent and authority of the founder :
and the text of this copy thus correſted, is that which is now
in uſe. Many of theſe alterations appear to have been made
in this book, between them both at Tyttenhanger, or Clerkenwell, as I colleſt from a letter from the founder to the vice-
preſident, dat. 28. Jan. 1557, in which he ſays, that he ſhall
ſend by the preſident, an altered and.improved copy of. his
ſtatutes, which he had ordered to be forthwith ingroſſed in
parchment. In another letter to the preſident, dat. 25. Feb.
1557, the founder tells him, " I truſt ye will not forget to
" make an INDEX CAPITULORUM STATUTORUM, which we
". forgott when we were together." In this copy, correſted by
Slythurſte's hand, London, the place from which they were originally dated, is ſtruck out for TYTTENHANGER. The altered
and improved copy, mentioned above, ingroſſed on parchment,
and ſigned with his own hand throughout, with the ADDITA-
MENT annexed, appears to have been delivered to the ſociety,
but with the original date of 1556 preſerved, in, or ſoon after,
April, 1558. See his letter, Append. Numb. XXV. Under
JOHN PERTE.

was

was ejected from his headſhip by the Queen's viſitors, and committed a priſoner to the Tower of London; where he died of grief, 1560, partly for the death of his honored friend and munificent patron, the founder, and partly for the loſs of his preferments.

SECT.

✝✝✝✝✝✝✝✝✝✝✝✝✝✝✝✝✝✝✝✝✝✝✝✝✝✝✝✝✝✝✝✝✝

## S E C T.  VIII.

A N anecdote equally ridiculous and fcandalous, has been propagated by Antony
Wood, highly injurious to the honor of fir
THOMAS POPE; which, notwithftanding it
appears at firft fight ftrongly to confute itfelf,
I fhall here examine and difprove ². It originated from Henry Cuffe, the famous fecretary
of the unfortunate earl of Effex, who was
executed, foon after his mafter, in 1601.

Cuffe, being a boy of the moft promifing
abilities and uncommon proficiency in literature, was fent at fifteen years of age, by Lady
Elizabeth Powlett, often mentioned above,
from Hinton faint George in Somerfetfhire,
to Trinity college in Oxford, where he was
elected fcholar on the twentyfifth of May,

---

ª Although poffeffed of the proper information and evidence,
I had long ago, and for many reafons refolved, never to enter
into a particular difcuffion of this idle calumny. But as, fince
the appearance of my firft edition of this work, it has been
circulated both in converfation, and by more biographers than
one, as a pleafant ancedote, I could no longer forbear ufing the
means in my power of expofing its falfity and futility.

1578.

1578 [b]. Within five years he was admitted
fellow, May 30, 1583 [c]. But even in this
fituation, the fame difcontented and arro-
gant fpirit, which afterwards hurried him to
an ignominious end, could not be fuppreffed.
Soon after his admiffion, when he was now
not more than twenty years of age, and in
the year of his probation, he endeavoured to
defame his founder by a falfe infinuation,
which favored alike of petulance and ingrati-
tude; and which, had it been true, deferved
animadverfion. The matter being reported to
Lady Powlett the foundrefs, fhe tranfmitted a
mandate to the college, ordering him to be
inftantly removed from his fellowfhip. This
we learn from the words of the college regifter. " *Refignante* CUFFO, *et locum Litteris*
" *Fundatricis dante* [d]." The caufe of his amo-
tion is twice mentioned by the Oxford anti-
quary. In the ATHENÆ he fays, that Cuffe
" was forced to refign his fellowfhip of Tri-
" nity college, for fpeaking certain matters
" though true, which redounded to the *great*
" *difcredit* of the FOUNDER [e]." In another
place, however, he tells the whole ftory with-

[b] REGISTR. PRIM. fol. 37. b.
[c] Ibid. fol. 42.
[d] Ibid. fol. 42. b.
[e] ATHEN. OXON. vol. i. col. 307. edit. 2.

out

out referve, and produces his authority.
" Doctor Bathurſt told me that our Cuffe
" was of Trinity college, and expelled from
" thence upon this account: the founder,
". ſir Thomas Pope, would, wherfoever he
" he went viſiting his friend, *ſteal* one thing
" or other he could lay his hands on, put it
" in his pocket, or under his gown. This
" was, ſuppoſed rather an *humour* than of
" *diſhoneſty*. Now Cuffe, upon a time, with
" his fellows being merry, ſaid, a pox this
" is a poor beggarly college indeed, the
" plate that our founder ſtole would build
" ſuch another, which coming to the Pre-
" ſident's ears, he was thereupon ejected '."
The reader muſt have already noticed the
glaring inconſiſtency of theſe two curious
narratives. In the firſt, ſir Thomas Pope, is
by implication at leaſt, repreſented as a
thief: in the next, his diſhoneſty is ſoftened
into humour and jocularity. That the whole
is a miſrepreſentation, and a jumble of circumſtances, appears from an original paper
in the hand-writing of Doctor Bathurſt.
" Secretary Cuffe was expelled from a fel-
" lowſhip of Trinity college, on this ac-
" count. Our founder, when upon a viſit,
" would often carry away a ſilver cup under

---

' See Hearne's LIB. NIG. SCAC. p. 593.

" his

" his gown for the joke-fake, fending it
" back the next day to laugh at his friend.
" Cuffe being merry at: ANOTHER COLLEGE
" with fome of his boon companions, faid,
" *A pox this is a beggarlie college indeed, the*
" *plate that our founder ftole would build another*
" *as good.* Thefe words being told to the
" Prefident, he was ejected. This I have
" often heard from my predeceffour doctor
" prefident Kettell who was contemporarie
" with Cuffe <sup>s</sup>." In the margin, Bathurft
has recorded the name of the other college,
which Cuffe was pleafed to treat in fuch
terms of contempt, and which needs not here
to be mentioned. Indeed, it was no part of
the accufation againft Cuffe, that, as Wood's
context infinuates, his pleafantry led him to
depreciate the buildings of his founder : but
that he wantonly converted one of his practi-
cal jokes, a fpecies of humour not uncommon
among our feftive anceftors, into a petty
larceny. On the whole, we now perceive
that Wood has inaccurately related this ftory
from a cafual converfation with Bathurft,
which he remembered as imperfectly. As
to Cuffe, I know not whether he ftill continued at Oxford after this ejection. But

---

<sup>s</sup> BATHURST PAPERS, MSS. In the poffeffion of the late Mr.
Payne, canon of Wells.

having

having great addrefs, and much real merit, about three years afterwards, that is in the year 1586, he was chofen fellow of Merton college. Being an admirable Grecian, he was about the fame time made profeffor of Greek in the univerfity. It was in this department, that he affifted Columbanius in the firft edition of Longus's elegant PASTORAL ROMANCE, which was printed at Florence in 1598[h]. He was no lefs eminent as a logician and a difputant. His intimate friend Camden, to whofe BRITANNIA, at its firft appearance, he prefixed an excellent Greek epigram, characterizes Cuffe, as a man of exquifite learning and genius, but of a factious and perverfe temper[i]. Notwithftanding the fevere check he received at Trinity college, he generoufly prefented to the library there feveral volumes. Perhaps fome readers will be candid enough to think, that his expulfion from this fociety was rather owing to an unguarded vivacity of difpofition, than to any malignity of mind. Our hiftorians fay, that the earl of Effex, who began, after a

---

[h] COLL. MSS. T. Hearne, vol. xiii. p. 236. Columbanius fays in the Dedication, p. ii. " Qua in re operam mihi fuam, " non ingratam illam quidem, navarunt viri omnium literatiffi- " mi atque officiofiffimi Herricus CUFFUS Anglus, &c."

[i] Camd. ELIZ. p. 869. edit. Hearn.

tedious

tedious confinement, to feel the dangers of his fituation, difmiffed Cuffe from his fervice and family, for turbulence and infolence [k]. Effex was unfortunate in not having before perceived thefe qualities, in a man who fhared fo much of his confidence.

[k] Camden, ubi fupr. p. 827. 833.

SECT.

++++++++++++++++++++++++++++++++++++

## S E C T.  IX.

FROM a recapitulation of what has been said, the following character of fir THO-MAS POPE arifes. He appears to have been a man eminently qualified for bufinefs ; and although not employed in the very principal departments of ftate, he poffeffed peculiar talents and addrefs for the management and execution of public affairs. His natural abilities were ftrong, his knowledge of the world deep and extenfive, his judgment folid and difcerning. His circumfpection and prudence in the conduct of negociations entrufted to his charge, were equalled by his fidelity and perfeverance. He is a confpicuous inftance of one, not bred to the church, who without the advantages of birth and patrimony, by the force of underftanding and induftry, raifed himfelf to opulence and honorable employments. He lived in an age when the peculiar circumftances of the times afforded obvious temptations to the moft abject defertion of principle : and few periods of our hiftory can be found, which exhibit more numerous examples of occafional compliance

with

with frequent changes. Yet he remained unbiassed and uncorrupted amid the general depravity. Under Henry the eighth, when on the dissolution of the monasteries, he was enabled by the opportunities of his situation to enrich himself with their revenues by fraudulent or oppressive practices, he behaved with disinterested integrity; nor does a single instance occur upon record which impeaches his honor. In the succeeding reign of Edward the sixth, a sudden check was given to his career of popularity and prosperity: he retained his original attachment to the catholic religion; and on that account, lost those marks of favor or distinction which were so liberally dispensed to the sycophants of Somerset, and which he might have easily secured by a temporary submission to the reigning system. At the accession of Mary, he was restored to favor; yet he was never instrumental or active in the tyrannies of that queen which disgrace our annals. He was armed with discretionary powers for the suppression of heretical innovations; yet he forbore to gratify the arbitrary demands of his bigotted mistress to their utmost extent, nor would he participate in forwarding the barbarities of her bloody persecutions. In the guardianship of the princess Elizabeth,

R                              the

the unhappy victim of united superstition, jealousy, revenge and cruelty, his humanity prevailed over his interest; and he less regarded the displeasure of the vigilant and unforgiving queen, than the claims of injured innocence. If it be his crime to have accumulated riches, let it be remembered, that he confecrated a part of those riches, not amid the terrors of a death-bed, nor in the dreams of old age, but in the prime of life, and the vigour of understanding, to the public fervice of his country; that he gave them to future generations, for the perpetual support of literature and religion.

*F I N I S.*

# APPENDIX.

## CONTAINING

Original EVIDENCES and PAPERS.

### NEVER BEFORE PRINTED.

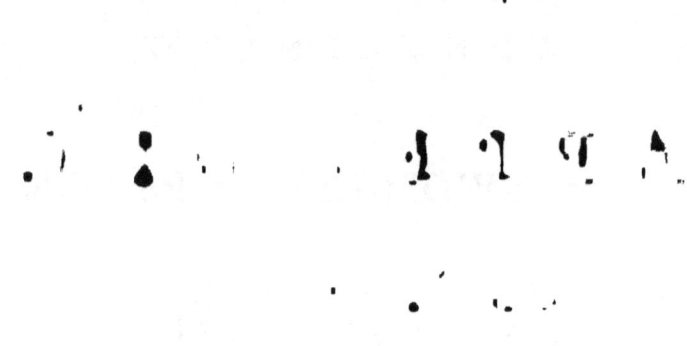

# CONTENTS

O F T H E

# APPENDIX.

R 3

NUMB.

+⊹+⊹+⊹+⊹+⊹+⊹+⊹+⊹+⊹+⊹+⊹+⊹+⊹+⊹+⊹+⊹+⊹+⊹+

## N U M B. I.

The laſt Will of William Pope of Dedington, father of ſir Thomas Pope,
Dat. 1523 [a].

IN the name of our Lorde, Amen. The ſecond day of Februarie in the yeare of our
lorde one thouſand five hundreth and twentie. I
WILLIAM POPE, hole of minde, make my will in
this maner. Firſt, I bequeathe my ſoul to allmighty
god to his bliſſed moder Mary : and my bodie
to be buried in the pariſhe chirche of Dadington.
To the mother chirche of Lincoln iij *s.* iiij *d.* My
londe, my wiffe to have the one halffe of the rent,
and the reſt to bee kept to the uſe of my ſonne till
hee bee of lawfull age. Item, I bequeathe to THO-
MAS POPE an hundreth more ; and to everie dough-
ter fourtie pownde : and if enie of them dye, their
parte to remaine to other. And to have a preſte
ſynginge one yeare. And my wyffe and my ſonne to
occupie my holdinges, the which I hold now, as
longe as ſhe is widowe, and after, THOMAS POPE to
have the occupying and thuſe of theym. And the

---

[a] Muſ. Aſhmol. MSS. D. 15. 4to. pag. 31. b. Inter Codd.
A. Wood, Manu. Rad. Sheldon. Et Regiſtr. Bodefelde, Cur.
Prærog. qu. vii..

*reſidew*

refidew of my goodes I gyve and bequeathe to
THOMAS POPE my fonne, Margarett my wyffe, Ro-
berte Edmondes, and Richarde Swifte, myne execu-
tours, to difpofe for the welthe of my fowle; and
maifter William Farmer to be overfeer to the perfor-
maunce of my will. Item, I bequeathe to the tor-
chis, the bellis, our ladie beame, faint Thomas
beame, to everyche one of theym, iij *s.* iiij *d.* Item,
to Clifton chapel, vj *s.* viiij *d.* Item, to everie god-
childe a fchepe.


Præfentib. temp. lecturæ fupradicti Teftam. Willielmo Farmer, · vicario de Dadington. Joanne
Smith, et Thoma Anne.


*Proved before the Commiffaries of Cardinal Wolfey, and
William Wareham, archbifhop of Canterbury, in the
cathedral church of faint Paul, London, May* 11, 1523.

N U M B.

++++++++++++++++++++++++++++++++++++

# N U M B.   *II*.

An INQUISITIO POST MORTEM relating to the eſtate of William Pope,
father of ſir THOMAS [b].

POPE. Terræ et poſſeſſiones Will. Pope in
Com. Oxon. Duo meſſuagia, ſex virgatæ
terræ, decem acræ prati, viginti acræ paſturæ, et tres
acræ boſci cum pertin. in Whithill, tent. de dom.
rege, ut de hundredo ſuo de Wotton, pro redditu
xij *d.* per annum, et ſecta ad curiam hundredi prædicti. Et valent per ann. in omnibus exitibus, ultra repriſas, lx *s.* Prout per quandam Inquiſitionem
inde compertam apud Oxon, xv° die Septembr. anno
dicti domini regis xv°, coram Roberto Woodcock ar-
migero, eſcheatore ibidem, (virtute brevis ejuſdem regis de *diem clauſit extremum*, eidem eſcheatori poſt
mortem Willielmi Pope directi : qui obiit xvi° die
Marcii, anno dicti dom. regis xiiii° : cujus filius et
hæres propinquior eſt Thomas Pope, ætatis xvi annorum et amplius,) plenius continetur. Dicta Meſſuagia, quatuor virgatæ terræ, decem acræ prati, viginti acræ paſturæ, et tres acræ boſci, cum pertin.
in Hokenorton, tenentur de Carolo duce Suffolciæ,

[b] Ex INQUISIT. POST MORTEM in Anglia, Temp. Hen.
viii. MSS. Rawlinſ. Num. 1386. Bibl. Bodl. fol.

ut

ut de manerio fuo de Hokenorton, per quæ fervicia
ignoratur. Et valent in omnibus exitibus ultra reprifas, ut per dictam Inquifitionem, lxs. De quibus
quidem præmiffis, quidam Rogerus Lupton et alii
fuerunt feifiti ficut de feodo, ad ufum Willielmi
Pope et hæredum, ficut in dicta Inquifitione plenius
patet [b].

SUMMA totalis valoris terrarum ⎫
et poffeffionum nuper Willielmi ⎬ vi. l.
Pope in Comitatu prædicto, ⎭

[b] See fupr. p. 5. 265.

NUMB.

✝✝✝✝✝✝✝✝✝✝✝✝✝✝✝✝✝✝✝✝✝✝✝✝✝✝✝✝✝✝✝✝✝✝✝

## N U M B. II.

## Grant of Arms to Thomas Pope, efquire, dat. Jun. 26. 1535 ᶜ.

TO all prefent and to come, thies prefent letters receyving or heyring. I Chriftofore Berker, efquier, alias gartier chief and principall kýng of armes of Englifhmen, fend due humble recommendation and greeting. Equite willith, and reafon ordainith, that men virtuofe and of commendable difpoficion and lyvyng, be by their merits renoumed and had in perpetuall memory, for their good name and fame. And not all oonly they in their parfons in this mortall lyfe fo bryef and tranfitory; but alfo, after theym, Thofe that of their bodies˙ fhall come, difcende, and procreate, to be in all placys of honnour and worfhip, with other, renoumed and ennobled by fhewing certeyn enfignes and demonftracions of honnour and nobles: That is to witt, the Blafon of Armes Helme and Creft, with their appertenaunces: to the intente, that by their enfample other fhall the more enforce theym perfeverantly to ufe their tyme in deeds of honnour and worfhip, and other virtuoufe workes, to obteyn and gett the renoume of auncyent nobleneffe in their ligne and pof-

---

ᶜ Ex Orig. penes Honoratiff. Francifc. Com. de Guidford.

terite.

terite. And therefore, I the said gartier principall kyng of armes, which not all-only by comon renoume, but also by the reporte and witness of sundry noble gentilmen of name and of armes, with other credable and noble parsons, am verily informed and advertysed: That THOMAS POPE, of Dodyngton in the countie of Oxenford, esquire, hath long continued in Vertue, so that he hath deserved, and is well worthy, he and his posteritie to be in all places of honnour and worship renoumed, compted, nombred, admitted, accepted and receyved, into the nombre, and of the company, of other auncyent gentilman; And for the remembrance and consideracion of the same his Vertue, Gentilness, and Abilitie; By authorite and power unto myne office annexed and attributed, have devised, ordeyned, and assigned, unto and for the said THOMAS POPE, and his Posteritie, the Armes, Helme, and Creste, in manner and fourme following. THAT IS TO SAY, *Party per pale, gold and asure, a chiveron thereon 4 flourdeluces, between 3 griffons beddes rafyd counterchangyd on the fielde. Upon his Crest, 2 dragons beddes indorsant, rafyd, a crownette abowte their necks langued counterchaunged, set on a wreathe gold and vert, the mantlets gueules doubled silver botoned gold,* . . . . . . . To HAVE and to hold, unto the said THOMAS POPE, and to his Posteritie, with their due difference to to be revested to their honour for evermore. In witness whereof, I the said gartier principall king of armes, have signed these presents with myne owne hande, and sett thereto the seall of myne Office, with the seall of myne Armes. GIVEN at London the 26th daye

of

of June, in the yere of our lorde god 1535, and
of reighn of our foveraigne lord king Henry the
eighth, by the grace of God king of England
and of Fraunce, defenfor of the feith, lorde of Ire-
lande, and in earth under Chrift the fupreme head
of the church of England, the 27th yere [a].

---

[a] In lord Guildford's Pedigree of POPE, which is on
parchment beginning with " Thomas Pope Com. Cant.
" Armiger," before or about the reign of Edward the third,
and continued below fir Thomas Pope, a different coat of
arms, curiofly depicted, is affixed to each perfon throughout; without any infertion at the proper place, or continuance
afterwards, of the new coat granted in this inftrument. However it is evident that the family had no real title to that antient coat, otherwife fir Thomas Pope would never have procured a new grant of arms : and it appears from tombs and
painted glafs at Wroxton, that the family after him conftantly
ufed this new coat granted by Barker, xxvii. Hen. viii.

Chriftopher Barker who grants this patent, was famous in his
office. Carte fays, that he proclaimed Q. Mary in Cheapfide,
1553. But this is a miftake ; for he died Jan. 2.--iii Ed. vi.
Anftis, Ord. Gart. ii. 378. Compare Carte, Hist. iii. 285.

N U M B.

# N U M B. III.

Grant from Henry the eighth to Thomas Pope, gent. of Warden of the Mint, &c. in the Tower, Nov. 13. 1535 ª.

*Pro Th. Pope,*
*De Conceſſione.* } R E X omnibus ad quos, etc. SALUTEM. Cum Henricus nuper rex Angliæ ſeptimus, pater noſter cariſſimus, de gratia ſua ſpeciali, per Literas ſuas patentes gerentes datum viceſimo quinto die Septembris, anno regni ſui primo, dederit et conceſſerit dilecto ſibi Willielmo Stafford ª tam officium Cuſtodis Cambii et Monete infra Turrim ſuam London, quam Cuſtodiam Cunagiorum auri et argenti infra Turrim predictam et alibi infra regnum

ª Sec. Part. Lit. Pat. Hen. viii. An. Reg. 26ᵗᵒ. Ex Orig. in Capella Rotulorum.

ᵇ In the Britiſh Muſeum may be ſeen, " Particule Compoti " Willelmi Stafford Armigeri, Cuſtodis Cambii et Monete in- " fra Turrim London. viz. de Auro et Argento ibidem ope- " ratis, fabricatis, et monetatis, a feſto S. Michaelis Archan- " geli, Anno 14 RR. Henrici vii. uſque feſtum S. Michaelis " Archangeli, Anno 16to." MSS. Harl. 698. 29. p. 76. See alſo.—3ª. pag. 62.

• ſuum

ſuum Anglie; habend. et occupand. Officium et Cuſtodiam illam per ſe vel per ſuum ſufficientem deputatum, aut ſuos ſufficientes deputatos, a viceſimo ſecundo die Auguſti tunc ultimo preterito, ad terminum vite ipſius Willielmi; percipiendo in et pro dictis Officio et Cuſtodia vadia, ultimo Edwardi tercii, et primo Ricardi ſecundi, nuper regum Anglie, annis, eiſdem Officio et Cuſtodie debita et conſueta, de exitibus et proficuis Cambii et Monete, et Cunagiorum, predictorum, provenientia, per manus ſuas proprias, una cum omnibus feodis, proficuis, regardis, commoditatibus, domibus, manſionibus, juriſdictionibus, libertatibus, et aliis emolumentis, eiſdem Officio et Cuſtodie, ſeu eorum alteri, qualitercunque pertinentibus ſive ſpectantibus, in tam amplis modo et forma prout aliquis alius, ſive aliqui alii, Officium et Cuſtodiam prædicta, tempore prefati dni Edwardi tercii, aut aliquo alio tempore, melius tenuit et occupavit, tenuerunt et occupaverunt, ac in eiſdem percepit et perceperunt, prout in eiſdem literis patentibus plenius apparet. Cumque eciam Nos, per alias literas noſtras patentes gerentes datum duodecimo die Auguſti, anno regni noſtri ſeptimo, de gracia noſtra ſpeciali, dederimus et conceſſerimus dilecto Servienti noſtro Johanni Copynger ᵇ generoſo, ac pagetto officii noſtre garderobe ro-

---

ᵇ But I find an abſolute grant of this office made to him three years before, Priv. Sigill. Hen. viii. an. reg. 4. April. vi. I find alſo the following grants made to the ſaid John Copynger within the fifteen firſt years of Henry viii. viz.— Priv. Sigill. Hen. viii. an. reg. 1 April. x. He, with James Worſley, has from the king, certain tenements within the pa-

riſh

barum, tam Officium predictum Cuftodie Cambii et
Monete infra turrim noftram London, quam Cuftodiam cunagiorum auri et argenti infra Turrim predictam et alibi infra regnum noftrum Anglie predictum, habend et occupand. Officium et Cuftodiam
illam, per fe vel per fuum fufficientem deputatum,
aut per fuos fufficientes deputatos, quandocumque
primo et proxime idem officium, feu cuftodia, per
mortem predicti Willielmi, aut per furfum reddicio-

rifh of faint Auftin, in London, *ad placitum.*—Priv. Sigill. Hen.
viii. an. reg. 3. Novemb. xiii.  He has the office *Ballivi Domi-
nii de Grays-thurk, co. Effex, ad vitam.*—Bill. Signat. Hen. viii.
an. reg. 6. Octobr. xix.  He has the office *Clerici Exituum Curiæ
de Banco, cum vadio,* x l. —Priv. Sigill. Hen. viii. an. reg. 6.
Novemb. xxvii.  He has the office *Cuftodis Parci de Ockley co.
Gloucefr.*—Priv. Sigill. Hen. viii. an. reg. 8. Maii. xx.  He
has the office of keeper of the king's wardrobe within the
caftle of Nottingham, *ad vitam.*  He being then " *Pagettus
" Garderobe noftre.*"—Bill. Signat. Hen. viii. an. reg. 8. Febr.
xii.  He being *de Hofpitio noftro,* has a fpecial pardon.—Bill.
Signat. Hen. viii. an. reg. 9. Octobr. xvii.  He has a fpecial
pardon.—Priv. Sigill. Hen. viii. an. reg. 10. Jul. xvi.  He
has the office of keeper of the king's wood *de Cheftenwoode
co. Cant. cum. vadio ii d. per diem ad vitam.*—Bill. Signat. Hen.
viii. an. reg. 15. Decembr. 12.  The king grants to John
Copynger *Grometto robarum fuarum , cuftodiam placea vocat.*
Bridewell *cum Pertin. juxta Civit. London. cum vad.* iv d. *per
diem ad vitam,* from the revenues of the duchy of Cornwall.—
Bill. Signat. Hen. viii. an. reg. 7. Febr. viii.  Thomas Ryder,
and *John Copynger,* have grant of a corrody within the monaftery of Milton in Dorfetfhire.

What was the ftipend of the *Gardianus Monetæ in Turri,* does
not appear.  But John Browne has an annuity of xviij l. vj s.
viij d. in confideration of refigning this office.  Priv. Sigill.
xxiv. Maii, an. 36. Hen. vii.

nem

nem predictarum literarum patenciõn, feu quocumque alio modo, vacare contigiffet, pro termino vite
ipfius Johannis; percipiendo annuatim, in et pro
dictis Officio et Cuftodia, vadia, ultimo Edwardi
tercii, et primo Ricardi fecundi, nuper regum
Angliæ, annis, eifdem Officio et Cuftodie debita et
confueta, de exitibus et proficuis Cambii et Monete
ac cunagii predictorum provenientia, per manus
fuas proprias, una cum omnibus feodis, proficuis, regardis, commoditatibus, domibus, manfionibus, ju-
risdictionibus, libertatibus, et aliis emolumentis
eidem Officio et Cuftodie, et eorum alteri, qualitercumque pertinentibus five fpectantibus, in tam amplis modo et forma prout aliquis alius, five aliqui
alii, Officium et Cuftodium predicta, tempore prefati dni Edwardi tercii, aut aliquo alio tempore, melius tenuerit et occupaverit, tenuerint et occupaverint,
ac in eifdem percepit et perceperint, prout in eifdem
literis noftris patentibus plenius apparet. Ac JAM
intelleximus, quod prefatus Gulielmus Stafford mor-
tuus eft; cujus pretextu prefatus Johannes Copynger
officium predictum, virtute literarum noftrarum predictarum, adhuc exercuit et occupavit, et ad prefens
exercet et occupat: Ac modo prefatus Johannes Copynger in voluntate exiftit literas predictas, fibi in
forma predicta factas, nobis reftituere in cancellariam noftram, ibidem cancellandas; ea intencione
quod nos alias literas noftras patentes de officio predicto ac ceteris premiffis, Dilecto nobis THOME
POPE, Generofo, pro termino vite ipfius THOME,
concedere dignaremur. Nos premiffa confiderantes,
pro eo quod litere patentes, dicto Johanni, ut pre-

mittitur

mittitur, facte, ad prefens cancellate exiftunt, de gracia noftra fpeciali, necnon in confideracione veri et fidelis fervicii, nobis per predictum THOMAM antehac impenfi, et impofterum impendendi, dedimus et conceffimus, ac per prefentes damus et concedimus, eidem THOME, tam predictum officium Cuftodie Cambii et Monete infra Turrim noftram London, quam predictam Cuftodiam Cunagiorum auri et argenti infra Turrim predictam, et alibi infra regnum noftrum Anglie : Habend. et occupand. Officium et Cuftodiam illam per fe, vel per fufficientem deputatum fuum aut per fuos deputatos fufficientes, a fefto fancti Michaelis ultimo preterito ad terminum vite ipfius THOME : Percipiendo, in et pro dicto Officio et Cuftodia, vadia ultimo Edwardi tercii et primo Ricardi fecundi, nuper regum Anglie, annis, eifdem Officio et Cuftodie debita et confueta de exitibus et proficuis Cambii et Monete, ac Cunagiorum predictorum, provenientia, per manus fuas proprias, una cum omnibus feodis, proficuis, regardis, commoditatibus, domibus, manfionibus, jurifdictionibus, libertatibus, et aliis emolumentis, eifdem Officio et Cuftodie, feu earum alteri, qualitercumque pertinentibus five fpectantibus, in tam amplis modo et forma prout aliquis alius, five aliqui alii, Officium et Cuftodiam predicta, tempore prefati Edwardi tercii, aut aliquo alio tempore, melius tenuit et occupavit, tenuerunt et occupaverunt, ac in eifdem percepit et perceperunt. Eo quod expreffa

mencio,

mencio, etc. In Cujus, etc. T. R. apud Weftmon. xiii. die Novembr.

P. ipfum Regem et de dat. predict. etc.

*Concordat cum Orig. in Capella Rotul.*

H e n. R o o k e, *Cler. Rotul.* (1764.)

NUMB.

+++++++++++++++++++++++++++++++++++

# N U M B. IV.

Grant from Henry the eighth to Thomas Pope and William Smyth ᵃ, for
their joint exercife of the office of
Clerk of the briefs in the ftar-chamber. Decemb. 23. 1536 ᵇ.

*De Conceſs. pro Thoma* R E X omnibus ad quos,
*Pope, et Will. Smyth.* etc. falutem. cum
nos per literas noftras patentes, quarum dat. eft
quinto die Octobris, anno regni noftri vicefimo
quarto, inter alia fecerimus, conftituerimus, et or-
dinaverimus, dilectum nobis Thomam Pope, cle-
ricum omnium fingulorum brevium et proceffuum
noftrorum, coram nobis et concilio noftro in camera
noftra *Stellata* apud Weftmonafterium, tam ad fectam
noftram, quam ad fectam alicujus ligeorum noftrorum, et aliorum quorumcunque, faciendorum et
retornandorum ; viz. quod idem Thomas extunc de
tempore in tempus, durante vita fua, per fe vel per

---

ᵃ Another patent is herein recited, by which the faid king
granted to Thomas Pope the office of clerk of the briefs in
the ftar-chamber. an. reg. 24. Octobr. v. viz. A. D. 1533.

ᵇ Prim. Part. Lit. Pat. Hen. viii. Anno Reg. 26. Ex Orig. in
Capell. Rot.

fufficientem

fufficientem deputatum fuum five fufficientes deputatos fuos, omnia et fingula brevia de fubpena, atta-
chiamenta, commiffiones, tam ad examinandos teftes,
quam ad recipiendas refponfiones; nec non ad quafcumque materias finaliter determinandas, quam alias
commiffiones quafcumque, injunctiones, brevia de
executione judicii, et alios proceffus quofcumque,
cujufcumque nominis generis feu nature forent, coram nobis et confilio noftro apud Weftmon. retorna-
tos, feu quoquo modo ibidem per decretum confilii
noftri predicti qualitercunque emanantes, feu per
dicti confilii noftri decretum ibidem faciendos, Scri-
beret, faceret, et componeret, et cujuflibet [cuilibet]
hujufmodi brevium et proceffuum nomen fuum ap-
poneret feu apponi faceret; ita quod nullus clericus
cancellarie noftre predicte, neque aliquis alius in
fcribendo feu faciendo hujufmodi brevia feu proceffus, feu aliqua eorumdem, quoquomodo fe intro-
mitteret, feu intromitterent, fine licentia ipfius
Thome Pope. Habend. occupand. gaudend. et exercend. officium predictum prefato Thome Pope, per
fe, vel fufficientem deputatum fuum, five deputatos
fuos fufficientes, durante vita fua, cum vadiis et feodis [a], pro hujufmodi brevibus et proceffibus faciendis, ab antiquo debitis et confuetis abfque aliquo
compoto, feu aliquo alio, proinde nobis vel heredibus noftris reddendo, folvendo, feu faciendo, prout
in eifdem literis noftris predictis inter alia plenius

---

[c] Edmund Martyn and Thomas Powle were appointed to
this office, with an annual fee of xx l.   Bill. Signat. Hen. viii.
an. reg. 38.

contine-

continetur. Et quia prefatus Thomas in voluntate exiftit, literas noftras predictas, fibi in forma
predicta factas, quoad dictum Officium clerici
omnium et fingulorum brevium et proceffuum
noftrorum, coram nobis et confilio noftro in camera noftra *Stellata* apud Weftmon. faciendorum
et retornandorum, nobis in cancellariam noftram
reftituere ibidem cancellandas ; ea intencione, quod
nos alias literas noftras patentes prefato Thome
Pope, ac cuidam *Willielmo Smyth*, de dicto Officio
clerici proceffuum noftrorum predictorum in forma
fequenti concedere dignaremur : Nos, pro eo quod
litere noftre predicte quoad dictum Officium clerici
proceffuum noftrorum predict. prefato Thome Pope
facte, ad prefens cancellate exiftunt, de gratia noftra
fpeciali ac ex certa fciencia et mero motu noftris, fecimus, conftituimus, ordinavimus ipfos Thomam
Pope et *Willielmum Smyth* et eorum alterum diutius
viventem, clericos omnium et fingulorum brevium
et proceffuum noftrorum coram nobis et concilio
noftro in Camera noftra *Stellata* apud Weftmon. tam
ad fectam noftram quam fectam alicujus ligeorum
noftrorum et aliorum quorumcunque faciendorum et
retornandorum : viz. quod idem Thomas Pope et
Willielmus Smyth, et eorum diutius vivens, ex nunc
de tempore in tempus durante vita fua per fe vel per
fufficientem deputatum fuum, five fufficientes deputatos fuos, omnia et fingula, brevia de fubpena, atta-
chiamenta, commiffiones, tam ad examinando teftes
ad recipiend. refponfiones, necnon ad quafcunque
materias finaliter determinandas, quam alias commiffiones quafcunque cujufcumque nominis, generis, feu

nature,

nature, fuerint, coram nobis et confilio noftro apud
Weftmon. retornat. feu quoquomodo ibidem per decretum confilii noftri predicti faciend. vel e dicto
confilio noftro extra predictam cameram *Stellatam*
per decretum confilii noftri predicti qualitercumque
emanantes, feu per dicti confilii noftri decretum
ibidem faciendas, fcribant, faciant, et componant,
et cujuflibet [cuilibet] hujufmodi brevium, et proceffuum nomina fua propria, vel nomen eorum alterius
apponant feu apponat, vel faciat ; ita quod nullus
clericus cancellarie noftre predicte, neque aliquis
alius in fcribendo feu faciendo hujufmodi brevia vel
proceffus, feu aliqua eorundem, quoquomodo etc.
intromittant vel intromittat, fine licencia ipforum
Thome Pope et Willielmi Smyth. Habend. occupand. gaudend. et exercend. officium predictum prefatis Thome Pope et Willielmo Smyth, et eorum
alteri diutius viventi, per fe vel per fufficientem deputatum fuum, five deputatos fuos fufficientes, durante vita ipforum Thome Pope et Willielmi Smyth,
et eorum diutius viventis, cum vadiis et feodis pro
hujufmodi brevibus et proceffibus faciendis ab antiquo debitis et confuetis, abfque aliquo compoto feu
aliquo alio, proinde nobis vel heredibus noftris reddendo folvendo feu faciendo. Et ulterius de uberiori
gracia noftra, dedimus et licentiam conceffimus prefato Willielmo Smyth, quod ipfe omnia et fingula
brevia, proceffus, necnon literas noftras patentes quofcunque, ac alios proceffus quofcunque cujufcumque
nominis generis feu nature fuerint in eadem curia
cancellarie noftre faciendos, ex nunc durante vita fua
predicta, nomine fuo proprio, vel nomine magiftri
rotulorum,

rotulorum, aut nomine alicujus magiftri de curia
cancellarie noftre predicte pro tempore exiftentis, ad
libitum fuum fcribere, facere, et componere poffit
et valeat licite et.impune, abfque moleftatione, con-
tradictione, feu impedimento, magiftri rotulorum
cancellarie noftre pro tempore exiftentis, feu alicujus
alterius perfone, five aliquarum aliarum perfonarum
quarumcunque, in curia cancellarie noftre predicte
nunc exiftentis, aut in pofterum fiendi; proceffibus
officii clerici. corone ejufdem cancellarie noftre, fex
clericorum cancellarie noftre predicte ac clericorum
de parva baga ejufdem cancellarie noftre quoquomodo pertinentibus five fpectantibus duntaxat ex-
ceptis. Et hoc abfque fine feu feodo magno et
parvo in hanaperio cancellarie noftre predicte proinde reddendo, folvendo, feu faciendo. Et quod expreffa mencio de vero valore annuo, aut de certitu-
dine premifforum, feu eorum alicujus, aut de aliis
donis five conceffionibus per nos prefatis THOME
POPE et Willielmo Smyth ante hæc tempora factis
in prefentibus minime facta exiftit, aliquo ftatuto
actu ordinacione provifione feu reftrictione inde in
contrarium habito, facto, ordinato, five provifo :
aut aliqua alia re caufa vel materia quacumque in
aliqua re non obftante. In cujus, etc. T. R. apud
Weftmon. vicefimo tercio die Decembr.

Per ipfum regem, et data predicta auctoritate parliamenti.

*Concordat cum Orig. in Capell. Rot.*

HEN. ROOKE. (1764.)

NUMB.

✝.✝✝↓✝↓✝↓✝↑✝↓✝↓✝↓✝↓✝↑✝↓✝↓✝↓✝↑✝↓✝↑✝↓✝↓✝

# N U M B.  V.

Grant from Henry the eighth to Thomas Pope and John Lucas, of Clerk
of the Crown in Chancery ᵃ, February
xxviii. 1538 ᵇ.

*Pro Thoma Pope, et Joh.*    **R** E X omnibus ad quos,
*Lucas, de Conceſſione ad*   etc. Salutem. C U M
*Vitam.*            N o s decimo quinto die
Octobris, anno regni noſtri viceſimo quarto per
literas noſtras patentes, recitantes in eiſdem, quod
nos per alias literas. patentes, quarum quedam date
fuerunt ſexto die Marcii, anno regni noſtri tercio decimo. de gratia noſtra ſpeciali, ac ex certa ſciencia et
mero motu noſtris, dederimus et conceſſerimus dilecto nobis Radulpho Pexall ᶜ Officium Clerici Co-

---

  ᵃ Specifying a former grant of the ſame made to *Thomas Pope*
alone, Octob. xv. 1533. an. reg. 24.

  ᵇ Quint. Part. Lit. Pat. Hen. viii. An. Reg. 29°. Ex Orig.
in Capel. Rotul.

  ᶜ Bill. Signat. Hen. viii. an. reg. 6. Decembr. xvi. and an.
reg. 4. The ſaid Rad. Pexall, and Edith his wife, have
*ſpecialem liberationem.* — Bill. Signat. Hen. viii. an. reg. 11.
April. xvi. The king appoints the ſaid Ralph *Feodarium ſuum*
*co. Suthamton.*—Bill. Signat. Hen. viii. an, reg. 15. Septembr.
xvi. He has a grant of a corrody within the monaſtery of
Thetford.

rone Cancellarie Anglie : habend. occupand. et exercend. Officium illud eidem Radulpho ad terminum
vite fue, per fe, vel per fufficientem deputatum fuum,
five per fufficientes deputatos fuos, cum omnibus juribus, proficuis, commoditatibus, et emolumentis,
eidem Officio qualitercumque pertinentibus five
fpectantibus, in tam amplis modo et forma prout
Johannes Tanworth, Galfridus Marten, et Thomas
Ive, temporibus Edwardi quarti, nuper regum Anglie, ac Willielmus Porter nuper Officium illud habens tempore noftro, feparatim tenuerint, occupaverint, et exercuerint : ac eciam viginti libras annuas
prefato Radulpho, pro occupatione et exercicio Officii predicti, dederimus et concefferimus, per predictas literas noftras patentes, habend. et fingulis
annis percipiend. prefato Radulpho, durante vita
fua, de exitibus, proficuis, et revencionibus Hanaperii Cancellarie noftre predicte, per manus cuftodis
ejufdem Hanaperii pro tempore exiftentis, prout
dicti Johannes Tanworth, Galfridus Marten, et
Thomas Ive, temporibus predictis, ac Clemens
Clerke tempore bone memorie dni Henrici regis
patris noftri, ac dictus Willielmus Porter tempore

Thetford.—Bill. Signat. Hen. viii. an. reg. 16. Mar. yi. He
is made Clerk of the Crown.—Bill. Signat. Hen. viii. an.
reg. 19. [*Sine D. Menf.*] He has licence " quod ipfe pannos
" laneos latos, ac pannos laneos vocat. *Kerfeys*, ac quofcunque
" pannos, plumbum, etc. unde cuftume et fubfidia ad fum-
" mam cccc *l.* attingent, folvendo cuftumas ad finem an. quin-
" que poft eftimacionem, etc. poffit emere, etc." I find a grant
of the priory of Bradenftocke to one *Richard* Pexall. Bill. Signat. Hen. viii. an. reg. 38. Octobr. viii.

noftro,

noftro, in Officio predicto, feparatim tenuerunt, et perceperunt : necnon Liberatam Vefturam et Furruram [d], prout Ricardus Sturgyon et Thomas Ive, tempore bone memorie dni Henrici fexti nuper regis Anglie progenitoris noftri, et dictus Willielmus Porter tempore noftro, tenuerunt et perceperunt, habend. et percipiend. annuatim prefato Radulpho, pro termino vite fue, ad magnam Garderobam noftram, per manus cuftodis ejufdem Garderobe noftre pro tempore exiftentis, erga fefta Natalis Domini et

---

[d] In the reign of Edward the fourth, the expenee of *furring* the liveries or robes of the fellows of New college, Oxford, for one year, is very confiderable. Rot. Comp. COLL. Nov. Oxon. A. D. 1479. " SOLUTIO PRO FURRURA. Et Sol. pro lv " fociis pro Furrura hoc anno, xviij *l.* vj *s.* viij *d.*" The following notices alfo fhew the very general and early ufe of this article of drefs, with its prices. COMP. Coll.Winton. A. D. 1399. " CUSTUS CONSANGUINEORUM DOMINI.—In ftipendio j pel- " liparii furrantis ij togas de albo ruffetto [for two fcholars] " erga feftum Omnium Sanctorum viij *d.* In ij novis furruris " emptis pro eifdem fimul cum ftipendio pelliparii furrantis ij " togas de Liberata [Livery] DOMINI Epifcopi [fundatoris] " erga feftum Natalis Domini iij *s.* x *d.*" COMP. Coll. Winton. A. D. 1396. " LIBERATA. Et in xxj furruris albis emptis pro " LIBERATA Capellanorum [the fellows] VALECTORUM et " BALLIVORUM erga feftum Natalis Domini xxxj *s.* vj *d.*"— COMP. ibid. A. D. 1394. — " LIBERATA. Et in iiij fur- " ruris emptis pro LIBERATA Willielmi Pope [fteward] et " iij ferviencium Collegii (pret. furrure xviij *d.*) vj *s.*"— Milton, in COMUS, ufes the word *fur* for *robe* in general, in confequence of its conftantly making a part of the fcholaftic habit. ver. 707.
　　——Doctors of the ftoick *Furr.*
The poet means, thofe morofe and unfeeling teachers, who wear the gown which diftinguifhes the fect of the ftoic philofophers.

Pentecoftis,

Pentecoſtis, prout in literis illis plenius continebatur : GRANDES labores, laudabiliaque obſequia, quæ dilectus nobis THOMAS POPE, attendens negociis noſtris in Cancellaria noſtra predicta multipliciter impendebat, indiesque impendere intendebat, merito contemplantes ; de gracia noſtra ſpeciali, ac ex certa ſciencia, et mero motu noſtris, dederimus et conceſſerimus prefato THOME POPE, inter alia, predictum Officium Clerici Corone Cancellarie Anglie, habend. occupand. et exercend. Officium illud eidem THOME POPE, ad terminum vite ſue, per ſe, vel per ſufficientem deputatum ſuum, ſive ſufficientes deputatos ſuos, cum omnibus juribus, proficuis, commoditatibus, et emolumentis, eidem Officio qualitercumque pertinentibus ſive ſpectantibus, immediate poſt mortem, dimiſſionem, ſurſum reddicionem, ſeu foriſ-facturam ipſius Radulphi, vel quam cito Officium illud ad manus noſtras quocumque alio modo devenire contigiſſet, ac eciam viginti libras annuas prefato THOME POPE, pro occupacione et exercicio Officii predicti, dederimus et conceſſerimus, per eaſdem literas noſtras patentes, · habend. et ſingulis annis percipiend. prefato THOME POPE, durante vita ſua, immediate poſt mortem, dimiſſionem, ſurſum reddicionem, ſeu ſorisfacturam, ipſius Radulphi, vel quam cito Officium illud ad manus noſtras quocumque alio modo devenire contigiſſet, de exitibus, proficuis, et revencionibus, Hanaperii Cancellarie noſtre predicte, per manus cuſtodis ejuſdem Hanaperii pro tempore exiſtentis, necnon Liberatam Veſturam et Furruram, habend. et annuatim percipiend. prefato THOME POPE, pro termino vite ſue, ad magnam

Garderobam

Garderobam noſtram, per manus cuſtodis ejuſdem
Garderobe noſtre pro tempore exiſtentis, erga feſta
Natalis Domini et Pentecoſtis, immediate poſt mortem, dimiſſionem, furſum reddicionem, feu forisfac-
turam ipſius Radulphi, aut quam cito Officium illud ad manus noſtras quocumque alio modo devenire contigiſſet, in tam amplis modo et forma prout
prediſtus Radulphus Officium prediſtum tunc habens, feu aliquis alius, five aliqui alii, Officium
prediſtum ante ea tempore habens, feu habentes,
habuiſſet feu percepiſſet, vel percepiſſent, in et pro
exercicio ejuſdem, prout in literis noſtris patentibus
prediſtis, datis decimo quinto die Oſtobris anno
regni noſtri viceſimo quarto fupradiſto, plenius
continetur. Ac poſtmodum diſtus Radulphus diem
fuum clauſit extremum ; quo pretextu, Officium
illud ad prefatum THOMAM POPE, virtute literarum
noſtrarum patencium prediſtarum, devenit ; ipſeque
in Officium prediſtum, poſt mortem prediſti Radulphi intravit, illudque exercuit et occupavit, et adhuc occupat, juxta tenorem literarum noſtrarum
prediſtarum : Quas quidem literas noſtras patentes,
eidem THOME POPE de Officio prediſto faſtas, prefatus THOMAS POPE in voluntate exiſtit nobis in
Cancellariam noſtram, quoad Officium prediſtum
necnon omnia et fingula premiſſa idem Officium
concernentia, reſtituere, ibidem cancellandas ; ea intencione, quod nos alias literas noſtras patentes de
Officio illo eidem THOME POPE et cuidam Johanni
Lucas concedere dignaremur. Nos premiſſa conſi-
derantes, ac pro eo quod litere patentes prediſte,
prefato THOME POPE in forma prediſta faſte, ad

preſens

prefens cancellate exiftunt, de gratia noftra fpeciali, ac ex certa fcientia et mero motu noftris, dedimus et conceffimus, ac per prefentes damus et concedimus, prefatis THOME POPE et Johanni Lucas dictum Officium Clerici Corone Anglie; ipfofque, et eorum Utruimque, Clericos Corone Cancellarie Anglie facimus, conftituimus, et ordinamus, per prefentes : Habend. occupand. et exercend. Officium illud eifdem THOME POPE et Johanni Lucas, ad terminum vite ipforum THOME POPE et Johannis Lucas, et eorum alterius diutius viventis, per fe, vel per eorum alterum, aut per fufficientem deputatum fuum, five deputatos fuos fufficientes, cum omnibus juribus, proficuis, commoditatibus, et emolumentis, eidem Officio qualitercumque pertinentibus five fpectantibus : Ac eciam viginti libras annuas prefatis THOME POPE et Johanni Lucas, pro occupacione et exercicio Officii predicti damus et concedimus per prefentes : Habend. et fingulis annis percipiend. prefatis THOME POPE et Johanni Lucas, durante vita ipforum THOME POPE et Johannis Lucas, et eorum alterius diutius viventis, de exitibus, proficuis, et revencionibus, Hanaperii, pro tempore exiftentis : Necnon liberatam vefturam et Furruram, habend. et annuatim percipiend. prefatis THOME POPE et Johanni Lucas, pro termino vite ipforum THOME POPE et Johannis Lucas, et eorum alterius diutius viventis, ad magnam Garderobam noftram, per manus cuftodis ejufdem Garderobe noftre pro tempore exiftentis, erga fefta Natalis Domini et Pentecoftis, in tam amplis modo et forma prout predictus Radulphus, feu aliquis alius, five aliqui

alii,.

alii, Officium predictum ante hæc tempore habens, feu habentes, tenuerit five perceperit, tenuerunt vel perceperunt, in et pro exercicio Officii predicti : Et hoc abfque fine feu foedo, magno vel parvo, in Hanaperio Cancellarie noftre, feu alibi, ad opus noftrum proinde reddendo, folvendo, aut faciendo. Eo quod expreffa mencio, etc. IN CUJUS, etc. T. R. apud Weftmon. xxviii. die Februarii.

Per ipfum Regem, etc.

*Concordat cum Orig. in Capella Rotul.*

HEN. ROOKE, *Cler. Rotul.* (1764.)

T                    N U M B.

## N U M B. VI.

The Charter of Mabill Abbeſſe of Godſtowe ᵃ, made to God and oure lady
and to ſeynt Cuthberte, and to the
Priour and Convent of Dureham,
from a certeyne diche thurte over in
Bewmounte ᵇ.

T H E ſentence of this charter is, that Mabile
Abbeſſe of Godſtowe, and the convent of the
ſame place, with one aſſent and conſent, yave, etc.

ᵃ Her name was Mabile Wafre.  She was the eighth abbeſs,
and preſided about the year 1286. Willis, Mitr. Abb. ii. 178.
ᵇ From the Chartulary of the Nunnery of Godſtow. MSS.
Rawlinſ. 1300. fol. Bibl. Bodl.

Viz. All the charters and evidences of the ſaid nunnery,
from the foundation, abſtraƈted into Engliſh, by " a pore bro-
" der and welwyſher to the good Abbes of Godeſtowe, dame
" Alice Henly, and to all hyr covent." Alice Henly, or Alice
of Henly, was abbeſs about 1464. Temp. Edw. iv.  In the
prologue or preface, (fol. 1.) the writer ſays, that he tranſlates
their regiſter, or ledger book, into Engliſh, for the benefit of
religious women, who are not ſuppoſed to underſtand Latin.
It is the original, on vellum.—Tanner, (Not. Mon. fol. p.
423.) informs us, that this curious manuſcript formerly belonged to ſir James Ware, and afterwards to Henry earl of Clarendon. The nuns are here often called *Mynchons*.  So the nunnery

at

to god, and to oure lady feynt Maria, and to feynt
Cuthberte, and to the priour and convent of Dureham, and to ther fucceffoures, or their affignes, all
what fo ever they were, all ther arable londs, the·
which they had fro a diche thurte over in *Bewmonte*ᵈ,
that is to fay, fro the londe of Philipp Ho Burgeys
of Oxenforde, unto the londe that was of Roger
Semer, in the fame tilthe ᵉ, in the fubarbis of Oxenforde ; whereof thre acres lye befide the londe of
Walter Boft of the north parte, and one acre lieth
of the fouthe parte of the londe of the faid Walter
Boft, bitwene the londe of Thomas Lewes and the

at Littlemore near Oxford, is called the *Minchery*, that is, the
MINCHIONRY, or houfe of nuns. Hearne gives another in-
terpretation of *Minchery*. HIST. ANTIQ. GLASTONB. Pref. p.
xxi. edit. 1722. It was cuftomary for the bifhops in their vifi-
tations of the religious houfes, to deliver their Injunctions, not
only to the monks, but even to the female convents, drawn up in
the Latin language ; which the nuns underftood juft as well as
their Latin leafes, and had therefore a fair excufe for not obferving. Sometimes, however, but very early, they were given
to the nunneries in French.

ᵈ Some antiquaries fuppofe that Oxford was a Roman City,
called BELLOSITUM : an hypothefis almoft as chimerical as the
fable of Brutus being the founder of the univerfity. The
truth is, King Henry the firft gave his palace at Oxford, the
Norman or French appellation BEAUMONT. This was foon
latinifed into BELLOSITUM : which at length became a name
for the town in general. Others pretend, that the original
antient univerfity which flourifhed before king Alfred's time,
was ftyled BELLOSITUM, and that it ftood detached from the
prefent, in or about Saint Giles's field. This is another fiction
of the monks, which originated after the eleventh century.

ᵉ Tillage. A field.

T 2                                          londe

londe of the fame Roger Semer: and one hede of all the faid londe buttith to the walles ᶠ towarde the weſt, and another hede buttith unto the kyngis hye waye of *Bewmonte*, toward the eſt. Alſo with vi penyworth of yerely rente to be taken of one acre of the londe of Thomas Lewes, with the tythes of the fame acre, ·and the tythes of an acre of Walter Boſte in the fame tylthe; with all his pertynantis, longyng ᵍ bothe to the londe, and to the rent and tythes. They willed alſo and graunted to the fame priour and covent aforefaid, that they ſhold have whatfoever right they had in voide groundes befide ʰ*Peralowfe Hall* in *Horfemonger ſtrete* ⁱ. To be had and to be hold to the priour and convent of Dureham, and to ther fucceſſoures or ther aſſigns, All of Them, and ther church of Godſtowe, frely, quyetly, holy, wele, and in peafe, for ever; with all liberties, efchetes, cuſtomes, tithes, eyfementis ᵏ, with en-

ᶠ Of the city.

ᵍ Belonging.

ʰ Aula Periculofa.

ⁱ Where a large ſtone-edifice now ſtands called *Kettel-Hall*; built by Dr. Ralph Kettel, prefident of Trinity college, about 1615. For building this Kettel-hall, a houfe was pulled down inhabited by George Cawfield, recorder of Oxford, who was buried in faint Mary Magdalene's church, xx. Octob. 1603. MSS. Wood, Muf. Afhm. Collectan. e *Regiſtr. Parochial. Civitat.* Oxon. D. 5. 4to. During Cromwell's ufurpation, fuch of the academics as had been famous for acting plays in the late king's time, ufed to act plays by ſtealth in this Hall. Wood's LIFE, vol. 2. p. 148. edit. 1772.

ᵏ Eafments.

tryngis

tryngis and goyng owte, aud futes of courte; and
all other thynges and actions in only wife longyng to
the faid londe, rente and tythes, with all ther pertynantis. Yelding thereof yerely to them, and to
ther fucceffoures, or to their affignes whofoever the
be, x s. of filver, and at michelmaffe v s. of filver,
for all fervyce, cuftoms, exactions, futis of courtes,
and fecular demaundes. And yf. hit happen the faid
priour and convent, and ther fucceffoures, or ony
maner affignes of them, to be behynde, of [or] to
faile in the payment of the faid yerely rente, (that
god forbede;) the forefaide priour and convente
grauntith for them and their fucceffoures, and all
maner of affignes, that hit fholde be wele lawfull
to the forefaid abbeffe and convente of Godftowe
and to ther fucceffoures, or mynyftris or fervauntis,
who foever the be, to entre, deftrayne, and nyme[1],
all tenements that they had, or myght have, in the
fubarbis of Oxenforde towarde the northe fro the
the fornamed diche thurte over *Bewmounte*, unto *Horfemonger ftrete* alfo; and all the londes aforefaid, from
day unto day, for the forefaid yearely x s. without
ony agayn fayinge[m] or lette of the forefayde priour,
covente, fucceffours, or affignes, whofoever they be,
tille hit were fully fatisfyed to the fayde abbeffe and
covente of Godeftowe, and to ther fucceffoures and
affignes, all of the forfaide rente. And the forefaid

---

[1] To take for a pledge. To feize. See Dufrefne, LAT. GL.
V. Namium, Namiare, &c. And Lye's Sax. Goth. Dictionary,
V. Niman.

[m] Gainfaying.

abbeffe

abbeſſe and covente of Godeſtowe, and ther ſucceſſoures, warrantized, aquyted, and defended for the
forſaide rente of x ſ. all the foreſaide londes, ſixe
penyworthe of yercly rent, and tythes of ii acres of
Walter Boſt, and Thomas Lewes, with all ther pertynantis as hit is ſaid afore, to the foreſaide priour
and covente of Durham, and to ther ſucceſſoures,
and to ther aſſignes, ayenſt all men and women.
Furthermore, the ſaid abbeſſe and covente of Godeſtowe willed and graunted for them and ther ſucceſſoures, or aſſignes, whych ſoever they ſholde be,
that they ſholde be quyte from yevyng all tythes,
bothe of more and leſſe [n], in the forſaid covente for
ever. And for this gyfte, etc. the foreſaide prior
and covente yaf to them aforehandes xx marke of
ſterlyngis. In witneſs of all thoſe thyngis, &c. [o]

[n] Great and Small Tythes.

[o] The original is in Theſauriar. coll. Div. Joh. Bapt. Oxon.
among other inſtruments of Godſtowe nunnery. In an abſtract
from which, Wood gives the names of the witneſſes, viz.
" Phil. de Ho, tunc Majori Oxon. Henr. Howayne, Johan.
" de Ho, Will. le Specer, Tho. Sowey." Muſ. Aſhm. 8513.—
Philip de Ho, O, or Eu, occurs mayor of Oxon, 1276, 1286,
1295, 1296, 1299. A. Wood's *Cat. of Mayors, etc. of Oxford*,
pag. 66. ſeq. MSS. ut ſupr. D. 7.

About the ſame time, two plots of ground lying in Magdalene pariſh, were confirmed to them by the convent of ſaint
Frideſwide's. [See Br. Twyne, MSS. ℛ. p. 259.] And in 1291,
their precincts and poſſeſſions were enlarged by grants of more
ground lying in and about their houſe. Wood's CITY of Oxford, MSS. Muſ. Aſhmol. All this they enjoyed till their
diſſolution.

N U M B.

✝✝✝✝✝✝✝✝✝✝✝✝✝✝✝✝✝✝✝✝✝✝✝✝✝✝✝✝✝✝✝✝

## N U M B.  VII.

Grant from Henry the eighth of *Barnard College*, with half the Grove of Durham College, to the Dean and Chapter of Chrift Church, Oxford, Decemb. 11. 1548 [a].

R E X, etc. Salutem, fciatis quod nos, de gracia noftra fpeciali, ac ex certa fciencia et mero motu noftris, Dedimus et conceffimus, ac per præfentes damus et conceffimus, decano et capitulo ecclefie cathedralis Chrifti Oxon, ex fundatione noftra, inter multa alia Totum illum fcitum, feptum, circuitum, ambitum, et precinctum, totius illius collegii, vulgaritur nuncupati BARNARDES COLLEDGE [b] in civitate noftra Oxon, cum fuis juribus

[a] In Capell. Rot.

[b] Bernard college, (now faint John's) was inhabited by ftudents, under that name, in the year 1549; and, as I conjecture, two or three years afterwards. I find a *Manciple of Bernard college* fuing for *battels* in the vice-chancellor's court, 1549. Regiftr. cur. cancell. Oxon. G G. fol. 37. Its laft prefect, called *Provifor*, before its endowment by fir Thomas Whyte, was Dr. Kennall. It had been an academical convent of Bernardines, built by archbifhop Chichely. Pat. ann. 15. Henr. vi. membr. 24. [A. D. 1437.] The king fets forth, that

whereas

membris, et pertinenciis univerfis; Ac omnia et fingula domos, edificia, ftructuras, ortos, pomeria,
gardina, ftagna, vivaria, terras, et folum noftra,
infra dictum fcitum, feptum, circuitum, ambitum,
feu precinctum, dicti collegii vocati BARNARDES
COLLEGE, exiftentia; ac omnia et fingula, muros,
menia, foffata, parietes, et cetera inclofamenta quecunque, eundem fcitum, feptum, circuitum, ambitum feu precinctum, ambientia aut quocunque modo
includentia : Ac eciam Dimidium, five Medietatem,
totius illius Horti collegii vocati *Durham Colledge* in
parochia fancte Marie Magdalene in fuburbiis dicte
civitatis Oxon, collegio vocato *Durham Colledge* dudum fpectantis et pertinentis : Habend. tenend. et
gaudend. predictum fcitum, et cetera Premiffa predicta, eifdem Decano et capitulo, et fucceſſoribus
fuis imperpetuum. Tefte R. apud Weftmon. xi. die
Decembris, anno R. Hen. octavi xxxviii.

whereas Henry [Chicheley] archbifhop of Canterbury intends
to found " quoddam congruum et notabile manfum collegiale,
" in honorem gloriofiffimæ virginis Mariæ fanctique Bernardi,
" in vico vulgariter nuncupato *Northgates ftrete*, vel faltem
" prope dictum vicum, in parochia fanctæ Mariæ Magdalenæ,
" juxta et extra portam borealem villæ Oxon, in folo ipfius ar
" chiepifcopi continente quinque acras terræ vel circiter, quæ
" de nobis tenentur in capite, &c." In a roll, in the Court
of augmentations, the fite and garden of Bernard college containing two acres, with all its edifices, and the garden of
Durham college, is valued at xx s. per ann. Pyx. S. FRIDES
WYDE. OXON.

N U M B.

✝✦✝✦✝✝✦✝✦✝✝✦✝✦✝✦✝✝✦✝✦✝✝✦✝✦✝✝✦✝✝✦✝✝✦✝✦✝✝

# N U M B.    * VII *.

## Part of the Charter of foundation of the Dean and Chapter of Durham cathedral, given by King Henry the eighth, A. D. 1541 [a].

" **D**AMUS etiam, ac per præfentes concedimus, præfato Decano et Capitulo, totum illud fci- tum, circuitum, ambitum, et præcinctum, cujuf- dam nuper Collegii vocati *Durefme College* infra vil- lam Oxon, in com. noftro Oxon. Ac totam illam ·ecclefiam five capellam, campanile, cœmeterium, ejufdem nuper collegii, una cum omnibus domibus, ædificiis, pomariis, gardinis, hortis, et folo, tam in- tra quam extra, juxta et prope fcitum, ambitum, et præcinctum ejufdem nuper collegii. Ac totum illud tenementum in HAMBORGWE in dicto com. noftro Oxon. Ac totam illam rectoriam et ecclefiam nof- tram de FRAMPTON in com noftro Lincoln. Ac to- tam illam rectoriam et ecclefiam noftram de RODING- TON in com. noftro Nottingham. Ac omnes illas rectorias et ecclefias noftras de FISHLAKE, BOSSAL,

---

[a] In Archivis Eccl. Cathedr. Dunelm. MS. Et in Capell. Rotul. viz. Lit. Pat. Henr. viii. ann. reg. 33.

et

et BRANTINGHAM, in com. noftro Ebor. Ac quandam annuitatem five annualem redditum quatuor
librarum exeuntium et annuatim percipiendarum de
rectoria five ecclefia noftra de NORTH ALLERTON
in dicto com. noftro Ebor, ad fefta Annunciatio-
nis beatæ MARIÆ VIRGINIS et fancti MICHAELIS
ARCHANGELI, annuatim folvendum. Ac totam illam
penfionem, five annuum redditum, fedecim librarum
exeuntium et annuatim percipiendarum de VICARIO
de NORTH ALLERTON prædicti pro tempore exif-
tente. Quæ quidem rectoriæ, annuitates, et penfio-
nes prædictæ dicti nuper Collegii, prædicto nuper
MONASTERIO fancti Cuthberti Dunelmenfis prædicti
fpectabant et pertinebant, aut parcellæ et poffeffiones
ejufdem nuper COLLEGII et dicti nuper MONASTERII
extiterunt ᵇ."

ᵇ Durham College, after its diffolution, was inhabited for
fome time by Walter Wryght archdeacon of Oxford, who pre-
fided in it over a few ftudents. But before or about the year
1552, it was totally defolated, and the buildings being intirely
neglected, began to be ruinous. Wood, MSS. Muf. Afhmol.
D. 3. pag. 208. See alfo Regiftr. CUR. CANCELL. Oxon. G G.
fol. 55. 68. 76. And Stevens, MONAST. i. 343. Alfo, AP-
PEND. Numb. viii. Wood tells us, that before the reign of
Edward the fixth, " Collegium vero Dunelmenfe et Bernardi-
" num [now faint John's college] vacua pæne jacebant . . . .
" unde canilia luftra, joco populari, vocabantur : ufquedum
" THOMÆ POPE et THOMÆ WHYTE militum, pietate, latifun-
" diis effent locupletata." HIST. ANTIQ. Univ. Oxon. i. 281.
col. 1. [From Br. Twyne, MSS. ARCHIV. Oxon. 8. fol. 235.
4to.] And Camden BRITANN. p. 271. DOBUN. edit. 1607.
fol. viz. " Noftra itidem memoria, ut novis etiam beneficiis Mu-
" fas complecterentur, Thomas Pope vir ordinis equeftris Du-
" nelmenfe collegium, et Thomas White civis fenatorque Lon-
                                                    " dinenfis,

" dinenfis, et equeftris itidem ordinis, Bernardi collegium, quæ
" fuis ruderibus fepulta jacuerunt, excitarunt, novis ædificiis
" inftaurarunt, latifundiis locupletarunt, et novis nominibus
" exornarunt. Hoc enim S. Joanni Baptiftæ, illud Sacrofanctæ
" Trinitati dicarunt." Doctor T. Cay thus fpeaks of Durham
college, in a paffage which for the elegance of its latinity alone
deferves to be tranfcribed. " Fuit aula illa de qua mentio eft
" apud eundem Aungervillium, aula Dunelmenfis, intra paucos
" annos Collegium Dunelmenfe, et hodie Collegium Trinitatis,
" vocata. Hanc bonus ille epifcopus primus erexit, conftructa
" inibi bibliotheca optimis libris referta, ceteraque ibi difpo-
" fuit juxta formam illam a fe in Philobiblo defcriptam, qui
" deinceps habitus eft ejufdem fundator. Donec regnante Ri-
" cardo ejus appellationis fecundo, Ricardus Hatefelde epifco-
" pus item Dunelmenfis ordinaret, ut fecularibus aulæ Aunger-
" villianæ Scholafticis certus monachorum Dunelmenfium
" numerus adjungeretur, qui Oxoniam, ftudendi caufa, Prioris
" femper Dunelmenfis nutu perpetuis poft temporibus aman-
" daretur, domumque revocaretur. His ita profpectum eft ab
" Hatefeldo, ut datis abunde ad illorum fuftentationem reddi-
" tibus, fine ullis monafterii impenfis ibi ftuderent. Quo bene-
" ficio ita fibi monachos demeruit, ut, oblivioni tradito Aunger-
" villii nomine, folus ille collegii fundator ufque ad monafte-
" riorum everfionem haberetur. Hodie tamen infigne Musaeum
" fub nomine, ut dixi, Trinitatis, a bonæ memoriæ Domino
" Thoma Pope equeftris ordinis viro refufcitatum; qui id
" longe quam antea præftantius, atque adeo ftudiofis quos fre-
" quentes alit commodius effecit. In ejus collegii bibliotheca,
" poftremis Henrici octavi annis, vidi ac perlegi hunc Aunger-
" villii librum cui Philobibli titulum indidit, eundem ipfum
" indubie, quem ipfemet bibliothecæ illi vivus contulerat."
Thomæ Caii Vindiciæ Antiquitat. Acad. Oxon. edit. Hearne,
Oxon. 1730. vol. ii. pag. 432.

\*₊\* Catalogue of the Wardens of Durham College.

The governors of this houfe were not ftyled Wardens, but
Priors, till the foundation was fully fettled. They were appointed by the Priors of the cathedral-convent of Durham.

I. John

I. John of Beverly occurs about the year 1333. See Stevens, Monast. i. p. 340. Twyne, Apol. Acad. Oxon. p. 170. edit. 1609.

II. William Appulby was appointed by John of Hemingburgh, Prior of Durham, Aug. 14. 1404. Stevens, ubi fupr. He was buried in the college. Wood, MSS. Muf. Ashmol. D. 19. 4to. It may be doubted whether he was the fecond.

III. Thomas Rome occurs in 1413. Stevens, ibid. He was Prior of Perfhore in Worcefterfhire. Reyner, p. 175. He was buried in Durham-college. Wood, MSS. ut fupr.

IV. William Ebchester, D. D. occurs about the year 1440. Stevens, ubi fupr. He was made Prior of Durham in 1446, and dying in 1456, was buried in his church. Wharton, Angl. Sacr. i. 777. See Rites of Durham Cathedral, &c. by I. D. 1672. p. 50.

V. Robert Ebchester. He was made bachelor of divinity, Dec. 24. 1469. Being then ftyled *Gardianus Collegii Dunelm.* Wood, MSS. Muf. Ashm. D. 3. fol. 126. Compare Stevens, ubi fupr. p. 343. col. 2. He was made Prior of Durham in 1478, and died and was buried there in 1484. Wharton, ut fupr. p. 778. 789. Rites of Durham, ut fupr. p. 51.

VI. Thomas Swawell occurs in 1502. Stevens, ut fupr. p. 342. He was made doftor in divinity, in 1501. Wood, Fast. Oxon. i. p. 4.

VII. Thomas Castell occurs in 1511. Stevens, ubi modo fupr. He was made bachelor of divinity at Oxford in 1510. Wood, MSS. Muf Ashmol. D. 3. fol. 15. And D. D. in 1511. Wood, Fast. i. 18. 20. He muft not be confounded with *Thomas* Caftell, who died Prior of Durham in 1519. Wharton, ut fupr. p. 781.

VIII. Hugh Whithead fucceeded Caftell in 1512. Proceded bachelor of divinity at Oxford Mar. 14. 1511. Wood, Ath. Oxon. Faft. i. 17. See alfo MSS. Wood, E. 9. ubi fupr. viz. Oppon. in Theology. Created Doftor, May 13. 1513. Ath. Oxon. i. Faft. 20. Appointed Prior of Durham in 1524.

1524. During his priorate, which he held twenty four years, he rebuilt many houses at Bear-park; and at Pittintown erected a new hall called the *Prior's hall*, with other edifices annexed. He was the last Prior of Durham; and, on the change of the foundation by Henry the eighth, was constituted the first Dean in 1541. He died in 1547, and was buried in the church of the Minories at London. Wharton, ubi supr. p. 782. Wood, ATH. OXON. i. Fast. 20. Willis's Cathedrals, DURHAM, p. 252. RITES of DURHAM, p. 92.

IX. EDWARD HENMARSH occurs in 1527. Stevens, ut supr. p. 342. He was made S. T. B. in 1513. ATH. OXON. i. Fast. p. 20. See Wood, MSS. Mus. Ashmol. D. fol. 177. 180. He probably presided till the final Dissolution of this college in 1540.

## N U M B. VIII.

Grant of Durham College in Oxford, from Edward the fixth, to George Owen, and William Martyn. Dat. Feb. iv. 1553 ª.

EDWARDUS fextus dei gratia, etc. omnibus ad quos, etc. falutem. Sciatis, quod nos in confideratione boni, veri, fidelis, et acceptabilis fervicii, per fervientem noftrum dilectum, Georgium Owen, armigerum, unum medicorum noftrorum, etc. de gratia noftra fpeciali, etc. Dedimus et conceffimus, etc. prefato Georgio Owen, etc. Ac etiam totum illud meffuagium, five nuper Collegium noftrum, vocatum DURHAM COLLEDGE, in univ. Oxon. Ac totum illud Scitum, Circuitum, Ambitum, et Precinctum dicti nuper collegii vocati DURHAM COLLEDGE in univ. Oxon. predicta, cum fuis juribus, membris, et pertinenciis, univerfis: Ac omnia et fingula, domos, edificia, ortos, pomaria, gardinos, terras, tenementa, et folum noftrum, infra dictum fcitum, circuitum, feu precinctum ejufdem nuper

---

ª **Ex copia** quadam abbreviat. In Thefauriario Coll. Trin. **Oxon.** Compared with the original by fir Thomas Pope.

collegii

collegii exiftentia, ac modo, vel nuper, in tenura
five occupatione Walteri Wryght [b], doctoris in jure
civili, vel affignatorum fuorum : Necnon omnes
illos bofcos noftros, et arbores noftras, vulgariter
nuncupatas ELMES, crefcentes et exiftentes in *le*
BACKSIDE dicti nuper collegii, vocati DURHAM
COLLEDGE, et eidem nuper collegio dudum fpectan-
tes et pertinentes: Ac terram, fundum, et folum,
eorundem bofcorum et arborum, habend. tenend. et
gaudend. etc. ac prædictum fcitum dicti nuper collegii, prefato Georgio Owen, et Willielmo Martyn, ac
hæredibus et affignatis ipfius Georgii imperpetuum [c].

[b] About the year 1540, he was principal of Peckwater-inn
at Oxford. In 1543, he was made archdeacon of Oxford,
while the cathedral fubfifted at Ofeney. Inftalled a prebendary
of Winchefter cathedral, Jan xi. 1559. A prebendary of
North-Grantham in the church of Salifbury. He was feveral
times a commiffary, and vifitor, of the univerfity of Oxford.
Wood, ATH. i. F. 63. Willis's CATHEDRALS, cath. Oxford,
p. 447. Gale's WINCHESTER, p. 119. On the ruin or demolition of Durham college, where he lived a few years after its
diffolution, he retired to Exeter college, where he died, May x.
1561. viz. " D. pientiffimus Walterus Wryght, mortem obiit
" in fuo infra collegium noftrum, cubiculo, anno pofteriore
" [viz. 1561.] x. Maii. Et voti compos, in facra æde B. M.
" in Oxon. fepultus eft. Qui ex teftamento nobis dono dedit
" craterem unum deauratum, feptem libris ponder. cum iii.
" libr. in pecunia." E REGISTR. coll. Exon. Oxon. fol. 76.

[c] I have before obferved [LIFE, pag. 115.] that all the
eftates of Durham college, together with its *fite* here fpecified,
were granted by Henry viii. May xii. 1541, to the new dean
and chapter of Durham. The faid eftates ftill remain in the
poffeffion of that cathedral. But how or when the faid *fite* reverted to the crown, fo as to be granted by Edward the fixth to
Owen

Tenend. etc. etc. ac prædictum fcitum dicti nuper collegii, etc. de nobis, hæredibus et fucceſſoribus noſtris, in focagio, ut de Honore noſtro de EWELME in dicto com. noſtro Berks ᵈ. per fidelitatem tantum, et non in capite. Ac reddend. annuatim nobis, etc. de et pro prædicto fcitu et terris dicti nuper collegii vocati DURHAM COLLEDGE, viginti fex folidos et octo denarios legalis monetæ Angliæ, etc. ad feſtum fancti Michaelis archangeli fingulis annis folvendos, pro omnibus redditibus, ſerviciis, et demandis quibuſcunque, proinde nobis, hæredibus, vel fucceſſoribus noſtris, quoquomodo reddendis, folvendis, vel faciendis, etc. In cujus Rei, etc. Teſte meipfo apud Weſtmon. quarto die Feb. anno regni noſtri feptimo.

" *Exam. et concordat cum Liter. pat. remanent. penes*
" *dom. G. Owen.* THO. POPE" ᵉ.

Jur. in *Officio* ᶠ Johannis Pycharell auditoris ibid ᵍ.

Owen and Martyn, I know not ; unleſs this refumption was made, when the biſhoprick of Durham was diſſolved by Edward the fixth, An. reg. vii. 1552.

ᵈ In Oxfordſhire. Theſe inaccuracies are not uncommon in antient inſtruments.

ᵉ Manu fua.

ᶠ Lege, *Officina*.

ᵍ Sc. Scaccarii.

NUMB.

✛✛✛✛✛✛✛✛✛✛✛✛✛✛✛✛✛✛✛✛✛✛✛✛✛✛✛✛✛✛✛✛

## N U M B.   IX.

Purchafe of Durham college aforefaid,
by fir Thomas Pope, of G. Owen
and W. Martyn. Dat. Feb. xx. 1554ᵃ.

OMNIBUS Chrifti fidelibus, ad quos hæc
præfens carta noftra indentata pervenerit,
Georgius Owen, armiger, unus medicorum regis et
reginæ ᵇ, et Willielmus Martyn, generofus, falutem
in domino fempiternam. Sciatis nos prefatos G.
Owen, et W. Martyn, pro quadam competenti pe-
cuniæ fumma nobis per THOMAM POPE de Tytten-

---

ᵃ Thefaur. ut fupr.

ᵇ GEORGE OWEN was a man of great learning, and eminent in his profeffion. He was fucceffively phyfician to Henry
the eighth, Edward the fixth, and Philip and Mary. He attended Henry on his death-bed, who made him a witnefs to
his laft will, in which he bequeathed him 100 l. He was alfo
prefent at the death of Edward the fixth, and attended the
princefs Elizabeth in her imprifonment. Leland has complimented him in his ENCOMIA of the learned men of thofe times.
Edit. 1589. p. 96. He died 1558. Befide the grant of Durham college from Edward the fixth, he received with its adjoining eftates a grant of the nunnery of Godftowe, near Oxford ;
the buildings of which he converted into a dwelling-houfe,
with fome few alterations and improvements.

U                              hanger

hanger in Co.Hertf. militem,præ manibus bene et fideliter perfoluta, unde fatemur nos et quemlibet noftrum fore plenarie fatisfaƈt. et content. eundemque Thomam Pope, militem, heredes, et adminiftratores fuos inde acquietat. et exornerat. effe per præfentes, Dediffe et conceffiffe, et præfenti carta confirmaffe prefato Thomæ Pope, militi, totum illud meffuagium, five nuper collegium noftrum, vocatum *Dyrram College* in univ. Oxon. Ac totum illum fcitum, circuitum, ambitum et præcinƈtum noftrum, diƈti nuper collegii, vocati *Dyrram College* in univ. Oxon. prediƈta; cum fuis juribus, membris, et pertinenciis univerfis: Ac omnia et fingula, domos, edificia, ortos, pomaria, gardina, terras, tenementa, et folum noftrum, infra diƈtum fcitum, feptum, circuitum, feu præcinƈtum, ejufdem nuper collegii exiftentia, ac modo, vel nuper in tenura five occupatione Walteri Wryght, doƈtoris in jure civili, vel affignatorum fuorum : Necnon omnes illos bofcos noftros, et arbores noftras, vulgariter vocatas *Elmes*, crefcentes et exiftentes in *le Backfide* diƈti nuper collegii vocati *Dyrram College*, et eidem nuper collegio dudum fpeƈtantes et petinentes: Ac terram, fundum, et folum noftrum eorundem bofcorum et arborum [c] :

---

[c] The grove of Durham college was much larger at the diffolution of the faid college, than at the time of this purchafe. Part of it was rented by Lernard College, now faint John's. Bernard college was diffolved by Henry the eighth, who gave the faid college and its appurtenances, together with a part, called *half*, of Durham college grove, to his new cathedral of Chrift church, 1545. This part, or *half*, I prefume, was *that* which had been rented, as above, by Bernard college, and

was

Ac reverſionem et reverſiones quaſcunque omnium ac
ſingulorum præmiſſorum, et cujuſlibet inde parcellæ,
necnon redditus et annualia proficua quæcunque
reſervata ſuper quibuſcunque dimiſſionibus et con-
ceſſionibus de præmiſſis, ſeu de aliqua inde parcella

was therefore conſidered, at the time of this donation, as its
uſual appendage. In the year 1555, ſir Thomas Whyte, pur-
chaſing from Chriſt-church the ſaid Bernard college, purchaſed
likewiſe of the ſame, the part or *half* of Durham college grove
above-mentioned. This part, or *half*, is what now makes the
outer grove, and perhaps much more, of ſaint John's college.
See Wood, Hiſt. Ant. ii. 252.—Stevens, Monaſt. ii. 53. Wood,.
MSS. Muſ. Aſhm. 8513.—And eſpecially, Numb. VII. Append.
Thus the outlet, or *grove*, in the text, included only what remained to Durham college after the aforeſaid alienation made
by Henry the eighth. When Trinity college and ſaint John's
were founded, the two founders jointly erected the ſtone wall
which now ſeparates the groves, or gardens, of the two colleges. That this was done by agreement between them both, I
collect from the words of a letter from ſir Thomas Pope, to the
preſident, dat. Jul. xxiv. 1557, in which, he deſires the preſident to beſpeak for him, a certain large quantity of ſtone, " for
" ſo much I think I ſhall occupie *for my part* of Mr. [ſir Tho-
" mas] White's wall." Afterwards, ſir T. Pope ſurrounded the
whole grove of Trinity college with a ſtone-wall: and I find expended thereon cxx, *l.* The ſtone was purchaſed of William
Freere of Oxford, who, with Agnes his wife, got poſſeſſion of
the houſes called Dominican and Franciſcan Friers at Oxford,
ſoon after their diſſolution, and demoliſhing the buildings ſold
the materials. See LIFE, p. 125. . And Wood, Hiſt. Antiq.
Univ. Oxon. lib. i. pag. 66. col. 2. William's elder brother
Edward was afterwards ſettled at Water-Eaton near Oxford.
Arms in the windows of the houſe of Mr. Freer, at Oxford,
are deſcribed by Lee, 1575. ARMS, & Muſ. Aſhmol. MSS.
Codd. A. Wood. D. 14.

U 2 factis:

factis : Adeo plene, libere, et integre, ac in tam
amplis modo et forma, prout illuſtriſſimus princeps,
nuper rex Edwardus, ejus nominis ſextus, prædictum
meſſuagium ſive collegium et cetera ſingula premiſſa
nobis prefato G. Owen et W. Martyn, ac heredibus
et aſſignatis Mei prefati Georgii imperpetuum, per
literas ſuas patentes, ſub magno ſigillo ſuo Angliæ
confectas, gerentes datum apud Weſtmon. iv. Feb.
anno nuper regni ſui ſeptimo, dedit et conceſſit.
Adeo plene ac libere et integre, ac in tam amplis
modo et forma, prout prædictum meſſuagium ſive
collegium ac cetera premiſſa modo habemus ſeu tene-
mus, virtute et vigore literarum patentium prædictarum dicti nuper dom. regis, aut aliter quocumque modo.   Habend. tenend. et gaudend. predictum
meſſuagium ſive collegium vocatum *Dyrram College*
in dicta univ. Oxon. et cætera premiſſa, cum eorum
pertinentiis univerſis prefato Thomæ Pope, militi,
heredibus, et aſſignatis ſuis, ad ſolum Opus et Uſum
ipſius Thomæ Pope, militis, hæredum et aſſignato-
rum ſuorum, imperpetuum. Tenend. per redditus et
ſervicia inde prius debita et de jure conſueta.  Et nos
vero præfatus G. Owen, ac W. Martyn, ac hæredes
et aſſignati Mei præfati Georgii, dictum meſſuagium
ſive collegium vocatum *Dyrrham Colledge*, et cætera
præmiſſa, cum pertinentiis præfato Thomæ Pope,
ac hæredibus et aſſignatis ſuis, contra nos et hæredes
noſtros warrantizabimus et imperpetuum defendemus.
per præſentes. Et cum per prædictas lit. pat. quidam annualis redditus viginti ſex ſolidorum et duorum denariorum reſervatus ſit, annuatim ſolvendus
dicto nuper regi hæredibus et ſucceſſoribus ſuis, ſi-

cut

cut ibidem plenius apparet, Sciatis me prefatum G. Owen, conveniſſe et conceſſiſſe per præſentes, pro me, hæredibus, executoribus, ac adminiſtratoribus meis cum præfato Thoma Pope, hæredibus et aſſignatis ſuis, non modo quod eos et eorum quemlibet indempnes et ſine dampno et detrimento de ſolucione dicti redditus, et cujuſlibet inde parcellæ, de cætero imperpetuum ſervabo, ac de omnibus oneribus et incumberantiis quibuſcunque dictum collegium et cætera præmiſſa, ſeu eorum aliquod concernentibus per ipſos Georgium et Willielmum, ſeu eorum alterum, antehac habit. fact. aut præmiſſis, ſed etiam, quod quandocunque et quoties contigerit, dictum redditum, ſeu aliquam inde parcellam, levari de prædicto collegio, ſitu et cæteris præmiſſis præconceſſis ſeu de aliqua inde parcella, quod tunc et toties, ego præfatus Georgius, et hæredes ac aſſignati mei forisfaciemus prædicto Thomæ hæredibus et aſſignatis ſuis quadraginta Solidos nomine Pænæ: Et quod tunc et toties bene licebit prædicto Thomæ Pope hæredibus et aſſignatis ſuis, in omnia maneria, terras, tenementa, et hæreditamenta mea infra com. Oxon. et Berkſ. intrare, et diſtringere, tam pro prædictis redditu, ſeu arreragiis ejuſdem, aut aliqua inde parcella, ſic ut præfertur, aliquo tempore poſthac de eodem collegio, et cæteris, præmiſſis, levatis, quam pro foriſfactura pænæ prædictæ, levatis, quam ac pro omnibus expenſis et coſtagiis per eundem Thomam Pope, hæredes, vel aſſignatos ſuos, per circa et concernentibus ſolucionem dicti redditus, pænæ, aut arreragionem ejuſdem, ſuſtinendis ac ſolvendis : Et

U 3                          diſtric-

diſtrictiones ſic captas abducere et aſportare, et penes
ſe retinere, quouſque idem Thomas Pope, hære-
des et aſſignati ſui, ſint inde plenarie ſatisfacti et contenti. Sciatis inſuper, nos prefatos G. Owen, et W.
Martyn, feciſſe, ordinaſſe, conſtituiſſe, deputaſſe, et in
loco noſtro poſuiſſe dilectos nobis in Chriſto, *Willielmum Hemerford* [d], theologiæ bachalarium, *Johannem
Heywood* [e], *Edwardum Love*, et *Johanem Milwarde* [f], gene-

[d] Concerning whom I find nothing more, than that he was
of Oxford; where he took the degree of A. B. in December,
1558, as *Capellanus ſecularis*. Alſo Mar. xx, 1541, the degree of maſter of arts. MSS. A. Wood, Muſ. Aſhmol. E. 29.
And E. 6.

[e] Probably the ſame whom ſir T. Pope calls, in his Will,
his " trewe frynd," and to whom he bequeathes a memorial.
See Life, p. 164. *John Heywood* is alſo one of the witneſſes to
the codicil of ſaid Will.

[f] Sir T. Pope, in his Will, calls this *John Milwarde* his
*Clerk*, and leaves him a legacy of xx *l*. He appears to have
been related to Dame Elizabeth Powlett, widow of ſir T.
Pope, and was probably of her neighbourhood in Derbyſhire.
Ex Teſtam. More of the name are mentioned in her Will.
William and Robert are witneſſes to her deed of gift at Burton
upon Trent. Life, p. 200. Sir T. Pope, in a letter to the preſident of his college, without date, ſpeaks of " Henry Mil-
" warde my friend ;" and one of that name occurs among the
firſt Famuli of the college at the foundation. Comp. Burſſ.
1556.--7. As to the ſaid *John Milwarde*, mentioned in the
text, he was, beſide what has been already ſaid, one of the
witneſſes to the codicil of ſir T. Pope's will. He was alſo a
witneſs to the inſtrument concerning the dirge at Much-Waltham. Life, p. 132. On ſir T. Pope's death he became ſteward,
or receiver, to ſir Hugh Powlett. Regiſtr. prim. coll. Trin.
fol. 24. b. In 1561, Decemb. vii, the ſaid college appointed

rofos, noftros veros et legitimos attornatos, conjunctim
etdivifim, ad intrandum et ingrediendum in prædictum
meffuagium, five collegium et cætera præmiffa et in
quamlibet inde parcellam, ac plenam et pacificam po-
feffionem ftatum et feifinam inde, vice et nominibus
noftris, capiendum : Et poft hujufmodi poffeffionem
ftatum et feifinam inde fic captam et habitam, deinde eadem ad dandum et deliberandum præfato Tho-
MÆ Pope, militi, aut fuo in ea parte attornato, fecundum vim, formam, et effectum hujus prefentis
carte noftre: Ratum ac firmum habentes, et habituri,
totum et quicquid attornati noftri fecerint, feu eorum
aliquis fecerit, in premiffis. · In cujus rei teftimo-
nium huic prefenti carte indentate partes prædicte fi-

ed him their attorney in a certain law-fuit, calling him in
their Appointment, " Joannem Milwarde generofum, clariffimi
" Hugonis Paulet militis famulum." Regiftr. ut fupr. fol. 29.
He·occurs often as an agent between the faid college and Dame
Powlett the foundreffe ; as I collect from thefe articles, viz.
Comp. Burff. 1561.--2. " Sol. pro uno pari chirothecarum
" dat. Mag. Joh. Milwarde ex mandato præfidis et officiario-
" rum, ij s. iv d."—Comp. 1563.--4. " Sol. Jul. xxii. pro
" cena mag. Milwarde adferentis mandatum a domina funda-
" trice de luftranda porcione filvæ, ij s. viij d." Again in the
fame year. " Sol. pro epulis infumptis in mag. [Simon.] Par-
" rett, etc. et Joannem Milwarde, v s. viij d." He fometimes
acted as deputy-fteward to Dame Elizabeth Powlett. I find him
more than once, prefenting a new-year's gift to the college ;
and as late as 1582. He alfo occurs on fome other occafions.
One Arderne Milwarde is elected fchol. coll. Trin. è com. Oxon.
in 1583. Ex regiftr. That the family was of Derbyfhire, as
above hinted, I conclude from the following entry. " Henri-
" cus Milwarde filius Johannis de Snitterton, co. Derb. &c." Ex
Regiftr. in pergamen. ab A°. 1665. fol. 7.

gilla

312 A P P E N D I X.

gilla fua alternatim appofuerunt. DATUM vicefimo die Februarii, Annis regnorum Philippi et Mariæ, etc. etc. primo et fecundo ⁵.

Per me GEORGIUM OWEN.

WILLIELMUS MARTYN.

⁵ It appears, that in procefs of time, the penfion of xxvj *s.* viij *d.* herein mentioned, remained unpaid into the exchequer for feveral years, through the neglect of the heirs or affigns of George Owen: infomuch, that the payment of the fame fell on the new college, to the amount of about twenty pounds. Where-upon, on due reprefentation, James the firft orders Abbot arch-bifhop of Canterbury, Williams bifhop of Lincoln, and lord keeper, and Andrewes bifhop of Winchefter, " out of his gra-" cious and princely care of the good of all colledges," to direct a precept to the faid heirs, requiring them forthwith to repair to the prefident; and to make full fatisfaction for the paft, and entirely to relieve the college for the future. Which they did, by an inftrument dated at Whitehall, Feb. xix. 1622. and figned with their own hands. In Thefauriar. coll. Trin.

NUMB.

++++++++++++++++++++++++++++++++++++

## N U M B.  X.

Preamble of Letters Patent, from Philip and Mary, for founding Trinity College at Oxford. Dat. Mar. viii. 1554.--5 [a].

PHILIPPUS et Maria, dei gratia, rex et regina Angliæ, Franciæ, Neapolis, Jerufalem, et Hiberniæ, fidei defenfores, principes Hifpaniarum et Siciliæ, archiduces Auftriæ, duces Mediolani, Burgundiæ et Brabantiæ, comites Hafpurgiæ, Flandriæ, et Tirolis, omnibus ad quos præfentes literæ pervenerint falutem. Cum prædilectus et fidelis confiliarius nofter THOMAS POPE, miles, inftinctu charitatis, divina præveniente gratia, in animum induxerit quoddam COLLEGIUM de uno præfidente, prefbitero, et de duodecem fociis, graduatis, quorum quatuor femper erunt prefbyteri, ac de octo fcholaribus, infra univerfitatem noftram Oxon, in quadam domo five meffuagium vulgariter vocato *Derham Colledge*, ac infra et fcitum et precinctum ejufdem, de novo

---

[a] Thef. ut fupr. in Cift. Et in 1. Part. Orig. de Ann. 1, 2. Phil. et Mar. In Offic. Rememorat. Scaccar. Et inter Lit. Pat. Phil. et Mar. Ann. Reg. 1, 2. Part. 5. In Capel. Rotul.

erigere,

erigere, creare, et in tempus perpetuum ftabilire, in honorem fanctæ et individuæ TRINITATIS, et dei omnipotentis gloriam : Ac etiam unam liberam Scolam, infra villam de Hokenorton, vel alibi infra com. Oxon. in honorem nominis JESU, vulgariter vocandam *Jefus Scolehowfe*: Ac idem Collegium, maneriis, terris, redditibus, et proventibus, ex fua munificentia, ad fufficientem fuftentationem eorundem Collegii et Schole, liberaliter dotare, ac ornamentis, utenfilibus, et aliis bonis convenientibus, fufficienter ornare, in maximum fcolarium literis ibidem incumbenitum folamen et incitamentum, optimumque omnibus fimile pofthac imitandum præbens exemplum; ac etiam in communem utilitatem omnium fubditorum noftrorum : Nofque igitur, ut hæc fua devota intentio debitum et perpetuum, noftra regia mediante auctoritate et facultate, fortiatur effectum, ad humilem petitionem ejufdem THOMÆ, etc. etc. etc.

*Teftibus nobis ipfis apud Weftmon. octavo die Marcii, annis regnorum noftrorum primo et fecundo. Per ipfos Reg. et Regin* [b].

[b] Signed HARE, i. e. fir *Nicholas Hare*, mafter of the rolls.

NUMB.

†↓†↓†↓†↓†↓†↓†↓†↓†↓†↓†↓†↓†↓†↓†↓†↓†↓†↓†↓†

# N U M B.  XI.

Part of the Charter of Establishment of the said college, in consequence of the foregoing Letters Patent. Dat. Mar. xxviii. 1555 [a].

O MNIBUS Chrifti fidelibus ad quos hoc fcriptum pervenerit. Thomas Pope, de Tyttenhanger in com Hertf. miles, falutem in domino fempiternam. Sciatis, quod ego prefatus Thomas, licentia regia ad omnia et fingula fubfcripta perficienda primitus habita et obtenta, prout per literas fuas patentes, gerentes datum apud Weftmon. octavo die Marcii, annis regnorum fuorum primo et fecundo, plenius liquet et apparet : Ad dei omnipotentis gloriam, ac in honorem fanctæ et individuæ Trinitatis, per præfentes, virtute licenciæ prædictæ, erigo, creo, ftabilio, et fundo, unum collegium de uno præfidente prefbytero, duodecem fociis graduatis, quorum quatuor erunt prefbiteri, ac de octo fcholaribus, perpetuis duraturis temporibus infra fcitum et præcinctum cujufdam domus meæ, vulgariter vocatæ *Derham College*, fituatæ et exiftentis infra

---

[a] In Thefauriar. prædict.

univ.

univ. Oxon. Et ulterius volo et ordino, quod idem collegium, fic per me creatum et erectum, *Collegium fanctæ et individuæ Trinitatis in univerfitate Oxon. ex fundatione Thomæ Pope militis*, nuncupabitur et appellabitur. Et ut collegium prædictum de perfonis congruis et convenientibus adimpleatur et decoretur; fciatis, Me prefatum Thomam Pope, de moribus, doctrina ac induftria, dilecti mihi in Chrifto Thome Slythurft, clerici, fancte Theologiæ Baccalarei, et cæterorum hic per me nominandorum, plurimum confidentem; conftituiffe et ordinaffe prefatum Thomam Slythurft primum et modernum præfidentem prefbyterum dicti collegii: et Stephanum Markes, artium magiftrum, Robertum Newton [b], Joannem Barwyke, Jacobum Bell, Rogerum Crifpyn, Johannem Rychardefon, Thomam Scotte, Georgium Sympfon, artium baccalareos, primos et modernos focios et fcholares dicti collegii: et Johannem Arden, Johannem Comporte, Johannem Perte, et Johannem Langfterre, primos et modernos fcholares ejufdem collegii: Refervans mihi, et executoribus meis, authoritatem et plenam poteftatem nominandi et eligendi refiduos focios et fcholares, ufque ad completionem numeri in licentia regia contenti.— Sciatifque ulterius, ut omnia et fingula premiffa debitum et perpetuum fortiantur effectum, quod ego

---

[b] At this time fellow of Exeter college. The next year, viz. xvii. Oct. 1557, he was elected *annual* rector of the faid houfe. Wood MSS. Muf. Afhm. E. 29. Afterwards he was elected the fecond *perpetual* rector of that college, Nov. ii. 1570. This office he refigned Oct. iv. 1578. Wood, Hift. Antiq. Univ. Oxon. ii. 94. col. 2.

Thomas

Thomas Pope, do, ac per præfentes concedo, eifdem præfidenti, fociis, et fcholaribus, totum illud ´mef-fuagium (five nuper collegium) meum, vocatum *Derham college* in univ. Oxon. ac totum illum fcitum, etc. adeo plene, libere, integre, ac in tam amplis modo ac forma, prout prædictum meffuagium—nuper habui, virtute ac vigore perquifitionis inde per me factæ de Georgio Owen, etc. etc*.

Dat. Mar. xxviii. 1, 2. Phil. Mar.

*Sub Sigillo et Manu Dom.* THOMÆ POPE.

* The remainder, in which it is fpecified that they fhall be a body politick *in nomine and re*, fhall plead and be impleaded, with other privileges ufual in forms of this kind, is therefore omitted. Together with a Grant of new Lands, &c.

# N U M B.  XII.

Letter of Attorney from Thomas Slythurfte, for taking poffeffion of a certain meffuage in Oxford, called *Trinity College.* Dat. Mar. xxiii. 1555ᵃ.

NOVERINT univerfi per præfentes, me Thomam Slythurfte, Canonicum five Prebendarium libere capelle fancti Georgii martyris infra caftrum regium de Wyndefore in com Barkf. facre theologie bacalarium, feciffe, conftituiffe, et in loco meo pofuiffe, dilectos mihi in Chrifto Stephanum Markes, artium magiftrum, et Robertum Newton, artium bacalarium, meos veros et legitimos attornatos conjunctim et divifim, ad intrandum et ingrediendum, pro me, vice et nomine meo, in unum meffuagium cum pertinenciis fuis univerfis in univ. Oxon. vocatum *Collegium fancte et individue Trinitatis in univ. Oxon.* prædicta, ex fundatione venerabilis viri Thome Pope, militis, ac plenam et pacificam poffeffionem et feifinam inde capiendam : et poft hujufmodi feifinam fic inde receptam et habitam, eandem ad meum proprium ufum retinend. et cufto-

---

ᵃ Thefauriar. ut fupr.

diend.

diend. fecundum vim, formam et effectum cujufdam
donationis, Mihi et aliis facte per prefatum venera-
rabilem Thomam Pope, militem, ut per eandem do-
nationem inde confectam, cujus Dat. xxviii. die
menfis Martii annnis reg. Phil. et Mar. reg. et regin.
prim. et fec. manifefte liquet et apparet. Cæteraque
omnia ac fingula quæ in premiffis, vel circa ea, neceffaria fuerint feu quomodolibet oportuna, vice et
nomine meo facienda, exequenda, et finienda, adeo
plenarie ac integre prout facere poffem feu deberem,
fi in premiffis perfonaliter intereffem. Ratum gra-
tumque habens et habiturus, totum et quicquid dicti
mei attornati conjunctim et divifim meo nomine fecerint in premiffis per præfentes. In cujus rei tefti-
monium, figillum meum appofui. Dat. apud Chalfont fancti Petri, xxviii. Marcii, annis regnor. Phil.
et Mar. etc: primo et fecundo.

Per me Thomam Slythurste [b].

[b] Manu et figill. ipfius.

N U M B.

# N U M B. XIII.

Admiſſion of the firſt Preſident, Fellows, and Scholars, of the ſaid college, on the Eve of Trinity-Sunday, May, xxx, 1556 [a].

OMNIBUS Chriſti fidelibus ad quos hoc præſens Scriptum pervenerit, Salutem in Domino ſempiternam. Sciatis, quod anno domini milleſimo quingenteſimo quinquageſimo ſexto, triceſimo die menſis Maii, qui eo anno vigilia ſanctiſſimæ Trinitatis extitit, in preſentia Mri Roberti Morwent [b], præſidis collegii Corporis Chriſti in univ.

[a] Regiſtr. prim. dict. coll. fol. 1. a.

[b] I find the ſame perſon, at the time of founding ſaint John's college, employed by ſir T. Whyte, xviii. Jun. 1, 2. Phil. Mar. to take poſſeſſion of Bernard college, and its appurtenances, juſt before granted from Chriſt Church to the ſaid ſir Thomas Whyte for the foundation of ſaint John's college. Collectan. MSS. Wood, Muf. Aſhmol. 8513.——He was nominated one of the firſt fellows of C. C. C. by biſhop Fox, the founder, and appointed by him, perpetual vice-preſident. He died 1558. Wood, Hiſt. Antiq. Univ. Oxon. ii. 232. He was eminent for his learning, and a ſingular encourager of literature. Fulman, in his manuſcript corrections of Wood's HIST.

and

Oxon. et notarii publici infrafcripti, ac aliorum quorum nomina inferius in hoc inftrumento continentur: Magifter *Thomas Slythurfte*, facræ theologiæ
bacalarius, et canonicus prebendarius liberæ capellæ
regis et reginæ in caftro fuo de Wyndefore, oriundus
ex com. Berks. Sarum diocef. primus PRÆSES no-
minatus ac affignatus collegii fanctiffimæ et individuæ Trinitatis in univ. Oxon. prædicta, ex fundatione venerabilis viri domini THOMÆ POPE militis,
juramentum fubiit in Sacello dicti collegii de Officio
PRÆSIDIS rite et fideliter ibidem adminiftrando ;
magiftro Roberto Morwent prædicto hujufmodi juramentum, virtute literarum fibi a Fundatore mif-
farum ac ibidem palam et publice lectarum, exi-
gente. Forma autem juramenti ab eodem præftiti
de verbo in verbum fequitur. *Ego Thomas Slythurfte,*
*&c, &c.* Qui quidem PRÆSES fic juratus, eifdem
die, loco, et anno, a magiftris, *Arthuro Yeldarde,*
com. Northumberl. Diocef. Dunelm. et *Stephano*
*Markes*, com. Cornub. Diocef. Exon.—in facultate
artium magiftris : Et magiftro *Joanne Barwyke*, com.
Devon. Diocef. Exon. in facultate artium incep-
tore : et dominis *Joanne Bell*, com. Somerfet. Bath.
et Well. Diocef.—*Joanne Richardfon*, com. Cumberland. Diocef. Carliol. — *Georgio Rudde*, com.
Weftmoreland. Diocef. Dunelm. — *Thoma Scotte*,
com. Cumberland. Diocef. Carliol.—*Rogero Crifpyn*,

and·ANTIQ. OXON. informs us, that Morwent was appointed
by bifhop Fox to fucceed Claymond, the firft prefident of that
college, without election. MSS. Muf. Afhmol. D. 9. 4to.
pag. 40.

com.

com. Devon. Diocef. Exon.—*Roberto Evans*, com.
Cornub. Diocef. Exon.—*Joanne Perte*, com. Warwic. Diocef. Litchf. et Cov. — *Roberto Bellamie*,
com. et Diocef. Eboraci, artium bacalariis, et in
Socios dicti collegii per prefatum Fundatorum nominatis et afcitis, juramentum ad SOCIORUM Officium, juxta ftatutorum dicti collegii normam, bene et
fideliter præftandum, exigebat. Tenor autem juramenti ab ipfis tunc præftiti fic habet. *Ego. &c. &c.*
Eodem etiam die, fine temporis intervallo domini
*Johannes Langfterre*, com. et Diocef. Ebor. annos
natus novemdecim ad feftum divi Joannis Baptiftæ proxime precedens, et *Reginaldus Braye*, com. Bedford. Diocef. Lincoln. annorum octodecim ad feftum
divi Johannis prædictum, artium bacalarii : *Joannes
Arden*, com. et Diocef. Oxon. annorum octodecim
ad feftum Pafche proxime precedens, *Joannes Comporte*, com. Middlefex. Diocef. London. annorum
octodecim ad initium quadragefime precedentis, *Robertus Thraſke*, com. Somerfet. diocef. Exon. annorum octodecim ad feftum purificationis precedens,
*Gulielmus Saltmarſhe*, com. et diocef. Ebor. annorum
octodecim ad feftum divi Lucæ precedens, et Jacobus *Harrys*, com. Glouc. diocef. Briftol. annorum
feptemdecim ad feftum divi Johannis Baptiftæ precedens, in facultate artium ftudentes non graduati, in
SCOLARES dicti collegii per Fundatorem nominati
et afciti ; dicto Præfidi juramentum, de officio Scolarium in ipfo collegio humiliter et prompte per
ipfos et ipforum quemlibet præftando, dederunt, in
hunc qui fequitur modum. *Ego, &c. &c.* Sociis

autem

autem et Scholaribus fic juratis, ad OFFICIARIO-
RUM electionem proceſſum eſt pro anno illo inſtanti.
In qua quidem electione, magiſter Markes ad VICE-
PÆSIDENTIS officium, ex mandato domini Funda-
toris deputatus eſt: magiſter Barwyke in DECA-
NUM, dominus Richardſon ac dominus Perte, in
BURSARIOS, per electionem aſſumpti ſunt: ma-
giſter Yeldarde, ex Domini Fundatoris voluntate
LECTORIS PHILOSOPHICI, dominus Bell, LECTO-
RIS RETORICI, per electionem, onera ſuſcipiunt.
Horumque ſinguli, juxta ſtatuta de ſuo cujuſ-
que fideliter obeundo officio, corporale juramentum
dederunt, in preſentia omnium Sociorum et Scholarium. His demum ita peractis, prefatus magiſter
Robertus Morwent, Præſidis et Officiariorum manibus ſigillum commune collegii, a Fundatore prius
acceptum et apud ſe interea temporis reſervatum, tra-
didit: quo in collegii Gazophilacio firmiter repoſito,
dictus Præſes, Socii, et Scolares, veſpertinas preces,
cum cantu et nota, ſolemniter factiſſimæ Trinitati ea
nocte perſolverunt. Ac in craſtino, matutinas, et
alias diei horas, una cum miſſa honorifice celebra-
runt. Inter cujus quidem miſſæ ſolennia, habita eſt
a Præſide concio ad populum ᶜ, qui frequens illuc

ᶜ This SERMON, (improperly ſtyled ad populum,) of the firſt.
Preſident, was in the hands of Dr. Charlett: and I find the following ſhort extract from it, among the papers of Mr. Wiſe.
[MSS. F. Wiſe.] " Jam vero quibus orationis præconiis oportu-
" nam venerabilis admodum FUNDATORIS noſtri MUNIFICEN-
" TIAM prædicare pergam, qui caducam hujus Academiæ
" famam redintegrare, fortunasque bonarum literarum collapſas
" in ſolidum revocare, COLLEGIUM novum ſtabiliendo, pro-
" ventusque et poſſeſſiones ampliter elargiendo, ut videtis,
" obnixe

et multus confluxerat gratulabundus, et omnia faufta nafcenti collegio exoptaturus. Qui quidem univerfus, una cum collegiorum præfidibus, fplendido et magnifico, eo die, excepti funt convivio. Et ut hinc facile conjiciatur, quanto cum applaufu et gratulatione exordium fumpferit hoc collegium; ac præterea ut optime meriti beneficiorum fuorum memoria, ac debita laude, non fraudentur : vifum eft hic, in perpetuum rei monumentum, commemorare, quænam donaria a quamplurimis munificis viris, in ipfius veluti crepundiis, acceperit hoc collegium. Primo, a venerabili facerdote, magiftro Thoma Sothern [d], ecclefiæ cathedralis Exonienfis Thefaura-

" obnixe laborat? Studiorum tantæ jam nunc, et antea fue-
" runt anguftiæ, ut de artibus et fcientiis penitus actum effet,
" nifi hujus unius auctoritate, prudentia, gratia, voluntate, li-
" beralitate, res noftræ conftitiffent. Id quod vivus etiamnum
" valenfque præftitit; horum beneficiorum teftis oculatus ipfe
" futurus. Quam magnis et præmiis et commodis ex ejus in-
" figni pietate ftudia nunc inftaurabimus, hi parietes quafi
" pleno difertoque ore loquuntur. Taceo hoc in loco, ubi
" tot ejus ALUMNOS eruditione celebres afpicio, ut literatos
" homines unice femper amaverit, et muneribus et favore com-
" plexus affidue fuerit, VIR ampliffimus, et ipfe literis ac
" doctrinis rite excultus. Pariter etiam noviftis, quam largus
" eft in pauperes et egenos, in rebus gerendis dexter, ftrenuus,
" et officiofus, religionis avitæ tenax, &c." No great credit
is due to profeffed panegyrics. But thefe commendations are
neither extravagant, nor unfupported by facts.

[d] Thomas Southern was elected fellow of Magdalene college, Oxford, about 1500, and occurs as fuch at a vifitation of that college by bifhop Fox, in 1506. He is otherwife called one of Ingledew's chaplains there, with a falary of ten marcs. Regiftr. Fox. Winton. lib. ii. fol. 44, 51, b. 52.

rio, ᵉ viginti libras aureas monetæ optimæ, dono ac-
cepit ; ultra quinquaginta libras, quas eidem poſt
mortem ſuam, per teſtamentum legaverat. Deinde,
ad convivium in ipſo ſanctiſſimæ Trinitatis die ſplen-
didius ac liberalius faciendum, Mag. Edovardus
Love ᶠ, generoſus, collegio miſit cunicellos quadra-

b. et ſeq. He was elected boreal proctor of the univerſity
of Oxford, May 2, 1511. Wood, Hiſt. Antiq. univ. Oxon. ii.
417. He was alſo fellow of Eton college, in 1512. Willis,
MSS. collectan. co. Bucks. fol. Nᵒ. 23. in bibl. Bodl. He
was inſtituted vicar of Modbury, co. Devon. Mar. 17. 1517,
at the preſentation of Eton college. regiſtr. Oldham, Exon.
This vicarage he reſigned in 1523. regiſtr. Veyſey, Exon.
He was inſtituted rector of Farringdon, co. Hants, Jun. 5.
1519, being then ſtyled A. M. at the preſentation of Hugh
Oldham, biſhop of Exeter : which rectory he reſigned in 1524.
regiſtr. Fox. Winton. lib. iv. fol. 15. b. and lib. v. fol. 168.
He was made treaſurer of Exeter cathedral, May 8, 1531.
Le Neve's Faſti, p. 91. He was appointed, by the name of
" Thomas Sothern clerke," a commiſſioner, with others, for
ſuppreſſing hereſies in the dioceſe of Exeter, Feb. 16, 1556.
Wilkins, Concil. iii. 140. He died in 1557. Wood. Athen.
Oxon. i. f. 8. His will is dated April 30, 1556. Proved Jul.
24, 1557. In regiſtr. Wreſtley. qu. 25. cur. prærog. Cant.
The legacy mentioned in the text proved to be a miſtake.
By the ſaid will, he bequeathes the ſum of xiij l. vj s. viij d.
to the fabric of Exeter cathedral ; and orders the whole choir
of the church to attend his obſequies : from whence it may be
concluded that he was buried in his cathedral. He likewiſe
founds an obit in the ſaid church. Ingledew's chaplains, or
fellows, abovementioned, were reſtrained to natives of the dioceſe of York and Durham.

ᵉ See Life, p. 127.
ᶠ The founder's brother in law, and ſteward. See Life,
p. 182. Theſe things, I preſume, he ſent by the founder's
orders.

ginta

ginta octo, agnos tres, capones novemdecim, por-
cellos tres, anferulos quatuordecim, pipiones quin-
quies duodenas, damas duos, et vitulum unum:
Dominus Georgius Gyfforde [s], miles, cunicellos
viginti quatuor, et pullos gallinaceos duodecem:
Magifter Crocker [h], generofus, dimidiatum bovem,
et agnum unum: Magifter Edmundes [i], generofus,
damam unum, et vitulum unum.: Magifter Anto-

[s] George Gyfford occurs dubbed a knight of the carpet,
by queen Mary, the day following her coronation, in the chamber of prefence at Weftminfter. MSS. Dugd. Muf. Afhm.
B. 173. A vifitor of the monafteries. Dugd. Warw. p. 800.
A fupervifor of chantries in com. Bucks, 1549. Willis, Mitr.
Abb. ii. 38. He interceded with lord Cromwell for the prefervation of the monaftery of Wolftrope, and other houfes,
which he vifited. See LIFE, p. 27. He was buried, Jan. 7,
1557, according to Strype, with much magnificence. Eccl.
Mem. iii. 389. He was of Buckinghamfhire; of which county
he was a reprefentative in queen Mary's firft parliament held at
Oxford, 1554. Willis, Not. parl. ed. 1730. p. 89. Compare
MISCELLANEOUS ANTIQUITIES, pp. 37. 40. Numb. i. Printed at Strawberry Hill, 1772. 4to.

[h] The founder mentions him in a letter to the prefident,
15 Feb. 1557. " I have fent you by Mr. Crocker your Crofs
" with a cafe." He was probably of Hook-Norton, co. Oxon.
See Strype's Annals, Vol. iv. 123. N. 79. App. One John
Crocker, efquire, of Hook-norton, is mentioned by Dugdale, prefenting to the church of Warmington, in Warwickfhire, Sept.
10, 1554. WARWICKSHIRE, p. 417. Many of the name are
buried in Hook-Norton church. Particularly John Croker,
1568. See alfo Lee's Vifitation, MSS. ut fupr. p. 26. I find
Sir Edward North alienating to John Croker the manor of
Melcomb, co. Oxon. Licent. Alienat. 7 Feb. 35 Hen. viii.
Part. 18.

[i] The founder's uncle. See LIFE, p. 2.

nius

nius Ardern[k], generofus, vitulum dimidiatum, anferulos duos, porcellum unum, et caponem unum :
Magifter Ricardus Ardern, generofus, panes fex folidorum : Magifter Platte [l], generofus, ovem unam,
et anferulos duos : Magifter Yates[m], generofus, ovem
unam : Orpewoode[n] de Northlea ovem unam : Bri-
anus de Cogges[o] anferulos duos, et pullos duos :
Magiftra Irifhe[p], oppidana, lagenam vini unam :

[k] The founder's relations. See LIFE, p. 121. 183. He
mentions John Arden of Cottisford, co. Oxon. in his will.
And in Comp. Burff. 1587.—8. I find,

   " Sol. magiftro Seller equitanti Kirtleton cum xeniolo ad
   Mag. Ardern. iv *d*. [This was *Antony* [*].]
   " Sol. pro chirothecis magiftri Ardern. v *s*.

This name is often written *Arden*. It was an ancient family,
originally of Warwickfhire. Dugd. Warw. and MSS. Lee,Vifit.
Oxfordfh. I cannot find out " Panes fex folidorum," but fuppofe it was fome fine fpecies of manchet. In lord Guilford's
pedigree of POPE, *Arden* occurs very early.

[l] Or Plotte. Bartholomew Plotte of Sparfholt, in Berkfhire,
appears to have married the founder's uncle's daughter. Afhmole's Berkf. iii. 285.

[m] A college tenant, and one of the founder's mother's relations. See LIFE, p. 2. and Indentur. in Regiftr. prim. coll.
fol. 13.

[n] Alice Orpwood, mother of Rob. Parrot, whofe defcendants
were connected with Northly, died 1558. See LIFE, p. 183.
and App. XXI.

[o] Both, the founder's brothers in law, and, I fuppofe his
tenants or retainers. See LIFE, p. 184.

[p] In whofe houfe Cranmer and Ridley were confined, at Oxford ; her hufband, a vintner, being mayor of the city. Rid-

   * (See Regiftr. PERROT, infra citat; NUMB. xxi, fol, 112, a,)

X 4                                                    ley

Magifter Furfe [q], oppidanus, lagenam vini unam :
Magifter Bridgeman [r], oppidanus, dimidiatam vini
lagenam, cum fragis. Convivio autem finito [s], et
actis Altiffimo gratiis, decedentes hofpites et extranei
omnes, Sociis et Scolaribus fuum collegium bene

ley particularly mentions her in a letter, dat. May 31, 1555,
but with no very favorable circumftances. " Viro, in cujus
" aedibus ego cuftodior, uxor dominatur—vir ipfe, *Irifchius*
" uomine, fatis mitis eft omnibus : uxori vero plufquam obfe-
" quentiffimus." Ridley's LIFE of Ridley, 589, 663.— She
was buried in St. Martin's church, Oxon. 1556. MSS. Wood.
Bib. Bodl. Rawl.

[q] I find Thomas Furres, or Firfe, fenior bailiff of the city,
1556. Wood's Cat. of Mayors, &c. MSS. Muf. Afhm D. 7.
—p. 118. I find alfo John Bridgeman, fenior bailiff, 1531.
ibid. with Wood's note, in marg. that he married Mary the
fifter of fir Thomas Whyte, founder of St. John's, p. 114.

[r] Bridgeman was perhaps a vintner of the city of Oxford,
as were Furfe and Irifhe, here alfo mentioned. Regiftr. Cur.
Cancell. Oxon. notat. GG. fol. 32. " Feb. iii. 1548. Quo die
" compar. perfonaliter, Magifter *Edmundus Iryfhe*, &c. &c.
" *Thomas Furfe*, &c. &c. and in the prefens of them all, Mr·
" Chauncellor dyd decreye, that they and every of theym
" fhall fell redde wyne, claret wyne, and whyte wyne, after
" xiiij *d.* the gallon. And all other, fellynge the fame wynes
" within the citie of Oxforde, fhall felle after the fame rate."
ARCHIV. Univ. Oxon.

[s] Concerning this feaft, I find the following articles, Comp.
Burff. 1556.

" Sol. in regardo famulis diverforum generoforum appor-
tantibus a dominis fuis miffa munera, et aliis occupatis
in curandis cibis, aliifque negotiis, in die fanfte Trinitatis. xviij *s.* v *d.*

" Sol. in expenfis factis in fefto fanctiff. Trin. ultra omnem
allocationem. xxvij *s.* v *d.*

precantes

precantes relinquunt; aptum poft quietem adeptam, futurum mufis ac bonis literis domicilium ᵗ.

Acta funt hæc, eo quo fcribuntur modo, Anno Dom. prædict. necnon die et menfe prædictis, in prefentia publici notarii . fubfcripti, et Magiftrorum Roberti Morwent, Arthuri Yeldarde, teftium meo-rum, et aliorum plurimorum. Et ego, &c. [*Deeft, nomen notarii.*]

At antient feafts it was the cuftom for friends to fend in prefents of provifion. Thus at the inthronifation-feaft of arch-bifhop Wareham, in 1504. "In Expenfis neceffariis, una "cum regardis datis diverfis perfonis venientibus cum diverfis "exhenniis." Batteley's Canterbury. Lond. 1703. Append. Suppl. p. 28.

ᵗ It appears however that although the whole number, one fchólar excepted, was firft admitted in a formal and legal· manner on this day, that ten fellows and feven fcholars had' lived in the college, and received all emoluments and alloca-tions, for nine weeks before, viz. from the feaft of the Annun-ciation preceeding, with which day the firft Computus begins. In which nine weeks, I find alfo,

"Sol. pro quatuor diebus pietanciæ in feptimana Pafchæ præcedentis, viz pro ipfo die Pafchæ, et tribus feriis fe-quentibus. xxvj. s. viij. d.

"Sol. pro quatuor diebus pietanciæ in feptimana Pente-coftes præterlapfæ, dominica viz. et tribus feriis fe-quentibus. xxvj. s viij. d.

And although this Computus ends at Michaelmas following, I find,

"Sol. pro uno die pictantiæ anticipato ex mandato Funda-toris, viz. pro obitu Fundatoris in menfe novembris futu-ro [die 16.]

Which obit was afterwards appointed to the feventh of Auguft, on which it is ftill continued. And though the obit for his wife

Margaret

Margaret was then on Jan. 16, yet they kept it within the time of this Accompt. viz Term. ii Septim i.

" Sol. pro uno die pietantiæ, viz. pro obitu Domine Mar garete uxoris noftri Fundatoris. vj *s*. viij *d*.

This Computus begins with the feaft of the Annunciation, and ends with the Michaelmas following. Some articles are charged for one term, or quarter, that is from Trinity to Michaelmas, and fome for the whole half year, viz.

" Sol. lectori philofophico *per annum dimidiatum*.....

" Sol. lectori linguæ latinæ pro *uno* termino . . . .

" Sol pulfanti organa pro *uno* termino. . .

" Sol. celebrantibus miſſam matutinalem pro 1 termino, *et tertia parte precedentis* . . .

" Sol. pro focalibus, viz. pro carbonibus et ligno *ab initio collegii* ufque ad feft. S. Michaelis archangeli proxime feq. per *xvii Septimanas* . . . .

From all which circumftances, taken together, it is manifeft, that they were refident, though perhaps not fully fettled, in the college, before the formal admiffion fpecified in this inftrument.

N U M B.

✚✚✚✚✚✚✚✚✚✚✚✚✚✚✚✚✚✚✚✚✚✚✚✚✚✚✚✚✚✚

# N U M B. XVI.

Conditions relating to the intended Foundation of a free grammar-School, at Dedington, Co. Oxon. by Sir Thomas Pope[a].

" THE faid prefident, fellowes, and fchollers,
" [*of Trinity college Oxford,*] fhall yerely for
" evermore give and pay unto one hable perfon,
" well and fufficiently lerned and inftructed in
" gramer and humanitie, which fhall be SCHOLE-
" MASTER of and at a frefcole, to be called Jhefus
" Scole of the foundation of the faid fir Thomas
" Pope, to be erected at Dedington in the faid
" countie of Oxon, and to teach children gramer
" and humanitie there frely, for his yerely falarye
" and wages, xx markes, of good and lawfull
" money: And to one other hable and lerned per-
" fon in gramer to be USHER within the faid fre-
" fchole, yerely viii *l* of good and lawfull money, to
" teache children likewife ther frely. The fame feve-
" rall falaries and wages to be paid to the faid fcole-

---

[a] Ex Indentura quadripart. Dat. April 1. 1, 2. Phil. et Mar.
1555. In Thefauriar. prædict.

" mafter

" mafter and ufher yerely, at two termes in the
" yeare: that is to faye, at the feaft of Thannun-
" ciacion of our ladie faint Marie and faint Mighell
" Tharchaungell, or within one quarter of a yere
" next after any of the faid feaftes, by even portions.
" And that the faid fcolemafter and ufher, after the
" erection of the faid fcole, to be in the faid fcole,
" as is aforefaid, fhall be from tyme to tyme for
" ever namyd and appoynted by the prefident, fel-
" lows, and fcollers, of the faid colledge, and of their
" fucceffoures or the moft part of them. And the
" faid fcolemafter and ufher fo to be namyd and ap-
" poyntyd, to have and enjoye the faid offices of
" fcolemafter and ufherfhipp during lyf; unlefs fome
" fawlt, offence, or notable cryme, be commytted
" or don by any of them, and fufficiently proved
" agaynft any of them, that then uppon fuch
" fawlt or cryme fo commytted or don, and pro-
" ved, as is aforefaid, the partie commyttinge
" fuch fawlt, offence, or cryme, to lofe his faid
" rome, and a new to be namyd for him, as is
" aforefaid. And the faid fcolemafter, and ufher
" and fcollers, that fhall be in the faid fcole, to be
" furder and otherwife ordered concerninge the order
" and rules of the faid Scole, and good contynu-
" aunce thereof, as fhal be appoynted by the faid fir
" Thomas Pope in his life, or after his death by the
" faid dame Elifabeth his wife, within the ftatutes of
" the faid colledge, or by any other writing fealed
" and fubfcribed by the handes of either of them.
" And the refidew of the faid revenues and profitts
" [befides certain other ufes] for the charge of the re-
"           " paracions

" paracions of the faid fcolehoufe and other reafon-
" able charges that fuch of the faid colledge as fhall
" yearlie furvey the faid fcolehoufe, for the perfor-
" mance of the good orders therein to be con-
" tinualie kept, fhall be put unto, about the faid
" furvey.—"

N U M B.

# N U M B.  XV.

Account of a petition referred to the princefs Elifabeth at Hatfield, by fir Thomas Pope, in Augufl, 1556[a].

AD futuram rei memoriam, atque ut alienis pe-
riculis edocti præfentes ac futuri hujus collegii focii ac fcolares, cautius quod ad ftatutorum
obfervantiam pertinet fefe gerere difcant. Sciatis,
quod vicefimo die Augufti, anno Domini millefimo
quingentefimo quinquagefimo fexto, et hujus collegii
anno primo; Dominus Geogius Sympfon, lector
philofophicus, et Dominus Georgius Rudde, artium
bachalarii, et dicti collegii focii, ob violatum ftatu-
tum *De muris noctu non fcandendis*, juxta ejufdem fta-
tuti exigentiam perpetuæ amotionis et expulfionis
a collegio pœna fuiffe punitos, fine fpe regreffus
quam ullo modo in eodem habebant reliquam.
Unde ad venerabilem virum Dominum Thomam
Pope, dicti collegii Fundatorem, tanquam ad *Sacram
Anchoram*, confugere conati, de perpetrato crimi-
ne impunitatem, aut faltem pœnæ mitigationem,
fuppliciter petituri. Ægre tandem, ac nonnifi medi-

---

[a] Regiftr. prim. Coll. prædict. fol. 7. a.

antibus

antibus ac intercedentibus excellentiſſima principe Domina ¡Elizabetha, fereniſſimæ Mariæ forore, cui tunc ab intimis conſiliis dictus Fundator fuit, ac etiam propria conjuge, prænobili femina Domina item Elizabetha, exauditi funt. Atque ita datis literis ad mag. Thomam Slythurſte, tum collegii fui Præfidem, dicti duo bachalarii publice in communi collegii aula, crimen fuum coram omnibus tum fociis tum fcolaribus agnofcentes, in focietatem denuo recepti funt: indicta illis per dictum præfidem et officiarios mulcta viz. vj. s. viij. d. ad duas cortinas bombycinas emendas, pro Summi Altaris, in Sacello collegii, ampliori ornatu. Literarum autem proditarum tenor de verbo in verbum ad hunc qui fequitur modum fe habet ᵇ.

ᵇ Inferted in LIFE, pag. 84.

✝✝✝✝✝✝✝✝✝✝✝✝✝✝✝✝✝✝✝✝✝✝✝✝✝✝✝✝✝✝✝✝✝

# N U M B.  XVI.

An indenture made May 5, 1556,
" witneſſing that the preſident, fel-
" lows, and ſchollers of Trinity col-
" lege Oxford, have received of their
" founder, ſuch parcells of churche
" playte and ornamentes of the
" church, as hereafter followethe[a]."

F FYRST, a chalice with a patent [paten] gilt,
weyingee xx. oz. iii. quarters[b]. Item, one

[a] E Regiſtro prædict. fol. 8. a.

[b] Of all the plate given by the founder, this is the only
piece now remaining. All that he gave, enumerated in various
parts of this work, was either aboliſhed as ſuperſtitious
in the year 1570, this piece excepted, or granted to king
Charles the firſt in the year 1642. It is well known that all
the colleges in Oxford contributed their plate to that monarch's
neceſſities. A laudable and very ſeaſonable proof of loyalty,
but much regretted by the lovers of antient art, as it deſtroyed many valuable ſpecimens of curious workmanſhip not elſewhere preſerved, in an article which our magnificent anceſtors
carried to a moſt ſuperb and ſumptuous exceſs.—I take this occaſion of mentioning here two pieces of plate formerly belonging
to the ſaid college, granted with the reſt to king Charles,
which

other chalice with a patent[c], parcell gilt, poz. xiii.
oz. di. Item, a pipe of fylver, parcell gilt, poz. xiii.
oz. di. Item a pax of ivory garnyſhed with fylver
and gilt, and fett with counterfeete ſtones. Item, a
chappel-croſſe of copper, with Marye and John,
and a foote to the fame, gilt. Item, a pair of cen-
fors of copper. Item, ii. pair of latten candleſtickes
for the altar. Item, a holye water-ſtop of latten. ,
Item ii crewettes of tynne. Item a pint bottell of
tynne for the chappell. Item a deſke to lay a mafs
booke upon, pained grene. Item, a lectorne[d] of
waynſcott for the quere [choir.] Item, ii. fair anty-
phoners[e] of parchmente lymned[f] with gold. Item,
a fair legeant[g] [legend] of parchmente lymned with

which would at prefent have been great curiofities : their infcriptions are thus recorded. " Poculum collegii S. et indivi-
" duæ Trinitatis Oxon. ex dono Joannis Denham unici filii
" Joannis Denham militis et unius baronum fcaccarii. 1631."
17 oz. This was Denham the poet, author of Cooper's Hill,
&c. The other was infcribed, " Ex dono Jacobi Harrington·
" equitis aurati filii natu maximi et hujus collegii comm."
13 oz. dim. 3. d. No date. This was Harrington, author of the
Oceana. [Ex quadam fchedul. in thefauriar. Coll. antedict.]
Who little fufpected, that this innocent memorial of gratitude
to the place of his education, would be converted into a contri-
bution, however inconfiderable, for the fupport of royalty. .

    c Paten.
    d Properly a defk for reading the leffons. Lutrin. Fr.
    e Antiphonarium. - Lat.
    f Illuminated.
    g Or Lectionary, which contained all the leffons, whether
from fcripture, or other books, which were directed to be read
in the courfe of the year. Rot. Comp. Coll. Winton. A. D.
1479. MS. " Pro reparacione magne Legende, iij s. iv d.

                    Y                              gold.

gold. Item, iiii. grayles[h] of parchmente lymned with gold. Item a rector chori of parchmente lymned with gold. Item, a fair mafs booke of parchmente lymned with gold, and covered with blacke velvette. Item, a mafs-booke of parchmente covered with leather. Item, a pfalter for the quere printed with note. Item a fuite of veftmentes of red clothe of tiffue orphryfed with needle worke, with iii. albes, ftoles, and fannels[i], agreeable to the fame. Item, ii. copes of red clothe of tyffue, orphryfed with needle worke, and a running orphrife of green clothe tyffue. Item, ii. copes of yellowe baudkyn, woven with fcallop-fhells, orphrifed with grene clothe of tyffue. Item, a fuite of veftmentes of blewe velvette, orprifed with needle worke, with albes ftoles and fannels agreeable to the fame. Item, a fuite of veftmentes of red clothe of bawdkyn, orphrifed with needle-worke, with albes, ftoles, and fannells, agreeable to the fame. Item, a fuite of veftmentes of red bawdkyn, woven with birds. orphrifed with blewe bawdkyn, with albes, ftoles, and fannels, agreeable to the fame. Item, a cope of blewe baudkyn, woven with fonnes [funs], orphrifed with needle worke. Item, a cope of red bawdkyn woven with birdes of gold, orphrifed with needle-worke. Item, a cope of whyte damafke with flowers of gold, orphrifed with needle-worke. Item, a veftment of white damafke orphrifed with needle worke, with an albe, ftole, and fan-

[h] The Grail or *Gradual* contained all that was fung by the choir at high·mafs.

[i] See Dufrefne, LAT. GLOSS. V. FANO vel PHANO.

nell,

nell, to the fame. Item, a veftmente of blacke velvette for a maffe of requiem [k]. Item, a veftment of
blewe grogreyn [l] powdered with crownes of needle-
worke, with albe, &c. Item, a veftmene of whyte
fatten of Brydges [Bruges], with a grene croffe of
fatten of Brydge, powdered with flowers, with albe,
&c. Item, a veftment of whyte ..... for Lent, with
an albe, &c. Item a yeftmente of whyte fuftion
for Lent having a croffe of reade [red] fuftion, with
an albe, &c. Item, ii. alter-clothes for the high
alter; that is to fay, i. for the upper parte, and i.
for the nether part, of checker bawdkyn, pained [m]
with crymfon velvette, powdered with flowers and
angels of gold, Item, ii. like alter-clothes for the
faid alter of blewe bawdkyn, pained with red velvette
woven with bookes of golde. Item ii. like alter-
clothes, for the faid alter, of whyte fatten of Brydges,
powdered with birdes of gold. Item, ii. nether alter-

[k] In marg. " Note the albe, ftole, and fannel to the blacke
" veftmente is lacking, which fhall be fent."

[l] I know not exactly the meaning of this word, but it is ufed
in the INVENTORY of the goods of Curtefs bifhop of Chichefter, who died in 1587. " One filk *grograine* gowne faced
" with velvet.—Another *grograine* gowne, &c." Strype, ANN.
REF. vol. i. B. i. ch. 26. pag. 332. edit. 1728. I fuppofe it to
be from the French *gros grain*, and that grogram is its cor-
ruption.

[m] Striped or edged. In the romance of IWAIN AND GAWAYN
(MSS. Cott. GALB. E. xi.) we have this appofite paffage.

" And with a mantell fche me clad. · It was of purpur fayre
" and fyne. And the *pane* of riche ermine." That is, The
*border* was of ermine.

clothes

clothes for the alters in the Body of the chappell, of
read bawdekyn woven with flowers and caftles of
gold, and payned with white damafke, and greene
ᵇ brydge-fatten powdered with droppes of velvette,
and Jefus of gold. Item, the upper and nether
clothe for the Sepulchre ᶜ, pained with whyte and
red brydge-fatten. Item, a herfe clothe of blacke
fuftion of Naples powdered with images, birdes,
and rolles of needle-worke, with a croffe of whyte
fuftion, and the dove in the myddeft, of needle-
worke. Item, a clothe for the Sacrament of whyte
taffata edged with bone worke and taffels of gold.
Item, a corporas caife [cafe] of blewe cloth of golde,
and reade velvette, with Jefus on it of ftole-worke of
golde wherein is alfo a fyne corporas. Item, i. other
corporas cafe of reade bawdkyn wherein is alfo a fyne
corporas. Item, ii. other corporas cafes, whereof
the one is of taffata, and other of whyte fuftion,
in every of which cafes is alfo a fyne corporas. Item
a clothe of canvaffe to lye uppon the high alter iii.
yerdes long. Item, ii. lynnen clothes to lay uppon

ᵇ Bruges.

ᶜ The following appointment occurs in the Founder's ADDI-
TAMENTUM before-cited. fol. ult. " Volo, ut duodecim de-
" narii annuatim concedantur, ad SEPULCRUM DOMINI in
" facello collegii mei, in die Parafceves et VIGILIA PASCHÆ,
" pernoctantibus et vigilantibus, ad laborum fuorum ea in re
" compenfationem." See an account of a pompous SEPULCHRE
of this fort made for Radcliffe church at Briftol, in 1470, in
Walpole's ANECD. PAINT. vol. i. pag. 45. edit. i.—Rot. Comp.
Coll. Wint. 1395. MS. " Et in i. carpentario conducto per
" ii. dies ad faciendam domum SEPULCRI in choro, &c. vj d.

the

the altars in the Bodie of the chappell, cont. iii.
elles and a quarter the pece. Item, iiii. Towelles for
the High͜ altar, and iiii. towelles for the nether
altars ᴾ. Item, ii. cufshens, of redde fylke for the
chappel woven with flowers of golde. Item, a great
waynfcot coffer to put in all the ornaments aforefaid.
ALL which parcells, &c. IN witnefs, whereof, &c.

*Moreover*, the within named prefident, fellowes,
and fcholers, have receaved of the faid fir Thomas
Pope, their founder, ii. proceffionalls, and a gof-
pell boke.

ᴾ " Quatuordecim Tualliæ de panno lineo pro͂ fummo altari,
" &c.—Quinque parvæ Tualliæ pro manibus tergendis." [Coll.
Windef.] Dugd. Mon. iii. Eccl. Coll. p. 85. col. 2. " Duo
" Abfterforia de panno lineo ad extergendum digitos poft per-
" fufionem in majori altari." Dugd. Append. Hift. Eccl. S.
Paul. p. 217.—Rot. Comp. Coll. Winton. MS. 1395. " Et in xi
" ulnis de panno de Weftnale emptis per dictum Thefaurarium
" [de Wolvefey] et liberatis collegio xix die Marcii pro tuellis
" altarium capellæ, v ʃ. iij *d*."

✝✝✝✝✝✝✝✝✝✝✝✝✝✝✝✝✝✝✝✝✝✝✝✝✝✝✝✝✝✝✝

## N U M B. XVII.

Indentura de ornamentis et jocalibus miſſis per dominum Fundatorem, tam ad ornátuḿ Sacelli quam Aulæ, Jan. xx. 1557 [a].

F FIRSTE, a ffayre cope of rede ſylke lyned with taffata, and having images of gold wrought upon the ſame, the orphiſes [orphreis] being needle-worke, and having a narrowe cape. Item, i. veſt-ment of red velvette, with a Croſſe of gold of ſtole-wotke, and ymbrawdered with floure de luces, an-gels, and ſpred eagles of gold, with ſtole, and ffan-nell of blacke velvette, with an albe; belonginge to a veſtment of blacke velvett, which is mentioned in the *ffirſt indenture* made by the colledge, declaringe the receyte of the ffirſt church-ſtuffe and playte, and the lacke of the ſaid ſtole, fannel, and albe, noted in the margent of the ſaide indenture. Item, a veſtment of blewe ſilke lyned with taffata, and woven with burdes and flowers of Colen [Cologn [b]] gold, with ſtole, &c. Item, a rich clothe or ca-

[a] Regiſtr. ut ſupr. fol. 17. a.
[b] Or, Colonia in Italy.

napye

napye to hange over the bleſſed ſacrament on the
altar made with cypers ᶜ, and perled with golde, and
frynged with ſylver, being hemmede with a lace of
ſilke and golde. Item, a faire canapye to cary over
the bleſſed ſacrament upon Corpus Chriſti daye,
made of yalowe ſilke, velvet, and clothe of golde
fryngede. Item, iiii. paynted ſtaves to cary the ſaid
canapye uppon. Item, a ffaire corporas caſe of
clothe of golde, and a fine lynen clothe within the
ſame. Item, one other fair rich corporas caſe, with
images of golde of bothe ſydes, having a border
about the ſame on both ſydes, garniſhed with ſeed
perle ; on the one ſyde of which corporas caſe is our
Lady and her ſonne on horſe-backe, and on the
other ſyde our ladye and her ſonne ſittinge in a
chaire, and a fyne lynnen clothe within the ſame.
Item, one other corporas caſe of red ſilke and golde,
with a fyne lynnen clothe ᵈ within the ſame. Item,
ii. faire quyſhions of red ſilke, and flowers of golde
wrought in the ſame, for the chappell. Item, a fair
payr of Organs ᵉ, which, with the carryage from

ᶜ Q. Cyprus-lawn. " Quinque aurifrygia, quorum tria ſunt
" OPERE CYPRENSI nobiliſſimo, et unum eſt de opere Angli-
" cano." Lib. Anniv. BASILIC. VATICAN. apud Rubeum in
VIT. Bonifacii. viii. PP. p. 345. Alſo Carpentier's SUPPL. GL.
Cang. tom. i. col. 391. " Unum pluviale de canceo rubeo
" cum aurifrixio de opere CYPRENSI."

Milton's *cyprus lawn*, in IL PENSEROSO, is written *cipres*, in
the firſt edition.

ᵈ In marg. " The clothe promyſed but not ſent."

ᵉ In the college-ſtatutes the following clauſe occurs, " In
" die Veneris Officium de Nomine Jeſu, in die Sabbati vero, de

Y 4                                benedicta

London to Oxford, coft x *l*[.] Item, a depe bayfon
of puter to ftand in the bodye of the chappel inftede

" benedicta Virgine matre, cum cantu et organis folemniter
" feptimanatim celebrari debere ftatuo." And in the fame
ftatute it is injoined. " Primas ac fecundas vefperas, completo-
" ria, et matutinas et altas miffas, ac proceffiones, devote ac
" diftincte, cum cantu et nota, fecundum confuetudinem et
" ufum ecclefiæ cathedralis Sarum, celebrent et cantent."
Cap. xii. *De Horis canonicis, Miffis et aliis fuffragiis dicendis, de
modo in Choro fedendi.* [See LIFE, p. 129.] The organ, mentioned in the text, was removed from the chapel, where it
ftood over the fcreen, into the burfary, about the year 1645.
At length, under the adminiftration of the prefbyterians, it
totally difappeared. After the parliamentary ORDINANCE made
in the year 1644, it is extraordinary, that the magnificent
organ on the north fide of the chapel of faint John's college,
Oxford, (which continued in ufe till the year 1768,) fhould
have been fuffered to remain : more efpecially, as it had been
erected under the patronage of archbifhop Laud ; and as Cromwell's vifitors had ordered fir William Paddy's donation for
founding the choral fervice in that chapel, to be entirely applied to the augmentation of the Prefident's falary. *Original
Regifter of the Vifitation of univ. Oxon.* A. D. 1648. MS. Archiv.
Oxon. 4to. At New-college, the organ, given by William
Port in the year 1458, which ftood at the ftall-end of the
north fide of the choir near the veftry, fupported by wooden
pillars, was deftroyed in the year 1646. Wood's *manufcript
Englifh Hiftory of the Univerfity of Oxford*, vol. ii. fol. 245.
The prefent organ in that chapel was erected in the year 1663.
But the beautiful fcreen, on which it is placed, without any
defign of fupporting an organ, was conftructed in the year
1636 : and in the fame year, continues Wood, " the old ftalls
" and deskes being pulled downe, *thofe that are now ftanding* were
" fet up ; and the wainfcott adorned with curious painting,
" containing the figures of apoftles, faints, &c." MS. ibid.
fol. 246.

*f* A new organ was bought, in 1529, for the new, large and
beautiful

of a fonte. Item, a faire ſtaffe to carry the beſt croſſe withall, covered and garniſhed with copper and gilt. Item, a ſhipp of puter to putt in franken-ſence. Jtem, a paire of crewettes of pewter. Item, a pax of everie [ivory]. Item ii. faire bell candle-ſtickes of latten, to ſett tallow candles in upon the altar. Item, iii. Antiphoners of parchmente, bought by Mr. Parret for the queere. Item, ii. proceſſio-nalls and a goſpell-boke, which were conteyned in the backſide of the ſaid *firſt indenture* made by the colledge for receipt of the firſt plate and ornamentes of the churche. Item, ii. altar clothes, the one for the upper parte, and the other for the nether parte

beautiful church of Holbech in Lincolnſhire, for 3 *l.* 6 *s.* 8 *d.* Stukeley's ITIN. CURIOS. p. 20. Gray, archdeacon of Berks, bequeathed 4 *l.* in 1521, to St. Mary's church at Oxford, *for a new payr of organs.* Regiſtr. univ. Oxon. Archiv. A. 166. fol. 66. According to Dugdale, an organ was purchaſed for the church of Sutton-Colfield in Warwickſhire, by Veſey biſhop of Exeter in the reign of Henry the eighth, at the coſt of 14 *l.* 2 *s.* 8 *d.* WARWICKSH. p. 667. In the year 1439, a new organ was made for the choir of Merton-college, by William Wootton, organ-builder at Oxford, for the ſum of 28 *l.* Ant. Wood's MERTON-PAPERS, MS. Bibl. Bodl. [Cod. BALLARD.] Whethamſtede abbot of Saint Alban's, about the year 1450, gave to his church a pair of organs; for which, and their erec-tion, he expended fifty pounds. No organ in any monaſtery of England was comparable to this inſtrument, for its tone and workmanſhip. CHRON. WHETHAMST. per Hearne, vol. ii. p. 539. About the year 1476, Thomas Wyrceſter, abbot of Hyde near Wincheſter, gave eight marcs and a horſe, to purchaſe an organ for his church. " Octo marcas et unum equum bonum " pro novis organis muſicalibus." MSS. ARCHIV. WOLVES. apud Winton.

of

of the altar, paned with red clothe of tyſſue and purple-velvett, rychlie imbrowdered with angels and ſkitchins [eſcutcheons] of the paſſion. Item, a deſke-clothe paynede with bawdkyn of ſundry collers and edgede with whyte. Item, a cope of blacke ſilke with ſtripes of golde, having a rich orphes.

Item, a ſtondinge cup of ſilver gilt, with a cover graven with the pommegranet and a ſheiff of ar-rowes, poz. xxxiii. oz. Item, ii, gilte ſaltes without a cover, poz xxxix. oz. iii. quarters. Item, iii. playne drynkin potts of ſilver gilt, whereof one hath a cover, poz. xxxi. oz, iii. quarters. Item, ii. crewettes of ſilver gilt, poz. ix. oz. Item, a holie-water ſtoppe and a ſprinkell of ſilver, parcell gilt, poz. xviii. oz. iii. quarters. Item, a ſacringe bell of ſilver gilte, poz. v. oz. quarter. Item, a pax of ſilver gilt, with a crucifix and Mary and John, poz. xvi. oz. iii. quarters. Item, ii. pair of ſilver ſenſers, parcell gilt, poz. lxx, oz. Item, a ſhip of ſilver with a lyttell ſpone for frankenſens[g], parcell gilt, poz. xvii. oz. di. Item, ii. chappell bayſens of ſilver, parcell gilte, poz. xxxvii. oz. di. Item, a ffaire croſſe of ſilver and gilte with Marye and John, garnyſhede with cryſtall and ſtones, with a foote of ſilver and gilt to the ſame, weinge together, beſydes the gar-nyſhing of cryſtall and ſtones, xxiiii. l. v. oz. Item, ii. candleſtickes of ſilver parcell gilte, poz. xxxi. oz. iii. quarters. All whiche parcells, &c. In witneſſe whereoff, &c.

[g] A ſpecies of Cenſer. _See Dugd. Mon. iii. 276. 311. 294. Ibid. Eccl. Coll. 84.

*Item,*

[h] *Item*, receved from the Founder, iii. Marche, a baner of grene fylke, wrapped in grene bokram, with ii, knoppes gylted for the fame.—Item, receeived the fecond day of Aprile, an image of Chriftes refurrection, with a cafe for the fame having locke and kaye. Item, received from our faid founder the vi. daye of Aprile, a defke-clothe of dyverfe-coloured fylke.

[h] Added in the regifter, ad calc. inftrumenti,

N U M B.

✛✛✛✛✛✛✛✛✛✛✛✛✛✛✛✛✛✛✛✛✛✛✛✛✛

# N U M B. XVIII.

Indentura de ornamentis et jocalibus, miſſis per dominum Fundatorem ad collegium tertia vice. April. 12, 1557 [a].

F FIRST, two tunicles for a diacon and ſub-diacon of white ſatten with flowres of gold, with albes, ſtoles and parrys to the ſame to matche with the veſtment of white damaſke — [*before recei-ved.*] Item, a banner clothe for the Croſſe, of grene ſarcenett; on the one ſide whereoff is paynted the *Trinitie*, and on the other ſyde our Ladye. Item, a crucifix of woodde, paynted, with the foure evangeliſtes, to ſet at the Entry of the Queere [b] in the ſaide college. Item, one image of woode of the reſurrectyon paynted, to ſett upon the altar at Eaſ-ter; and a box, lyned with cotten with a locke and kaye to putt the ſame image in. Item, ii. bookes of parchment lymned with gold; the one of which, beinge a goſpellar, is covered on the one ſyde with ſylver, and havinge a crucifix on the ſame copper

[a] Regiſtr. fol. 10.
[b] Choir.

and

and gilte: And the other boke, being a piftoler[c], is lykewife covered on the one fyde with fylver, having upon the fame-an image of St. Paule being fylver and gilte. Item, a faire cope of clothe of golde, with an orphrefe[d] of clothe of fylver, and a running orphrefe embrodered. Item, a veftment and ii. tunicles of clothe of fylver, having orphrefes of clothe of golde, and a running orphrefe embrodered, as the cope hath, with faire fyne new albes, ftoles, phannells, and gyrdles, for the fame, with iii. bags of lynen clothe to put the fame in. Item, a faire canapie of blue clothe of gold, paned with riche redde tynfell, with thredes of golde and a faire fringe of fylke, and the infide of the valence lyned with fatten of Bridges. Item, a hearfe-clothe of the fame blue clothe of golde and red tynfell frynged with fylke. Item, fix albes furnifhed for Boyes to

---

[c] Epiftoler. For the Epiftle.

[d] That is an embroidered edging. From AURIFRASIUM, corrupted from AURIFRISIUM, properly perhaps AURIPHRI-GIUM. Fr. Orfray. Hence the Italian fregiato d' oro, that is, as our elder poets exprefs the phrafe, fretted with gold. Ariofto has, " D' ORO FREGIATA l' armatura," ORL. FUR. xxv. 97. And, " Ricche di gioie, e ben PREGIATA D' ORO," Ibid. xxxviii. 78. Menage fuppofes AURIPHRYGIUM to be " Phry-" gian work or embroidery in gold." It is certain that PHRY-GIUM is ufed fimply and fubftantively for this fort of ornament in a robe. " Obtulit S. Benedicto planetam [a Cope] aureis " PHRYGIIS, menfium 12 figna infra habentibus, ornatam." Leo Oftienf. CHRON. CAS. Lib. ii. c. 24. In Chaucer's DREME of CHAUCER, PHRYGIUS is written FREGIUS, v. 1070. Some difficulty is thrown on this fpecious etymology by the Anglo-faxon verb ᚠᚱᚫᛏᚦᚪᚾ, to adorn.

carye candleftickes and fenfors, whareof two of them
be hymmede [e] with clothe of golde, of the fame
clothe of gold that the cope before remembered js
of. Item, ii. tunicles of white Brydges faten, or-
phrefed with grene Brydges faten, for fuch to weare
as fhall carye the croffe and holie-water ftoppe. Item,
ii. faire copes of tyffue, with fair orphefes of nedle-
worke. Item, a cope of blewe baudkin with flowres
of golde, and with an orphrefe of yelowe tyffue,
havinge a running orphefe of red velvet. Item,
another faire cope of white damafke with angells and
arch-angells of gold, havinge a faire orphefe of needle worke. Item a faire veftment and two tunicles
belonging to the fame, of the fame redde clothe of
tyffue that the ii copes before remembered are of,
having orphefes of needleworke and armes upon the
fame, and having new albes, ftoles, and parrys belonging to the fame. Item, a defke-clothe made of
olde churche ftuffe of fundry fortes. Item, a quiffion
to lay the croffe on in the Sepulchre, made of iiii.
fcochyns wherein armes are wrought. Item, a monftrans [f] of fylver gilt, poz. xxi. oz. ALL which parcells of plate, books, and ornaments, &c. In wit-
neffe, &c.

[g] *Item*, Receyved from our founder, in the month
of June, 1558, thefe bookes followinge. In primis,
Jofephus Græce. One booke [ volume ] of St.
Beede's works. Another, intitled Sanctiones Eccle-

---

[e] Hemmed.
[f] A box for relics, or the Sacrament.
[g] Ad calc. inftrumenti, in Regiftr.

fiafticæ.

fiaſticæ. One other of St. Juſtines workes the mar-
tir. And one Greeke Pſalter covered with clothe of
golde. Item ſyx proceſſionalls printed. — *Item*, two
clothes of payned velvett for the ſepulcher. Item,
two clothes of ſaten Brydges for the lowe alters.
Item, eight ſconſys. Item, a bible in Engliſhe,
with a Pſalter, and a . . . , booke. Item ii books of
common prayer[h] in latten[i].

[h] Maſs-book.
[i] See Numb. XIX.

✝↓✝↓✝↓✝↓✝↓✝↓✝↓✝↓✝↓✝↓✝↓✝↓✝↓✝↓✝↓✝↓✝↓✝↓✝↓↓✝

## N U M B. XIX.

Bifhop Horne's Letter to Trinity college concerning the Removal of fuperftitious ornaments from the chapel ². Dat. 1570 ᵇ.

*To the worfhipfull my loving friends the prefident and fellowes of Trynitie college in Oxford.*

AFTER my hartie commendations : Whereas I am informed that certaine monuments

---

ª Regiftr. fol. 138. b.

ᵇ Soon after the Act of Uniformity had been promulged in 1558, in the firft year of queen Elifabeth, inftead of removing the fopperies of the antient worfhip, or at leaft fuffering them gradually to wear away by time and negleft, this fociety appears to have fpared no expence to retain and renew thefe folemn toys. This may be gathered from the following articles in Comp. Burff. 1560,–1.

" Sol. pro quatuor ulnis panni vocatl *Fetwich* pro altari-
" bus, ij *s.* vij *d.* ob.—Sol. pro clavis exiguis ad eadem pendi-
" lia [curtains] affigenda, ij *d.*—Sol. pro longis *lathes* quæ in-
" ferviebant circa pendilia altarium, xxij *d.*—Sol. pro ulna
" canabei panni ex qua fiebant pendilia fupra oftium CRUCI-
" FIXORII, xj *d.* ob." The laft article is for a curtain to hang over the little folding-doors which inclofed the CRUCIFIX ftanding on the principal altar.

tending

tending to idolatrie and popifh or devills fervice, as Croffes, Cenfares, and fuch lyke fylthie ftuffe ufed in the idolatrous temple, more meter for the fame than for the houfe of god, remaynethe in your college as yet undefaced; I am moved thereby to judge great want of good will in fome of you, and no lefs neglygence in other fome, as in beinge fo remiffe to performe your duties towards god, and obedience unto the prince. Wherefore I can do no leffe, as in refpecte of my Office and Care I have of you, but verie earneftlie forthwith, uppon the receite hereof, will you to deface all manner fuche trafhe, as in the church of Chrifte is fo noyfome and unfeemlie; and to convert the matter thereof to the *godlie* ufe, profett, and behoofe of your houfe. And further to have in mynde the motion made by the graunde commiffioners *. If anie do make doubt of your

---

* Notwithftanding this Injunction, I find Bifhop Horne vifit-. ing the college, by his commiffary, G. Acworth, L. L. D. four years before, Nov. 19, 1566, who finds " Nihil reformatione " dignum." Regiftr. Horne, fol. 52.

I fhall give fome other inftances of his reforming genius, from his faid Regifter, penes Officiar. Epifc. Winton.

INJUNCTIONS, among others, At a *Vifitation of the Cathedral of Winchefter*, Oct. 2, 1571. Reg. ut fupr. fol. 83.

" *Item*, That the roode loft in the bodye of churche be " mured upp, and fome parcell of fcriptur be written ther. " *Item*, That the tabernacles of images now ftanding voyde " in the bodye of the churche may be taken away, or filled " upp, and the places made plane. *Item*, That all images " of the Trinitye in the glaffe windows, or other places of the " churche, be putt oute and extinguifhed, together with the " ftone croffe in the churche-yarde. *Item*, That the inven-

Z " torye

ſtatutes, in that parte, as ſome more obſtinate than *zealous* may doe ; I do ſignifye unto you, That I

" torye of all the churche ſtuffe, as copes, veſtiments, albes,
" chalices, pixes, ſervice books, and ſuch other whatſoever, be
" brought and exhibited to the ordinarye within two monthes
" next after, with a certificate of all the images that wer in
" the churche."

At a *Viſitation of Wincheſter College*, Oct. 2. 1571. fol. 88.
ſeqq.  " *Item*, That the organs be no more uſed in ſervyce-
" tyme, and the ſtipende for the orgayne-player, and that
" which was allowed to a chapplen to ſay maſſe in the chappell
" in the cloyſter, ſhalbe hereafter torned to ſome other *godlye*
" uſe and neceſſarye purpoſe in the colledge chappell. *Item,*
" The prayers which the choriſters uſe dailye to ſaye in lattyn
" in *fromons* § chappell, ſhallbe no mor uſed, but inſtead there-
" of ſome other prayers, or *pſalmodie. Item,* That for the ſer-
" mons aforeſaid, to be preached by the warden and fellowes,
" there be a decent pulpit made removeable, and to be ſett
" upp by the greces beneath the communion-table for the ſer-
" mon tyme ; and that the rood-lofte be taken down to a com-
" petent height for hindering the hearers. *Item,* That the holie
" communion ſhall be miniſtered in the ſaid colledge, withoute
" any cope having images or pictures."

At a *Viſitation of New college in Oxford*, Aug. 29, 1567. fol.
65.  " *Item*, Ut tabulata inter chorum capellæ et navem ejuſ-
" dem amoveantur et proſternautur, uſque ad altitudinem ſedi-
" lium ejuſdem chori, et ut omnes et ſingulæ imagines ibidem
" olim ſtantes igni committantur. *Item*, Ut amotis tegminibus
" orientalis partis chori ejuſdem capelle, parietes ibidem obum-
" brentur plane, dealbentur, et ſententie ſacre ſcripture ibidem
" ſcribantur.——Neque ſocii, ſcholares, aut miniſtri chori, ſe
" convertant in divinis, more papiſtico, ad orientem, cum can-
" tatur *Gloria Patri.*" Againſt the eaſtern wall of this magnificent chapel over the altar, the pride of Gothic architecture

§ Fromond's.

have perufed the ftatutes, and do fynde, that, the fame well confidered, and the words thereof trulie

was richly difplayed in imagery, niches, pinnacles, groupes of tracery, and other fumptuous ornaments of curious workmanfhip. Thefe were deftroyed or defaced by this injunction of bifhop Horne; who not only removed the ftatues, but broke or filled up the niches, and reduced the whole, which muft have formed a beautiful and characteriftical termination of the vifto from the choir-door, to a plain fuperficies of plaifter and whitewafh. This wall, or fcreen, is thus defcribed by the founder in the ftatutes of the college. STATUT. COLL. Nov. *Rubr.* lxiii. "*Item, quia in intermedio capitali five tranfverfali muro* "*capelle noftri collegii fupradicti, ubi quidam murus lapideus inter* "*ipfam capellam et aulam ipfius collegii mediare nofcitur ac eciam fe-* "*parare; ymago fanctiffime ac individue.Trinitatis, patibulum fancte* "*crucis, cum ymagine crucifixi, beate Marie virginis, fanctorumque* "*plurium aliorum ymagines, fculpture, feneftre vitree, ac picture* "*varie, nonnullaque alia opera fumptuofa, ad dei laudem gloriam et* "*honorem ipfiufque matris predicte, fubtiliter fabricata, variifque* "*coloribus perornata, devotiffime fituantur, ac multipharie collocan-* "*tur, &c."* In the year 1695, in refitting the altar and its environs, it was found that much of this antient Gothic workmanfhip ftill remained under the furface of the wall, covered with a thick coat of cement or plaifter, in tolerable prefervation. See LIFE of A. Wood. vol. ii. p. 392. edit. 1772.

To return to Horne. That he might contribute all the affiftance in his power, towards purging away the dregs of popery, I find him while bifhop of Winchefter, very frequently vifiting, his cathedral, Winchefter college, New college, Magdalene, Corpus Chrifti, and Trinity, colleges, in Oxford; but St. John's not once. Ex Regiftr. Horne, prædict. He began this bufinefs the year after his entrance into the bifhoprick. At Trinity college he vifited in perfon, 24 Sept. 1561, when I find expended upon him in dinner, wine, and gloves, iv*l.* ix*s.* x*d.* Afterwards the following notices occur.

Comp.

interpreted, you may lawfullie withoute infringinge of any parte thereof, deface the fame abufes, and receave the commoditie that may be had thereof, to thufe of your houfe. So truftinge to hear fhortlie that the fame fhall be accomplifhed effectualie, I wilhe to you all the encreafe of the grace of godes holie fpirite. From *Waltham*, the xixth day of July, 1570. Your loving friende,

ROBERT [HORNE] WINTON[d].

Comp. Burff. Coll. Trin. 1565.—6. " Alloc. in epulis datis
" commiffario epifcopi Winton. vifitanti collegium, die Sept.
" [Nov.] 19, 1566. xl*s*.

Comp. 1575.—6. " Sol. 6. Jul. 1576. Apparatori D. Epif-
" copi Wynton. adferenti literas citatorias. v*s*.
" Sol. pro i Pari chirothecarum dato Dom. Epifc. Winton. iv*s*.
" Allocat. in epulis datis Dom. Epifcopo Winton, vifitanti
" collegium, fec. die Augufti, A. D. 1576. vj*l*. ij*s*. ij*d*. *qu*.

Horne was a learned man, but a zealous and active puritan. While Dean of Durham in the reign of Edward vi. he demolifhed many very elegant and very harmlefs monuments of ancient art, in that noble cathedral. The author of a curious book, entitled *Ancient Rites of the Church of Durham*, Lond. 1672. p. 122. written by one who lived while the monaftery fubfifted, tells us, that he deftroyed the hiftory of St. Cuthbert beautifully painted in glafs throughout the cloyfter-windows. This havock, he adds, was made by dean Horne, " who could never abide " any ancient monuments, acts, or deeds."

d See the next Article.

✝✝✝✝✝✝✝✝✝✝✝✝✝✝✝✝✝✝✝✝✝✝✝✝✝✝✝✝✝✝✝✝

# N U M B.   XX.

Letter from Queen Elizabeth's Commiffioners relating to the Bufinefs
of the laft-mentioned Letter, dat.
1570[a].

*To the prefident, fellowes, and fcollers, of Trynitie
college, Oxford.*

WE will and commaunde you, by vertue of
the Quenes majefties commiffion to us directed, that before the xiith daye of Julye next en-
fuenge the date hereof, you caufe to be defaced all
the church Plate and church Stuffe, belonging to
your colledge; in fuch forte, that it never maye be
ufed agayne, as it hath bin. Otherwife, as to you
fhall feeme beft, to the moft profett and behoffe of
your faid colledge. And that you fo doe it, as
either one of her Majefties commiffioners may fe it;
or you the prefident, by your othe, teftifie to us, or
our colleagues, to be doen, according to the tenour
herof, the next court daye after the daye abovementioned. Returnyng then agayne this our Precept

[a] Ibid. fol. 139.

Z 3                                              with

with you. Whereof fayle you not, as you will
anſwer to the contrarie at your perrel [b]. This xxviii.
June, 1570. *Thomas Cooper, L. Humfrie, H. Weſtphalinge, W. Cole* [c].

[b] However, a few months before, they demoliſhed the ſtone-
altars in the chapel, and placed in their ſtead, a communion-
table, &c. as appears by the following entries.
Comp. Burſſ. 1569.—70. " Sol. lapicidinis per duos dies in
" facello laborantibus. iv *s*. iv *d.*

" Sol. 10. feb. pro *communionis menſa et pluteis* in facello, xj *s.*

Soon afterwards, the *Metrical* pſalms, after the plan of Geneva, growing faſhionable, I find the firſt mention of the following article.
Comp 1575.—6. " Expoſ. a decano pro ſex libris pſalmorum
" in uſum facelli. xij *s*."

[c] The queen's commiſſioners for aboliſhing popiſh ſuperſtition in the univerſity of Oxford. They ſate in the divinity
chapel, in Chriſt-church cathedral. Cooper was dean of
Glouceſter, afterwards biſhop of Wincheſter. Humphrey was
preſident of Magdalene. Weſtphalinge was canon of Chriſt-
church, afterwards biſhop of Hereford. Cole was preſident of
C. C. C. Oxon. See Wood Hiſt. Antiq. univ. Oxon. i. 291.
Godwyn informs us, that Weſtphalinge was a perſon of ſuch
conſummate *gravity,* that during a familiar acquaintance with
him for many years, he never once ſaw him *laugh.*—" *Nun-*
" *quam in riſum viderim ſolutum.*" De Præful. ed. 1616. pag.
546. ed. 4to. His arms are elegantly painted in the great
window of the Chapter-houſe at Chriſt-church, with an Inſcription, and the date 1601.

†↓†↓†↓†↓†↓†↓†↓†↓†↓†↓†↓†↓†↓†↓†↓†↓†↓†↓†↓†↓†↓†↓†

# N U M B.  XXI.

Compofitio quædam Collegiorum, Coll.
Magd. et Coll. Trin. Oxon. Dat.
Feb. 26, 1558[a].

OMNIBUS Chrifti fidelibus, ad quos hoc
præfens fcriptum indentatum pervenerit : Nos
Thomas Coveney, præfidens collegii B. Mariæ Magdalenæ in univerfitate Oxon. et fcholares ejufdem
collegii, falutem in domino fempiternam.    Cum
Alicia[b] PARRET, nuper de parochia fancti Petri in
oriente Oxon. vidua, ac bonæ memoriæ matrona,
ejufque [c] teftamenti unicus executor SIMON PAR-
RET [d], generofus, nuper prædicti collegii focius, ob
magnæ devotionis fervorem, et affectionem in præ-

---

[a] In Thefauriar. Coll. Trin. et Regiftr. prim. fol. 22. b. Et
Muniment. Coll. Magd.

[b] Daughter of Robert Gardiner, mentioned below, of Sun-
ningwell, Berkfhire, and Alice Orpewood. See p. 327.

[c] Dat. fuit teftamentum 21 Mar. 1556. Probat. 4 Jul. 1556.
Offic. Teftam. Oxon.

[d] In the Britifh Mufeum are manufcript letters of one Simon
Parrett, certainly not the fame, dat. Oxon. 1582. concerning a
new edition of Fox's *Book of Martyrs,* written to Fox. MSS.
Harl. 416.

Z 4                              fatum

fatum collegium, inter fe dederint, et manibus fuis propriis tradiderint, partim Owino Oglethorpe nuper præfidenti collegii prædicti, et fcholaribus ejufdem collegii, partim nobis præfato Thomæ Coveney nunc præfidenti dicti collegii, et fcholaribus ejufdem collegii, centum viginti et quatuor libras bonæ ac legalis monetæ Angliæ, ad emendum et perquiren‧ dum terras et redditus ad verum annuum valorem fex librarum, ultra omnes reprifas, quas vocant, habend. et tenend. nobis præfatis præfidenti et fcholaribus collegii B. Mariæ Magdalenæ in univerfitate Oxon. et fucceſſoribus noftris, in perpetuum ; ad effectus quofdam pios infra-fcriptos : præcipue vero, pro perpetuis duabus Exhibitionibus in dicto collegio fundandis, et aliis non minus piis, quam neceſſariis, fuftentationibus pauperum fcholarium ftudentium in dicto collegio. Nos igitur, præfati præfidens et fcholares, tam infigni pietate moti, rurfus nec ferentes tam pium defiderium præfatorum ALICIÆ et SIMONIS effectu fpoliari, nec defunctam fua extrema voluntate fraudari, fed mandatum ejus ad effectum perducere conantes ; præfatam fummam, vel faltem majorem ejus partem, quadruplo erogavimus in emptionem terrarum, nuper de Roberto Radborne de Stanlake in com. Oxon. perquifitarum, et reliquam fummam, prout opportunitas fe offeret, in fimiles ufus applicabimus. Quos quidem redditus fex librarum per annum, nos præfati præfidens et fcholares promittimus, et per præfentes obligamus nos et fucceffores noftros, ad fpecialem requifitionem præfati SIMONIS PARRET, *Præfidenti Sociis et Scholaribus Collegii fanctæ et individuæ Trinitatis in univerfitate*

*univerfitate Oxon. ex fundatione* Thomæ Pope *militis*,
quod nos et fucceffores noftri deinceps perpetuis fu-
turis temporibus, deo volente, colligemus, exponë-
mus, et folvemus, vel folvi faciemus, per manus
burfariorum dicti collegii, fecundum voluntatem
prædictæ Aliciæ, ad hunc qui fequitur modum.
In Primis, promittimus, et obligamus nos et fucceffores noftros, quod deinceps in perpetuum erit
unus fociorum dict collegii B. Mariæ Magdalenæ in
univerfitate Oxon. facris initiatus, viz. prefbiter bonæ
converfationis integræque famæ, qui orabit pro animabus Roberti Parret et Aliciæ uxoris ejus,
Simonis Parret et Elisabethæ uxoris ejus, Johannis Kele et Edmundi Kele, Roberti Gardenar
et Aliciæ uxoris ejus, et pro animabus omnium Fide- ·
lium defunctorum, bis fingulis hebdomadis, cum
celebraverit Miffam. Qui quidem prefbiter recipiet in
fine cujuflibet anni termini decem folidos, de prædictis fex libris ; viz. in toto per annum, et fic de anno
in annum, quadraginta folidos. Cujus electio ac ·
præfectio deinceps erit penes præfidentem prædicti
collegii B. Mariæ Magdalenæ pro tempore exiften-
tem, fi domi fuerit, vel fi intra unum menfem ad
dictum collegium redierit poft receffum, deceffum,
obitum, refignationem, vel deprivationem, prædicti
focii, fic ad hanc electionem admiffi. Quod fi præfidens ultra menfem abfuerit a prædicto collegio, tum
penes vice-præfidentem erit novum fufficere prefbite-
rum in vacantis locum. Tenebiturque admittendus
ad hanc exibitionem, eodem die, aut faltem intra tres
dies immediate fequentes ejus admiffionem, hanc
Compositionem legere. Insuper, nos præfati præfidens

fidens et fcholares obligamus nos et fucceffores noftros ad celebrandas Exequias dominica fecunda poft
feftum Pafchatis quo die obiit præfatus ROBERTUS
PARRET, et miffam die fequenti fingulis annis in
perpetuum, pro animabus fupranominatorum, cum
expreffione nominum eorum. Et ad diftribuendos
viginti folidos inter præfidentem dicti collegii et focios ejufdem, qui interfuerint exequiis et miffæ prædictis folummodo: nifi forte præfidens, aut fociorum
aliquis abfuerit in negotiis collegii; in quo cafu
nolumus eorum aliquem fua fraudari portione. Necnon ad folvendum Choriftis dicti collegii, vel eorum locum tenentibus, quinque folidos et quatuor
denarios; et Præceptori eorum fexdecim denarios,
fingulis annis in perpetum. Et ulterius promittimus,
quod eodem die quo celebrabitur Miffa pro animabus fupranominatorum, trefdecim folidi et quatuor
denarii infumentur in uberiorem refectionem præfidentis et fcholarium prædictorum, prout fieri confue-
vit in exequiis aliorum Benefactorum dicti collegii.
Decernimus etiam, ut qui admiffus fit ad hanc exhi-
bitionem, fingulis annis, eodem die celebrabit Miffam, et vocabitur Capellanus ALICIÆ PARRET.
Item, quod communi campanario, more Oxoniæ
folito, pro animabus prædictorum publice procla-
manti, in die dictarum Exequiarum, annuatim da-
buntur quatuor denarii, pro labore ejus. Præterea,
nos præfati præfidens et fcholares obligamus nos et
fucceffores noftros, per præfentes, quod deinceps
fingulis annis ad terminum viginti annorum, primo
die Maii, quo die obiit præfata ALICIA, nos præfati præfidens et fcholares, et fucceffores noftri, deliberabimus

liberabimus viginti folidos capellano fic electo ; ut is, et unus Gardianorum ecclefiæ fancti Petri in oriente Oxon. fingulis annis, in exequiis celebrandis in parochia prædicta fancti Petri pro animabus prædictorum, juxta eorum difcretionem, fingulis annis, durante termino prædicto, diftribuant et erogent in pios ufus : viz. in neceffarios fumptus Exequiarum et Miffæ, et in fuftentationem Indigentium commorantium in dicta parochia fancti Petri. Et ulterius decernimus, quod elapfis viginti annis, et debitis factis diftributionibus in parochia prædicta, quod extunc nos præfati præfidens et fcholares, fingulis annis imperpetuum, deliberabimus, per manus burfariorum prædicti collegii, viginti folidos alicui focio dicti collegii, vel fcholari, eligendo et nominando, more capellani prædicti, ad orandum pro animabus prædictorum. Præterea ordinavimus, quod refiduum fex librarum prædictarum remaneat ad opus et ufum dicti collegii imperpetuum. POSTREMO, ut COMPOSITIO et hæc præfens Ordinatio firma fit et perpetua, nullifque injuriis antiquanda, nos præfati præfidens et fcholares concedimus per præfentes, pro nobis et fuccefforibus noftris imperpetuum ; quod fi per nos præfatum præfidentem et fcholares, vel fucceffores noftros, fteterit, quo minus hæc Ordinatio non plenarie fuerit fatisfacta, fed incuria vel culpa noftra aut exhibitiones non folvantur, vel defunctis Jufta non perfolvantur, vel diftributiones omittantur ; quod tunc, quoties id contigerit, bené licebit *Præfidenti Sociis et Scholaribus Collegii fanctæ et individuæ Trinitatis in univerfitate Oxon. ex fundatione* THOMÆ POPE *militis,* imperpetuum, in omnes terras

ras noſtras, nuper perquiſitas de præfato Roberto
Radborne in Stanlake prædicta, intrare et diſtringere, diſtrictioneſque ſic captas licite aſportare, ab-
• ducere, effugare, et penes ſe retinere, ac ad eorum
uſum recipere et habere, ad tantum valorem quanti
valoris fuerit onus ſive exhibitio dicti ſocii vacantis ſupra tempus limitatum, aut diſtributio ulla, ut
ſuperius conſtituitur, omiſſa. In cujus rei teſti-
monium, uni parti hujus ſcripti indentati penes nos
præfatos præſidentem et ſcholares collegii B. Mariæ
Magdalenæ in univerſitate Oxon. et ſucceſſores noſtros remanenti, *Præſidens Socii et Scholares Collegii
ſanctæ et individuæ Trinitatis in univerſitate Oxon. ex
fundatione* THOMÆ POPE *militis*, Sigillum ſuum
commune appoſuerunt ; et alteri parti hujus ſcripti
indentati, penes præfatos *Præſidentem Socios et Scholares Collegii ſanctæ et individuæ Trinitatis in univerſitate Oxon. ex fundatione* THOMÆ POPE *militis*, et
ſucceſſores eorum, remanenti, nos præfati præſidens
et ſcholares collegii B. Mariæ Magdalenæ Oxon.
Sigillum noſtrum commune appoſuimus. DATUM
xxvi. die februarii, anno regni sereniſſimæ noſtræ
principis Eliſabethæ, dei gratia, Angliæ, Franciæ,
et Hiberniæ Reginæ, fidei defenſoris, etc. primo *.
[1558.—9 ]

---

ᶜ By another inſtrument, mutually given as above, bearing
date Sept. 1, 1579, this *Compoſition*, on account of the reformation of religion, was altered, as it is to this day obſerved
by Magdalene college. *In Regiſtr. Coll. Trin. prim.* fol. 40.
*Et in Munim. Coll Trin. et Magd.* ut ſupr.—Wood is miſtaken in
ſaying, that this *Alicia Parret* was the *wife* of Simon, for ſhe
was his *mother.* Hiſt. Antiq. Univ. Oxon. ii. 190. But he afterwards

wards corrected the miſtake, Athen. Oxon. i. faſt. 23. col. 1.
Vide Lee's MSS. Viſitat. Oxfordſh. pp. 12, 13.   In the altered
Compoſition, where mention is made of the *diſtributio in choriſ-*
*tas*, it is added, " Quia dictus *Robertus* Perott, al. Parret, pater
" dicti *Simonis*, fuit olim præceptor choriſtarum in dicto colle-
" gio." He was an eminent muſician for his time ; and gra-
duated in muſic at Oxford, before the year 1515. And dying
April 21, 1550, aged 72, was buried in the church of St. Peter
in the Eaſt at Oxford.   The ſame Robert Perrot was a ſharer
of abbey-land, and bought Rewley abbey at Oxford on the
diſſolution.  Wood, *MSS. Cit. Oxf.* No. 8491.  Muſ. Aſhm.
He alſo occurs receiver general of the archdeaconry of Bucking-
ham, in 1534, Willis, *Cath. Oxf.* p. 119. He was alſo receiver
of rents for Chriſt-church, Oxford, in the twenty-ſixth year of
Hen. viii. *MSS. in Offic. Primit.* He is mentioned, in lord Williams's Charter for founding Thame-ſchool in Oxfordſhire, dated
1574, to have been receiver of the rents for Littlemore Pri ry
near Oxford.  Compare LIFE, p. 117, 183. and Append. Numb.
IX. *in the notes.*  And p. 327. *notes.*  Alſo Wood, FAST. OXON.
i. 69, 70.   And Morton's Northamptonſh. p. 460.

But a curious authentic manuſcript has lately been communicated to me, containing various evidences and notices of the
family of Perrot : the following extracts from which will confirm or correct what is here, or has been before in other parts
of this work, either imperfectly or erroneouſly obſerved concerning the ſaid family. viz. " fol. 5. b. Simon Parret is made
" notary public, 22 May, 1546.—fol. 7. a.  S. Parret is con-
" ſtituted regiſtrar of Bucks, with a fee of five marks and a
" robe annually, 20 Jul. 1547.—fol. 3. a.  S Parret, of Ox-
" ford, gentleman, is appointed ſteward of divers manors, to
" dame Elizabeth Pope, widow, 20 Jan. 1559.—fol. 6. b.
" He is made, by Edward the ſixth, bailiff of the chantry-
" lands within the county of Oxon. 2. Feb. 1550, with a fee
" of v*l.* vj*s.* viij *d.*—fol. 111. b.  He, then aged xxxvi years,
" marries Elizabeth Love of Aynhoe, 28 Sept. 1550.—fol. 78.
" b.  He ſells his leaſe of the parſonage of Stoke-lyne to his
" brother in law Edward Love, 1561.—fol. 7. a.  His ſon

" Simon

" Simon comes to a court at Northleigh, co. Oxon. 1568.—
" fol. 111. a.   He dies aged 71, 24 Sept. 1584, and is buried
" in St. Peter's church in the East at Oxford.—fol. 111. a.  His
" wife Elizabeth, married at nineteen years of age, and by
" whom he has nineteen children, dies in 1572, and is buried
" in the said church.—fol. 72. a.   Robert Parret of Oxford
" esquire, [the musician] father of the first Simon, occurs in
" 1549.—fol. 12. a.   Robert's will is dated 18 Apr. 1550, he
" being then of St. Peter's, Oxon.   Therein he gives to his
" wife Alice his patent of 4 marcs annually from the king,
" ending with the life of G. Pigott.   In the same he mentions
" his son Simon.—fol. 111. b.   He dies 21 Apr. following,
" buried ibid.—fol. 13. a.   The will of the said Alice is dated
" 21 Mar. 1556.   Therein she mentions Elizabeth the wife of
" her son Simon, to whom she gives *her best cassocke of clothe and*
" *sattin kyrtell.*   She dies [Alice] 2 Jul. 1558.—fol. 111. b.
" The same Alice, mother of the said Simon, daughter of Alice
" Orpewood, dying 1558, is buried in the said church.—fol.
" 37. a.   Articles of marriage between Simon Parret [the
" younger] and Avis White, dated 1573." *MS. fil. olim Gulielmi*
*Perrot, armig. de Northleigh co. Oxon. Nunc penes me, ex dono R. V.*
*Joannis Price, Protobibl. Bodl.*

On the whole it appears, that *Simon,* fellow of Magdalene
college, mentioned in this instrument, who married *Elisabeth*
*Love,* was the person whose name occurs in papers and accounts
(See LIFE, 183.) at the foundation of Trinity college, and who
was the founder's agent.

The manor of Northleigh aforesaid, being parcel of Nettley
abbey in Hampshire, was granted to fir Thomas Pope and his
heirs in the year 1545, by patent of Henry the eighth, anno
regn. 36. Jul. 28. par. 8.   From him it descended to his widow
dame Elisabeth.   Late in the reign of queen Elisabeth, it appears to have been vested in the descendants of Robert Parrot,
or rather Perrot, abovementioned; whose son Simon, as we
have seen, married Elisabeth Love, fir Thomas Pope's niece.
Wood [Ath. Oxon. i. Fast. 27. ut supr.] is mistaken in saying,
that the said Robert, the founder of this family in Oxfordshire,
was

was the second son of George Perrot of Haroldston near Haverford west in Pembrokshire. It is proved from better authority, that he was born at Hacknes in the North riding of Yorkshire. MS. Registr. Parrot, ut supr. fol. 111. b. The family of Perrot lived at Northleigh, in their antient capital mansion house, till within these few years : but are now extinct, at least in the lineal succession. This estate was lately purchased by the duke of Marlborough.

NUMB.

# N U M B. XXII.

## Articles relating to certain Buildings and Utenfils of Wroxton Priory in Oxfordfhire, foon after the Diffolution. Dat. Aug. 16, 1537 ᵃ.

H Ereafter enfueth, afwell certeyne buildyngs belonging to the late Monaftery of Wroxtone

ᵃ In Thefaur. Coll. Trin. prædict. Manu Dom. Thomæ Pope. Where are feveral original inftruments relating to this monaftery. The moft antient (not yet printed) are the two following, being nearly coeval with the foundation.

I. " Univerfis fancte matris ecclefie filiis literas iftas fufpec-
" turis vel audituris,magifter MICHAELBELET falutem in domino.
" Noverit univerfitas veftra, quod ego dedi et conceffi domine
" abbatiffe de GODESTHOUGH et monialibus ibidem deo fervi-
" entibus, redditum quadraginta folidorum annuatim percipien-
" dorum ad duos terminos: fcil. viginti folidos ad octabas Pen-
" tecoftes, et viginti ad octabas fancti Martini in hyeme. Quos
" predictos quadraginta folidos predicte moniales recipiant an-
" nuatim per manum prioris et canonicorum de WROKSTAN:
" quibus ego affignavi certum redditum in certo loco ad cer-
" tum terminum in manerio meo de Sycheftan. Ut fine omni
" impedimento poffint eos percipere, et predictis monialibus
" reddere ad predictos terminos. Feci et predictos canonicos
" . . . . . . . . in periculo animarum fuarum, et jurare, vifis
" facro-fanctis, quod fine dolo et fraude, omni impedimento et
" occafione

fold by William Rayneſeford, eſquier, to Thomas
Pope, eſqyer, the xvith day of Auguſt, A°. xxix.

" occaſione ceſſante, ſolvant prediƈtum redditum prediƈtis mo-
" nialibus ; Ut autem hæc mea donatio et conceſſio rata ſit
" et firma, preſens ſcriptum ſigilli mei munimine roboravi.
" Hiis teſtibus, domino *Rad. de ſanƈto Amando*, dom. *Joh. de*
" *Bruchton, Alex. de Barton, Herveo Belet, Philip de Merula,*
" *Roberto de Sycheſtan.* *Rob. Parvo de Wroxton, Rob. de Cerce-*
" *dene, Nich de Wroxſtan,* et multis aliis." No date. cum ſigill.
*Michael Belet founded the monaſtery early in the reign of Henry the*
*third, about the year* 1230.

II. " Univerſis ſanƈte matris eccleſie filiis literas iſtas viſu-
" ris vel audituris. HUGO, Prior loci ſanƈte Marie de WROKES-
" TAN, et totus conventus qui ibidem ſerviunt deo et beate
" Marie, Salutem in domino. Noverit univerſitas veſtra, quod
" nos obligamus nos et ſucceſſores noſtros in perpetuum, ad
" reddendum abbatiſſe et conventui de Godeſtowe annuatim
" quadraginta ſolidos argenti : ſcil. viginti ſolidos ad oƈtabas
" ſanƈti Martini in hyeme et viginti ad oƈtab. Pentecoſtes.
" Quos quadraginta ſolidos patronus noſter magiſter MICHAEL
" BELET aſſignavit nobis percipiendos in manerio ſuo de *Sicheſ-*
" *tan :* ubi ipſe dedit nobis decem libratas terre. Sicut carta
" ejus teſtatur quam habemus. Et prediƈtam obligationem
" multis modis fecimus, quia juravimus in animas noſtras.
" quod prediƈtam ſolutionem trium marcarum ſine fraude et
" occaſione, ceſſante omni contradiƈtione et impedimento, fa-
" ciemus ad prediƈtos terminos : et ſigillo noſtro conventuali,
" quod huic ſcripto appenſum eſt, confirmavimus ; ſub pena
" viginti ſolidorum pro quolibet defeƈtu ſi contingat. Subjeci-
" mus etiam nos ſpecialiter in hac parte juriſdiƈtioni epiſcopi
" *Lincoln.* qui fuerit pro tempore, et ſimiliter Archidiacono
" *Oxon :* ut illi duo, vel unus eorum, poſſit nos ſine omni
" contradiƈtione compellere ad prediƈtam ſolutionem, et ad
" penam ſi fuerit commiſſa. Et quicunque eleƈtus fuerit in
" priorem, jurabit quod fideliter hanc obligationem obſervabit.
" Hiis teſtibus, domino *Nicolao* reƈtore ecleſie de *Brocktun,*

" dom.

[Hen. viii.] as alfo certeyne utenfils belonging to the
faid monaftery, being fold unto the faid William

" dom. *Bernardo* ˙vicario eclefie de *Blokkefham*, *Jacobo de*
" *Hawntya* tunc fenefcallo de *Godeftowe*, *Petro le Butelir de*
" *Mildecumb, Henr. de Lingitre, Rad. de Middletun, Will. de Hed-*
" *dindun, Henr. Meryet,* et aliis." With the feal of the monaftery ; reverfed with Saint Michael killing the dragon, and
exergue Eleemosina Michaelis Belet. Hugh was the fecond prior, and died before the year 1263.

Our next original inftrument, in point of antiquity, is a char-
ter of Henry the ivth, granting free warren to Richard the
prior, and his convent, in the manors of, *Wroxton* Oxfordfhire,
*Thorpe Underwood* Northamptonfhire, and *Sifton* Lincolnfhire,
" Hiis teftibus, Th. Cantuar, H. Ebor, R. London, H. Wyn-
" ton, Th. Dunolm, N. Bathon. et Wellenf, Henr. principe
" Wall. filio noftro primogenito, cariffimo confanguineo noftro,
" Edwardo Duce Ebor, Thoma Arundell, Ric. Warr. et Rad.
" Weftmorl. comitibus, Thoma Beaufort cancellario noftro,
" Joh. Stanley fenefcallo hofpicii noftri, et Mag. Joh. Prophete
" cuftode privati figilli noftri, ac aliis. Dat. &c. decimo die
" octobr. ann reg. noftri duodecimo." A. D. 1410. with the
broad feal in green wax.

Here is alfo a charter of King John (printed by Dugdale)
recited by infpeximus of Henry the fourth, ann. regn. 12.
Octobr. 25. cum magn. figill. [See Dugdal. Mon. ii. p. 326.
50.] This infpeximus recites a charter of Richard the fecond,
who cites Edward the third, who cites Henry the third his
father, who cites John his father. In this infpeximus Edward
the third confirms the previous charters. " Hiis teftibus, J.
" Archiep. Cant. W. Winton. epifc. Thefaurar. noftro. Henr.
" com. Lancaftr. Will. de Bohun. com. Northampt. Henr. de
" Percy, Thoma Wake de Lydell, Ric. Talebott fenefcallo
" hofpicii noftri, et aliis. Dat. per manum noftram apud Weft-
" mon. 26. die Jan. ann. reg. 22." A. D. 1348.

From thefe evidences, Willis's lift of the priors of this monaftery might be enlarged or authenticated, viz. Hugh occurs

Prior,

Raynesford by our Souveraigne lord the king's officers. That is to faye.

Prior, ut fupr.—Richard, ut fupr.—Thomas Grove, without date.—William Braddenham, A. D. 1490. Alfo Feb.
1, 5 Hen. vii.—Richard, 1504. For, Dec. 6, that year, T.
Sidnall Capellanus de Wroxftan, by will, bequeaths to the faid
Richard and his convent many legacies : particularly his body
to be buried in the conventual church before the great crofs,
and one pound of wax to burn before the crofs in the parochial
church of Wroxftan.—Thomas Smith, ann. 4. 7. 20. Hen.
viii. He continued to the diffolution. See Willis Mitr. Abb.
ii. p. 188, 334. Concerning the abovementioned penfion of
forty fhillings, paid by this monaftery to Godftowe nunnery, I
find the following original inftrument, made in 1539. "This
" byll made the xxift day of October, the xxxth yere of the
" reign of our foueraign lord kyng Henry the viiith, witneff-
" eth, that I Richard Gwent clerk, Deane of the Arches,
" have, received of Thomas Pope efquier, thirtie poundes fter-
" lyng, to the ufe of Dame Kateryn Bukley, Abbes of the
" monaftery of Godftowe in the countie of Oxford, and the
" convent of the fame, for the purches of a certayn annuytie
" of xl s. by yere goyng out of certayne londes and tenements,
" &c. being parcell of the poffeffions of the late monaftery of
" Wroxton in the faid countie. In witnes whereof, I have
" fubfcrybed this byll with my own hond, the daye and yere
" above written, per Me Richard Gwent." In the Burfary of Trinity college Oxford. Where is alfo a Releafe for
the fame by the faid abbefs, with the beautiful feal of Godftowe
abbey appendant. Catharine Bukley, or Bulkley, was the laft
abbefs. See her Letter to lord, Cromwell, complaining of the
injuftifiable proceedings of Dr. London, who came with a pretended commiffion for diffolving her convent. Burnet. Ref. vol.
iii. p. 130. Rec. Num. 54. I alfo find [Thefaur. Coll. Trin.]
a fragment of a letter from her, to fir Thomas Pope, defiring
him to intercede with lord Cromwell on this bufinefs. See
fupr. Life, p. 184.

A a 2                              Firft,

Firft, the Wall of the Churche on the outfide next the cloyfter from the foote of the great window downwards.

Item, The fouth ile joyning to the dorter [b], with ii. litell iles north eft from that joyning to the fame ile.

Item, The dorter, with the roffe thereof.

Item, The ffrater howfe on both fides.

### IMPLEMENTS and UTENSILS.

Item, The condyte as it is, with all the Lede thereto belonging.

Item, ii. braffe Potts in the Kichyn to fythe mete in.

Item, In the Brewhowfe ii. grete ledes ffaft fett in a frame. ii. fmall ledes fett in curbes. One greate troffe of lede fett in the grounde.

All which implements before reherfed, I the faid William Raynfeford covenenteth and promyfeth by thef prefents at fuch time as I fhall leve the ffarme which I nowe hold of the faid Thomas Pope in Wroxton, to leve well and fufficyently repayred and mainteyned, and in as good cafe as they be now at the makyng of thes prefents.

THO. POPE. W. RAYNESFORD [c].

[b] Dormitory.
[c] Of Great-Tew, in Oxfordfhire.

Witnes

Witnes at the making thereof John Edmondes[d], gent. John Marſhall. Richard Hochynſon[e]. John Ridley. and John Menefye.

[d] He occurs ſupr. See LIFE, p. 117, 326.

[e] He received a grant of lands with Sir T. Pope, pat, 30, Hen. viii. par. 8. ſupr. citat.

✝✝✝✝✝✝✝✝✝✝✝✝✝✝✝✝✝✝✝✝✝✝✝✝✝✝✝✝✝✝✝✝✝

# N U M B. XXIII.

Rate of the Purchafe of the Rectory of Garfington [a], in Oxfordfhire by Sir Thomas Pope, from Philip and Mary, under certain Confiderations. Jan. 22, 1557. An Extract [b].

Philip and Marie. By the *King* and *Queen*.— Forafmoche as Sir Thomas Pope, knighte, as as we are credybly enformed, entendeth, if he might purchafe the faid parfonage, to gyve the fame to the prefydent fellows and fcollers of Trinitie college in the univerfitie of Oxford, and to their fucceffours

[a] It was given by Richard ii. to the cell of the holy Trinity at Wallingford, Berks, ann. reg. 15. Feb. 9. A. D. 1392.— Anthony South prior, and the convent of the faid cell, prefented William Dayfote, bachelor in decrees, to the faid rectory : faving a penfion of 100 *s.* due to themfelves, and of 40 *s.* due to S. Fridefwides, at Oxford. Dat. in dom. capit. Jun. 4. 1479. E. Regiftr. Mon. S. Albani. MSS. Tanner. Bibl. Bodl. fol. This priory was annexed to S. Alban's abbey. It was granted to Cardinal Wolfey : but by forfeiture reverted to the crown.

[b] E Lib. fec. Les Rates, 3, 4. Phil. Mar. Britifh Muf. MSS. Harl. 607. fol. 7. b. ut fupr.

for

for ever, and at his chardge to erect an howfe there, for the faid prefident, fellows, and fcollers, to repofe them in, when any plage fhall happen within the faid univerfitie: We mindinge the furtherance of that good acte, and therwithal confideringe the Buyldinge of the fame howfe will be no lytle chardge to the faid Sir Thomas, are pleafed, *etc. etc. Dat.* 22 Jun. 1557.

†+†+†+†+†+†+†+†+†+†+†+†+†+†+†+†+†+†+†+†+†+†+

# N U M B. XXIV.

*In the year* 1577, *when a mortal epidemical diftemper* [a] *prevailed at Oxford, the College retired to the aforefaid houfe at Garfington* [b] : *relating to which occafion the following very fingular inftrument, dat. April* 3, 1577, *ftill remains.*

Inftrument concerning the Receflion of Trinity College from the Univerfity to Garfington aforefaid, in time of the Plague, 1577.

TO all chriftian people to whom this prefent writinge fhall come to be reade or hard. Ar-

---

[a] In the Statutes of Trinity college, given in 1556, the Founder allows a falary of vj *l.* xiij *s.* iv*d.* to the Prefident, if removed and rendered incapable of ferving his office, *propter infirmitatem contagiofam, quæ nunc videtur perpetua futura.* Cap. xviii. This difeafe, I prefume, was the Sweating Sicknefs.

[b] E Regiftr. prim. Coll. Trin. Oxon. fol. 144. a. They likewife had before retired hither in the year 1570, or the next, the plague then raging at Oxford. Ex Comp. 1570, --1. In which plague fix hundred perfons died at Oxford. Wood, Hift. Antiqu. Univ. Oxon. i. 291. In this houfe they lived as at the college, and performed here, not only the collegiate, according to their own ftatutes, but all academical

exercifes

thur Yeldarde prefident of the college of the holie
and undivided Trinitie in the univerfitie of Oxforde,

exercifes neceffary for their degrees, by permiffion of the univerfity. In the Computus of the laft-mentioned year, I find
many curious particulars relating to their manner of living in
this retirement, and to the general diftrefs of the times. Among
others, more than once, this article.—" Sol. pro *armis* ad *tuen-*
" *dam domum.* viz. iii. black [iron] bpllet. iiij *s.* vj *d.*" Again,
1570.-1.—" Pro carta ad ufum Burfariorum apud Garfington.—
" Pro epulis peregrinorum, piftoris aliorumque potum adferen-
" tium.—Pro equo Mag. Orpwoode euntis ad Abington ad pa-
" randum panem et potum pro collegio apud Garfington.—Pro
" expenfis ejufdem apud Woodftocke et apud Kidlington variis
" temporibus circa panem et potum parandum pro iis qui re-
" manent Oxoniæ.". It appears that they carried with them,
from the college,. to this place, proper neceffaries and utenfils,
not only for their kitchen and buttery, but alfo for divine fervice. This was by the founder's directions; who moreover
leaves this roftriction, " Reliqua vero jocalia, et vafa argentea,
" tam facelli quam aulæ ufui a me conceffa, et alia ornamenta
" *majoris pretii,* in alium *tutiorem* locum infra univerfitatem
" Oxonienfem, curabunt perferenda." ADDITAM.. ad ftatut.
ut fupr. fol. 104. During this feceffion, they are alfo directed
to leave four perfons in the college, " ad tutiorem collegii cuf-
" todiam." *Ibid.* Concerning whom this article often occurs.

Comp. 1570.--1. Pro antidoto contra peftem ad ufum eorum
qui domi remanferunt. v *s.* iv *d.*—

Alfo, Datum N. pro labore fuo in cuftodiendis Januis, et aliter,
tempore peftis . . . . .

And, Oct. 25. Sol. T. C. pro labore fuo in proficifcendo heb-
domadatim, pro decem hebdomadis, Woodftockiam, ad
emenda obfonia pro iis qui domi remanent.—

By which laft article, as in fome preceeding, it appears, that it
was unfafe, or perhaps impoffible, to purchafe provifions at Oxford, in this calamitous feafon. Again, in the fame year. " Pro
" expenf.

of the ffoundation of Sir Thomas Pope, kt. and the fellows and fcollers of the fame colledge, fend greeting in our lord god everlafting. Know yee, that wee the faid prefident, fellowes and fcollers, have appointed, conftituted, and affigned, and do by thefe prefents ap. conf. and aff. Thomas Blockfome, of Garfington in the Countye of Oxforde, butcher, to provide and bye for us foe many calfes, and the fame to kill, as fhall ferve to our neceffarye ufe for the fayde colledge and companye there, from the making hereof, unto the ffirft day of June next folowinge

" expenf. Mag. Orpewood et Chambrelen apud Weodftocke
" quando folvebant pecuniam piftori, et *confirmabatur pactum*
" *cum eodem* pro pane et potu pro Collegio [apud] Oxon." I find a great reparation of this houfe, 1596. Ex Comp. Anni. In the year 1603, the plague broke out again at Oxford, when they probably retired hither as before. But the chief notice that occurs, under that year, concerning it, is,

Alloc. pro expenf. tempore peftis, xiij *l.* iij *s.* iv*d.*

In the year 1563, the plague raging at Oxford, before this houfe was finifhed, I find them retiring to Woodftock, where they hired houfes for their accommodation. About which fingular migration I have extracted thefe entries, from Comp. 1563 --4.

Sol. per totum tempus peftis pro præfervantibus mithridato et pillulis, diverfis temporibus, xij *s.* x *d.*
—— Pro prandio infumpto in medicum noftrum, i'j *s.* iv*d.*
—— Pro ftipendio miniftri ecclefiæ Woodeftock, ij *s.*
—— Ad ufum templi in Woodeftock, xx *d.*
—— Pro expenf. Greenwoodi [ a fellow ] pefte mortui, iv*s.* ix *d.*
—— Pro expenf. Burfariorum dum profecti funt ad Woodeftock ad Computum [*generalem*] faciendum . . . .
—— Sol. Woodftockii pro nocturnis vigiliis.——

the

the date hereof : prayinge all justices of peace, and
and others the quenes majesties officers, quietlye to
permitt the said Thomas Blockfome to carye, drive
and passe throughe their libertyes, with all such
Wares as he shall bye [buy] for such purpose before
named. In witness whereoff, we the sayd president,
fellowes, and scollers, have sett our common seale to
these presents, the thirde daye of Aprill in the year
of our soveraigne ladye Elizabeth, by the grace of
God, quene of England, Ffraunce and Ireland, de-
fenderesse of the faithe, the xixth. [1577. ᶜ]

ᶜ In an exhibitory bill, or schedule, of expences for their removal this year, as it seems, mention is made of carrying the
Cl ck from the college-hall to Garsington-house. Also for carriage of surplices. viz. " Sol. operariis pro vectura li ostolio-
" rum Mag. Præsidis, Sociorum, et Scholarium, ad ecclesiam
" de Garsington." And the two following articles occur. "Pro
" lectis et hospitiis extra domum pro firmariis [farmers] aliis-
" que in Computo Bursariorum et Ballivorum tento apud Gar-
" sington hoc anno."—" Pro luminibus in choro ecclesiæ de
" Garsington, xvij s. iv d."

N U M B.

# N U M B. XXV.

Account of the firſt PRESIDENT, FEL-
LOWS, and SCHOLARS, of Trinity
College, Oxford, nominated by Sir
THOMAS POPE, and admitted May
30, 1556. And of ſuch others as
were afterwards *nominated* by the
ſame Authority.

### FIRST PRESIDENT.

### THOMAS SLYTHURSTE.

**B**ORN in Berkſhire. He took the degree of
A. B. at Oxford, Feb. 27, 1529 [a]. He determined in the ſame term [b]. Made M. A. at Oxford,
Feb. 25, 1533 [c]. Theſe are ſufficient proofs that he
was educated at Oxford ; but in what college is un-

[a] Wood, Extracts from Regg. univ. Oxon. MSS. Muſ.
Aſhm. E. 6.

[b] Id. Ib. F. 14.

[c] Id. Ib. E. 29. where it is not ſaid that he was *incorporated*
M. A. Theſe extracts from the Univ. Regg. were made by
Wood, after the publication of Hiſt. et Antiq. Univ. Oxon.

certain.

certain. Probably at Brazen-nofe, or Magdalen.
Antony Wood affirms, that he was incorporated
Mafter of Arts from Cambridge[d]. But no fuch
perfon occurs taking any degree in that univerfity[e].
He was admitted at Oxford B. D. Nov. 21, 1543[f].
He was inftituted Feb. 11, 1545, to the vicarage of
Chalfont St. Peters, Bucks, at the prefentation of
Robert Drury, efquire[g]; and on the deceafe of Ro-
bert Harrifon[h]. On Feb. 21, 1554, he fupplicated
for the degree of D. D. et Oxford[i], which he never
took. He was created canon of Windfor by letters
patent of Queen Mary, Apr. 2, 1554[k]. He was

---

[d] Hift. et Antiq. ii. 295. col. 1. But he retracts this affer-
tion in his Englifh MS. copy of that work; and owns that he
had applied a reference, belonging to Yeldarde nextmentioned,
to Slythurfte.

[e] In Regiftr. Univ. Cant. And Dr. Richardfon's MS. index
to Cambridge graduates from 1500. See alfo the laft note.

[f] Wood Athen. Oxon. faft. 67. col. 1. [In Sion College
library there is a quarto manufcript entitled FASTI CANTABRI-
GIENSES *ab ann.* 1500 *ad ann.* 1658.]

[g] MSS. Br. Willis, fpectant. ad Co. Bucks, No. xii. part 2.
pag. 12. fol. In Bibl. Bodl.

[h] Willis, ibid. He is buried in the church, with this Infcription. " Of your charity pray for the fowl of Sir Robert
" Harifon fum tyme vycar of thys church and of lyttyl Myffen-
" den which deceffid the xxv day of Auguft, A°. Dni. M° V°
" XLV. whofe fowl God pardon."

[i] Wood MSS. ut fupr. E. 9. But no mention occurs of the
*fupplication* under the year in his FASTI. It is thus entered in
the regiftr, " Quatenus ftudium in eadem facultate per 20 an-
" nos hic et alibi, &c." Regiftr. I. fol. 149. a.

[k] Rymer, Foed. xv. pag. 382. col. 2. But he did not fucceed

inſtituted, Feb. 13, 1555. to the rectory of Chalfonte St. Giles's Bucks at the preſentation of William Sothold [1]; and on the death [a] of William
Franklyn, fellow of King's college Cambridge [b],
prebendary of York and Lincoln [c], arch-deacon [d] and
chancellour [e] of Durham, maſter of St. Giles's [f]
hoſpital at Kepyer near Durham, and dean of Windfor [g]. He was inſtalled preſident of Trinity College
Oxford, according to the founder's nomination, May
30, 1556. About the ſame time he reſigned the
vicarage of Chalfonte St. Peter's [h]. I find him appointed, by the convocation of the univerſity of Oxford, with others, Nov. 11, 1556, to regulate or
ſuperviſe the exerciſes in theology, on the election of
cardinal Pole to the chancellorſhip [i]. He was deprived of the preſidentſhip of Trinity college by
queen Eliſabeth's viſitors in September, 1559. On

ceed to the canonry of Richard Arche, deprived; as Willis
obſerves in MS. notes on Le Neve's FASTI, MSS. W.llis, Bibl.
Bodl. For ſee Rymer, ubi ſupr. 365.

[1] MSS. Willis, ſpect. ad co. Bucks. No. 33. fol. ubi ſupr.

[a] Willis, ibid.

[b] Frithe's Catal. MS. decan. et canon. Vinſor.

[c] Willis, CATHEDR. York, p. 165. And Lincoln, p. 199.

[d] Ibid. Durham. p. 259.

[e] Rymer, Fœd. xix. 282.

[f] Willis, ibid.

[g] MSS. Frithe, ut ſupr.

[h] For Edm. Dorman occurs vicar in 1557. Willis, MSS. ut
ſupr. No. 33.

[i] Regiſtr. I. Congr. et Conv. fol. 163. b. Select delegates
are alſo appointed for other ſervices, " diſpicere quid in una-
" quaque re optimum fuerit." See alſo fol. 166. b.

which,

which, being commited to the Tower of London,
he died there, about 1560[v].

Richard Slythurst, with Thomas Broke, was
made keeper of the park of Ewelme, Oxfordshire,
by licence from Henry viii. with a fee of ij d.
per diem, Apr. 24, 1513[x]. William Slythurst received a lease from Henry viii. of certain possessions in
Watlington, Oxfordshire, Jan. 27, 1522[y]. Another Richard Slythurst, of Berkshire, and of Brasen-
nose college Oxford, occurs taking the degree of
M. D. at Oxford, 1566[z]. He was a physician at
Oxford, and died there in the parish of St. Peter in
the East, 1586[a]. Another Richard Slythurst also
was fellow of Magdalene college in Oxford, and
supplicated for the degree of B. D. in 1543[b]. John
Slythurst was a monk of the monastery of Missen-

---

[v] Wood. Hist. et antiq. ut supr. ii. 295. col. 1.

[x] Priv. sigill. Hen. viii. an. reg. 4. Apr. 24.

[y] Bill. signat. Hen. viii. an. reg. 13. Jan. 27. " Ad finem
" 21 annorum. reddendo [regi] annuatim, liij s. iiij d. And
" xiij s. iv d."—Part of these possessions is called " le keybease
" Milpok."

[z] Wood, MSS. ut supr. E. 9. Some of his dispensations
for the said degree are granted, amongst others, " ut crearetur
" doctor ante adventum reginæ, et paratus fit ad disputandum
" coram illa." Ex Registr. Univ. ibid. citat.

[a] Wood, ibid. Et ex Testam. dat. 20. Jan. 1586. Prob.
23. Feb. seq. Registr. AB. cur. cancellar. Oxon. GG. fol. 253.

[b] Wood, MSS. ut supr. E. 5. compared with MSS. E. 9.

den,

den, Bucks, and a prieſt, 1539 [c]. Probably theſe perſons were all of the family of THOMAS SLY-THURST, the ſubjeƈt of this article; ſome of them being conneƈted with his neighbourhood in the country, and others with the univerſity of Oxford : Eſpecially, as the Name is very ſingular [d]. He certainly had a brother, named John [e]; whom I conclude to have been the monk abovementioned.

### FIRST FELLOWS.

#### 1. ARTHUR YELDARD.

Born at Houghton-Strother near the river Tyne, in the county of Tindall, in Northumberland [f]. He was educated in grammar and ſinging, as a boy of the almonry, or choriſter, in the Benediƈtine convent, now the Dean and chapter, of Durham [g]. He

[c] Willis, Mitr. Abb. ii. p. 31. I likewiſe find one Henry Slythurſte preſented to the vicarage of Dedham, co. Eſſex, by the biſhop of London, Oƈtob. 11, 1555. Newcourt, Repertor. ii. p. 210.

[d] It is ſometimes written *Slighurſt*; as in a Will, where *Thomas*, the ſubjeƈt of this article, is remembered, dat. 1553. In regiſtr. teſtam. archidiaconat. Buckingh. temp. regin. Mar. His ejeƈtion from his preferments is mentioned by Sanders, VISIBIL. MONARCH. lib. vii. p. 668. edit. 1592. fol.

[e] From an entry in a book in the library of Trinity college, viz. POLYANTHEA, Baſil. 1512, fol. given, among others, by Thomas Slythurſt the preſident.

[f] Regiſtr. prim. coll. Trin fol. 1, b. et 25.

[g] MSS. F. Wiſe.

became

became afterwards one of the masters or assistants of
Rotheram college in Yorkshire[h]. He was admitted
a sizar of Clare-Hall in Cambridge, 1544[i]. He took
the degree of A. B. in January 1547[k], and was
elected fellow of Pembroke-Hall before 1550[l]. He
occurs junior treasurer of that house 1551[m]. He
took the degree of M. A. in the same university
1552[n]. At Pembroke-hall he became tutor to
Henry and Antony, sons to sir Antony Denny[o], who
were matriculated Nov. 27. 1552[p]. He afterwards

---

[h] Ibid. For an account of this college, see Hearne's Lib.
Nig. Scacc. p. 683. It had a provost, three fellows, six choristers,
two masters in grammar, and another in music.

[i] Lib. Matric. univ. Cant. Where his name is spelt *Yildart*.

[k] Regiftr. Univ. Cant. et Collectan. MSS. V. rev. et doctiss.
Gul. Richardson, coll. Eman. Mag.

[l] Collectan. MSS. mag. Atwood, olim aul. Pemb. foc.

[m] In bishop Wren's manuscript Historiola of the master
and fellows of Pembroke-hall, collected, as it seems, about
1624, these notices occur concerning Arthur Yeldard. " *Yelder*
" vel *Yelderd*. Northumbranus, artium baccalaureus, et thesau-
" rarius junior, anno 1551. Post biennium desiit nominari.
" Illud nomen nunc forte pronuntiamus *Geldar* :—Arthurus
" Yeldar ei nomen est. SS. theologiæ doctor, et secundus
" præfectus collegii SS. Trinitatis apud Oxonienses, &c." MSS.
penes magistr. aul. Pembr. Cant.

[n] Regiftr. Univ. Cant. et collectan. MSS. D. Richardson,
ut supr.

[o] See *Dedication*, infra citat. *Notes*. Denny was the only person
of the court, who dared to inform king Henry the eighth of
the probability of his approaching Death, and one of the executors of that king's will.

[p] Lib. Matric. univ. Cant.

B b                              attended

attended thefe young gentlemen on their travels[q].
While at Cambridge, for his better fupport in ftudy,
he received an annual exhibition from the princefs,
afterwards queen, Mary, by the hands of Dr. Francis Mallet, her chaplain and confeffor, the laft mafter of Michael-houfe in Cambridge, and, befide
other promotions in the church, dean of Lincoln[r].
In the year 1553, he appears to have been at Dilling
in Flanders[s] : but he certainly did not go abroad,
as Wood infinuates[t], on account of the reformation
of religion in the reign of Edward the fixth; dur-
all which it is manifeft that he was refident at Cambridge. He feems to have left the kingdom on account of his two pupils above mentioned; with
whom he travelled, as I have before obferved. In
the firft year of queen Mary, 1553, while at Dilling, he tranflated from greek into latin, *Documen-
ta quædam admonitoria Agapeti diaconi*[u]. It is dedicated to the queen; and in the dedication, dated
at Dilling, he mentions her majefty's many rare
accomplifhments; in particular, her knowledge of
the latin and greek tongues[w]. A manufcript of

[q] Sed *Dedication*, infra citat. *not.*

[r] Tanner Bibl. pag. 504.

[s] See *Dedication*, infra citat. not.

[t] Hift. Antiq. Univ. Oxon. i. 282. col. 2.

[u] Autograph. MSS. Brit. Muf.—Inter. MSS. Bibl. Reg. 7.
D. iv.

[w] To confirm and illuftrate this and other paffages in the
text, I give the following Extracts from this Dedication.——
" Ut difficillimis his chriftianæ reipublicæ temporibus, charitate
" ubique frigefcente, vera religione oppreffa et prope extincta,
atque

this piece is in the royal library, now part of the
Britiſh Muſeum ; and is the ſame that was preſented

" atque (ut uno verbo dicam) rebus omnibus fere ad ſummam
" deſperationem adduĉtis ; eam nobis [D. O. M.] donavit
" REGINAM, quæ ita eſt omni ſcientiarum cognitione exculta,
" ita et Græce quæ rara eſt in ſæmina virtus, et Latine doĉta,
" ut in pauciſſimis Viris par ſimiliſque doĉtrina inveniatur ; ut
" nulla his fere in rebus ei admonitore ſit opus. Quippe quæ
" omnium præclarorum principum exempla quæ quidem literis
" continentur, ad mores reĉte formandos pertinentia, in
" promptu habeat, eorumque optima ſemper in rebus gerendis
" imitetur et exprimat. Quæ, etiam ab infaotia, ita pietatis
" ſemper et veri cultus divini fuit ſtudioſa ; ut ob vitæ ſanc-
" titatem, quantum homines conjeĉtura aſſequi poſſunt, digna
" ſit adeo judicata, ad quam Religio hoc toto fere regno
" exulans, tanquam in portum profugeret, &c."—" Quum
" ergo viderem admonitorias haſce Agapeti Sententias, et
" breves et nervoſas, a nemine haĉtenus quod ſciam digne
" donatas Latinitate ; et ſtatuiſſem aliquo grati animi indicio
" ſignificaŕe, me non eſſe immemorcm beneficiorum, a Celſitu-
" dine tua per manus Doĉtoris MALLETTI acceptorum, quibus
" CANTABRIGIÆ juvenis in ſtudiis alebar : Judicavi eas eſſe
" dignas in quibus ita elaborarem, &c."—" Reſtat ergo, ut
" immortales gracias Majeſtati tuæ habeam perpetuo, quod
" Diſcipulos meos mihi a parentibus erudiendos traditos, nobi-
" les illos quidem ſummæque ſpei adoleſcentulos DENNEIOS, et
" patre et matre jam orbatos, tanto amore proſequuta fueris,
" eorumque tutelam tam charam habueris, ut ne mater quidem
" indulgentius illorum incolumitati providere potuiſſet, quam
" eſt a te proviſum : Quæ, etſi eam ipſis longinquas regiones
" petendi facultatem annuere non es dedignata, quam parentes
" in vita ſæpe promiſerant ; tamen id omnino permittere noluit
" pietas tua eximia, antequam et Puerorum educationem ex-
" ploraveras, et de tutorum etiam fide quorum curæ commiſſi
" ſunt accurate inquiſiveras. Verumenimvero hujus tantæ in
" illos indulgentiæ uberrimi, deo favente, brevi percipientur

fruĉtus :

to queen Mary. He tranflated into Greek Sir Thomas More's CONSOLATORY DIALOGUE AGAINST
TRIBULACION, .written in the year 1534, and in the
TOWER of London ˣ. On the foundation of Trinity college at Oxford, he was admitted, by the
founder's nomination, a fellow of the fame, May
30, 1556, and was incorporated M. A. in that univerfity, Nov. 12, the fame year ʸ. The circumftance
of his having been patronifed in his ftudies at Cambridge by the princefs Mary who was now queen,
and his connection with the family of Denny, muft
have been inftrumental to this nomination. He appears to have been in high favor and efteem with
the founder; who appointed him the firft philofo-

" fruƈtus : Quum, tua providéntia, fcientiarum linguarumque
" variarum cognitione ornati, et multarum rerum ufu atque
" experientia inftruƈti, Viri in patriam redibunt ; Majeftatique
" tuæ et reipublicæ huic florentiffimæ ea fide fervient, qua
" Patri tuo primum, deinde Fratri, regibus æterna memoria
" dignifiimis, fervivit ipforum pater prudentiffimus ANTHO-
" NIUS DENNEIUS miles. Quod ut fiat, non modo precibus
" affiduis D. O. M. urgebo, verum etiam ipfe opera et in-
" duftria mea, quantum potero, juvabo."—" Datum DAL-
" LANCIÆ duodecimo Die Decemb. Anno regni tui auguftifs.
" primo." Infcribed, " MARIÆ, Angliæ, Ffranciæ et Hy-
" berniæ, Reginæ ferenifimæ, ARTHURUS YELDARDUS Salu-
" tem optat æternam."

ˣ MS. F. Wife. Who fays he had feen it among the curious
manufcripts of Mr. Farmer of Tufmore in Oxfordfhire. But it
is not, I believe, to be found there at prefent. More's book is
fuppofed by fome to have been tranflated from the Latin of one
Hungarus : and was printed at Antwerp by John Fowler in
1573. 12mo.

ʸ Wood Ath. Oxon. i. f. 85.

phy-

phy-lecturer in his college, yet permitted him to be absent, and to serve that office by deputy, for many months[z]. I have before taken notice[a], that the founder placed his son in law, John Beresford, at Trinity college, under the tuition[b] of this learned and experienced preceptor : to whom on that occasion, he sent the following letter.

  " Mr. Yelder, *with my right herty commendations.*

  " I send to yow my son Mr. Basford, whom with
 " the rest committed to your charge I requyre yow
 " so to instruct as theye may proffytt in lernynge :
 " ffor doing whereoff ye shall not fynde me unthank-
 " full. I will not forget yow, so soon as I shall see
 " convenyent tyme. and thus fare ye well. Written
 " at London the xiiith of July, anno 1557.

Your loving ffrend,

T H O. P O P E [c].

---

[z] Ex Comp. Burff. 1556.

[a] Supr. p. 188.

[b] All the *Convictores* admitted into the college, are ordered to be placed under the tuition of one of the fellows. It seems also, that these were attended by their *private* preceptors. For in the Statutes of the college, where mention is made of the number of *Convictores* to be admitted, it is immediately added, " cum DIDASCALIS *suis ipsos comitantibus.*" Cap. x.

[c] Ex Autograph. ubi supr.

B b 3
He

He wrote latin profe with great elegance and perfpi-
cuity. He feems to have been employed in the verbal
compofition of· the college-ftatutes; for the founder
in a letter to the prefident, Nov. 26, 1556, orders
a reward to " Maifter Yeldard, in confideration of
" the paynes he took to *pen* my ftatutes." On the
deprivation of Slythurfte, the firft prefident, above-
mentioned, 1559, he was prefented, with Stephen
Markes, mentioned in the next article, to Dame
Elifabeth Pope, the foundrefs; who nominated him
prefident, and he was accordingly admitted Sept. 26,
1559 [d], to the great fatisfaction of the fociety [e]. He
took the degree of B. D. Jun. 24, 1563 [f]. And of
D. D. Feb. 15, 1565 [g]. He was prefented by the
fame Dame Elifabeth, Feb. 12, 1571, to vicarage of
Much-Waltham in Effex [h]. In September, 1566,

---

[d] Wood fays, " Vifitatorum juffu fucceffit." Hift. Ant.
univ. Oxon. i. 282. But this is a miftake; for he was regularly and duly nominated and admitted. Regiftr. prædict.
fol. 24.

[e] From their letter to the foundrefs, *ibid*. In which they
fey, that both the candidates are, " mofte worthye the office,
" bothe for the meyntenaunce of good and godlie livinge,
" and alfo for the commoditie of the coledge in politike af-
" faires." The foundrefs, in her anfwer, fays, fhe has chofen
him, trufting " it fhall be for the comoditie of the coledge, and
" alfo for all your comfrethe and quietnefs." *ibid*, fol. 24. b.

[f] Wood Ath. Oxon. i. Faft. 92.

[g] Ibid. 95.

[h] The next perfon prefented to the fame, but by the prefident and fellows of Trinity college, Oxon. was Nicholas Yeldard; I fuppofe, his brother, but not of the college, Sept. 10,

1574.

he difputed in divinity before queen Elifabeth, during her magnificent reception at Oxford; Juel,
bifhop of Salifbbury, being the moderator [1]. He
was appointed, Jul. 13, 1580, by the earl of Leicefter, vice-chancellor of the univerfity [k]. I find
him commiffioned, Jun. 10, 1583, with four other
Doctors, to recieved Albertus de Lafco a prince of
Poland, accompanied by lord Leicefter and other
nobles, at their public entry into Oxford : who
were entertained in the univerfity for the four following days, with fumptuous banquets, difputations, orations, fermons, and two plays prefented
in Chrift Church hall [l]. In the year 1576, he was
empowered, in conjunction with others, to correct
and reform the whole body of the ftatutes of the
univerfity [m]. He continued prefident of the college
thirty-nine years, four months and three days [n]. He
died Feb. 2, 1598-9 [o], and was buried in the chapel

1574. Regiftr. prim. coll. fol. 29. b. And Newcourt, Repertor. ii. 632. Afterwards the fame dame Elifabeth made over
the advowfon, pro hac vice, to the faid Arthur Yeldard, and he
prefented Rob. Palmer, not a fellow, Octob. 6, 1585. Regiftr.
Grindall, epifc. London. And Newcourt, ut fupr. 633.

[l] MSS. Baker. vol. vi. p. 141. b. Brit. Muf. Harl. MSS.
7033.

[k] Wood, Hift. antiq. univ. Oxon. ii. 429.

[l] Ibid. i. 299. Hollinfh. Chron. iii. 1355.

[m] Wood, Hift. antiq. univ. Oxon. i. 294. col. 1.

[n] Regiftr. prim. dicti coll. fol. 53.

[o] Ibid.

of

of the college ᵖ. He has a copy of latin verſes, among others of the capital ſcholars of thoſe times, viz. Alexander Nowell, Herbert Weſtphalinge, Thomas Bodley, George Buchanan, *etc.* at the end of Humphreys's Life of biſhop Jewel, 1573 ᑫ. He has likewiſe a latin poem prefixed to John Caſe's *Speculum Moralium Quæſtionum, Oxon.* 1585. It appears that he died very old, by another latin copy of verſes ʳ written by him, in a collection of Oxford verſes, on the death of Sir Richard Unton ˢ.

ᵖ As I collect from the following articles in Comp. Burſſ. 1598—9.

" Sol. operariis et cænæ funebri defuncti præſidentis, et pro " jentaculis ſociorum proficiſc. ad epiſcopum Winton, et " pro cæna eorundem poſt reditum. xl ſ. *ob. q.*

" Sol. pulſanti campanam. ij *d.*

" Sol. pro *ly* bellman. ij *d.*

ᑫ Johannis Juelli Vita, &c. Lond. 4to.

ʳ Of which he ſays,

Quæ dolor atque amor extorſere ſeni meditanti.

His will is dated Jan. 8, 1598. Proved April 16, 1599. Apud Regiſtr. *Aſtor. cur. cancellar. Oxon.* G G. fol. 178. b. archiv. acad. Oxon. It contains nothing remarkable. He leaves all his effects, of every kind, to Eleanor his wife; whom he likewiſe appoints executrix. Except that he bequeathes ſix volumes of the *Centuriæ Magdeburgenſes* to the college library.

ˢ Intitled, " Funebria nobiliſſimi et præſtantiſſimi equitis D. " Henrici Untoni ad Gallos bis legati regii, &c. a. Muſis " Oxonienſibus apparata, 1596. 4to." It was made and publiſhed by Doctor Robert Wright, fellow of Trinity college, Oxford, afterwards biſhop of Lichfield and Coventry. Who has alſo prefixed a good latin preface. Wood (Ath. Oxon. ii. 1137.) does not mention this publication by Dr. Wright. The collection is cloſed with two copies by Wright; the laſt of which,

which, being in a fingular ftrain, and much fuperior to the tafte
of thofe times, I am tempted to infert.

Hæc, Untone, tuo cecinere in funere mufæ
    Oxonides, triftes munera ad inferias :
Oxonides mufæ, quarum es nutritus in ulnis :
    Heu, teneras lacrymarum imbre rigante genas !
Quæ tibi poftremo noftri pro munere amoris,
    Curavi in memores jam referenda typos.
Accipiant læti manes ftudia ifta tuorum,
    At tu, patrone o dulcis, ave atque vale !

By the former of thefe two copies, it appears, that Wright accompanied fir Henry Unton, in one of his embaffies into France,
to the French king's camp at Lafere, in which fir Henry died,
1595. See Afhm. BERKSH. i. 190. iii. 313. In Thomas Newton's ENCOMIA, printed 1589, is an epigram addreffed, " Ad
" eruditiffimum virum ROBERTUM WRIGHTUM nobiliffimi
" Effexiæ comitis famulum primarium." p. 124. This I judge
to be the fame Robert Wright ; efpecially from the two concluding lines.

Ubera cui Charites dant, et favet innuba Pallas,
    Quemque beat docta doctus Apollo chely.

Dr. Robert Wright was born at Saint Alban's, and elected
fcholar of Trinity college, Oxford, aged fifteen, jun. 7. 1574.
Regiftr. Coll. prim. f. 36. Fellow, being then bachelor of
Arts, May 25, 1581. Ibid. f. 39. He was fucceffively chaplain to queen Elifabeth, and king James the firft. He was prefented, by lord keeper Egerton, to the rectory of Brixton De-
verel in Wiltfhire, Nov. 29. 1596. MS. Tanner, ad Wood's
ATHEN. ii. 1135. He was inftituted Rector of Hayes in Middlefex, on the prefentation of William lord Pembroke, Apr. 4.
1601. Admitted Dec. 21. in the fame year canon refidentiary
and treafurer of Wells. He was alfo vicar of Sunning in
Berkfhire, and Rector of Bourton upon the Water in Gloucefterfhire. See Newc. REPERTOR. i. 641. In 1613 he was appointed the Firft Warden of Wadham college, by the foundrefs
dame Dorothy Wadham. In 1622, confecrated bifhop of
Briftol ; and in 1632, tranflated to the fee of Lichfield and
                                    , Coventry.

## 2. STEPHEN MARKES.

Born in Cornwall. He was a fellow of Exeter college, Oxford, where he took the degree of A. B. 1552 [t]. Made A. M. Jul, 11, 1554 [u]. On Octob. 17, 1555, he was elected rector of the said college,

Coventry. Prynne fay, that bifhop Wright placed a " goodly " crucifixe in a frame with the pictures of men and women de- " voutly praying to it," above the altar in Litchfield cathedral, and that he was greatly concerned in compofing the *late* canons, oaths, &c. That at Briftol, he fued the Dean and chapter for oppofing him in placing *Images* in the cathedral, and other churches, there. That he introduced many fuperftitious inno- vations at Briftol " to humour Canterbury [Laud,] by whofe " means he was tranflated to Coventry and Litchfield." *Anti- pathie of the Englifh Lordly Prelacie, &c.* Lond. 1641. 4to. ch. v. pag. 292. ch. vi. BRISTOLL.

In 1641. he was one of the protefting bifhops, with eleven more : and before his committment to the Tower, fpoke an eloquent oration at the bar of the Houfe of Commons, which is extant. He died in the year 1643, at his palace at Ecclefhall while it was befieged by the rebels. Of this venerable prelate there is preferved a good old portrait on board at Trinity col- lege, concerning which the following notice occurs, COMP. Burff. coll. Trin. 1632.—3. " Pro imagine epifcopi Lichfield- " enfis adornanda, xvj s." At fir Charles Adderley's houfe in Warwickfhire, there was a picture of bifhop Wright, with a long infcription. ANTIQUITIES OF LITCHFIELD CATHEDR. Lond. 1717. pag. 51. Another belonging to fir John Davies at Bere-Court in Berkfhire, Afhm. BERKSH. ii. 337. (See alfo ibid. 397.) There is another at Wadham-college.

[t] Wood. MSS. ut fupr. E. 5.

[u] Id. ib. E. 29.

then

then an annual office, and held by the fellows ʷ. In the year of his rectorfhip he was admitted, as above, a fellow of Trin. coll. Oxon. May 30, 1556. At the fame time he was appointed vice-prefident of the fame by the founder. He was in nomination for the prefidentfhip with Arthur Yeldard, in Sept. 1559, on the deprivation of Slythurfte; as was obferved in the preceding article. He fupplicated for the degree of B. D. Octob. 10, 1559ˣ. He had quitted his fellowfhip before the end of the year 1560ʸ.

### 3. JOHN BARWYKE.

Born in Devonfhire. He was of Magdalene college, Oxford. He appears to have been recommended to the founder by Alexander Belfire, the Firft Prefident of Saint John's ᶻ. Took the degree of A. B. 1549. And of M. A. April 27, 1556ᵃ.

ʷ Id. D. 2. pag. 306.

ˣ Regiftr. I. Congreg. et Conv. fol. 185.

ʸ Ut patet ex Regiftr. coll. prim. fol. 140.

ᶻ MSS. F. Wife. Formerly fellow of New college, and canon of Chrift Church.

ᵃ Wood, MSS. Ib. D. 6. And E. 29. One John Barwicke was ordained an Accolyte in Baliol college chapel, Mar. 9, 1554. Being then SCHOLARIS *collegii Magdalenæ.* REGISTR. Rob. King, Epifcop. Oxon. f. 80. Alfo a John Barwicke occurs, at the fame time and place, ordained Subdeacon, he being then bachelor of arts and fellow of Magdalene college. *Ibid.* By the way, it appears from this regifter, which begins 1543, that bifhop King, the firft bifhop of Oxford and laft abbot of

Ofeney,

Admitted fellow of Trin. coll. Oxon. by nomination as above. At the fame time appointed dean by election. He quitted his fellowfhip about the year 1565 [b].

## 4. JAMES BELL.

Born in Somerfetfhire. Was fcholar of C. C. C. Oxon, where he took the degree of B. A. 1551 [c]. From thence admitted fellow of Trin. coll. Oxon. as above. At the fame time appointed rhetoric-lecturer by election. He left his fellowfhip about Michaelmas, in the year of his admiffion [d], and fuddenly became a zealous affertor of the reformation; in

Ofeney, ufually held his ordinations *in Capella Manerii de Thame-Parke.*

[b] Comp. Burff. 1564—5.

[c] Wood, MSS. ut fupr. D. 6. and Athen. Oxon. i. f. 75.

[d] Regiftr. KETTELL. viz. cui tit. " ALUMNI illi quos venerabilis vir, THOMAS, cognomento POPE, ordinis militaris, " in hoc domicilio alendos ftatuit: et non folum ipforum vic-" tui moribufque profpexit, verum etiam ut bona ingenia " bonis artibus et difciplinis imbuerentur, ad finceram Chrifti " Religionem populo Chrifti ftrenue commendandam, impenfe " curavit." Apud Coll. Trin. in pergamen. fol. It was drawn up by Dr. Kettel, prefident; and continued, by him, from the foundation to the year 1602, incluf. The original draught of this Regifter, in Kettel's own hand, is in the Afhmolean Mufeum, codd. A. Wood, 8490. fol. 28. with many interpolations, corrections, and additions, in the hand of its collector. This laft-mentioned copy of the faid regifter, which feems to have been given to A. Wood by Dr. Buthurft, prefident, is here cited, and will be often afterwards, in the courfe of this article of the APPENDIX.

defence

defence of which he publifhed feveral pieces, here
enumerated. A tranflation of *Luther's treatife of
Chriftian Liberty*. Lond. 1579. 8vo. A tranflation
of *John Fox's Sermon of the Evangelical Olive*. Lond.
1578. A tranflation of *Fox's Sermon preached at the
Chriftening of a certain Jew at London*, 1577. 16mo.
A tranflation of *Fox's* and *Haddon's Anfwer apologe-
tical to Hierome Oforius his flanderous Invective*. 1581.
4to [e]. A tranflation of *Fox's Pope confuted*. Lond.
1580. 4to. In the preface of this laft piece, the
tranflator, Bell, mentions his happy converfion to
proteftantifm from popery.  " I wandered long in
" the felfsame mizmaze, noofeled therein by the
" grayheaded of that fchoole, whofe countenance
" carried me from my Chrifte to the fwinftie of
" the Sorbone, which had fwalowed me up, if the
" Lord had not prevented me betimes." In the
fame, he takes notice of being " taxed by a friend
" with apoftafy." Wood calls our author " a great
" admirer of John Fox, the martyrologift [f]."
Among the manufcripts of the royal library, now
in the Britifh Mufeum, is one entitled, *James Bell's
account of Cæcilia princefs of Sweeden her travelling
into England*, 1564, dedicated to Q. Elifabeth [g]. He
was inftalled, Feb. 13, 1595, into the prebend of
Holcombe in the cathedral church of Wells ; and
Octob. 11, the fame year, into the prebend of

[e] See Strype, Ann. Ref. i. p. 433.
[f] Athen. Oxon. i. 232.
[g] 17. C. XXIX. charta.

Combe

Combe in the fame church [h]. Tanner, having mentioned Bell's preferments at Wells, adds, " Hic " *Jacobus Bell* mihi videtur ille Somerfetenfis, qui • " primo fcholaris collegii Corporis Chrifti Oxon, " baccalaureus artium admiffus A. 1551, et poftea " fub finem menfis Maii, A. 1556, focius collegii " Trinitatis electus. *Refragari tamen videtur ætas.*" Tanner means, that he was rather too old, to have lived to take thefe preferments. But he might be admitted at the univerfity, as was antiently the cuftom, very young: and, befide the circumftance of his county, his fudden departure from the college, and the hiftory of his religious principles, all taken together, render it highly probable that he was the fame perfon.

### 5. John Richardson.

Born in Cumberland. Was fcholar of Queen's college [1], Oxford; where he took the degree of

---

[h] Tanner, BIBL. pag. 95.

[1] I know not if *fcholar* is here the proper ftyle. Nor do I fully comprehend the fyftem of the antient foundation of Queen's college. But the members are thus diftinguifhed in the eftablifhment of an Obit in the chapel there, dated Oct. 6. 1538. The provoft if prefent is to receive ij *s.* " Every " felowe and fcoler beyng prefent, xx*d.* Every chaplayne, " vj *d.* Every mayfter of the chyldrene, vj *d.* Every chylde " of the taberd, iiij *d.* Every clerk of the chapell, iiij *d.* " Every poyr [poor] chylde, ij *d.* Archiv. Coll. Regin. Oxon. " [MSS. Ed. R. MORES, fol. 116.]" And in another Obit, dated Febr. 21. 1516. " To every felowe, chaplayne, mayfter " of the chyldren, and to the chyldren of the howfe, the " clerkes

B. A. in March 1553 [k]. From thence admitted fellow of Trin. coll. Oxon. as above. At the fame time appointed burfar by election. He had quitted the college before the end of 1560 [l]. He was afterwards, as I collect, inftituted to be rectory of St. Saviour's, in York, 1567, where he died 1591 [m].

## 6. George Sympson.

Born in Cumberland. Was fcholar of Queen's college, Oxford; where he took the degree of B. A. in March, 1553 [n]. From thence admitted fellow of Trin. coll. Oxon. as above. Made M. A. Jul. 8, 1558 [o]. He was ejected for popery about 1561, and ordered, with others, not to be feen within twenty miles of either of the univerfities, under fevere penalties [p].

## 7. George Rudde.

Born in Weftmoreland. Was fcholar of Queen's college, Oxford; where he took the degree of B. A.

" clerkes of the chapel, and to every fcoler beyng poyr chylde, " &c." Ibid. [MSS. ut fupr. fol. 113.]

[k] Wood, MSS. ut fupr. D. 6. and E. 5. He was ordained fubdeacon, ratione *ftudii ultra decennium continuati*, in Oxford cathedral, Sept. 19. 1556. Regiftr. Epifc. Oxon. fol. 90.

[l] Ex Comp. Burff.

[m] Drake's Ebor. p. 311.

[n] Wood, Ibid.

[o] Wood, MSS. E. 29.

[p] See Strype, Ann. Ref. iv. 275. compared with MSS. Kettel. fupr. citat.

in

in March, 1553 [q]. From thence admitted fellow of Trin. coll. Oxon. as above. He was made M. A. Jul. 8, 1558 [r]. He quitted his fellowſhip about Eaſter, in 1563 [s].

## 8. THOMAS SCOTTE.

Born in Cumberland. Was ſcholar of Queen's college, Oxford ; where he took the degree of B. A. Jul. 5, 1554 [t]. Admitted, from thence, fellow of Trin. coll. Oxon. as above. He took the degree of M. A. Jul. 6, 1556 [u]. He was elected one of the proctors of the univerſity, Apr. 25, 1560 [w]. But the ſame year, or very ſoon afterwards, he was ejected from his fellowſhip, with others, for re-fuſing the oath of ſupremacy to queen Eliſabeth [x].

## 9. ROGER CRISPIN.

Born in Devonſhire. Elected fellow of Exeter college, Oxford, 1550 [y], where he took the degree of B. A. Dec. 8, 1554 [z]. From thence admitted

[q] Wood, D. 6. E. 5.
[r] Wood, MSS. E. 29.
[s] MSS. Kettel.
[t] Wood, E. 6. and E. 5.
[u] Id. E. 29.
[w] Wood, Hiſt. antiq. ii. 426.
[x] Ibid. i. 284.
[y] Wood, MSS. D. 2. p. 42.
[z] Ibid. D. 6. This perſon, and ſome others of Exeter col-lege, recited in theſe two LISTS of the FIRST FELLOWS and SCHOLARS, were recommended to the Founder by John Holy-man,

fellow of Trin. coll. Oxon. as above. He took
the degree of M. A. Jul. 8, 1558 [a]. He quitted
his fellowſhip about the feaſt of All Saints in 1562 [b].

## 10. ROGER EVANS.

Born in Cornwall. Perhaps of Exeter college.
I find nothing of him in the univerſity regiſters, or
elſewhere, but that he was admitted when A. B. a
fellow as above; and that he left his fellowſhip at
the end of 1559 [c], I ſuppoſe on the acceſſion of
Eliſabeth, and the change of religion.

man, the ſecond biſhop of Briſtol in 1554, originally fellow of
New-college, then a monk of Reading abbey, and afterwards,
on the diſſolution of his monaſtery, a retired ſtudent in Exeter
college till about 1553. MSS. F. Wife. In an Epiſtle to the
Univerſity of Oxford, dated 1530, from Hugh Faringdon abbot
of Reading, he is charaĉteriſed as a theologiſt and a preacher of
great erudition. Regiſtr. FF. fol. 101, 102. Alexander Belſire
his cotemporary in New-college, and the Firſt Preſident of
Saint John's, was his intimate friend to his death. Dying in
1558, he bequeathed ſeveral books to the library of Wincheſter
college.—For the charaĉter of abbot Hugh Faringdon, above-
mentioned, Holyman's patron, ſee HIST. ENGL. POETR. vol.
ii. p. 446. And Willis, MITR. ABB. i. 161. See alſo Wood,
HIST. ANTIQ. Univ. Oxon. i. 252. a. ii. 95. b. 136. a.

[a] Wood, MSS. E. 29.

[b] MSS. Kettel. The following article occurs concerning
him in the beginning of the ſame year, Comp. Burſſ. 1591--2.
" Solut. 16 Jan. pro expenſ. magiſtri Criſpin equitantis ad
" Londinum ad emenda falſamenta et halecia pro quadrageſi-
" ma, x ſ.

[c] Regiſtr. MSS. Rad. Kettel. ut ſupr.

C c                            11. JOHN

## 11. JOHN PERTE.

Born in Warwickfhire. Took the degree of A. B.
May 8, 1556 [d]. Admitted fellow of Trin. coll. by
the founder's nomination, as above. Admitted, at
the fame time, one of the burfars by election. I
find him often mentioned in the founder's letters,
as employed in tranfcribing the college-ftatutes [e].
He left the college in 1558 [f], being, as I fufpect,

[d] MSS. Wood, ut fupr. D. 6.

[e] This is the oldeft copy now remaining in the college; except the original one, figned and fealed by the founder. It is
on parchment. The next, in point of antiquity, is one fent to
the bifhop of Winchefter, which is alfo on parchment, and
bears the following infcription prefixed.

" Reverendiffimo in Chrifto patri, et digniffimo patrono pro-
tectorique noftro unico, domino Epifcopo Winton."

" QUOD per hos decem annos fubinde defideravit amplitudo
veftra, clariffime PRÆSUL, curavimus tandem effectum dare.
Humillime offerimus exemplar STATUTORUM illorum, quæ in-
junxit nobis beatæ memoriæ FUNDATOR nofter fingularis, dominus THOMAS POPE, miles; et quorum obfervantiæ invigilat
feliciter eximia veftra follicitudo. Unaque cum ipfis, nofmet,
noftrum ftatum fidemque noftram, veftræ, colendiffime ANTIS-
TES, fidiffimæ tutelæ, favorique benigniffimo, unanimiter et
fuppliciffime cupimus effe in perpetuum concreditos et commen-
datos. Dat. Oxon. April 1. A. D. 1609. Veftræ amplitudini
devotiffime devincti, Præf. et Soc. Coll. Trin. Oxon. &c."
[Compare p. 125. fupr. Note, g. And p 248. Note, a ] In
the beginning of Cromwell's ufurpation, on the diffolution of
the bifhopricks, this copy was returned to the college, by the
deprived bifhop Morley, where it now remains.

[f] Regiftr. Ketell.

removed

removed for turbulence and contumacy. It appears
by the founder's letters, that he had excited and
encouraged a faction in the college, under pretence
that the statutes were unreasonably strict[t]. This
affair seems to have given the founder much un-
easiness and concern; and he frequently speaks of
it in his letters to the president. At length, it oc-
casioned the following address in form to the whole
society.

[t] By the same letters it appears, that he was ordered to
appear before the founder, I suppose, at London; and to bring
with him his objections to the statutes drawn out in form,
which now remain. These objections the founder intended to
lay before the dean of St. Paul's: this was Dr. Henry Cole,
who also was, or had been, warden of New college Oxford,
provost of Eton, prebendary of saint Paul's and Salisbury, archdeacon of Ely, and vicar general of the spiritualties under Cardinal Pole. He was likewise an eminent civilian, and joined
in a commission with Sir Thomas Pope. He is celebrated as a
classical scholar in Leland's Encom. p. 79. edit. 1589.

Ascham has left this testimony of Cole's literature and humanity. "Tantum ego et communi omnium voci de tua
"eruditione, et frequenti Morysini sermoni de tua humanitate
"semper tribui, doctissime humanissimeque Cole, ut imperitus
"ipse si te non colerem, et inhumanus si non amarem, merito
"videri possim." Epistol. R. Ascham. lib. iii. Asch. Colo.
edit. Lond. 1581. p. 154 b 12mo. with a present of Aristae-
us, &c. Sir Richard Morysine, or Morison, here mentioned,
was one of Ascham's most distinguished literary friends, a great
friend to the Reformation, and sent by Henry the eighth, and
his successor, an embassador to the emperour Charles the fifth.
He died, an exile for religion, at Strasburgh in 1556.

　　　　" To

" To his lovinge ffriends the fellowes of Trinitie
" college in Oxforde.

" With my hartie commendations. As I was
" not a little greved of the reporte of late made
" unto me, that, contrarie to my expeƈtations, there
" sholde be any such lyghtnefs amonge you, as not
" to approve thofe my Statutes which I fent you;
" being drawen and colleƈtede, as well oute of the
" good orders of other colleges, as alfo by the ad-
" vife and cownfell of diverfe moft fage and wife
" heddes; and that for the *rigour* of them, as it
" was termed, mofte parte of you would wantonlie
" forfake my college, and the Benefit you had by
" me there: So fyndinge by letters comynge from
" diverfe of you, the fame reporte to be untrue;
" have conceived better opinion of you, occafion-
" inge me the lefe to repente my Charge, which
" I have, and shall[h], beftowe amonge you. And
" as I cannot but much commende and allowe the

[h] In a letter from him to the prefident, dat. Whitmonday,
1558, he fays, " I shall by [buy] of the maƚter of the Rolls
" ii. ffaier manors with ii. advowfons in Lyncolnshere, which
" I entende to gyve to my collegge." Amongft others, he
might perhaps here mean this intended donation; which, however, never took effeƈt. I fuppofe, on account of the founder's
death, which happened a few months afterwards. In another
letter, from and to the fame, without date, but written 1558,
he promifes to affure to the college three other advowfons with
all convenient fpeed. But, I fuppofe, for the reaɯn abovementioned, they never came to the college.

" ftayed

" ſtayed witte and mature diſcretion of thoſe among
" you, which do declare themſelves content with
" ſuch my Ordinances as I gave unto you, whom
" as occaſion ſhall ſerve I muſt allwaye thynke
" worthye to be had in my memorie; ſo I require
" you All, quietlie to receive theſe Statutes which
" I eftſones ¹ ſend you, ſealed and ſubſcribed with
" my hande ᵏ: myndinge not for any man's plea-
" ſure, hereafter, to alter and change any of them.
" Signifieinge the gryeffes that have been exhibited
" unto me by ſome of you; and [that] being pe-
" ruſed and ſeene of diverſe honorable, wiſe, and
" learned men, with the Statutes thereunto apper-
" tayninge ¹, [they] are in no wiſe ᵐ lyked or
" thought mete to be altered. Wherefore, if any
" among yowe cannot perſuade himſelfe to be con-
" tent with theſe my Orders and Decrees, I hartyly
" require the ſame, without diſturbance, to gyve
" place unto ſuch others as will obedientlie lyve
" under the ſame; and, when he ſhall ſee his tyme,
" to departe from my ſaide college, which to do
" he ſhall have my goode wille and favour. And
" thus praying you to have me in remembrance,
" with your prayers to God, I bid you all fare-

¹ Forthwith, *or* again.

ᵏ See note in pag. 248.

¹. *Additamentum.* See ibid.

ᵐ " *Lyked—to be altered.*" i. e. No alteration is approved or
*lyked.*

C c 3                    " well.

" well.  Written at London, the xxvth of Aprill,
" 1558.

" Your loving ffrende,

" T.  P o p e ª."


*₊* When this perſon was removed from his fellowſhip, the founder intended, partly on the recommendation of cardinal Pole, to place in his room
the learned William Alan, a name equally celebrated
among the catholics, and proſcribed by the proteſtants.  But that deſign did not take effect ; he being
promoted about the ſame time, and probably by the
intereſt of ſir Thomas Pope, to a canonry in the
cathedral of York º.  Alan was an able controver-
ſialiſt in defence of the declining doctrines of the
church of Rome : educated at Oriel college, and
about the year 1556, appointed Principal of ſaint
Mary's H a l l, and elected one of the proctors of
the univerſity of Oxford.  Upon the acceſſion of
queen Eliſabeth, he retired to Louvain, where he
wrote his famous book on P u r g a t o r y and P r a y e r s
f o r  t h e  D e a d, which abounds in rhetoric more
than argument, and contains much ingenious declamation and ſophiſtry.  Soon afterwards he returned
to England, where he publiſhed many ſpecious apo-
logies for his religion, which he diſperſed with
great art and induſtry.  But the treatiſe juſt men-

ª E Regiſtr. primo coll. prædict. fol. 16. b.
º MSS. F. Wiſe, ut ſupr.

tioned

tioned was the bafis of his polemical reputation.
As he wrote chiefly for the conviction of his countrymen, moft of his compofitions are in Englifh;
and are not inelegant fpecimens of ftyie, at a time
when the ftate of our language was rude and un-
fettled. A folid old Englifh critic pronounces one
of Alan's tracts to be " a princely, grave, and
" flourifhing piece of natural and exquifite Eng-
" lifh ᴾ." Being again driven abroad, he was rewarded with a canonry in each of the churches of
Cambray and Rheims. At length ftanding high in
the efteem of pope Sixtus the fifth, he was conftituted a Cardinal, and archbifhop of Mechlin in
Brabant ᵠ. It is not the leaft of his dignities, and
it is a proof of the univerfality of his literature,
that he was librarian of the Vatican ᶠ. His activity
was indefatigable in the fupport of his profeffion.
He was a principal inftrument in eftablifhing the
Englifh catholic feminaries at Doway and Rheims;
and feveral others in Spain and Italy. His intem-
perate papiftic zeal, which he imprudently carried
into the dangerous politics of the times, and which
prompted him to circulate feditious papers in England to prepare the way for the Spanifh invafion,
was cenfured even by thofe of his own intolerant
perfuafion. He died aged only fixty three years,

---

ᴾ Bolton's HYPERCRIT. iv. §. 2.

ᵠ Wood, ATH. OXON. i. 268. And his LIFE, written by
Nich. Fitzerbert. Antw. 1621. 8vo.

ᶠ Miræus, SCRIPT. SÆC. xvi. p. 68.

in 1594 '. Vertue had a curious caſt of his head, from an original medallion.

## 12. ROBERT BELLAMIE.

Born in Yorkſhire. Of Exeter college, as I col-
léct. Took the degree of B. A. May 8, 1556 '.
He was admitted fellow of Trin. coll. Oxon. as
above, viz. May 30, 1556. I find him nominated
one of the firſt fellows of St. John's college, Oxford, by ſir Thomas Whyte, the founder, in his
charter, dat. Mar. 7, 1557-8 ᵘ. This appointment
he did not, however, accept; for he occurs óne of
the burſars of Trinity college 1565 ʷ. He took the
degree of M. A. May 28, 1560 ˣ. He afterwards
proceeded in phyſic; and, as I ſuppoſe by diſpenſation, took the degree of M. B. Dec. 16, 1562 ʸ.
On Jun. 23, 1571, he took the degree of M. D.
having quitted his fellowſhip 1565, and removed to
St. John's college, as an independent member ᶻ.
Higgs, in his catalogue of fellows of St John's
college, mentions him as one of the firſt fellows of
the ſame; but Wood, in the margin, ſays he was

ˢ Wood, ut ſupr. Pitſ. 792.

ᵗ Wood, MSS. ut ſupr. D. 6.

ᵘ MSS. Catal. Gr. Higgs, ut inf.

ʷ Comp. Burſſ. 1564—5. And Regiſtr. PERROT, ſupr. citat. (Numb. xxi.) fol. 112. a.

ˣ Wood, MSS. ut ſupr. E. 8.

ʸ Ibid.

ᶻ Wood Ath. i. f. 105.

fellow

fellow of Trinity college². Wood alfo omits him
in his firft fellows of St, John's; where he was only
nominated, and never admitted ᵇ. In Nov. 1589,
he was made matter of Shireburne hofpital, near
Durham, by bifhop Hutton; who, in a letter to
the lord Treafurer, cálls him " an honéft man, a
" preacher and a phyfician; to have charge both
" of the fouls and bodies óf the poor, impotent,
" fick, perfons of that hofpital ᶜ." On Octob. 31,
1573, he was inftalled canon of the third ftall of
Durham cathedral. He was alfo rector of Hough-
ton in the bifhoprick of Durham ᵈ. He was living
1590 ᵉ. He is characterifed, with others of the
church of Durham, in a latin manufcript poém,
preferved among Wood's papers in the Afhmolean
Mufeum, entitled ITER BOREALE ᶠ, written by Dr. Richard Eedes, canon of Chrift Church, Oxon, and

---

ª MSS. Muf. Afhm. F. 28. fol. 204. b.

ᵇ Hift. Ant. ii. 303.

ᶜ Dat. March, 1590. apud Strype, Ann. iv. p. 15.

ᵈ Willis, CATHEDRALS. cath. Durham, p. 266, 278, 280.

ᵉ Hutton's letter in Strype, ubi fupr. Willis, ut fupra, fays,
by miftake, that he died 1588. One Robert Bellamie occurs a
feminary prieft in 1588. Strype, iii. 260. ut fupr.

ᶠ 8553. 91. It has *marginal notes* by the author. Concerning this Robert Bellamie, the fame, as I prefume, I find the
following entry in the Regifter of the Univerfity. " April 10,
" 1562. Suplicat Robertus Bellamie A. M. quatenus graciofe
" cum eo difpenfetur ut amplius *prælegere* non teneatur. Caufa
" eft, quia tot et tantis negotiis domi impeditur ut nullo pacto
" *prælegere* poffit. CONCESS. modo fubftituat alium. *Non ob-*
¶ *fervat conditionem.*" Regiftr. Congr. et Conv. I. fol. 203. a.

afterwards

afterwards dean of Worcefter. This journey was taken 1584.

## First Scholars.

### 1. John Langsterre. [or *Langafter*[f].]

Born in Yorkfhire. Of Brafen-nofe college, Oxford, where he took the degree of B. A. Mar. 26, 1556[g]. Admitted fcholar of Trin. coll. Oxon. May 30, 1556. Ætat. 19. Made probationer fellow, by the founder's mandate, Dec. 25, 1556[h], and actual, on Trinity Sunday, Jun. 7, 1558[i]. Made M. A. May 15, 1560[k]. He quitted his fellowfhip about the year 1563[l].

### 2. Reginald Braye.

Born in Bedfordfhire, and defcended from fir Reginald Bray of Eton-Bray in that county, famous in the reign of Edward the fourth[m]. Took the

[f] i. e. Lancafter.

[g] Wood, MSS. D. 6.

[h] Regiftr. prim. coll. fol. 4. b.

[i] Regiftr. ibid. fol. 4. b. His year of probation was protracted by the founder's command, who fays in a letter to the prefident, " Concerning fir Langefter's yeare of probation I " will he be ordered therein according to the ftatutes." Dat. 27 Nov. 1556.

[k] Wood, MSS. E. 29.

[l] Comp. Burff. 1562—3.

[m] Lee's Visit. Oxf. 1574. ut fupr. pag. 45.

degree

degree of A. B. at Oxford, May 8, 1556[n]. Admitted scholar of Trin. coll. Oxon. as above, aged 18. He left the college in Hilary term the same year[o].

### 3. JOHN ARDEN. [or *Ardern.*]

Born in Oxfordshire, and of an antient and respectable family settled at Cottisford, or Kirtlington. Admitted scholar of Trin. coll. Oxon. as above, Æt. 18. Related to the founder[p]. Left the college about Michaelmas, in 1558[q]. Afterwards he gave eighteen volumes or more to the library[r].

### 4. JOHN COMPORTE.

Born in Middlesex. Admitted scholar of Trin. coll. Oxon. as above. Æt. 18. He took the degree of A. B. May 23, 1558[s]. Made probationer fellow, by the founder's mandate, on Trinity Sunday, Jun. 7, 1558[t]. He left his fellowship in the end of the year 1560[u]. He gave to the library *Robert Holcot upon the Sentences*[w].

[n] Wood, MSS. D. 6.
[o] MSS. Kettel.
[p] See supr. p. 327.
[q] MSS. Kettel.
[r] In which he is stiled ARMIGER.
[s] Wood, MSS. E. 6.
[t] Regiſtr. coll. ut supr. fol. 4. b.
[u] MSS. Kettel.
[w] Fol. See Lib. Benef. bibl. coll. Trin. in pergam.

5. ROBERT

## 5. ROBERT THRAKSE.

Born in Somerſetſhire. Admitted ſcholar of Trin. coll. Oxon. as above, Æt. 18. He left the college about Michaelmas 1558 [x], having taken the degree of A. B. the ſame year, Feb. 1 [y].

## 6. WILLIAM SALTMARSHE.

Born in Yorkſhire. He ſeems to have been firſt of Brazen-noſe college [z]. Admitted ſcholar of Trinity college. Oxon. by the founder's nomination, as above, aged 18. Took the degree of A. B. May 23, 1558 [a]. Made probationer fellow, by the founder's mandate, on Trinity Sunday, Jun. 7, 1558 [b]. He took the degree of M. A. Decemb. 1, 1562 [c]. He is mentioned in the Will [d] of Edward Hyndmer, a fellow of the college [e], and a memorable benefactor to the library, viz. " I bequeathe to my old " good friende ſir Henrie Saville, knight, warden " of Merton colledge in Oxford, my houpe gold " ring ; and to Mr. Thomas Allen my old friende

[x] MSS. Kettel.

[y] Wood, MSS. E. 6.

[z] MSS. Wood, E. 6. in Marg. ſub. an. 1558.

[a] MSS. Wood, E. 6. ſcil. ut ſupr.

[b] Regiſtr. coll. fol. iv. 6.

[c] MSS. Wood, E. 29.

[d] In Theſauriar. coll. Trin. Oxon.

[e] Admiſ. ſchol. Jun. 4, 1561, ſoc. 1568, Jun. 7. Regiſtr. coll.

" and

" and fellowe in Trinitie colledge, but now of
" Gloucefter-halle, my golde ringe with deathes
" heade inameled, which was fometime our friende
" Mr. *Saltmarfhes*[f]." I conjeɗure, that he was inclined to the catholic perfuafion; not only from his
conneɗions with this Edward Hyndmer[g], and Tho-

[f] This will is dat. Novemb. 15, 1607.

[g] It feems probable that this Edward Hyndmer had a ftrong
tendency to the catholic perfuafion, from the circumftance of
his quitting his fellowfhip when he ought to have taken orders.
He was admitted M. A. on Decemb. 4, 1570, and left the
college about 1576. MSS. Wood, E. 29. and Comp. Burff.
coll. Trin. 1575—6. I likewife find in a book of his private
accounts, made long after he left the college, " Expended for
" a BREVIARIE, xvi*s*." In Thefauriar. coll. Trin. He appears
to have lived many years in the family of fir Robert Dormer,
at Winge in Bucks. Ex chartis, ibid. By his will, mentioned
in the text, and written with his own hand, he leaves to fir
Robert Dormer, " iij fpurr-royalls and a double duckatt," as
a fmall remembrance of great favours received from him. To
lady Elifabeth Dormer, " my honorable miftris," two twenty-
fhilling pieces; and to their fon, fir William Dormer, forty
fhillings in angels. He bequeathes legacies to all fir Robert
Dormer's fervants by name. He leaves to Trinity college,
legacies to the amount of 157 *l*. 14 *s*. part of which was expended in furnifhing the library with book-cafes. [Ex Chart.
ibid. et Comp. Burff.] Likewife to the library, a great number of books; many of them French and Italian. To the
poor of the parifh of Winge, v *l*. He appoints the fellows
of Trinity college, aforefaid, executors of his will; and fir
Henry Saville, " my verie honorable friende," overfeer. He
defires to be buried in the chapel of Trinity college; but by a
difcretionary power left with his executors, he was interred in
the church of Winge, Aug. 20, 1618. Ex chart. ut fupr. He
was near eighty years of age when he died, and was born in
Weftmore-

mas Allen, the famous mathematician and antiquarian, but becauſe he left his fellowſhip about the

Weſtmoreland. Regiſtr. coll. Trin. In the ſaid Will, he remembers many of his relations, of his own name, living at
Kirkbie-Stephen in Weſtmoreland.

He was in high favour with the foundréſs : as appears from
the following entry, written by Ralph Bathurſt, fellow, afterwards preſident of Trinity college, Oxford, in a blank leaf of
Budden's LIFE OF BISHOP WAINFLET, edit. 1602, in the
library of that college. " Bibliothecæ coll. Trin. Oxon. libellum
" hunc inter alios complures legavit D. EDWARDUS HINDMER.
" Quo procurante, auctor ejus, Johannes BUDDENUS, Scholaris lo-
" cum ex gratia dominæ fundatricis apud nos obtinuit, A. D. 1583.
" Inde poſt annos aliquammultos ad prælectoris philoſophici munus
" a Magdalenenſibus electus, hanc Wainfleti ſui Παλιγγεσιαν edidit.
" Quam egregii viri D. Joh. BOWMAN et D. Fr. FIELD, colleg.i
" noſtri tunc temporis ſocii, ejuſque ibidem coætanei, prout in regiſtro
" collegii patet, elogiis poeticis exornarunt. R. B. 1655." Budden,
Waynflet's biographer, was firſt of Merton college : where he
was taken particular notice of by ſir Henry Saville, who recommended him to his friend Edward Hyndmer above-mentioned,
as a proper candidate for a ſcholarſhip of Trinity college. To
which he was elected May 30, 1583. After five years, intend-
ing to ſtudy the civil law, he left Trinity college, and retired
to Glouceſter-hall ; chiefly for the converſation of the learned
Thomas Allen, mentioned in this article. Afterwards he was
appointed philoſophy-reader in Magdalene college, principal of
New Inn-Hall, king's profeſſor of civil law, and principal of
Broadgates-hall. He wrote ſome other pieces. He died 1620.

About the ſame time, and for the ſame reaſon, I find one
Thomas Warren, fellow of Trinity college, retiring to Gloceſter-hall. [Schol. Jun. 14, 1568. Soc Jun. 3. 1572. Regiſtr. Kettel.] The motives for his receſſion, hinted above,
expreſsly appear from the following entry concerning him.
Regiſtr. Theſauriar. 4to. " Poſt ſuſceptum gradum Art.um Ma-
" giſtri

year 1566, when he muſt have been called, by the
ſtatutes of his houſe, to take Orders[h]. It is not
improbable, that he retired to Gloucefter hall, or
Hart-hall; both which places, particularly the firſt,
were the receptacles, about this time, of ſuch fellows of colleges, as could not, on account of their
private attachment to popery, confiſtently or con-
ſcientiouſly retain their fellowſhips. I find him,
about the year 1570, vifiting Trinity college with
Leonard Fitzimmonds, mentioned below, who had

---

" giſtri anno quarto [1579] receſſit ad aulam Gloceſtrenſem." He
was afterwards buried in the chapel of Trinity college, April
28, 1598. Wood's Collectan. e Parochial. Regiſtr. Oxon, Paroch. S. Thome. Muſ. Aſhmol. D. 5. George Blackwell alſo,
fellow of the ſaid college, receded to Gloceſter-hall, " where
" he was held in good repute by Edm. Rainolds and Thomas
" Allen, the two learned ſeniors," about 1568. Wood. Ath.
Oxon. i. p. 382. Numb. 449. [See Lel. Itin. ii. 105. edit.
1745 ] Afterwards he went to Rome : where, by Henry Cardinal Cajetane he was conſtituted arch-preſbyter of the Engliſh clergy at Rome, and by Pope Clement the eighth, notary
of the apoſtolic ſee, in the year 1598. He was intimately
connected with Garnet, provincial of the jeſuits in England.
See Camd. Elizab. p. 900. edit. Hearn. His works, recited
by Wo d, are learned, and were much eſteemed by thoſe of
his perſuaſion. He is mentioned more than once by Caſaubon,
as the friend and coadjutor of Garnet, in a long epiſtle which
contains many curious anecdotes of Garnet's hiſtory, not elſewhere to be found. Caſaub. Epiſtol.—Epiſt. 624. Frontoni
Duc. Dat. I ondin. 1611. edit. 1656. p. 762, 796. He returned to England in 1607, and died in London 1612. [Schol,
Maii 27, 1562. Soc. Jun. 18, 1565. Com, Middl.]

h Comp Burſſ coll. Trin. 1566—7,

quitted

quitted his fellowſhip of that college, and retired tó
Hart-hall, for this reaſon'.

¹ As did Thomas Allen, above-mentioned, to Glouceſter-
hall, in 1570. See his Life by Campbell, in the *Biographia Brit.*
vol. i. And Hearne's Lɪв. Nɪɢ. Scᴀᴄᴄ. Præfat. p. xxx. §. x.
And Wood, Aᴛɪɪ. Oxon. i. col. 546, 106, 174, 467, 485. F.
248. Allen gave ſome manuſcripts to the Bodleian library.
One of them is *Auguſtinus de Civitate Dei,* to which is added
*Gregorii Moralia in Jobum.* MSS. Bodl. 198. The hiſtory of
this veneıable volume is curious, and deſerves to be developed
at large. It is beautifully written on vellum in folio; and originally belonged to Robert Groſthead biſhop of Lincoln in the
thirteenth century, in whoſe hand are many notes in the mar-
gins. Groſthead gave it to the convent of Friars Minors at
Oxford. Theſe Friars gave it to the famous theologiſt Thomas
Gaſcoigne, under their ſeal, about the year 1433. Gaſcoigne
preſented it to Durham college at Oxford, and at length
Allen placed it in the Bodleian library. At the end of this
manuſcript there is a long note written by Gaſcoigne, which
Tanner has printed, Bibl. p. 311. All the books belonging to
the library of Richard de Bury in Durham college, were diſperſed ſoon after the diſſolution of that houſe. Some were removed to the Humfredian library, and others to Baliol college;
but the greater part became the property of Doctor Owen, to
whom Durham college was granted.· Archbiſhop Parker procured many Saxon manuſcripts of Doctor Owen. In the Cotton
library, there is a volume conſiſting of a collection of charters,
and other antient writings, tranſcribed by Jocelyn, Parker's
chaplain : who has inſerted this note at many of the pieces.
*The archbiſhop of Canterbury had this charter from Dr. Owen.* At
ſome others, *The copy of this Dr. Talbot had of Dr. Owen.* Vɪ-
ᴛᴇʟʟ. D. 7. Robert Talbot, the annotator on Antoninus, was
employed by the archbiſhop to collect antient manuſcripts,
chiefly Saxon. Many of Parker's books, now in Bennet college
library at Cambridge, appear to have belonged to Talbot. The
archbiſhop's principal collector was Bateman, another of his
chaplains ;

chaplains; who fays, that he "gathered within four years, "under his graces commiffion, fix thoufand feven hundred "books." Bateman's Doom *warning all men to judgment, &c.* Lond. 1581. 4to. pag. 400. It fhould not be forgotten here, that Thomas Langley bifhop of Durham, by will dated Dec. 17. 1437, gave a large legacy of books to the library of Durham college. Wharton Angl. Sacr. i. p. 776. As did John Longland bifhop of Lincoln, who died in 1547. Tanner, Bibl. 485. But the college was diffolved, before that bequeft could take place. I fhould fpeak here of Bury. This prelate was one of the earlieft Englifh reftorers of literature. Of his Philobib- lon, I have fpoken at large in the second Dissertation prefixed to the firft volume of the History of Englis.a Poetry. He held fome of the higheft offices both in church and ftate under Edward the third, whofe education he had fu- perintended. In the year 1331, he was fent by that king to Avignon, to negotiate fome bufinefs with the pope. Rymer, Foed. ii. 59. He there lodged in the houfe of cardinal Colonne, where Petrarch at that time alfo refided. Petrarch embraced the fortunate opportunity of confulting this learned Englifhman, then only a private ecclefiaftic, about the fituation of the antient Thule, fuppofed to be one of the British iflands : for the geo- graphy of antiquity was one of Petrarch's favorite ftudies. Be- ing without his books, of which he had amaffed a prodigious collection, he promifed to tranfmitt to Petrarch the beft infor- mation he could obtain on this fubject, after his return to Eng- land. What had immediately given rife to Petrarch's curiofity about this ifland, probably was Giraldus's fabulous account of Thule, in his Mirabilia Hiberniæ, a work juft publifh- ed, and recently tranflated into French by John of Meun, author of the *Romaunt de la Rofe.* Petrarch wrote frequently to Richard of Bury to know the refult of his promifed enquiries about Thule : but, perhaps in confequence of Bury's important occu- pations, never received any anfwer. See Petrarchæ Epistol. iii. 1. In this epiftle, Petrarch calls Bury, "Virum ardentis "ingenii nec literarum infcium, abditarumque rerum fupra "fidem curiofum." The ingenious author of La Vie de Pe- trarque, thinks that Petrarch's letters to Bury are now in

fome

" Alloc. *pro epulis Mag.* Saltmarſhe *et Mag.* Fitzimmonds, xx *d*" [k].

## 7.  JOHN  HARRYS.

Born in Glouceſterſhire.  Related to the founder [l]. Admitted ſcholar of Trin. coll. Oxon as above, Ælt. 17.  Admitted probationer fellow on Trinity Sunday, 1559 [m].  He left the college about the latter end of the ſame year [n].

## 8.  EDMUND  HUTCHINS.

Born in Oxfordſhire.  the founder's nephew, and one of his heirs [o].  Admitted ſcholar of Trin coll. Oxon. Octob, 3, 1556, by the founders mandate [p],

---

ſome library of England. Tom. i. Liv. ii. p. 169. Amſt. 1764. 4to. I have ſearched for this treaſure, but without ſuccefs. See Wharton, ANGL. SACR. i. 765. Leland and his tranſcriber Trithemius are miſtaken in what they have aſſerted about Petrarch's correſpondence with this prelate.  From what is here ſaid, may be alſo corrected two ſlight miſtakes in the French ENCYCLOPEDE, under the article BIBLIOTHEQUE.

[k] Comp, Burſſ. ut ſupr. 1569—70.

[l] From the will of Edmund Hutchins, mentioned in the next article.

[m] MSS. Kettel.

[n] Ibid.

[o] See ſupr. p. 122. 168.  In a letter to the preſident without date, from Tyttenhanger, he ſays, " I befeech you ſee that " Mr. Basford and Huchyns applye their ſtudye."

[p] Regiſtr. coll. fol. iii. b. " per authoritatem et mandatum
" venerabilis

Æt. 22. He quitted the college about Chriſtmas 1558 [q]. He lived at Dumbleton in Glouceſterſhire, where he was Lord of the Manor, and married the Daughter of Thomas Cockes, eſquire [r]. By his will, dat Jan. 28. 44 Eliz. and proved ſoon afterwards, he left to Trinity college aforeſaid the advowſon to the church of Dumbleton. Alſo eſtates, worth per ann. 33 *l.* 6 *s.* 8 *d.* part of which the ſaid college was annually to pay to certain charitable uſes, and to have the reſidue [s]. But his coheirs claiming the premiſſes, the whole benefaction was ſet aſide by a decree of chancery [t]. He left beſides, other charitable bequeſts to places with which he was connected. He was a benefactor to the library, in 1592. On a buttreſs, on the ſouth ſide of the college [u], the following memorial of him remains, cut in the ſtone. "Jeſu have M. O. E. Hutchins." 1558. i. e. *Jeſus have mercy on Edmund Hutchins.*

"venerabilis viri dom. Thomæ Pope militis, coll. prædicti "fundatoris, ad ſupplendum *octonarium* in eodem collegio nu- "merum, aſcitus." He is placed here on account of the laſt mentioned circumſtance. For the time of his admiſſion does not *ſtrictly* correſpond with that of the ſeven preceding.

[q] MSS. Kettel.

[r] Atkyns's Glouceſterſhire, p. 406.

[s] In Theſauriar. coll. Trin. Oxon.

[t] Regiſtr. prim. ſol. 124. b. et chartis in Theſauriar. antedict.—His pedegree is in Muſ. Aſhmol. Codd. Aſhm. 836. pag. 67.

[u] Facing the north-ſide of the Chapel of Baliol college.

*Afterwards, as places became vacant, the* FOUNDER
*nominated the five following* SCHOLLARS[x].

#### .... PIGGOTT.

No notice of him occurs in the regiſter. But
ſuch a perſon was ſcholar 1557 [y], and I preſume was
nominated by the founder; who mentions him with
great regard in a letter to the preſident, dat. *Whitmonday,*"1558. Underſtandinge... that ſir Pigott woll
" at Trynite Sunday next yeld upp his ffellowſhip
" [ſcholarſhip] and neverthelefſe deſireth to remayne
" in the college as a ſojorner; I have thought good,
" for that he is honeſt and a vertuos yong man,
" to deſire you he may remayne in his chamber as a
" ſojorner, and that he be well entreatyd in everye
" condition : for to be playne with you, I entende
" afſoone as he ſhall be prieſt, to have hym in my
" houſe iff I maye." And again, in another to the
ſame, dat. 25 May, 1558. " Iff Pigott depart, then
" may the pore boye for whom the biſhopp of Briſ-
" towe's chanceller maketh ſute, be preferryd to his
" rome : but in any caſe let Pigott be a comoner in
" the houſe." Accordingly he quitted the founda-
" tion, 1558.

#### WALTER BLOUNT.

Born at Blount's Hall, in Staffordſhire. The
founder's nephew. Admitted ſcholar Jan. 9, 1556.

---

[x] One of whom he nominated to a fellowſhip.
[y] Comp. Burſſ. 1556—7. See ſupr. p. 366.

Æt.

Æt. 18 ᶻ. He left the college about Michaelmas, 1558 ᵃ. This was the laſt inſtance in which the founder ordered any perſon to be admitted, except at the ſtatutable time of election. Concerning which he tells the preſident in a letter, dat. 27 Nov. 1556. " When my wiffs brother is ons " placed, I woll for no man's ſute the ſtatutes of " my college be broken in that poynt : and that " the election ſhall alwaies be uppon Trynytie Son- " day." One Gualter Blount, eſquire, is returned a Juſtice of the peace for Worceſterſhire, " as very " honeſt and religious," among the reſt of that county, by Freake the biſhop, to the lord Trea- ſurer, Oct. 6, 1587 ᵇ.

## RICHARD SOUTHERN.

Born at Exeter. Admitted ſcholar on Trinity Sunday, Jun. 7, 1558. Æt. 16 ᶜ. I preſume he was a relation of Thomas Southern, the treaſurer of Exeter cathedral, mentioned above. In a letter to the preſident, dat. 27, Nov. 1556, the founder ſays, " Mr. Sowtherne ſhall have his ſcholler placed " as ſone as any rome [place] is voyd, and one " man ſped to whom I have made promyſe." And in another to the ſame, dat. 24 Jul. 1557, he ſays,

---

ᶻ Regiſtr. coll. fol. 4.

ᵃ MSS. Kettel. See ſupr. p. 204.

ᵇ Strype Ann. Ref. iii. App. 174. One Walter Blount oc- curs a ſeminary prieſt, 1588. Ibid. p. 260.

ᶜ Regiſtr. fol. 68. b.

" I am

" I am forye to here your vice-prefident is fick,
" but I hope in god he fhall fhortly rere his helth ;
" for which as I fhall pray, fo I requyre you tell
" hym, I am content young Sowtherne fhall be at
" the fcoler's commens, his ffrends peyinge for the
" fame, till he can be *placyd* in my collegge." He
left the college, 1560.

### F R A N C I S   B U T L E R.

Born at Briftol. Admitted fcholar the fame day.
Æt. 17 [d]. The founder, befide what is mentioned
in the article of Piggott, mentions him in a letter
to the prefident, dated Whitmonday preceding, " I
" will that the pore fcholer of Briftow, for whom
" Mr. Dalby [e] . . . labor, be admytted. Mr. Dal-
" bye is the bisfhoppes chanceller, and a man to
" whom I am beholdinge; and the pore man he
" laboreth for is very towardlye, and his ffryndes
" not habell to fynde hym to fcole." He left the
college 1560 [f]. The fudden departure of this perfon, and fome others, about this time, it may be
fuppofed, was owing to the change of religion at the
acceffion of queen Elizabeth.

[d] Regiftr. ibid.

[e] William Dalby was prefented to the rectory of Littleton,
Briftol. Diocef. 1556. He was made prebendary of Briftol,
1558, being then chancellor of that diocefe. He was ejected
from his preferments by Q. Elizabeth. Rym. Fœd. xv. 450.
And Willis, Cathedr. Briftol. p. 788. The bifhop of Briftol
was Holyman, mentioned above, p. 400.

[f] MSS. Kettel.

LEONARD

## LEONARD FITZSYMONS.

Born at Dublin [g]. Was chapel-clerk of C. C. C. Oxon [h]. Being a native of Ireland, he was, from thence, admitted ſcholar, not only by the nomination, but by the diſpenſation, of the founder, on Trinity Sunday above-mentioned, and at the earneſt ſuit of Thomas Marſhall, the ſecond dean of Chriſt-church, in 1558, aged ſeventeen [i]. He took the degree of A. B. the next year, 1559, May 8 [k]. By the ſame authority, without having paſſed through the uſual year of probation, he was admitted actual fellow, on Trinity Sunday, June 9, 1560 [l]. He took the degree of M. A. May 4, 1563. But being averſe to the rites and Orders of the church of England, he retired to Hart-hall about 1571 [m], and afterwards became a popiſh prieſt [n]. Hollinſhed, from Stanihurſt, calls him " a deepe and pithie clerke, well ſeene in the Greeke " and Latine tongue, ſometime fellow of Trinitie " colledge in Oxford, perfect in the mathemati-

[g] Regiſtr. prim. coll. Trin. fol. 4.

[h] Wood, Ath. Oxon i. 199.

[i] Regiſtr. ut ſupr. And MSS. F. Wife. Marſhall had been a fellow of C. C. C. Oxon.

[k] Wood, ubi ſupr. F. 88.

[l] It is ſaid in the Regiſter, " per diſpenſationem venerabilis " et præpotentis militis Thomæ Pope." fol. 26.

[m] Rather 1570.

[n] Wood, ubi ſupr. And F. 92.

D d 4                    " cals,

" cals, and a paynefull ftudent in divinitie °."
Wood acquaints us, that he was eminent for his
learning in Ireland in 1580, and that he publifhed
feveral pieces, the titles of which are unknown.
He feems to have died in Ireland, where he probably fpent the latter part of his life °. He had a
brother educated at Cambridge, and afterwards be-
neficed in Ireland °. To mathematics he joined a
knowledge of mufic, as appears from the following
article in Comp. Burff. coll. Trin. 1561--2.

" Solut. *dom.* Fitzfimmons *pulfanti organa per*
" *annum,* xx *s* '.

---

° Chron. vol. i. p. 41. c. vii. Stanihurft's words are " pro-
" fundus clericus, qui utrafque linguas, theologiam et mathe-
" maticam, admodum calluit et coluit." Defcript. Hibern.
cap. vii.

° Wood, ubi fupr. i. 199. And Tanner, Bibl. p. 285.

° Stanihurft, ubi fupr.

' The ftatutable falary, although he was a fellow of the college. In confequence of the diffolution of the monafteries, and
of the reformation of religion, church mufic received an almoft
irreparable blow. Few were then educated at leaft to the mechanical part of the profeffion ; and when the fplendor of the
popifh worfhip was reftored, after a long intermiffion, by queen
Mary, it was difficult to procure inftrumental practitioners, properly qualified to affift at the folemnities of the mafs. Under
thefe circumftances in order to facilitate and fecure fo precarious
an acquifition, Sir Thomas Pope found it neceffary to provide in
his ftatutes, that there fhould be conftantly one perfon admitted
into the fociety, competently fkilled in mufic, who might be
able to execute the office of organift to the college. That this
was the cafe, the provifion itfelf feems to imply ; as well as
the reafon which the founder exprefsly fuggefts for it, and the
manner

manner in which it is worded. "Hic autem, quoniam opus
"eft, et maxime convenit, ut per hanc electionem *provideatur*
"nequando dictum Collegium ORGANORUM PULSATORE fit
"*deftitutum*, nec *talis ubique inveniri poffit facile*, liberam dictis
"electoribus poteftatem facio et permitto, unum aliquem talem
"de quocunque poffint loco eligendi, qui ludendi organis pe-
"ritus, et in grammaticæ etiam rudimentis competenter erudi-
"tus, in dictorum fcholarium numerum, modo fit pauper, ad-
"mittatur; et organa in dictis feftis, aliafque in officiis divi-
"nis, more in ecclefiis confueto, pulfare tenebitur: nifi Socio-
"rum quifquam id præftare muneris melius noverit et poterit."
STATUT. coll. Trin. cap. vii. In the Additament, where the
falary mentioned in the text is affigned, he is likewife obliged,
"Scholares ad cantandum in choro idoneos reddere."

I am not in the mean time ignorant, that antiently in our
foundations of churches and colleges, no feparate or diftinct
officer, by the name of organift, was ever appointed. This
duty was fubordinate, and appears to have been commonly performed by one of the clerks. In the ftatutes of Corpus Chrifti
college at Oxford, given in 1517, two chapel-clerks are eftablifhed, one of whom is alfo to be the *Organorum pulfator*. Cap.
xvii. The firft inftance of the mention of an Organ in any
collegiate ftatutes which I have had the opportunity to examine,
occurs in thofe of Eton college, made about the year 1440.
Where one of the four clerks who is appointed to inftruct the
chorifters, is moreover ordered *jubilare organis*. Cap. x. Here
alfo, for the firft time, *Cantus organicus* is mentioned. In the
new cathedral-foundations of king Henry the eighth, a mafter
or teacher of the finging-boys is appointed: and befides, he is
to be "cantandi, et organa pulfandi, peritus." Statut. Ecclef.
Roffenf. dat. A. D. 1545. Cap. xxii. At New college Oxford,
King's at Cambridge, and Winchefter-college, in each of which
are ample choirs, there is no provifion by ftatute, not even for
an *Informator Choriftarum*. Although fuch an officer occurs in
the early rolls of New-college. At Magdalen college Oxford,
founded about the year 1459, there is alfo no mention of an
organift: but it is enjoined that one of the chaplains, or clerks,

. or.

or fome other fkillful perfon, fhall educate the chorifters in the plain chant and pricked fong. Cardinal Wolfey in the ftatutes of his college at Oxford, given 1525, mentions a *mufic-mufter*, not by the name of an *organift*, who is to be *muficæ peritiffimus*. MSS. JAMES, vol. vii. p. 89. Bibl. Bodl. In the year 1446, the abbot and convent of Muchelney in Somerfetfhire, granted a corrody of five marks, with feven gallons of ale, and feven loaves called *le old myches*, every week, and a gown and four loads of wood annually, to Ralph Drake *cantor*, or chanter, *pro fervicio nobis in illa fciencia mufica*; and on condition, that he attend the choir every day, and teach four boys, and one of the monks, or as many as chofe, to play on the organ. Hearne's AD. DOMERH. vol. i. APPEND. PRÆF. p. lxxxii. edit. Oxon. 1727. In a catalogue of the fervice-books of faint Paul's cathedral, taken in the year 1295, *Liber Organorum* occurs more than once. Dugd. Hift. p. 220. By which, I believe, we are not to underftand any fpecies of mufic-books for that inftrument. The Organ was fo effential a circumftance of divine worfhip, that the mafs, and other holy offices, were called *Organum*. Charpentier, SUPPL. Glofs. Lat. Du Cange. tom. iii. p. 89. in V.

To recur to the firft part of this note. There is a curious paffage in Erafmus's Annotations on the New Teftament, written about the year 1512, which admirably difplays the ftate of our church-mufic, juft before the Reformation. EPIST. Corinth. i. xiv. 19. [Opp. Tom. vi. C. 731. N. 26.] " We have in- " troduced into the churches, a certain elaborate and theatrical " fpecies of mufic, accompanied with a tumultuous diverfity of " voices. All is full of trumpets, cornets, pipes, fiddles, and " finging. We come to church as to a play-houfe. And for " this purpofe, ample falaries are expended on organifts, and " focieties of boys, whofe whole time is wafted in learning to " fing. Not to mention the vaft revenues which the church " fquanders away in the ftipends of finging-men, who are com- " monly great drunkards, buffoons, and chofen from the loweft " of the people. Thefe fooleries are become fo agreeable, that " the monks, efpecially in ENGLAND, think of nothing elfe. " To this end, even in the Benedictine MONASTERIES OF
" ENGLAND,

\*.\* In the year 1559, *nine* fcholars were admitted; and in the fame year, the founder's inftitution of *four* ADDITIONAL fcholars took place. My foregoing lift of the firft *eight*, would have been incomplete, without fome mention of the firft *four* ADDITIONAL fcholars; which are included in the following *nine* fcholars ', admitted in the year 1559 : concerning each of which, I fhall therefore fubjoin an account, however fhort and imperfect.

### LEONARDE PERSEY, [or *Piercie.*]

He left the college, 1562 ʰ.

### ... WOOD.

He left the college, 1560 ᵘ.

" ENGLAND, many youths, boys, and other vocal performers,
" are fuftained; who, early every morning, fing to the organ
" the mafs of the Virgin Mary with the moft harmonious mo-
" dulations of voice. And the bifhops are obliged to keep
" choirs of this fort in their families."

ª It is remarkable, that no mention is made at all of the four firft, in the *college regifter:* nor of the fcholarfhips of four others, (fellows) afterwards mentioned. This defect, as will appear by the references, I have fupplied from *Regiftr. Kettel.* Which is founded on evidences equally authentic, and ftill remaining.

ᵗ MSS. Kettel. Not in Regiftr. coll.

ᵘ Ibid. Not in Reg.

... DOWLE,

... Dowle, [or *Dowlie*.]

He left the college the fame year [w].

.... Prince.

He left the college, 1562 [x].

## Richard Basset [y].

Born in Yorkfhire. Afterwards admitted probationer fellow, by nomination of the foundrefs, Jun.
4, 1561 [z].

## Christopher Wharton [a].

Born in Yorkfhire. Afterwards admitted probationer fellow by nomination, and difpenfation, of
the foundrefs, his county being full, May 26,
1562 [b]. Soon after [c] the year 1564, he left his fel-

[w] Ibid. Not in Reg.

[x] Ibid. Not in Reg.

[y] MSS. Kettel. ex Comp. burff. 2. non in regiftr. ut fchol.

[z] Regiftr. fol. 27.

[a] MSS. Kettel. ut fupr. non in regiftr. ut fchol.

[b] " Qui virtute literarum domine fundatricis admiffus erat,
" alias admitti non potuit ex eo quod numerus ejufdem comi-
" tatus erat completus. Regiftr. fol. 26. b.

[c] I find the following entry in Regiftr. cur. cancell. Oxon.
GG. fupr. citat. fol. 89. " Nomina [cum tutoribus] fcholafti-
" corum degentium in domibus privatis, 1562.—Bartholomæus
" Chamberlayne, dominus Wharton tutor." Bartholomew
Chamber-

lowſhip, being averſe to the religion and orders of the church of England; and retiring to the college at Doway, an expedient not uncommon at this time, was made a catholic prieſt. He then returned to England, and officiated in that character; being in high reputation and eſteem for his learning and piety, among thoſe of his own perſuaſion [d]. At length being impriſoned for the public exerciſe of his pro-ſcribed function, and for diſclaiming the queen's ſupremacy, he was executed at York, in the ſixtieth year of his age, Mar. 28. 1600 [e].

## JOHN HALSEY [f], [or *Haulſei.*]

Born in Hertfordſhire. I find him nominated one of the firſt fellows of St. John's college Oxford, by the founder, ſir Thomas Whyte, in his charter, dated Mar. 28, 1557--8 [g], at which time he ſeems to have

Chamberlayne was perhaps a fellow of Trinity college after-wards, mentioned p. 195, 196. And his tutor, the ſubject of this article. Theſe tutors did not live with their pupils in the private houſes; the latter attended upon the former, who for the moſt part were fellows of colleges, occaſionally for inſtruc-tion, &c.

[d] See Thoreſby's *Leedes.* p. 521.

[e] Wood, Ath. Oxon. i. F. p. 93. col. 1. And Worthing-ton's *Catalogus Martyrum pro Religione Catholica in Anglia oc-ciſorum.* Edit. 1614. 8vo. pag. 43. where he is called, " Col-" legii Duaci alumnus."

[f] MSS. Kettel. ut ſupr. non in regiſtr. ut ſchol.

[g] Wood, Hiſt. antiq. univ. Oxon. ii. 303. col. 2. And Catal. ſoc. coll. di. Jo. Bapt. Oxon. per Griffin Higges. MSS. Muſ. Aſhmol. F. 28. fol. 204. ſupra citat.

been

been *convictor*, or commoner, in Trinity college[h]. It appears, however that he did not accept of this offer at St. John's college, being elected scholar of Trinity college, the following year, 1559. Afterwards admitted probationer fellow of the same, May 26, 1562[i].

## EDWARD TREWEL[k].

Born in Hertfordshire. Afterwards admitted probationer fellow, by nomination of the foundress, Jun. 9, 1560[l].

## THOMAS ORPEWOODE[m].

Born in Oxfordshire. The founder's nephew or near relation[n]. Afterwards admitted probationer fellow, by nomination of the foundress, Jun. 6, 1563[o].

[h] Wood, ut supr.

[i] Regiftr. ut supr. fol. 26. b.

[k] MSS. Kettel. ex Comp. 2. Burff. ut supr. non in Regiftr. ut supr.

[l] Regiftr. ut supr. fol. 26.

[m] MSS. Kettell. ut supr.

[n] See p. 327.

[o] Regiftr. ut supr. fol 3. " Ex nominatione piæ ac vene-" rabilis dominæ Pope, uxoris Thomæ Pope militis, Fundatoris " jam defuncti." Although she was now married to fir Hugh Paulet.

NUMB.

✝✝✝✝✝✝✝✝✝✝✝✝✝✝✝✝✝✝✝✝✝✝✝✝✝✝✝✝✝✝✝

# N U M B. XXVI.

## Account of the Marriages, and Defcendants, of John Pope, of Wroxton, efquire.

JOHN POPE, only brother to fir Thomas Pope, was fettled at Wroxton in Oxfordfhire, in or before the reign of Edward the fixth; where he was buried Jun. 24, 1583[a]. He was married thrice. His firft wife, was, as I conjecture, Anne Staveley[b], daughter of ——— Staveley of Bignell[c]

[a] Regiftr. parochial. de Wroxton, co. Oxon. See alfo Regiftr. PARRET, (citat. fupr. Numb. xxi.) fol. 6. b. fol. 3. a.

[b] Ex teftamento Dom. T. Pope.

[c] Concerning this family of Staveley, I find that William Staveley, lord of the manor of Bignell, who died 1498, bequeathes his body to be buried in the church of Bicefter, co. Oxon. and was a benefactor to Bicefter priory. By Alice his wife he had George, William, John, Mary, and Ifabell. The faid George, 16 Hen. viii. leaves provifion for certain maffes, &c. in Univerfity college. Kennet's PAROCH. ANTIQ. p. 680. feq. And Wood Hift. antiq. univ. Oxon. ii. 59. col. 2. Willis recites an epitaph to Thomas Giffard of Twiford, co. Bucks, marrying Mary, daughter of William Staveley of Bignell, who died 1450. Hift. of Bucks, p. 335. One of the name is buried in Bicefter church, with the date 1485. What is here

faid

in the faid county. She died before 1554 [d], and
was buried in St. Stephen's, Wallbrook [e]; leaving
one daughter, Elizabeth, to whom fir Thomas Pope
bequeathed 300 marks for her portion in marriage [f],
and who married, 1573, Edward Blount, of Burton
upon Trent in Staffordfhire [g]. The faid John Pope's
fecond wife was Elizabeth [h], daughter of fir John
Brockett, of Brockett-Hall at Hatfield in Hertfordfhire [i], to whom he was married before 1554 [k].
His third wife was Jane, daughter of fir Edmund

---

faid of the Staveley family, corrects a paffage in Leland, ITIN.
vii. fol. 8. " There is buried in the quier of the paroche
" churche of Burcefter, one William *Standley*, efquier, lord of
" Bygnelle, &c." Read *Staveley*. I take this opportunity of
obferving that Leland mentions fir T. Pope twice, Itin. vol.
iv. P. ii. pag. 91, 59. edit. 1744.

[d] Ex indentur. quadripartit. fupr. citat.

[e] See p. 167.

[f] Ex teftam. dom. T. P.

[g] From articles of agreement relating thereto, dat. Febr.
15. 14 Eliz.—Edward Blount occurs in dame Eliz. Paulet's will,
and, I fuppofe, was her nephew.

[h] Lee's MSS. Vifitat. ut fupr. pag. 32. And from other
evidences.

[i] See Chauncy's Hertf. p. 312. John Brockett receives, with
others, parcell of the poffeffions of St. Bartholomew's priory in
London, at the diffolution. Ibid. 324. Sir John Brockett, knt.
is member of parliament for Hertfordfhire, 1553. Willis, Not.
parl. ed. ii. p. 27. He was knighted 1 Edw. vi. Feb. 22. MSS.
Cotton. Claud. C. 3. fol. 172. b.

[k] She is mentioned in Indentur. quadripartit. fupr. citat.

Wyndham,

Wyndham, of Somerſetſhire, by whom he had no iſſue [l].

But by the ſecond wife, Elizabeth Brockett, the ſaid John Pope had iſſue three ſons, Thomas, George, and William; and ſix daughters, Georgia, Penelope, Mary, Suſannah, Anne, and Jane [m]. Thomas died an infant 1564 [n]. George appears to have ſtudied one year ùnder the tuition of John Sellar [o], in Trinity college, Oxford, which he left May 3, 1587, having been admitted in the rank of *conviƈtor primi ordinis* [p]. But he died ſoon afterwards. The only ſurviving ſon, and heir, William, in 1573 [q], and at fourteen years of age, was admitted, a *convictor primi ordinis*, into the aforeſaid college, Jul. 7,

[l] She is buried in the church of Fellbridge in Norfolk, with this epitaph. " Here lieth the bodie of Jane Conningſbie, " widdowe, and one of the daughters of ſir Edmond Wind- " ham, knt. deceaſed : firſt married to John Pope in the countie " of Oxford, eſquire, and after his deceaſe to Humphrie Con- " ningſbie, eſquire. She departed this life without iſſue of her " bodie, the xx daie of November, in the yeare of our Lord " 1608, and of her age 67." The ſaid Humphrie Conningſbie was of Hampton-court, co. Hereford. She muſt have been married to John Pope between 1573 and 1583. See CAT. of Mr. Weſt's Books, p. 220. Num. 4299.

[m] Lee's MSS. Viſit. ut ſupr.— Regiſtr. Wroxton.—Regiſtr. in 4to. in Theſauriar. coll. Trin.—And MSS. Pedigr. Rawlinſ.

[n] Regiſtr. Wroxton.

[o] B. D. Afterwards in 1597 reƈtor of Ickford in Buckinghamſhire.

[p] Ex regiſtr. quodam in 4to. in Theſ. coll. Trin. ſupr. citat.

[q] Regiſtr. Wroxton.

1587,

1587, which he quitted April 12, 1591 [r]. He was entered a ſtudent in Gray's-Inn, 1594 [s]. On the arrival of James the I. in England, he was created in the great gallery of St James's palace, Jul. 24, 1603, a knight of the bath [t]: and on May 22, 1611, a baronet, by the ſtyle of ſir William Pope

[r] Ex Regiſtr. in 4to ut ſupr.

[s] MSS. Harl. 1912. pag. 60.

[t] The ceremony of this creation is thus deſcribed by Howes, Stowe's continuator. " Sunday the twenty-foure [1603] was " performed the ſolempnity of knights of the bath riding " honorably from St. James to the courte, and made ſhewe " with their ſquires and pages about the Tilte-yarde; and " after went into the parke of St. James, and there lighted " all from their horſes, and went uppe to the king's majeſties " preſence in the gallerie where they received the order of " knighthood of thè bathe." Stowe's Ann. by Howes, pag. 827. But ſee Anſtis, who ſays this creation was on the day of the king's coronation, viz. Jul. 25. ` Knighthood of the Bath, App. pag. 57.

There is an old play addreſſed to this ſir WILLIAM POPE, written by Barnaby Barnes. It is a tragedy, entitled the DEVIL'S CHARTER, on the ſtory of pope Alexander the ſixth ; acted before James the firſt on Candlemas night, and printed Lond. 1607. quarto. " Dedicated to the honourable and his verie deare " friends ſir W. Herbert, and ſir W. Pope, knights, aſſociates " in the noble order of the Bath." This author Barnes wrote Four books of OFFICES about Princes, &c. Lond. 1606. fol. Alſo A divine century of ſpiritual ſonnets, Lond. 1595. Sir William Herbert, here mentioned, was afterwards earl of Pembroke, and Chancellor of the univerſity of Oxford. He was himſelf a writer of poetry, and publiſhed a book of poems. Some of his ſonnets were ſet to muſic by Henry Lawes. Pembroke college is named after him.

of

of Wilcott[a] in Oxfordſhire[w]. Afterwards, Octob.
16, 1629[x], he was made by Charles I. baron of
Bellturbett, and earl of Downe, in Ireland. On occaſion of the laſt mentioned dignity, ſupporters were

[a] *William Pope of Wilcott*, occurs high-ſheriff of Oxfordſhire,
43 Eliz.—Fuller's Worth. pag. 344. edit. 1662. The manor
of Wilcott, or Wivilcote, is ſaid by Plott to have been antiently the head of a barony ; and he ſuppoſes that one of its barons
is buried in the neighbouring church of Northleigh. See Plott's
Oxf. ch. x. §. 134. p. 154. But the perſon there interred,
with his wife, both whoſe recumbent figures, large as life, and
richly habited, are on a beautiful alabaſter tomb within an elegant chantry, is . . . . Wilcotes, or Willycotes, eſquire. They
have both a collar of eſſes, but no baronial badges ; and from
the ſtyle of the architecture, I take this chantry not to be older
than Henry the ſixth. The family were indeed lords of the
manor of Wilcott ; and they were of great note in Oxfordſhire,
but now long ſince extinct. See Kennet's Paroch. Antiq. p.
561. 527. Their eſcocheon was an eagle's head with wings.
The two figures on the tomb juſt mentioned, which are as large
as life, I take to be John and Alicia Wilcott, whoſe daughter
Elizabeth married into Raynesford of Great-Tew in this county, and whoſe arms appeared in the windows of the manor-
houſe there, with this remarkable inſcription. " **John Wyl-**
" **cotes et Alicia uxor ejus, ob.** 1400 **et ſemel.**" i. e. 1401.
or 1410. Leland ſays, " WIVELCOTE, *alias* WILCOTE, *a knight*
" *that was owner of the lordſhip of Tew, and dwelled in the*
" *maner place there, is leied in a faire tumbe of marble in Tewe*
" *churche.*" ITIN. iv. f. 16. pag. 14. edit. 1744. Compare
Hearne's TROKELOWE, Append. p. 329. 334. In the church
of Great Tew, if I recollect right, there is a tomb, perhaps
the ſame, with the *Croſs* of Raynesford and the *Eagle* of Wilcott.

[w] Dugd. Antient uſe of bearing arms, &c. 1682. pag. 82.
[x] Pat. Car. I. an. reg. 4. part 39.

granted

granted to the antient coat by Segar, otherwife
garter king at arms, on the twenty-third of December following [y]. He died Jul. 2, 1631 [z], at Wroxton, and was buried in the church, on the north
fide of the altar, under an alabafter monument of
elegant and coftly workmanfhip, on which are the
recumbent figures of himfelf and his lady, large as
life. This monument was made by Nicholas Stone [a].
He left by will to Trinity college, Oxford, one
hundred pounds [b], and a beautiful edition of Or-
telius's Geography, printed 1584 [c]. He married in
1595, or in the year following [d], Anne, daughter
of fir Owen Hopton, lieutenant of the tower of
London, and relict of Henry lord Wentworth, baron of Nettleftead [e]. She died at Wroxton, and

[y] MSS. F. Wife.

[z] Ex tumul. apud Wroxton.

[a] From Mr. Vertue.

[b] Comp. Burff. coll. Trin. 1630—1. Burfariis Antonio Far-
rington et GULIELMO CHILLINGWORTH.

[c] Ex lib. benefactor. biblioth. coll. Trin.

[d] See Collins, Peer. iii. p. 60. ed. i.

[e] MSS. pedigr. Rawlinf. And from empalements in paint-
ed glafs at Wroxton. At the fame place there is a fine old
portrait of fir Owen Hopton, dated 1590. His daughter,
Anne landy Wentworth, as mentioned in the text, had by
her former hufband, lord Wentworth, two fons, Thomas and
Henry. They were both fent together to Trinity college, Oxford, and matriculated Novemb. 12, 1602. Thomas, lord
Wentworth, being 11, and his brother Henry 8 years of age.
Collectan. e lib. Matric. MSS. A. Wood. Muf. Afhm. D. 1.
In the college-computus of that year, viz. 1601—2, I find the
following entry.

" Sol.

was buried there May 10, 1625[f]. In the reign of
James I. the faid William, lord Downe, built a
large manſion-houſe at Cogges in Oxfordſhire, now
partly ſtanding, on the ſite and ruins of the priory,
diſſolved by Henry VI[g]. He likewiſe built from

" Sol. pro chirothecis magiſtri Pope, xxxij s."
This, I ſuppoſe, was a compliment to their father-in-law William Pope, when he brought the boys to the college. Thomas,
now fourteen years old, appeared among the young nobility of
the univerſity, in the choir of Chriſt church cathedral, before
James the firſt and his queen, in the year 1605. Wake's REX
PLAT. p. 35. edit. 1607. In 1610, he was made knight of
the Bath, at the creation of prince Henry. He was in high
favour with James I. And by Charles I. with whom he was in
equal eſteem, he was created earl of Cleveland. His loyalty
and intrepidity make a conſpicuous figure in the grand rebellion. Dugd. BAR. iii. 310. col. 2. Lady Anne, abovementioned, alſo by her firſt huſband left a daughter, Jane, married to ſir John Finett, knight, of Weſtkele in Kent, who
was ſent an envoy into France, 1619, and knighted the next
year. In 1626, he was conſtituted maſter of the ceremonies
to Charles the firſt, having been aſſiſtant-maſter in the foregoing
reign, during which office, he wrote a book, now very ſcarce,
entit. FINETTI PHILOXENIS, *Some choice obſervations*, &c.
which contains a curious deſcription of the ceremonies of an
age of ceremony. See Collins, ut ſupr.—Birch's Pr. Henry,
p. 192.—Wood's Ath. Oxon. i. F. 270.—See alſo the PHI-
LOXENIS, p. 167, 199. edit. 1656. 8vo. This book has been
tranſlated into German.

At lord Guilford's, abovementioned, there is a picture large
as life, of Anne lady Wentworth, and her three children, Thomas, Henry, and Jane, which ſhe had by her firſt huſband, lord
Wentworth. It is painted by Vanſomer, 1596.

[f] Regiſtr. Wroxton.

[g] MSS. Wood, Muſ. Aſhm. E. 1. 4to. p. 45.

the

the ground, and finifhed in the year 1618[h], the prefent manfion - houfe at Wroxton; where his love of the Arts appears in the eaft-window of of the chapel, the glafs of which he caufed to be decorated, in 1623, by Van Ling[i], with hiftories from the new teftament, and family Arms[k]. At this place, but probably in the old abbey houfe[l], he was vifited by James I. in a progrefs; where he entertained the king with the fafhionable and courtly diverfions of hawking and bear-baiting. At the fame time his lady having been lately delivered of a daughter, the babe was prefented to the king, holding the following humorous epigram in her hand, with which his majefty was highly pleafed[m].

[h] Date ibid. in the hall.—In the year 1600, I find him living at Hook-norton, co. Oxon. *Ex chart. in thefaur. coll. prædict.* This was in a houfe built by the Brandons dukes of Suffolk. The manor of Hook-norton now belonging to the bifhoprick of Oxford, was granted to fir Thomas Pope, by Pat. 1. Mar. regin. Teft. Jun. 20. par. 5. " Cum pertinentiis in " com. Oxon. etc."

[i] From the window.

[k] Among the beautiful fragments of old painted glafs, with infcriptions, in lord Temple's Gothic temple, at Stowe, is a pane infcribed fir WILLIAM POPE and ANNE HOPTON; which, I fuppofe, came from this window.

[l] Which ftood in the Garden on the eaft fide of the prefent houfe.

[m] It is fuppofed to have been written by Dr. Richard Corbet then a young ftudent of Chrift Church, Oxon. afterwards Bifhop of Norwich. " In 1605, he was efteemed one of the " moft celebrated WITS in the univerfity, as his *poems, jefts, ro-* " *mantic fancies* and *exploits*, which he made and *performed ex-* " *tempore,*

See this little miftres here,
Did never fit in Peter's chaire,
Or a triple crowne ⬤ weare;
　　And yet fhe is a *Pope*.

No benefice fhe ever fold,
Nor did difpence with fins for gold;
She hardly is a fev'nnight old,
　　And yet fhe is a *Pope*.

No king her feet did ever kiffe,
Or had from her worfe look than this:
　　Nor did fhe ever hope,
　　To faint one with a rope;
　　And yet fhe is a *Pope*.
A female Pope youll fay, a fecond *Joan*;
No fure—fhe is POPE *Innocent* or none [n].

" *tempore*, fhewed. Afterwards entering into holy Orders, he
" became a moft *quaint* preacher, and therefore much followed
" by *ingenious* men. At length being made one of the chap-
" lains to his majefty king James the firft, who highly valued
" him for his *fine fancy* and preaching, he, was by his favour
" promoted, &c." Wood, ATH. OXON. i. col. 600. Corbet,
however, was a man of real wit, and poffeffed a vein of high
humour, which would have pleafed a more delicate tafte than
that of James. His POETICA STROMATA were printed in
1647.

　　[n]. Fuller's WORTHIES, LONDON, pag. 223. Ed. 1662. At
Wroxton there is a very curious picture of prince Henry while
a boy. The date is 1603, and the prince's age is marked 11.
But he was then only 9. Vertue could not difcover the painter.
He is reprefented large as life, cutting the throat of a ftag after

　　　　　　　　　　　　　hunting.

Before I ſpeak particulary of his Children, I return to his ſiſters above-mentioned. Of whom, Anne, the eldeſt, married John Spurling, eſquire, of Baldock in Hertfordſhire [o]. Georgia was born at Wroxton, 1563 [p], and married Robert Raynesford, eſquire, of Staverton in Northamptonſhire [q]. Jane, the third, married Francis Combes, eſquire, of

hunting. At ſome little diſtance is ſir John Harrington, a youth, the prince's intimate friend, as appears by his arms hung up in a tree. This piece was probably painted to compliment ſome boyiſh atchievement in hunting performed by the prince; for, almoſt from his infancy, he was remarkably fond of hunting. In the great hall of the old royal palace at Woodſtock, where he reſided, there was preſerved a prodigious pair of ſtag's horns, with an inſcription importing that the ſtag was hunted and killed by prince Henry. Probably the prince accompanied the king at this viſit.

[o] MSS. Pedigr. of Pope, penes honoratiſſ. com. de Guildford.—In the herald's office, there are two or three pedigrees of this family. But they are in general falſe and defective. That which I have cited, as being among *MSS. Rawlinſ. Bibl. Bodl.* Manu A. Wood. ſeems to be taken from one of theſe. Perhaps the moſt correct one in that office, is G. 3. 26. Offic. Arm. They have been obligingly compared for me by Ralph Bigland, eſquire, Somerſet-herald, and examined by Mr. Aſtle of the Paper Office.

[p] Regiſtr. Wroxton. Where it is ſaid that George Carleton, *eſquier*, was her godfather. He was of Brightwell, in Oxfordſhire, and related to this family by marrying Eliſabeth, daughter of ſir John Brockett, ſon of ſir John Brockett, mentioned above. See Chauncy's Hertf, p. 313.

[q] MSS. Wood, Muſ. Aſhmol. E. 1. pag. 115.

Hempſtead

Hempſtead in Hertfordſhire ʳ. Penelope was born
1568 ˢ. Mary was born 1569 ᵗ. Suſannah, the ſe-

ʳ MSS. pedigr. of Pope, penes honoratiſſ. ccm. de Guildford.
Their ſon Francis Combe, was gentleman-commoner of Trinity
college, Oxford, under the tuition of Mr. John Bowman,
which he quitted in 1602. Lɪʙ. Cᴀᴜᴛ. in quarto. He was an
elegant ſcholar, eſpecially in the Greek tongue. The books
which he left to Trinity college library, are a proof of his taſte
and learning. He died in 1641, and lies buried at Hempſtead
in Hertfordſhire. See Salmon's Hᴇʀᴛꜰᴏʀᴅꜱʜɪʀᴇ, pp. 95.
116. edit. fol. 1728. His numerous benefactions are recorded
on his wife's monument in the ſouthern chancel of the church
of Abbats Langley in Hertfordſhire.

ˢ Regiſtr. Wroxton. Where it is ſaid that Edward Boughton
was her godfather. He was of Lawford in Warwickſhire, and
married Suſannah a daughter, as it ſeems, of the firſt ſir John
Brockett. Dugd. Warw. p. 66. From Chauncy it appears,
that ſir Nicholas Barrington, who died 1521, married Eliſabeth,
a daughter of ſir John Brockett, afterwards married to William
Boughton, eſquire. Hertf. p. 367.

ᵗ Regiſtr. Wroxton. Her godfather, Anthony Buſtard, to
whom ſir Thomas Pope bequeathes by will x l. He was the
ſon of John Buſtarde, ſecond huſband to ſir Thomas Pope's mother Margaret, buried in a chapel on the ſouth ſide of Adderbury church, near Deddington, in Oxfordſhire, with this inſcription on a large monument of ſtone. " Nere unto this
" tombe lyeth buried the bodyes of John Buſtarde eſquire and
" Elizabeth his wife, and Jane Buſtarde wife to Anthonie Buſ-
" tarde, ſon and heire to the ſaid John: which John had by
" the ſaide Elizabethe xvii children. And the ſaid John dyed
" anno dom. 1534. The ſaid Elizabeth anno 1517, and the
" ſaide Jane anno 1568." Arms above. On a ――― between 3 roundells, 3 buſtardes, a bord. ingr. The ſame impal. a
cheveron ingr. between 3 unicorn's heads eraſed. See Lɪꜰᴇ. p. 5.
In the ſame church is a monument erected by the ſaid Anthony
to his daughter Mary, and her huſband Edward More who died
1586.

1586. Of the daughters of the faid John :—*Joanne* marries William Chauncey, efquire, of Edgcote, co. Northampt. who died 1585. She dies 1571. *Hiſt. of Northamptonſh.* i. 119. *Chriſtian* marries Edward Wilmot of Witney, co. Oxon. and, afterwards, William Bury of Culham, co. Berkſ. *MSS. Wood*, ut ſupr. E. 1. pag. 21. *Anne* marries Edward Frere, efquire, of the city of Oxford. See ſupr. p. 307. I find one John Buſtarde, a ſubſcribing witneſs to an inſtrument in Trinity college, Oxon. dat. Apr. 1. 22 Eliz. Alſo one John Buſtarde of Oxfordſhire, a fugitive for popery. *Strype's Reformat.* ii. App. 103. John Buſtarde is alſo removed from New college, Oxon. 1560. Wood. Ant. 283. The father of John Buſtarde, buried in Adderbury church, as above, if not the fame, is perhaps John Buſtarde mentioned in the will of Rich. Fox, of Bereford St. Michael's, co. Dorſet. dat. May 31, 1502. In which the faid Richard Fox leaves to the guild of Deddington, xx *s.* To buying a bell for ths church there, xij *s.* To the light of our lady of pity there, that is, of the holy virgin holding our ſaviour in her arms after his crucifixion, fometimes called the *image of Pite*, vj *s.* viij *d.* With other benefaĉtions and bequeſts. The reſidue of his goods to be diſpoſed of for his children by Rich. Fox, and JOHN BUSTARDE. *Ex Regiſtr. Blaymir.* qu. 15. cur. prær. Cant. Unleſs Dodynton in Somerfetſhire be here intended. The earlieſt notice I find of the name is in 7 Edw. ii. 1313, when one John Buſtarde is pardoned as an adhereut to Thomas earl of Lancaſter, concerned in the death of Pierce Gaveſton. Rym. Fœd. iii. 444. Gaveſton was detained a priſoner at Deddington for fome days before his execution near Warwick. Dugd. Bar. ii. 44. One William Buſtard, S. T. B who probably was of this family, was appointed one of the prieſts of the chantry of Guy-cliff, near Warwick, Jul. 29, 1520.—Priv. ſigill. Hen. viii. an. reg. 11. Jul. 29. Alſo Robert Buſtard is preſented to the vicarage of Newenhem by St. Alban's abbey, 24 Feb. 1468. Regiſtr. Mon. S. Alban. John Buſtard of Oxfordſhire, appears as a fugitive for religion, about the middle of Eliſabeth's reign. Peck's DESID. CURIOS. lib. ii. ad calc.——On mentioning the name

of

cond, was married, Nov. 12, 1583, to Daniel
Danvers, of Culworth in Northamptonſhire[u].

I now return to the iſſue of the aforeſaid William
Pope firſt earl of Downe, and his counteſs, Anne.
Theſe were two ſons, William and Thomas: and
one daughter, Anne[w], who died, as appears, unmarried, and was buried at Wroxton, Jul. 13,
1629[x]. As to the ſons, William Pope, anceſtor of
Henry earl of Litchfield, was born at, Wroxton,
1596[y]. He was knighted by James I. at the royal
manor of Woodſtock, Jul. 28, 1616[z]. He was mar-

of Freer in this note, I take this opportunity of inſerting the
following notice concerning William Freer, [p. 207.] extract d from the *Journal book of expences of building Cardinal Wol-
ſey's college*, now Chriſt Church, Oxford. MSS. Br. Twyne, notat. 8. archiv. Oxon. p. 351. It is ann. 20 Hen. viii. "Paid
" to William Freer of Oxford, for the new makinge, mend-
" inge, and repairinge of the high waye leadinge between
" Billſhipton and THE CROSSE ſtanding uppon Heddington-
" hills, for the more ſpeedy conveyance of ſtone, tymber, and
" lyme, to be carried from ſundrie places to the ſaide worke,
" over and above, xvl. paide by the handes of Mr. Nicholas
" Townly, maſter of the works, as by a booke of parcells
" thereof made by the ſaide William Freer, then being ſurvey-
" our of the ſaide workes, doth plainly appear at large,—
" xxxivl. viijs. vd."

[u] Regiſtr. Wroxton.

[w] Inſcript. ſepulchral, ibid. Perhaps the infant preſented to
king James.

[x] Regiſtr. ibid.

[y] Ibid.

[z] MSS. Dugdale. Muſ. Aſhmol. R. fol. 215.

ried,

ried, 1615, in St. Margaret's church Weſtminſter, to Eliſabeth ª, eldeſt daughter of ſir Thomas Watſon, knight, of Halſtead in Kent ᵇ. He died in 1624, while his father William was yet living, and was buried, Aug. 29, at Wroxton ᶜ. His relict afterwards married ſir Thomas Penniſtone, knight and baronet, of Cornwell in Oxfordſhire ᵈ. The ſaid William and Elizabeth Pope had iſſue three ſons, Thomas, William, and John; and two daughters, Anne and Elizabeth ᵉ. Anne born at Wroꞏn, 1617 ᶠ, married ſir Samuel Danvers, baronet, of Culworth aforeſaid ᵍ. They had a ſon chriſtened *Pope*, who gave a large emboſſed ſilver goblet to Trinity coꞏge, Oxford, which lately preſerved the following ꞏcription.

ª Regiſtr. Wroxton.

ᵇ A memorable benefactor to the church of Halſtead, 1610: adorning it with a beautiful painted window, ſteeple, porch, &c. In the ſame church is a ſtone to the memory of lady Watſon his wife, placed there by Thomas Pope, ſecond earl of Downe, her grandſon. See Harris's Kent, p. 141, 142. And Philpot's Villare Cant. p. 177. Whoſe miſtakes are here corrected.

ᶜ Regiſtr. Wroxton.

ᵈ MSS. Pedigrees in Muſ. Aſhmol. fol. F. 2. pag. 102.

ᵉ Ex Teſtamento Avi, Gulielmi Pope, dat. Dec. 31, 1630. when they were all living,

ᶠ Regiſtr. Wroxon.

ᵍ MSS. pedigr. Rawlinſ. ut ſupꞌr. Collins is here corrected, Peer. ii. 383. Ed. i. And Hiſt. Northamptonſhire, i. 164.

*Ex*

*Ex dono Pope Danvers, filii unici Samuelis Danvers
de Culworth in agro Northampton baronetti, ex matris parte Fundatoris confanguinei, et hujus collegii
primi ordinis commenfalis, an. dom.* 1662.

The younger fifter, Elizabeth, born at Halftead,
Decemb. 19, 1618[g], was married to George Ra-
leigh, efquire, of Farmborough in Warwickfhire[h].
To return to their Brothers above-mentioned, Thomas, William, and John. Of William I find no
more than his name recited in his grandfather's will :
and that he was born at Cogges, Jan. 11, 1624[i].
John was alfo born at Cogges Nov. 2, 1623, where
his father refided[k]. Of Thomas I muft fpeak more
at large, whom I therefore mention laft.

He was born at Cogges, 1622[l]. At the age of
nine years, on the death of his grandfather William,
viz. Jul. 1631, he became a baronet, and fecond
earl of Downe, by fucceffion. He was educated at
home under a careful tutor[m]; and in June, 1639,
was matriculated a nobleman of Chrift Church,

[g] Regiftr. Wroxton.

[h] MSS. Pedigr. Rawlinf.

[i] Regiftr. Cogges.

[k] Regiftr. Wroxton. Mrs. [i. e. Lady] Elizabeth Pope of
Cogges, occurs in 1636, in Regiftr. Parret, [citat. fupr.
Numb. xxi.] fol. 106. b. This muft have been their mother.

[l] Regiftr. Wroxton.

[m] Wood, Ath. Oxon. ii. 543.

Oxford.

Oxford[n]. He married Lucy, daughter of John
Dutton, efquire, of Sherborne in Glouceſterſhire[o].
She died Apr. 6, 1656, and lies buried in the
church of Cubberley, near Cheltenham, in the ſaid
county[p]. Having ſuffered ſeverely for his activity
in the royal cauſe during the grand rebellion, inſomuch that he was compelled to ſell his houſe and
eſtate at Cogges, he left the kingdom about the
beginning of Cromwell's uſurpation[q]: and making
an advantage of his perſecutions, took the opportunity of improving himſelf by viſiting foreign
countries[r]. About the time of the reſtoration he

[n] MSS. Wood, collectan. e lib. matric. ut ſupr.—See alſo
Laud's *Chancellorſhip*, p. 190. ſeq.

[o] And not Eliſabeth, as Wood ſays, Ath. Oxon. ubi ſupr.
See Atkyns's Glouceſterſhire, p. 377, 378, 646. Eliſabeth
married John Colt, eſquire. Atkyns, ibid.

[p] Inſcript. ſepulchral. ibid.

[q] Whitelock mentions a fine impoſed on the earl of Downe,
by the parliament, aſſigned to the garriſon at Abingdon, in
1645. Memor. p. 186. Other evidences ſpecify a fine of 6000l.
Theſe confiſcations were often granted to the preſbyterian miniſters, for the better ſupport of enthuſiaſtic prayer, and of
ſermons which had no end.

[r] In his diſtreſſes, Trinity college, Oxford, granted him ſums
of money, as appears by a ſchedule in the college-Treaſury.
" Mem. A. D. 1647, Given to the earl of Downe, *poſt finitum*
" COMPUTUM, by order of Mr. Preſident and Officers,
145l. 13s. 4d." And in the following year, the college gave
a preſent to ſir Thomas Pope, knight, his UNCLE, afterwards
a baronet, and in 1660, the third earl of Downe, hereafter-
mentioned, who was alſo a conſiderable ſufferer in the royal
cauſe. viz. COMP. BURSS. 1648. " Conceſſ. domino Thomæ
" Pope,

returned home; and dying at Oxford', Decemb.
28, 1660, was interred before the altar in the church
of Wroxton, with the following infcription, which
further illuftrates his character, and confirms many
particulars here mentiond.

## H. S. E.

ILLUSTRISSIMUS DOM. DOMINUS THOMAS POPE, DE
WILCOTT IN AGRO OXONIENSI BARONETTUS,
BARO BELLTURBET, COMES DUNENSIS, IN HI-
BERNIA.

*Vir, in quo nibil defideres præter vitam diuturnam :
cui ad eximiam corporis elegantiam, et miram felicitatem
ingenii, acceffit morum integritas, et rerum fcientia non
vulgaris. In quo eminere poffet erga patriam affectus,
nifi quod par effet ejus in amicitiis fides. In omnibus
recti et æqui obfervantiffimus ; fuper cætera, in regem
pius. Quem poftquam a perduellibus nefario bello la-
ceffitum, juftiffimis fed male felicibus juviffet armis ;
afflictis jam domi rebus, in exteras regiones proficifcitur :
Inter quas, ubi quæ Europæi mundi bumaniores funt
partes non incurius aut fruftra perluftraffet ; reverfus in
patriam, quum illic etiam fereniffimum principem tanto
patre dignum, Hæredem reducem vidiffet lætus ; faltem*

---

" Pope, xlv*l.*" One is furprifed at thofe donations, under the
government of doctor Robert Harris, Cromwell's prefbyterian
Prefident. But Harris was a man of candour, and I believe a
*majority* of the old loyal *fellows* ftill remained.

' MSS. Wood, ut fupr. No. 8466. 4. pag. 100;

*(quod*

*(quod unum reliquum erat) chariſſimæ filiæ dominæ Eli-*
*zabethæ* [t] *cum domino Franciſco Henrico Lee de Ditch-*
*ley, baronetto, auſpicatiſſimas feliciter celebraſſet nuptias,*
*(quia jam ſpes omnes ſic ſuas impleverat,) diuturni per-*
*vicaciis morbi patientia ſuperatis, non illibenter fato*
*ceſſit.*

$$\text{Anno} \left\{ \begin{array}{l} \text{\textit{Dom.} 1660.—\textit{Dec.} 28.} \\ \text{\textit{Æt.} 39.} \end{array} \right.$$

They had one only daughter, Elizabeth, who married ſir Francis Henry Lee, baronet, of Ditchley
in Oxfordſhire [u], by whom ſhe had two ſons, Ed-
ward-Henry, created earl of Litchfield by Charles
II [w], grandfather by this match to Henry earl of
Litchfield, chancellor of the univerſity of Oxford:
and Francis-Henry, a gentleman-commoner of Trinity college aforeſaid [x]. She was afterwards married to Robert earl of Lindſey [y]. Of this lady there

[t] Born at Cogges, April 15, 1645. Regiſtr. Cogges.

[u] Ex epitaph. modo citat.

[w] Collins, Peer. ii. 390. Ed. i.

[x] Ex Regiſtr. in Pergamen. coll. Trin. ab ann. 1683. fol. 6.

[y] Regiſtr. prædict. And MSS. Wood, modo citat. ——
Wood in another MS. mentions Philip Bertie, a younger ſon
of Rob. earl of Lindſey, of Trin. coll. who ſpeaks a copy of
Engliſh verſes, in the theatre at Oxford, 1683, to the duke
and dutcheſs of York, the lady Anne, &c. They were written
by Creech, then A. B. of Wadham college, and are printed in
Examen Poeticum, or vol. iii. of Miſcellany Poems. D. 19.
4to. pag. 56. MSS. Muſ. Ashm. In Monmouth's Rebellion,
in the year 1685, the ſame Philip Bertie, being half-nephew to
the

is a capital picture at lord Litchfield's at Ditchley,
by fir Peter Lely.

the Earl of Abingdon then Lord Lieutenant of Oxfordfhire, was
Captain of a company chiefly of his own college, in the militia
of the Univerfity, which he trained in Trinity college grove.
Wood, MSS. ibid. pag. 76. b. Under that year, I find the
following notices relating to this bufinefs in Comp. Burff. Coll.
Trin. Oxon. viz. 1685. " Dat. Tubicinibus Comitis de Ab-
" ingdon, x s." Again, " Pro armamentis Collegii expolien-
" dis et emendandis, xvi s."—And, " Pro feftivis ignibus
" [bonfires] poft devictos rebelles, i l. xij s. x d." In the fame
Computus are difburfements for horfes hired to ferve againft
the rebels.

Thefe notices relating to the troops raifed by the univerfity
of Oxford in Monmouth's rebellion, remind me of a curious
anecdote concerning Smith's famous Ode entitled Pocockius,
which I give from MSS. Cod. Ballard, vol. xix. Letter 104.
" In Monmouth's Rebellion, the univerfity of Oxford raifed
" a regiment for the King's fervice, and Chrift Church and
" Jefus college made one Company, of which lord Norris,
" fince earl of Abingdon, was captain: who prefented Mr.
" Urry a Corporal [Serjeant] therein with a halbard. Upon
" Dr. Pocock's death, Mr. Urry lugged Captain Rag [Smith]
" into his chamber in Peckwater, locked him in, put the key
" in his pocket, and ordered his bedmaker to fupply him with
" neceffaries through the window, and told him he fhould not
" come out, till he made a copy of verfes on the Doctor's death.
" The fentence being irreverfible, the captain made the Ode,
" and fent it with this Epiftle to Mr. Urry, who was a well
" built man, and large limbed: who [Smith] thereupon had
" his releafe." Pococke died in 1691. Urry, a ftudent of
Chrift-church, was the editor of Chaucer. The Epistle, here
mentioned, is a ludicrous profe analyfis of the Ode, beginning
*Opufculum tuum, Halberdarie ampliffime, &c.* and is lately printed
in Dr. Johnfon's English Poets. vol. 4. p. 62. The writer
of this anecdote is Mr. William Brome of Ewithington in

F f                                    Hereford-

I now return to Thomas Pope, the fecond fon or William firft earl of Downe, uncle to Thomas above-mentioned ·the fecond earl, and anceftor to Francis the prefent lord Guildford. He was born 1598 [z]. He was knighted by Charles I. at the royal manor of Woodftock, Aug. 1, 1625 [a]. He married at Wroxton, Apr. 20, 1636, Beata, Daughter of Sir Henry Poole of Saperton in Gloucefterfhire, baronet [b]. He appeared in arms for the royal caufe. On the death of his nephew Thomas, he became by fucceffion, Decemb. 28, 1660, a baronet, and third earl of Downe. He died Jan. 11, 1667, and was buried at Wroxton: as was his countefs Beata, Jul. 18, 1678 [c]. They had three fons, Thomas, Henry, and a fecond Henry; and five daughters, Elenor, Anne, Beata, Frances, and Finetta. Thomas was born, 1640, and on the death of his father, Jan. 11, 1667, became by fucceffion a baronet, and fourth

Herefordfhire, who died, aged 82, in 1745. He was of Merton college Oxford, an excellent fcholar, and a very learned anti-quary: intimately acquainted with Smith and Urry, and with Lord Oxford, John Philips, &c. In one of his LETTERS he fays, that Philips dedicated and fent to him the SPLENDID SHILLING in manufcript, and that he fent Philips in return a pound of tobacco. Ibid. LETT. 78. Compare LETTERS, 72. 74.

[z] At Wroxton there is a picture, dated 1606, of William Pope, aged 10, and of his brother Thomas, here mentioned, aged 8.

[a] MSS. Dugdale, Muf. Afhmol. R. fol. 232.

[b] Regiftr. Wroxton. There is a valuable portrait of this lady at Wroxton, by the fecond Vanfomer.

[c] Regiftr. Wroxton.

and

and laſt earl of Downe [d]. Theſe dignities he enjoyed but a few months; for he died May 18, 1668 [e], and was buried with his anceſtors, in a vault under the chancel at Wroxton. The firſt Henry was born Apr. 11, 1643, and died an infant [f]. The ſecond Henry was born Jan. 27, 1645 [g], and died at Oxford in Trinity college, where he was a ſtudent, aged 19, Jun. 20, 1665 [h]. Of the daughters, Elenor died an infant 1637 [i]. Anne was born 1637 [k], and married ſir Edward Boughton, baronet, of Lawford in Warwickſhire [l]. Beata, born 1639, was married Febr. 15, 1668, to William Soames, eſquire, of Thurlowe in Suffolk [m]. Frances, born 1647, was married March 5, 1671, to ſir Francis North, afterwards lord keeper, and lord North of of Guildford [n]; and from this match, grandfather to the preſent Francis lord North and Guildford. She died Nov. 15, 1678 [o], and was buried at Wrox-

[d] There are pictures at Ditchley of the two laſt earls of Downe.

[e] Regiſtr. Wroxton.

[f] Ibid.

[g] Ibid.

[h] Ex Tumul. ibid. I find the counteſs of Downe, his mother, making a preſent to the college, " in memoriam filii ſui " Dni Henrici Pope hujus collegii comm. defuncti." Regiſtr. ibid. in pergamen. ab ann. 1665, fol. 46. Where ſhe is called, by miſtake, Eliſabetha inſtead of Beata.

[i] Regiſtr. Wroxton.

[k] Ibid.

[l] MSS. Pedigr. Rawlinſ.

[m] Regiſtr. Wroxton.

[n] Ibid.

[o] Ex Epitaphio.

ton;

ton; where is an epitaph on her monument, written by Dr. Henry Paman, public orator of the univer-fity of Cambridge, who is faid to have been well acquainted with her amiable character [p]. The young-eft daughter, Finetta, was married May 4, 1674, to Robert Hyde, efquire [q], fon of Alexander Hyde, bifhop of Salifbury [r]. Thus by the death of male iffue, and marriage of the female, this family and name, at leaft in this branch, became extinct foon after the reftoration of Charles the fecond.

For from what is here collected on this fubject, it muft appear, that our great poet, ALEXANDER POPE, was related to this family only by fome colla-teral branch. I have mentioned all the male iffue, and their marriages; except the marriages of John

[p] North's Life of lord keeper North, 4to. p. 84.

[q] Regiftr. Wroxton. See Wood, Ath. Oxon. ii. 543.—f. 235.

[r] Whofe elder brother Laurence Hyde, efquire, of Heale near Salifbury, married MARY the daughter of ANTONY WARTON, rector of Bremor in Hamfhire, about the reign of Charles the firft, and great grandfather to the father of the author of this work. This lady, when a widow, for many days conceal-ed and accommodated in her houfe at Heale, aforefaid, king Charles the fecond after his hazardous flight from the battle of Worcefter, in the year 1651, and furnifhed the means for his efcape into France. At the reftoration, the king gave her a very valuable picture of himfelf, when a boy, a half-length, painted by Vandyck, and now in the poffeffion of my brother doctor Warton of Winchefter. See Clarendon's HIST. vol. iii. p. 331. edit. fol. 1704.

and

and William, two younger fons of fir William Pope knight, of Cogges: both which, I fufpect, died young; but if ever married, either of them may reafonably be fuppofed rather too young ' to have been the father of the elder Alexander Pope, who was born 1642 '. Befides, had the poet been de-fcended from either of thefe two younger fons, the title of earl of Downe could not have failed during his own and his father's life-time. Mr. Pope tells us, that, his " Father [Alexander] was of a gentle-
" man's family in Oxfordfhire, the head of which
" was the earl of Downe, whofe fole heirefs married
" the earl of Lindfey. His mother was the daughter
" of W. Turnor of York : She had three brothers,
" one of whom was killed, anothes died in the fer-
" vice of king Charles." Notwithftanding what I have here faid, I imagine that Mr. Pope alludes to Thomas Pope the fecond earl of Downe, whofe epi-taph I have given, no lefs than to his mother's bro-thers, in the following lines.

' The eldeft of them, John, was born Nov. 2, 1623. If it can be proved that he was the father of the elder Alexander Pope, it will follow that Thomas Pope, fecond earl of Downe, was his uncle : and confequently, that fir Thomas Pope, the founder of Trinity college, was the poet's uncle, to a high de-gree. It may perhaps be trifling to mention, that ALEXANDER POPE occurs twice as a name in this family, in, and about, Temp. Edw. iii.—MSS. Pedigr. penes honoratiff. com. de Guildford.

' Ex Epitaphio.

F f 3                                     Of

Of gentle blood, part fhed in *honour's caufe*,
While yet in Britain honour had applaufe,
EACH PARENT fprung ᵘ.——

And on the whole from my refearches on this
head I am inclined to determine, that our poet was
defcended from a branch of this family, viz. POPE
*of* DEDINGTON ᵛ, which fettled at Ginge, near Wantage in Berkfhire. They have ftill, or lately had, in
the family, which I believe has now loft the name
of *Pope*, a picture of fir Thomas Pope, and efcocheons of his arms.

For the convenience of the reader, the following
fhort Scheme, being a comprehenfive recapitulation
of what has been faid, both here and in the LIFE,
concerning this family, with fome improvements, is
annexed.

ᵘ Warb. POPE, iv. 43. ed. 1752.
ᵛ Thomas Pope, grandfather of William Pope, fir Thomas
Pope's father, had feven fons: William, the eldeft, married
*Jane Bonde*. MSS. Pedigr. modo citat. penes honoratiff. com.
de Guildford.

N U M B.

✝✝✝✝✝✝✝✝✝✝✝✝✝✝✝✝✝✝✝✝✝✝✝✝✝✝✝✝✝✝

# N U M B. XXVII.

GULIELMUS Pope de Dedington, co. Oxon. Gen. ob. 1523.

‖

Habuit Filium primogenitum

THOMAM POPE, MIL. FUNDATOREM COLL. TRIN. OXON.
1554. OB. 1558. JAN. 29.

Qui habuit Fratrem unicum, præter tres Sorores,
JOHANNEM Pope de Wroxton, co. Oxon. Armig. ob. 1583.

‖

Habuit Filium, præter duos alios, et sex Filias,
GULIELMUM Pope, nat. 1573. factum Equit. de Baln. 1603.
Baronett. 1611. Comitem de Downe, 1629. ob. 1631.

‖

Habuit Filios duos, præter unicam Filiam,

‖ | ‖

MAJOREM,
GULIELMUM Pope, nat. 1596. factum mil. 1616. ob. vivo Gulielmo Patre, 1624.

‖

Habuit filium, præter alios, et duas filias, THOMAM Pope, nat. 1622. baronett. et com. sec. de Downe, mortuo avo GULIELMO, 1631. ob. 1650.

‖

Habuit unicam filiam, et hæredem, ELISABETHAM Pope, nuptam D. FRANCISCO - HENRICO Lee de Ditchley, co. Oxon. Baronetto §.

‖

Habuere filium, præter alium, EDWARDUM-FRANCISCUM Lee, Baronett. factum comitem de Litchfield, 1674. ob. 1716.

‖

GEORGIUM-HENRICUM Lee. com. de Litchfield, 1716, ob. 1743.

‖

GEORGIUM-HENRICUM Lee, com. de Litchfield. 1743. Nuper academiæ Oxon. honoratissimum cancellarium, 1772.

MINOREM,
THOMAM Pope, nat. 1598. factum mil. 1625. baronett. et com. tert. de Downe, mortuo THOMA nepote, 1660. ob. 1668.

‖

Habuit filium, præter duos alios et filias quinqne, THOMAM Pope, nat. 1640. com. quart. et ult. de Downe, 1668. ob. eod. anno.

‖

Qui habuit in cohæredem, una eum duabus e filiabus prædictis, FRANCISCAM Pope, nat. 1647. ob. 1678. Nuptam D. FRANCISCO North, facto baroni de Guildford, 1683. ob. 1685.

‖

Habuere filium, præter tres alios, et filias duas, FRANCISCUM North, bar. de Guildford, 1685. ob. 1729.

‖

FRANCISCUM North, bar. de Guildford, 1729. com. 1752. Hodie superstitem, 1772. Titulis omnibus et honoribus majorem.

§ Renuptam Roberto Comiti de Lindsey.

✝✙✝✙✝✙✝✙✝✙✝✙✝✙✝✙✝✙✝✙✝✙✝✙✝✙✝✙✝✙✝✙✝✙✝

# N U M B. XXVIII.

## Account of Sir Thomas Pope's Burial, 1559 [a].

" THE vi day of ffebruary whent to the
churche to be beried at Clarkenwell [b] fir
" *Thomas Pope* knyght, with a ftandarde, a cott [c],
" pennon of armes, a targett, ellmett and fworde,
" and iiii dofen of armes, and xii for the branchys,
" and vi for the bodie, of bokeram : and ii ha-
" rolds [d] of armes, Mr. Clarenchus [e] and Mr.
" Yorke.   Mr. Clarenchus bare the cott, and Mr.
" Yorke bare the helmett and creft.   The gayff xl

[a] From MSS. Cotton. fol. Vitellius, F. 5. Brit. Muf. It
is a journal of occurrences chiefly in and about London, by
a cotemporary and a curious obferver, from 4 Edw. vi. to 5
Eliz. viz. 1563.   This article is almoft the only one, of any
length, now remaining clear and legible in the whole manufcript ; which in many parts is burnt to a cinder, and otherwife
much injured.

[b] This is inaccurately faid.   The body only laid in ftate in
the church of Clerkenwell.

[c] Coat.

[d] Heralds.

[e] Clarencieux.

mantyll

" mantyll ffrys gownes [to] xx men and xx wo-
" men : the xx men bare torchys, the women ii
" and ii together, with rayles. And ii grett whyt
" branchys and iv branchys [of] taperys of wax;
" garnifsfhed with armes and with iv dofen of pen-
" fels. Sir Richard Sowthwell, knyght, and fir
" Thomas Stradling, and dyvers oders morners in
" blake, to the nomber of lx and mo in blake.
" And all the howffe and the chyrche with blake
" and armes : And aftyr, to the playfe to drynke
" with fpyfe-brede and wyne[f]. And the morrow
" maffe iii fonges, with ii pryke fonges, and the iii
" [third] of Requiem, with the clarkes of Lon-
" don[g]. And after, he was beried : And that done,
" to the playfe to dener; for ther was a grett dener,
" and plente of all thynges, and a grett doll of
" money[h]."

[f] So at abbot Iflip's funeral in Weftminfter abbey, 1532.
The dirge being fung, they were entertained with " fpiced
" bread, fuckett, marmylate, fpiced plate, and divers forts of
" wine." Widmore's WEST. ABBEY, p. 208.

[g] A fociety of fingers who were hired to affift on thefe occafions. See HIST. ENGL. POETR. ii. p. 396.

[h] See LIFE, p. 178. From this paffage Strype drew what is
mentioned in his ANNALS. viz. " And fir Thomas Pope, a
" great man with the former queen [Mary,] buried with much
" much magnificence in Clerkenwell." [r. Walbroke.] Vol. i.
p. 32. Lond. 1725.

NUMB.

✝↓✝↓✝↓✝↓✝↓✝↓✝↓✝↓✝↓✝↓✝↓✝↓✝↓✝↓✝↓✝↓✝↓✝↓✝↓✝↓✝↓✝↓

# N U M B.  XXIX.

## Account of the Founder's Viſit to Trinity College Oxford, on St. Swithin's Day, 1556 ª.

SCIANT poſteri, quod ad collegium venit D. Fundator in feſto Sancti Swithini, A. D. 1556. Ei ab equo deſcendenti adſtitit ad frena magiſter

---

ª MSS. Wiſe. This paper was tranſcribed by the late Rev. Francis Wiſe, fellow of Trinity college, and Radclivian librarian, from the original, which was in the poſſeſſion of the learned Dr. Arthur Charlett, maſter of Univerſity college, and formerly fellow of Trinity college. It was written in the hand of Dr. Arthur Yeldard, the ſecond preſident of Trinity college ; and ſeemed to be intended for an entry in the college-regiſter, where it does not appear. Mr. Wiſe told me, that he ſaw other original papers relating to Trinity college in Dr. Charlett's library. Dr. Charlett ſeems to have made theſe collections for a work which he left behind him in manuſcript, entitled, " An " Alphabetical Catalogue of the Preſidents, Fellows, Scho- " lars, and Benefactors of Trinity college, Oxford, to the " year 1692." This catalogue was in the hands of Mr. Rawlins, of Pophills in Glouceſterſhire, but is not now to be found. See what is ſaid of it in Hearne's MSS. Collections, vol. 130. pag. 110. ſub. ann. Bibl. Bodl. cod. Rawlinſ. And compare LIFE, p. 178. in the notes. In a letter from Dr. Richard Rawlinſon to Mr. George Ballard, author of the LEARNED LADIES, dated

Præfidens : et mox, in porta collegii, oratione fatis longa et officii plena exceptus eſt a magiſtro Markes, vice-præfidente; ubi etiam humiliter eidem obtulerunt et donarunt burfarii cirothecas aurifrigiatas. Dein ad magnam præfidentis cameram eunt, fociis et fcholaribus utrinque ſtantibus. Comitabantur autem D. Fundatorem epifcopi Wintonienfis ᵇ et Elienfis, aliique plures ex aula magnates. Poſtquam Bibliothecam et Arbuſtum luſtraverant, ad prandium in magna aula collegii proceſſum eſt : ubi laute et opipare convivium inſtruebatur, ad lævum D. Fundatoris, paulo tamen ·diſtantius, adfidente Præfidente, ac dein ordine cæteris. In hoc convivium, in quo aderant etiam duodecim miniſtralli, et afferebantur inter alia plurima quatuor pingues damæ, necnon octo lagenæ Mufcadeli, allocabant burfarii xij *l.* xiv *s.* ix *d.* Quin et pro cirothecis xxiv *s.* xj *d.* Poſt, ad miſſam vefpertinam in choro capellæ præfens erat dictus D. Fundator, cum

dated Jun. 16, 1751, is the following paſſage. " Since my " laſt, I call to mind that our friend Mr. Rawlins actually fold " fome of his MSS. Particularly I remember a large folio of " Mifcellanies [mifcellaneous papers] moſtly relating to Ox- " ford, and partly in Dr. Charlet's hand, fold to Mr. Taylor " of Worceſterſhire : as alfo a copy of Wood's *Antiquities of* " *Oxford*, Latin, with originals [interpolations] by Mr. Wood " himfelf, &c." LETTERS, Cod. Ballard. vol. ii. LET. 138. folio. Bibl. Bodl.

ᵇ But he was not yet inthroned. He had cuſtody of the Temporalities, 16 Maii, 1556. Rym. Fœd. xv. 437. And the licence of election is dated Jul. 16. ib. 441. See fupr. LIFE, p. 237.

epifcopis

epifcopis et aliis, ubi divina celebrabat Præfidens
optima capa indutus ᶜ. Et ob'tulit D. Fundator
unam burfam plenam Angelorum. Hujus autem
diei totas expenfas ftatim ante difceffum, pro fua
munificentia, rependebat integre D. Fundator in manus burfariorum, in fcaccario computi, una cum ᵈ
ciffo argenteo deaurato. Dictus autem ciffus ftatim
ibidem implebatur vino mediato ᵉ, vocato *Ipocraffe*,
et ex eo fine mora propinabat D. Fundator Burfariis
et aliis præfentibus. Ac denique divertebat eo vef-
pere verfus Windleforam. Ac dedit D. Fundator
unicuique fcholarium propria manu unum marcam.

<hr/>

ᶜ Who is ordered to celebrate " in feftis magis duplicibus, et
" principalibus, et in die Exequiarum mearum, totum diei Offi-
" cium ac Miffam, cum diacono et fubdiacono." Statut.
Coll. Trin. Cap. xiii.

ᵈ Leg. Cypho.

ᵉ Legend. *f.* medicato.

# N U M B.  XXX.

## Teftimonium de Dom. Elifabetha Pau-let, D. Thomæ Pope uxore fecunda. A Radulpho Kettell confcriptum [a].

" $\mathbf{E}$ L I Z A B E T H A, inter clariffimas foeminas, ob corporis animique praeftantes dotes, in-

---

[a] Manu fua, inter chartas manufcriptas A. Wood, Bibl. Bodl. Oxon. Viz. A loofe paper inferted in A. Wood's MS. ENGLISH Hiftory of the Univerfity of Oxford, tom. ii. fol. 388. Dr. Ralph Kettel was prefident of Trinity college, and an ex. cellent governor, for near fifty years. He had been fellow and fcholar of the college for fourteen years, during the life-time of this lady. His family lived in her neighbourhood, at King's Langley in Hertfordfhire. She probably fent him to the col-lege, where he was admitted fcholar, Jun. 16, 1579. Regiftr. prim. fol. 30. He was chaplain to Bilfon bifhop of Winchef-ter, and to lady Walfingham, widow of the Secretary. A good, old portrait of him, in a brown furred gown, is in the college. Aubrey fays, that his picture was drawn by Mr. Bathurft, one of the foundation of Trinity college, from memory three years after his death, which was a ftrong likenefs. SURREY, tom, v. p. 406. His Life, but with many miftakes and abfurdities, is among Aubrey's manufcript LIVES in the Afhmolean Mu-feum.

The following anecdote is recorded of Dr. Kettel, which I relate, becaufe it is imperfectly told by Aubrey, and as it marks
the

" genium, multiplicem cognitionem, fermonis fa-
" cundiam, morum integritatem, pietatem, et muni-
" ficentiam merito celebranda, orta ex BLOUNTO-
" RUM fplendida familia in comitatu Staffordienfi de
" Burton ad Trent, connubio tradita eft ANTONIO
" BASFORD, viro inter armigeros infigni.  Qui, fuf-
" cepto filio unico JOANNE Basford, ELIZABETHAM
" reliquit fuperftitem, fama vitaque adeo celebrem,
" ut venerabilis Fundator nofter THOMAS POPE,
" tunc temporis, opibus, dignitate, et gratia, apud
" omnes ordines plurimum pollens, hanc fibi con-
" fortem digniffimam adfciverit.  Quae jam denuo
" conjux facta, propendebat admodum in opera
" quaeque infigniora; inter quae collegium hoc
" meritiffime reponimus.  Ad quod fundandum,
" omni conatu et fuafu Fundatorem noftrum con-

the times.  While prefident, it was his cuftom to attend daily
the DISPUTATIONS in the college-hall, on which occafion he
conftantly wore a large black-furred muff.  Before him ftood an
hour-glafs, brought by himfelf into the hall, and placed on a
table, for afcertaining the time of the continuance of the exercife, which was to laft an hour at leaft.  One morning, after
Cromwell's foldiers had taken poffeffion of Oxford, a halberdier
rufhed into the hall during this ceremony, and plucking off our
venerable doctor's muff, threw it in his face; and then with a
ftroke of his halberd broke the hour-glafs in pieces.  The doctor, though old and infirm, inftantly feized the foldier by the
collar, who was foon overpowered by the affiftance of the dif-
putants.  The halberd was carried out of the hall in triumph
before the doctor; but the prifoner, with his halberd, was
quickly refcued by a party of foldiers, who ftood at the bottom
of the hall, and had enjoyed the whole tranfaction. *MS. Papers
of Dr. Bathurft.*

" tinuo

" tinuo adhortata eſt. Unde evenit, ut ubi A.
" 1558 ᵇ, Januarii 29, dominica Sexageſima, a
" Clerkenwell ad electos ſuos ſpiritus deus dictum
" Thomam tranſtulerit, Elizabetham autem ad
" plebis ſuae Chriſtianae ſummum ſolatium ſuper-
" eſſe voluerit, Fundator huic ſummam auctorita-
" tem et poteſtatem in nos, Alumnos ipſius, de-
" mandaverit. Hinc, magis magiſque illuſtris, et
" conſpicua omnigenis virtutibus, nupſit venerabili
" atque inter ſplendidos militaris ordinis viros egre-
" gio, Hugoni Powlett Somerſetenſi. Ita nu-
" perrime *Domina Powlett* appellari coepit, apud
" George-Hinton inter Somerſetenſes, apud Titten-
" hanger inter Hartfordienſes, et apud Clerkenwell
" inter ſuburbanos Londinenſes, celeberrima. Hu-
" jus memoriam ſingulari cum pietate et obſervantia
" recolimus, collegii hujus alumni : cum ob aucto-
" tatem, quam ei, quouſque in vivis eſſet, Funda-
" tor contulit ; tum ob munificentiam, quam dum
" vixit exercuit in nos : quaque ad rem literariam
" confirmandam, et rem familiarem amplificandam,
" quotannis in perpetuum gaudere hoc collegium
" voluit electa Domina ᶜ. Utcunque enim veneranda


ᵇ Sc. 1558—9.

ᶜ The circumſtances of her whole benefaction where theſe.
Richard Blount of London §, eſquire, her nephew, bequeathed
by will 100 *l.* to maintain an exhibitioner in the ſaid college.
On his death, dame Eliſabeth Powlet covenanted with Blount's
executors, to give to the ſaid college, in conſideration of the

§ I find one Richard Blount, admitted a gentleman-commoner, Jan. 31. 1579.
And leaving the college, Feb. 28. 1581. E Libro primo Cautionum.

ſaid

" matrona, hinc a Tyttenhanger A. 1593, 27
" Octobris, ad superos concesserit; accesserunt ta-
" men ad Lectoris philosophici et rhetorici stipendia
" duplicanda, atque ad Focalium onus sublevandum,
" in annos singulos decem librae, ex ejusdem larga
" beneficentia."

said sum of 100 l. to her made over, the rectory of Ridge in
Hertfordshire, for the maintenance of the said exhibitioner,
and for the purposes mentioned in the text. She added also,
in the contract, the advowson to the vicarage of Ridge, now
lost. " For the great affection, good will, and favour, which
" she the same dame Elisabeth beareth towards the sayde col-
" lege, being founded by her late deare husband sir Thomas
" Pope." Ex Indentur. Dat. April 1, an. 22 Elizab. Regin.
A. D. 1581.

This Memoir was probably drawn up by Dr. Kettel, as was
the preceding narrative of the Founder's Visit to the College,
by Dr. Yeldard, with an intention of inserting it in the college-
register: but, like that, it was mislaid or forgotten, and never
entered. See p. 458. supr. in the notes. The manuscript seems
to have been procured by Antony Wood from Dr. Ralph Bathurst, who became possessed of many of Dr. Kettel's papers.